THE MAKER

BOOK TWO IN THE WREN TRILOGY

ROB WINTERS

Black Cube Press

Contact the author rawinters@me.com

Follow the author on twitter @robwinters

Sign up to the mailing list at https://www.robwinters.co.uk/books/wren

v1.5

For Mum and Dad

1

THE WATCHMAKER'S APPRENTICE

Paris, 1898

"It's magnificent," Victor Liouville said, holding the black pocket watch in his old but steady hands. He chuckled lightly as he admired it. "It's by far the finest you have made. Which, of course, means it is also the finest I have ever seen."

"Thank you," said Joseph Cartan, watching the old man with affection as he examined the timepiece. The two were sat at the counter at the back of the dim shop. The shop was closed, the early morning sun beginning to creep in through the gaps in the curtains.

"The finish and the fittings are perfect, the movement so smooth," Victor continued. He held it to his ear. "And so quiet," he whispered, shaking his head in awe. He picked up an eyeglass from the workbench and moved closer to the lamp to examine the piece in more detail, his bushy white eyebrows coming together to form a V as he spoke. "The markings around the face are very unusual. Not to my taste, I admit, but they have a prettiness to them. But overall... marvellous. For forty years, no one in this city has made a better watch than me. I have seen many come close. But as I look at this, I find myself unable to fathom how it has been made. It seems to have been created from the air itself." He removed his eyeglass and looked at Joseph. "Yet you use the tools I have given you." He smiled to himself and looked at the watch once more. "When a watchmaker examines the work of another, he is looking to fault it, looking for imperfections, not to praise it. So it pains me to say this, Joseph, but...this is a perfect watch."

"You are too kind," said Joseph.

"I am many things: *kind* is not one of them."

It was Joseph's turn to smile. "You've always been kind to me," he said, accepting the small timepiece back, looping its thin chain over his button, then slipping the perfect watch into the pocket of his waistcoat. "It has been an honour to be your apprentice, sir."

"Hah. One of us has been the apprentice," said Victor. "I'm just not sure it was you." He smiled again, reached over and gave the younger man a firm slap on the shoulder. He then stood and walked stiffly into the backroom, returning moments later with a bottle of Cognac and two glasses. "I know it is early, but I've been saving this for the right occasion," he said, removing the cork. "I should have opened it for dinner last night, but I preferred not to share it with them. It's far too good." He chuckled. "And this will be the last time we sit together. So I think now is a perfect time." He returned to his stool, handing Joseph a glass. They both nodded silent cheers and drank.

The old man slapped his lips together, savouring the taste, then looked around the dim shop with a content expression. "We did great work, you and I, and I'm sad to see you leave. When you first came to me, we were both young. Looking at you now, I see time has been kinder to you. Which makes me wonder if your watches have some magic in them." He laughed, and the laugh turned into a cough. "But I know not to ask such questions." He breathed a deep, laboured breath, then refilled their glasses. "However, I will ask about that stone." He looked at him, keenly, over the top of his glass.

Joseph tilted his head. "Stone?" He knew Victor would ask about it. He was old, but his eyes were sharp.

Victor gestured to Joseph's pocket. "The stone in the crown of that fine piece. At first, I thought it was a pearl. Milky white, smooth, reflective. But it's too...perfect."

Joseph said nothing; he just smiled, raised the glass to his mouth, and then drank.

"Very well," laughed Victor, "have your little secrets. I've always liked that about you; you have never lied to me. You keep much from me — I'm no fool. But you have never lied. So I'll not press you about the stone, and I won't even ask about the moon dial on the watch face, which to some might seem inaccurate." He pulled out and studied his own watch. "My moon will not be full for another three days." He smiled knowingly.

They finished their drinks, and Joseph stood and walked to the window, where he drew the heavy curtain, allowing the morning's dusty light to flood the long, narrow shop. Outside, people were beginning to go about their business. He watched them for a while. The small well-to-do street had been his home for a relatively short time, but he was going to miss it.

He helped Victor prepare the shop for opening, and when Victor's niece, a young sales assistant by the name of Delphine, arrived, Joseph climbed the narrow creaky stairs to his room to complete his packing.

The two said their final goodbye in the shop doorway, under the large sign in the shape of a watch. They shook hands, hugged, and then Joseph, suitcase in hand, turned and walked away. He didn't look back at the old man who watched him leave, and the old man didn't expect him to. He knew Joseph was different.

Joseph decided to walk the two miles to the station. It was a fine spring morning, and he could think of no better way to say goodbye to his beautiful city, his home for the last thirty years. He meandered down narrow roads that were getting busier as the sun climbed, the smells of ripe fruit engulfing his senses as he passed through a bustling market preparing for the day; the sounds of shutters opening, boxes being stacked, hooves beating the hay-covered cobbles. He wondered what London would be like. Then he wondered how long he'd stay *there* before feeling the need to move on again.

He had no desire to leave Paris, but there were only so many times he could, in good nature, dismiss the comments of his friends regarding his forever youthful appearance. The beard, artificially grey, had helped put pause to most of them, but they would start again in a few years as friends would become bent and fragile and turn to dust before him.

As he left the market behind, he felt a vibration in his pocket. He pulled out his black watch, flipped open its ornate cover, and frowned as he looked upon it. The main face of the clock informed him it was five minutes past eight: plenty of time to make his train. The markings circling the clock — the markings Victor had found not to his taste — had changed.

He looked around with a sudden desire to find somewhere private.

He left the street he was on, taking a narrow staircase and climbing to an alley running parallel, packed with tiny homes tightly squeezed together. But there was no privacy here; women talked around open doors while small grubby children played at their ankles. Dogs sniffed at him as he passed; old toothless men in vests eyed him suspiciously from upstairs windows. People dressed like him didn't walk down alleys like these.

After many more turns down crooked passageways, he eventually found a secluded spot behind a cloth factory that seemed to be closed. Between a damp wall and a row of wooden barrels, he knelt and pulled out his pocket watch once more. He flipped open the cover. The markings had changed again.

He put the watch away and opened his suitcase, pulling aside a layer of clothing to reveal a dark wooden box. Instead of a latch, it was sealed with a silver plate. When he placed his thumb on it, the box opened with a smooth movement, revealing three items within, held in place by the perfectly shaped indents carved into the wood. The largest of the three items was a dark grey, almost black, object that resembled a large lump of coal or perhaps a dark truffle. The second object was a wooden ring, smooth and varnished. The third was a milky white sphere, a circle of blue light around its circumference.

It was this last item that he removed from the box. He gripped it tightly in his hand, glancing around the still deserted alley, overlooked only by the pigeons of the rooftops. Confident he could not be seen, he squeezed the sphere, causing a bright blue disc of light to erupt around his fist.

About the size of a dinner plate, the disc was thin and made of many smaller discs, one of which left the others, drifting slowly away from Joseph, rotating ninety degrees until it lay flat before him.

He briefly reared his head above the barrels to look

down the alley; it was still empty. He was taking a risk, but he had to see this now.

With his focus back on the floating disc, he watched as a sphere, football-sized, emerged, as if rising from a pool of water. It was Earth.

The Earth faded, allowing Joseph to see a small, white, pulsating dot suspended above the planet's surface. He sighed and looked skyward in frustration, then back to the dot.

He thought he knew what it was, but he needed to be sure. With a gesture from his free hand, the dot grew until its shape became clear. It was a cube. With a flash of anger, he ended the light show then punched the barrel next to him with the side of his fist, causing the wood to crack and splinter, disturbing the pigeons watching above.

The corner was dim once more.

For a while, he didn't move. Then, with a soft and distant gaze, he extended his hand to the barrel's broken wood, placing his fingers on its damaged surface. The loose splinters fell to the ground, set free by the wood's new growth.

When he was done, he ran his hand over the smooth wood — like a carpenter examining his work. He returned the sphere to its box, his thoughts no longer on his new life in London. He would need a different plan now. After all these years, they had finally found his hiding place. They knew he was here.

2

AN INTERESTING FIND

Hurstwick, 2019

Under a grey November sky, with cold biting at her cheeks, Zoe Durkin swung the metal detector back and forth through the long grass.

The machine beeped, not for the first time that morning, and she knelt. With her gloved hand, she parted the tightly packed base of the grass and felt around. It was just a bottle top. She dropped the unwanted treasure into a carrier bag and, with a sigh, continued her circuit.

The professionals had already combed the clearing in Oban Wood over a year ago. She imagined a line of them on hands and knees, systematically scouring every millimetre. Travis, her technician, called her outings into the woods and the clearing, *a massive waste of time*. But to Zoe, they were a much-needed change to her routine. The fresh air, albeit *freezing*, was a welcome relief from the stuffy cabin, where she spent her time staring at a screen, trying to ignore Travis's tuneless humming. She was glad to be outside. It was peaceful. Cold but peaceful. And with progress on her *real work* moving at a dead snail's pace, it was the only thing keeping her sane.

Another beep, another bottle top.

Twenty metres ahead, she could see the fallen tree marking the end of her fruitless search. But there was no disappointment. Finding anything noteworthy would have been problematic; not only would she have to report her find, she'd have to invent a good reason for being out here in the first place. As an employee of GiaTek, a private company working as part of a government-run task force, her job was to investigate the anomalies known as the *Oban Energy Spikes* — spikes that originated a mile to the north in the woods, at a site known as *Place of Interest 1*. Poking around with her father's old metal detector, in the clearing known as *Place of Interest 2*, was *not* her job.

BEEP!

A rusty tent peg.

Still, there was a mystery to this site, and she often found herself wondering what happened here in the summer of 2018. The shallow crater had been found a few days after the energy spikes, but she'd seen no evidence connecting the two anomalies. The crater was first thought to be the result of the meteor shower that lit up the night sky around the same time. But it was the wrong type of crater for that.

Crunch.

She stepped back and looked down, then retrieved a shard of grey plastic, cracked by her boot. As she bagged it, she noticed a larger piece off to her right. She parted the grass for a better look. It was about the size of a sandwich and resembled one too, one left in the sandwich toaster for too long, two pieces of melted black plastic fused around a bundle of colourful wires. Whatever it once was, it was now crushed beyond recognition — probably nothing. But it was more interesting than bottle tops, so she placed it into a separate bag.

Not bothering to complete her circuit, she left the clearing with her find and followed the path through the woods, the dense but bare trees providing minimal protection from the chill wind.

The path she was on dropped and widened to meet the abandoned bypass, which was supposed to cut through the woods but was never completed. Construction was first paused in the summer of 2018 for the "removal of unexploded bombs from the Second World War" — a cover story given to the media. Work then resumed briefly until a mound of earth and uprooted trees were discovered in the woods. When the location was found to correspond precisely with the energy spikes, and ground-penetrating radar uncovered a thirty-metre-deep column of loose soil below the mound, the Oban Task Force was formed, and construction at the bypass was halted indefinitely.

Shortly after that, GiaTek, Zoe's employer, was invited to join the task force, and Zoe, a specialist in electromagnetic radiation, was ordered to drop everything and move to sleepy Hurstwick.

She didn't mind.

It was a pleasant enough town, and the work was interesting. Well, it was interesting at first. The data concerning the energy spikes, picked up by an orbiting satellite, were unlike anything she'd seen before, with readings off the charts. But since those spikes over eighteen months ago, there had been nothing more to record.

In the woods, excavation at Place of Interest 1 had failed to uncover a cause for the spikes. Cordoned off from the public, it was now a deep, well-like hole, rigged with sensors of every imaginable kind. However, whatever had occurred was a one-off. She was sure of it. Her overlords knew it too, for they'd been ordered to return to headquarters. And in just over a week from now, she'd be back in London. She couldn't wait.

Her company-provided Land Rover Defender was where she'd left it, parked among the long weeds sprouting through the now frozen, sandy track of the abandoned bypass. She opened its rear door and slid the metal detector inside, along with the plastic bags containing the rubbish and her crushed find.

Behind the wheel with the heaters on max, she sped along the track, slowing to glance at a weather-worn cabin, where the anomaly's effects had first been reported. A night-watchman, looking after construction vehicles, had witnessed total disruption to all electrical equipment on-site, the time of the outage matching the time of the first energy spike. There was more to his statement, but she'd only seen a heavily censored version. And it provided her with nothing useful.

She could now see the compound in the distance. Home to the Oban Task Force, it was a collection of squat grey buildings with narrow slits for windows, surrounded by a high wire fence and security cameras posted at each corner. At the gate, she pulled up to a card reader, lowered her window, and tapped her security card on the black frost-covered panel. The wire gate slowly slid open, and she drove across to Hut 4.

GiaTek was one of a handful of private companies based here, each occupying their own hut. She never spoke to anyone from the other companies; she wasn't allowed to. All findings and communications had to go through Duncan Clark, the government man in Hut 1. That way, only the government had the full picture of what was really going on. Everyone else involved just saw their tiny slice of it.

As Zoe passed Hut 1, she spied Duncan's Jaguar parked

outside and another car belonging to her boss, Greta Nilsson, the new GiaTek CEO who rarely visited the site. Zoe still hadn't met her in person and considered stopping by to introduce herself. She decided against it. No doubt she would get to see more of her back in London.

In Hut 4, Travis, wearing his bulky headphones, was still humming tunelessly, probably hadn't stopped since she left that morning. He looked up as she closed the door and shot her a mock salute. "Guess what happened when you were out?" he said in a dull tone, removing his headphones.

"Absolutely nothing?" she replied. She placed the metal detector in a locker and her plastic treasure on the table in the small kitchen area.

"It's like you're psychic or something." He leaned back in his chair, placed his hands behind his head, and yawned. "What's that?" he asked, eyeing the item on the table.

"Found it at the clearing. Probably junk."

Travis stood and walked to the table, leaning in with mild interest to look closer while Zoe worked the coffee machine. "I thought they searched the clearing?"

"It was right at the edge. I'd have missed it if I hadn't stepped on it. Did Greta come say hello?"

"Is she here?" Travis straightened up, tucked his shirt in and glanced to the window.

"Over at Hut 1 with Duncan. Probably discussing shutdown." Zoe spooned sugar into her coffee. "She wouldn't want to be seen talking to the likes of us, though."

"Probably not," said Travis, running a hand through his hair then flattening it with his palm.

Zoe smiled with a slow shake of her head as Travis dashed to the window to part the blind with his finger and thumb. Satisfied Greta wasn't on her way, he returned to the table and picked up the mangled plastic. He fingered the wires, holding it up, turning it over, looking at it from all angles. His eyebrows flicked. "There's a partial part number," he said. He took it to his desk, placed it carefully down, then typed the long serial number into Google. Zoe followed, blowing over the rim of her mug as she took the seat beside him.

"It's a drone," he said with a frown. "Well, it's a small part of a drone. Must be the one they shot at, right?" He picked it up to examine it again.

"Shot at?"

He swivelled in his chair to face her. "You're kidding me."

"What?"

"You didn't hear about the drone? It was all over the news. The army tried to shoot it down over the no-fly zone. They denied it, of course." He held up the plastic wire sandwich. "This could be it."

"Could be. No way of knowing, though, right?"

Travis stuck his thumbnails into a small gap and prised apart the two pieces of deformed plastic. "Well, would you look at that...." He retrieved a small, flat, fractured blue item from inside. It was cracked along its centre and bent slightly.

Zoe leaned in. "SD card?"

"Seems to be," he said, rummaging through a drawer from which he retrieved a small dongle. He plugged it into the side of his laptop, then inserted the card, careful not to damage it further. "Probably too mangled, but worth a try."

"Well?" she asked after a few seconds of watching him tap commands into a console window. "Anything?"

Travis frowned. "There's stuff on here, video files mostly, but I can't access any of them." He raised his eyebrows in surprise. "OK, for some reason I can access the photos...." A window opened with about twenty image files. He tabbed through them, each one showing aerial shots of green rolling hills. "Boring. Boring," he said as each one flicked up on screen before being replaced by another. "Boring. Boring, b—bingo." The last image showed three kids standing in what looked like a barn. Two boys and a girl looked straight at the camera; one was smiling, the other two seemed annoyed. Travis pointed at the remote control in the hands of the smiling kid. "There's our drone pilot."

Zoe moved her coffee aside and leaned in for a closer look. "When was it taken?"

"Day after the first energy spike."

"So it's the same drone."

"Has to be."

"But what about those video files? Can you extract them?"

Travis sighed and tapped some more on his keyboard. "No. I can see a manifest telling me they're there. The physical damage to the card isn't letting me get to them. The files might be fine," he said, offering hope. "We just need to fix the card."

"Can you fix it?"

He removed the card for a closer look. "I wouldn't know where to begin," he said, shaking his head slowly. "It's beyond even my level of genius. But Dinesh could do it."

She leaned back in the chair and crossed her arms. "No," she said after a while. "I should give it to Duncan. This is not within our area of responsibility."

"Really? You can't be serious. We've been here for over a year and still have no clue what's going on. This could hold all the answers. We give it to Duncan, and it'll get buried, and we'll never find out. We're gone in just over a week. Don't you want to know why we were here in the first place?"

"I do," she said. "But our job was to study the spikes and record further spikes—"

"There won't be any more spikes. *They* know that. This might tell us what caused them. And I know you still think there's a link between the site in the woods and the site in the clearing. What if there's something on here that confirms it? Come on," he urged playfully. "Let's at least try."

Zoe stood and picked up her coffee, cradled it in her hands, and began to pace. She stopped by the small window next to the door and parted the blind slightly. Greta Nilsson was leaving Hut 1. Tall, elegant, smartly dressed, she walked to her car, seemingly oblivious to the arctic gusts whipping her hair across her face. A moment later, she was speeding off towards the gates. She hadn't even glanced over. Just a wave would have been nice.

When the car was out of sight, Zoe turned to Travis. "Send it to Dinesh," she said. "Do you trust him to keep it quiet?"

Travis smiled and flicked his eyebrows. "Yeah. Remember last year's Christmas party?"

"Please, don't remind me—"

"If I tell him it's for you, he'll keep quiet."

"Good. If anyone finds out, it'll be our jobs."

"In the meantime," Travis said, returning his focus to the screen. "Might be worth tracking down those kids. The drone would've sent live video to the connected phone. They should have a backup."

"Wouldn't it be online by now? YouTube or TikTok or something?"

"Maybe. But I've probably seen everything online relating to this, and I've seen zero drone footage."

"Why would they not upload it?"

"Perhaps they didn't find it interesting? Anyway, it's worth speaking to them. If Dinesh can't retrieve the files, they might be willing to show us the video. Or at least tell us what they saw."

Zoe looked past Travis to a 3D map of the local terrain on the wall, two pins marking the two places of interest: the deep hole in the woods, the crater in the clearing. The prospect of something linking those sites *was* appealing. She then looked back to the photo of the kids and felt a sudden sense of excitement for the first time in months.

"OK," she said. "Send it to Dinesh, and I'll find those kids."

3

TRAINING AND TEA

"This felt like a much better idea in the summer," said Max, following Wren up the steep frost-covered hill as an ice wind blew down to greet them.

"We can stop your training at any time," said Wren, not looking back. He seemed to glide up the hill with ease, a single stride for every two of Max's. "Just say the word, and we'll head back."

"No, it's fine," replied Max, a smile hidden under his scarf.

"If you're certain. Before I met you, my Saturday mornings used to be backgammon with Frank at the bowls club. They do a nice hotpot for lunch, but you have to get your order in early or—"

"You sound like an old man sometimes."

Wren laughed and looked back at Max. "I'm the *oldest* of men, remember?"

He'd never been given a straight answer concerning Wren's age. As he looked at him now with his black shoulder-length hair, stubble that was almost a beard but not quite, dark eyes that were both calm and intense, he would have guessed he sat somewhere between thirty-five and forty-five. Which, of course, made it difficult for him to see Wren as his great-grandfather. Instead, he saw him as an unusual uncle, who spent a surprising amount of time in trees for a grown man, and was unbeatable at hide and seek.

It was ten in the morning. Windmill Hill was deserted. The only sounds were the crunch of their feet upon the frozen grass, and the calls of the crows gathered in the fields below them. It was a walk they made every Saturday morning. They'd meet on the path by the River Den, cross the fields together, skirt the southern edge of Moore's Farm, then climb the north face of the hill. Although they would occasionally see others on their journey, no one seemed to notice them.

"Maybe you could teach me to see through walls in the winter, from somewhere nice and warm," said Max. "And in the summer, we could practise distance viewing from up here."

"I'm sensing you're not a fan of the cold," replied Wren. "That's the Nim in you. Anyway, before all your complaining and talk of the weather, you may recall me asking you a question?"

"Sorry," said Max, remembering this was training and not just a walk in the countryside. "Yes. The two Gifts of a Watcher are perception...and...deception," he said, struggling to keep up with Wren's pace.

"The key to mastering both?"

"The breath," he answered, his breath now burning in his lungs as the hill's steepness increased.

Over the past year and a half, Max had learnt that breath was as important to his vision as his eyes were. For the first few months of training, it had been all they'd worked on. He learnt to slow his breathing and hold it for far longer than he'd thought possible. He'd learnt he could increase his awareness with each passing breath. Of all the skills Wren was teaching him, this widening of awareness came most easily to Max. At night before falling asleep, he would lie still and listen as every breath took his awareness further and wider, until he was no longer in his room but lying in the churchyard. There he would fall asleep, listening to the gentle stir of the trees.

With the basics of breathing and awareness under his belt, the focus of training was now *distance viewing*, which was precisely what it sounded like: viewing things at a distance.

They had started from the tall pine tree in Patrick's Corner, looking out over the town. Soon, that was not enough for Max; they needed to go higher, to push the horizon further. So they moved to the church spire. After a while, even that was not enough, so they took to Windmill Hill, where the world went beyond the reach of Max's eyes — for now.

"What about climbing?" asked Max.

"What about it?"

"Is that a Gift?"

"A gift with a small *g*. Not exclusive to Watchers."

Max nodded. He'd learnt that Gifts were brought about by genetic mutations during puberty. Certain combinations of these Gifts resulted in four main types of Gifted Nim: Watchers, Makers, Hunters, and Healers. There were other types, too, but they were rare, and Wren didn't talk about those.

Only a small number of Nim developed these Gifts, but all would benefit from them, for the Gifted played essential roles in Nim society. Wren was a Watcher, and the role of a Watcher was to protect their people from dangers.

The bitter wind intensified and clawed at Max's face as they climbed over the fence skirting the hilltop. They looked around. Animal tracks crisscrossed the icy grass, but the place was empty and mostly free from the mist clinging to the lower ground. It was just them.

"We'll look west today," said Wren, removing a flask from his thick coat. He unscrewed the cap, releasing a cloud of steam. "We'll look past the town and focus on the hills beyond." He took a swig of the tea, resealed it, then slid it back inside his coat.

Max looked out at the view. He couldn't see the hills, just the town, the surrounding chequerboard of fields, and hedgerows running from copse to wood. But the hills were there, somewhere, currently hidden behind grey curtains of dismal weather.

He readied himself.

He was nervous.

Recently, progress had slowed, maybe even halted. During their last two sessions, he struggled with his focus, finding it difficult to control his gaze, which seemed easily drawn to the slightest movements. The constant fight against his wandering eyes had resulted in headaches and dizziness, making training less enjoyable now. But he was determined to get past it. He told himself it was an obstacle that would soon be behind him.

His struggle to focus was not the only reason for his nervousness; he had something to tell Wren, something he'd been putting off for some time. But that could wait for another day.

"Ready?" Wren asked. "Open your eyes."

Max's eyes were open. What Wren meant was open them *fully*. He had to think of them as black holes pulling in all the light and information from the world, allowing nothing to escape. When Wren did this, his eyes turned oily black, instantly, leaving just a hint of white at their edge. For Max, it took longer and resulted only in slightly wider pupils, not quite extinguishing the browny-green set around them.

Max buried his nerves under a deep breath, and with a calm and still mind he focused his attention on the distant town, Hurstwick, a crooked hodgepodge of frost-covered rooftops and smoking chimneys, dominated by the tall spire of St Mary's Church.

He relaxed his eyes, allowing them to draw in as much light as possible. The longer he looked, the more he saw. Information poured in, building layer upon layer of detail until the clarity of the world around him, no matter the distance, sharpened to perfection.

He looked to the church clock, over two miles away. It was six minutes past ten. Gold paint was peeling up and flaking from the Roman numerals, and he noticed signs of rust around the bolt joining the hands.

It was strange to see things so far away in such perfect detail. The strangeness came from a numbness in the eyes; he felt no movement in them as his gaze travelled from point to point. Instead, it was like a large, fully immersive, high-resolution image panning and zooming before his *stationary* eyes.

"The town is clear," said Max. "I can see everything. But I can't see the hills, not through the cloud."

"Keep looking."

Max looked to the wall of weather beyond the town, noticing a cloud dumping its rain upon the countryside, the ghosts of trees and hedgerows briefly appearing through the veil, but still no hills.

When a dark patch, like a bruise, developed against the grey, Max locked his focus on it, but it faded and was soon gone.

"Don't try to see the hills," said Wren after a few minutes. "Try to ignore the clouds."

OK, Yoda, thought Max. Looking at something while trying to ignore it was not easy. As time passed and the cloud continued to resist his eyes, he became aware of a low rumble increasing in volume. It was a helicopter, probably circling the larger town of Denbridge to the southeast behind him. This persistent noise and the chill in his bones made it hard to maintain focus — not to mention the feeling of Wren watching him intently. But like Wren, Max was patient. He didn't give up.

After a while, he felt a gradual shift in himself. There was a heaviness in his limbs, and the sound of the distant helicopter had changed. It had slowed to a deep, penetrating thud, hammering through his chest, slowing until it matched the beat of his heart. A vibration lingered as each thud passed through him, resonating like a tuning fork. It wasn't an unpleasant feeling, just different. And as he got used to it, his mind returned to his breath, but that was now so slow he could not be sure he was breathing at all.

Then it happened; the unwelcome pull on his focus, like the week before. He felt it like gravity. He resisted at first, but it was too strong. His gaze, no longer under his control, drifted to a crow that flew between the town and the invisible hills; he saw the bird's feathers trembling as it flew against the wind. He tried to look away, back to the wall of shifting grey, but each time he did, gravity snapped him back to the bird.

"It's happening again, isn't it?" said Wren. His voice sounded muffled and slow to Max.

"What is?" he replied, trying to sound innocent.

"Your attention is being pulled away. Towards the bird."

Max sighed, and the trance was broken. He was back on the hill. The town was distant again, the helicopter still far behind him but no longer thumping in his chest. A headache was building. "Sorry," he said. "I couldn't help it. It was just like last time." He shook his head and looked to his boots.

Wren smiled thoughtfully. "I want you to try again," he said. "This time, if you find your attention drawn to the bird, or anything, just go with it. Don't fight it."

"Why?"

"Try it," Wren said, the edge of his lips forming a subtle smile.

After a few minutes, Max was again trying to catch a glimpse of the elusive hills beyond the wall of weather while the helicopter continued to provide its deep rhythmic soundtrack.

Soon another bird, or the same bird, fighting against the wind, appeared at the edge of his vision. He felt the pull, and he allowed his focus to drift, as Wren had instructed. When he did, something unexpected happened.

After a peaceful moment of his gaze resting upon the bird, there came a blinding flash of white light. It was somehow beautiful — like he'd glimpsed something other-worldly, something pure. The feeling faded with the light, and his vision took on an odd quality, less detailed than his usual sight, and warped as if looking through the spy-hole of a door. As he adjusted to this new way of seeing, he realised the hills were now visible to him, but not how he'd expected.

Snaking between the hills was the River Den, lined with bare trees. In the elbow of the river was an electricity pylon, sheep gathered at its base, their droppings blackening the frosty ground. Bronze-coloured footpaths of frozen clay crossed the silver hills, along with dark shiny roads twisting and turning in the creases of the countryside. All this came in a split-second barrage of imagery that caused Max to stumble, one hand to his temple, where he felt a sharp pain, the other reaching to find Wren for support, as a particularly vicious cold blast of air rushed up the hill to meet them.

"Max!" Wren called as he steadied him. "Are you OK?"

"Yeah, I think so."

"Do you need to sit?" Wren gestured to a bench behind them.

"No, it's fine. I'm fine. I just...wasn't expecting that." Short of breath, he pulled his scarf down to allow more air into his lungs.

"Expecting what?"

Max couldn't answer at first. A ringing began in his ears, accompanied by a dull pain in his head. He wasn't sure where to begin. Perhaps he *should* sit.

"What did you see, Max?"

"The hills," he answered once the ringing had lessened. "But..." he trailed off, trying to remember what had felt so strange about them, so different. He took a breath and then spoke slowly and deliberately. "I saw the crow. I allowed myself to go to it, as you said. Then I saw the hills. But...I think...I saw them from high above?" With an uncertain smile, Max looked to Wren. His smile faded when he saw Wren's confusion. "Is that...normal?" Max asked.

Wren straightened up and forced a smile. "Nothing about you is normal, Max Cannon." He slapped him on the back, then squeezed his shoulder.

When Max was feeling better, they walked along the top of the hill to keep themselves from freezing. He remained unsettled by his experience but said nothing to Wren.

They both looked out towards the abandoned bypass — abandoned, it was said, for *environmental concerns*. But Max suspected concerns of a different kind. Its wide and sandy track was now being reclaimed by nature; bushes and weeds covering most of it, the pale yellow of the sand only visible in parts. However, humanity was fighting back in the form of the compound, a collection of temporary buildings surrounded by a tall wire fence. The presence of it made Max uneasy. It was a reminder that events of a year and a half ago were still of interest to some. He didn't like the place, yet he felt drawn to it.

"Can we try the compound again?" Max asked. His tone was flat as if he'd rather not look inside, but curiosity demanded it.

"No more today."

"But I'm feeling better," pleaded Max. He wanted to finish on a high note, with no more weirdness.

Wren studied him silently for a while, then nodded. "If you're sure."

"I am."

They approached the wooden fence at the hilltop edge, then looked down and across to the bypass.

"Now, remember your breathing," said Wren, pulling up the collar of his coat. "When you're ready, I want you to—"

"Morning!"

A jogger, a man in his mid-twenties, had appeared from nowhere and was now using the fence to stretch. He was tall, not as tall as Wren, but larger, thick-set. He wore black trainers and a grey tracksuit that barely contained his bulk.

"Sorry," said the jogger, switching to stretch his other leg. "Didn't mean to startle you." He was wearing large headphones and spoke too loudly. "Lovely morning." His broad smile split his face in two as he stretched his back and rotated his hips.

Wren and Max smiled and nodded, but the morning felt far too cold to be described as *lovely*.

The jogger checked his watch, gave a small wave, then continued with his run, eventually disappearing over the brow of the hill, heading towards the car park.

"We need to work on our hearing, too," said Max, turning back to the bypass.

"Indeed," replied Wren, an eyebrow raised. "Now, choose a building. Focus on a small section of wall, and try to look beyond it. If you feel anything different — a pull on your focus or any pain — I want you to end it. OK?"

Max nodded. "OK."

He looked out to the four squat buildings, arranged in a square, doors facing inwards, a large grey shipping container at the centre, a satellite dish and antenna on its roof. He picked the building with the black Land Rover parked outside, and his breath fell quickly into its rhythm. The numbness in his eyes followed, and then the slow build-up of detail. He focused on an area beside the door, noticing the sign that read *GiaTek staff only* and the electronic keypad, some numbers worn more than others.

"Can you see the wall?" Wren asked. "The textures, the variations in the thickness of the paint, the scratches, the moisture from the frost?"

"I can."

"Good. Remember, there is more detail below the surface. You can't see it yet, but it's there. Light hits that *hidden* detail just as it hits the surface detail. But it's a different light. You need to find it."

The trick, according to Wren, for looking through anything, be it dense fog or a brick wall, was to force a shift in the light entering the eye, almost like adjusting the sliders of photo-editing software. Up the brightness, reduce the contrast, adjust the hue. Only, for Max, it wasn't that easy. Ever since the departure of Kelha, a year and a half ago, this particular skill had mostly evaded him.

Kelha was Wren's ship. A sentinel ship, she was designed to enhance the Gifts of a Watcher, allowing Wren to watch Earth from orbit. It had been Kelha who had awakened

Max's dormant Gifts, and her presence had amplified them. Now, with her gone, acting as a prison for a deranged Hunter, some of his abilities came less easily. Sometimes, under the right conditions, he could still see through solid objects, but it was harder now, and any success felt accidental.

Max continued to concentrate while listening to Wren's gentle guidance.

For the first few minutes, the grey, dirty walls of the cabin remained unyielding to his eyes. Then, to his surprise and delight, a light slowly grew from within the building. It was of a colour he had no name for and provided Max with a sense of depth within the cabin, where shadowy shapes formed, hinting at desks and chairs and...people. There were two people. Just vague smudges, but definitely people. It soon became clear to Max that the light allowing him to see was radiating from the electrical equipment within the building: computers, strip lighting, Wi-Fi routers, mobile phones.

"I can see inside," Max whispered, fearing the sound of his voice would break the spell. "Just vague shapes. There are people. And computers; lots of computers."

He focused on one of the shapes he believed to be a person, hoping it would sharpen. As soon as he did, the blinding flash of beautiful white light returned, this time bringing with it a cacophony of shrill beeps and static. Somewhere buried in the noise was...music?

A split second later, Max was back on the hill, Wren supporting him, sharp pain behind his eyes, ringing in his ears.

"Are you OK?" Wren asked as he held him.

He couldn't answer right away. The pain this time was too intense. He had to fight to maintain consciousness as a great pressure gripped his skull. He wanted to yell — to scream. Instead, he grimaced, fighting to control his breath.

"Are you OK?" Wren asked again.

This time Max managed a nod as he pinched the bridge of his nose. "I think I'm OK," he said eventually, smiling, but he wasn't. The pain had quickly lessened, but it was still there, and the hill was now spinning, and his stomach was going into spasm. But worse than all this was the disappointment. His Gift was broken.

Wren glanced at the cabins in the distance, then back to Max, concern etched on his ordinarily serene face. "That's enough for today." He placed a hand on Max's shoulder and led him to the bench a few feet away. "Sit."

They sat, Max leaning forwards, his head in his hands while Wren watched over him.

The sun soon broke through, causing the frost-covered grass that Max could see between the cracks in his fingers to shimmer and sparkle. He heard the call of the crows grow louder as if to welcome the sun. With caution, he sat upright and blinked. Windmill Hill was no longer spinning; he was starting to feel better.

"I'm sorry," Wren said after a while. "I've been pushing you too much. We'll pause the training. For just a short time," he added, quickly, as Max was about to protest. "I'm concerned. These episodes are unusual. I've not seen a young Watcher experience anything like them before. Also, you have your school studies to consider. We'll take a break over Christmas and start again, fresh, in the new year. We'll go slow. There is no rush, no exam to work towards. No test."

Max nodded reluctantly. It wasn't up for discussion, and he was in no state to argue. He looked sideways at Wren. Maybe now would be a good time to tell him his news — get it over with. He might as well. It wasn't as if he was going to ruin a great training session.

"Something's on your mind," said Wren, looking out into the distance.

"No, it isn't," said Max, losing his nerve.

"Are you sure? Because it seems to me you've wanted to tell me something for a while now."

Max sighed. "OK. But don't be mad."

"Uh-oh," said Wren, his mood seeming to lighten.

"I found the girl in my dream."

"The girl in your dream? Or the girl *of* your dreams?"

"I'm serious," Max managed a smile. "I found her."

Max had told Wren all about the dreams he'd been having since Kelha had awakened his Gifts. The dreams were recurring. He saw the same people time and time again, sometimes from a distance, sometimes as if looking through their eyes.

At first, Wren had shown little interest in Max's dreams. However, he'd listened more intently as Max spoke of them recently. He now seemed intrigued.

In the past, Max mostly believed they were just dreams. Only sometimes, soon after waking, did he believe they were something more, waking with a feeling that these people were real and that he was somehow connected to them. Now, he knew it to be true.

"I know I said I wasn't going to look for others," Max continued. "And I wasn't. But I got curious. I signed up to a website that helps you build a family tree. I entered my details, Mum's details, and when I added Dad's, the site found a matching record from another member—asked if I wanted to send them a message. So...I did. It's just...I've never had family before. Well, I have Mum, and now there's you, too. I just—"

"Want more."

Max nodded, then looked to his feet. "Is that wrong?"

"It's not wrong," Wren replied after a pause.

"Her name is Kira Furlong. She's an engineer. A pretty good one. She's working in Cambridge—"

"Please, Max," Wren said, holding up his hand. "I'd rather not know."

"But she's your great-granddaughter—"

"Please," Wren said calmly. "By all means, look for others. Meet them if you must. I can't stop you. But it's best I know nothing about them, and they know nothing about me."

"I'd never tell them about you. I just thought you might want to know about them."

"I don't. I'm sorry."

There was a silence, and Max fiddled with the Velcro strap on his glove.

They began to speak again after a while. But they spoke of other things. Wren asked about school, to which Max gave his default answer: *it's alright*. They discussed plans for Christmas, and Wren told Max of an upcoming birthday party for Father Elliot that he was helping to plan. Father Elliot was one of the Old Guard, a group of *very* old Hurst-wick residents who had known Wren for a long time. They were like family to him. Maybe that's why he wasn't inter-ested in finding family; perhaps he had enough already.

The weather was now improving, and the distant hills had emerged through the thinning clouds. "Come," said Wren as he stood and stamped his feet to keep warm, his hands deep in his pockets. "I'm freezing. Feeling good enough to walk?"

Max nodded and stood. Despite a dull pain behind his eyes and a fear that his abilities had peaked and were now diminishing, he managed a smile. The day hadn't gone as well as he'd hoped, but he'd spent time with Wren, and he loved spending time with Wren.

They made their way back down the hill, their warm

breath trailing behind them, their voices fading, leaving only the call of the crows carried on the icy wind.

Then the hilltop was empty.

But only for a short while.

The jogger returned.

He stopped by the fence, jogging on the spot before dropping to the cold ground to deliver an explosive burst of push-ups. When he was done, he sprung to his feet. Showing no signs of exertion, he looked out across to the compound and its drab buildings, his gaze slowly turning to the direction of the man and the boy he had seen moments earlier. They were now gone.

He crouched and reached behind the fence post, retrieving a small metallic object that he dropped into his pocket.

He inhaled deeply, breathed out slowly, then jogged back the way he came.

4

MEETING IN THE WOODS

The man in the grey tracksuit jogged through Windmill Hill's empty car park, then along the frozen gravel track, startling a deer who didn't see him coming. Not slowing, he watched it leap over a low hedge and disappear into the undergrowth.

At the end of the track, he turned right onto a two-lane road lined with trees, where he continued his steady, rhythmic pace.

All was quiet. The only sounds were his footfalls crunching on the gritted tarmac as he ran down the centre of the road, briefly moving aside for a passing car. His movements were fluid, a seasoned runner, a calm gaze.

As the road curved, a beaten-up white van with frosted windows came into view, parked in a lay-by. He slowed as he approached. The side of the van advertised that this was Neville's van, and that Neville could fix anything. To prove it, there was a long list of things that Neville was really good at fixing printed on the rear doors.

The jogger, now climbing into the van, did not look like a *Neville*.

Behind the wheel, he removed his headphones, leaving

them around his thick neck, started the engine, and cranked up the heater to defrost the windows. Then, from under the seat, he retrieved a chunky old laptop. He waited for it to boot, then opened a web browser.

He typed: *Kira Furlong Engineer Cambridge*. Then smashed the return key with a thick finger and glanced at the iced-up windscreen to check its progress. It was still mostly frosted, but with a small circle of clarity appearing just above the vinyl dashboard.

He looked back to the computer. The top result for his search was Wikipedia, followed by a long list of articles from the likes of *The New York Times*, *Harvard Business Review*, and *The Guardian*. He glanced at those, then clicked the Wikipedia entry.

Kira Furlong (born February 6, 1992) is a Canadian-born engineer working at Cambridge University's Artificial Architect Lab, where she leads the Generative Design Research Group. She is best known for her work combining artificial intelligence, robotics, and biomaterials to develop new ways of building inspired by nature.

"Geek," he muttered, then clicked to enlarge her photo. It showed her on stage behind a podium, in front of a large screen displaying the words 'Growing our Cities'. His eyebrows flicked. "*Pretty* geek." He noted the thick black curls pouring over her shoulders and her dark eyes. There was a strong resemblance to the boy.

After a few more clicks, he found himself on the Artificial Architect Lab's website, showing an artist's impression of a future city, dozens of organic-looking towers emerging from a lush forest.

Another page showed photos of all those involved in the project, with titles like Chief Programmer, Materials

Specialist and Data Scientist. There were details of an upcoming event, followed by a list of event sponsors: Clean Cities, The Foss Foundation, and the Council for Science and Technology.

He checked the windscreen again. It was almost clear enough to drive. He took one last look at the face of Kira Furlong, then closed the laptop and placed it back under the seat.

A small LED clock on the van's dashboard told him it was eleven forty-three—time to go.

Not checking his mirrors or bothering with his seatbelt, he pulled out of the lay-by and drove down the east side of the hill, away from Hurstwick, following a sign to Denbridge. For twenty minutes he sped down narrow country lanes, eventually taking the van off-road onto a dirt track, hedgerows as high as the van on each side.

The van complained about the uneven surface, threatening to drop its undercarriage and shed some of its dented panels. The tools in the back of the van joined in, crashing and clanking in protest, but then fell silent when the vehicle slowed to pass a wood of dark, bare trees. It left the track to enter the wood between two giant sycamores, slowly progressing as far as the other trees would allow.

He got out, opened the rear doors, retrieved two thick winter coats, donned one, placed the other over his arm, then headed north on foot through dense undergrowth. He soon found a path that led to a small river, partly frozen, which he followed for a short while as it meandered further into the wood. Eventually, the river disappeared underground. He carried on, catching an occasional glimpse of it as it reappeared at intervals. After a few minutes, he climbed a steep bank of frozen earth to emerge into a small, roughly circular clearing about ten metres wide. He stood at its centre, looking at the trees around him. Then up to the grey sky.

He inhaled deeply.

The location was suitable.

He pulled back the sleeve of his winter coat to reveal a large black wrist band. It covered a third of his forearm and was ornately carved with a smooth, reflective strip running its length. Bright markings ran across the strip. He studied them, then swiped them away, inviting more to appear. After tapping several of the markings, he covered the band with his sleeve, then made towards a fir tree at the clearing's edge, surrounded by dense brown bracken, curled and brushed silver by the frost. At the trunk, on a stub of a former branch, he hung the coat he was carrying. He leapt, disappearing into the branches high above.

There he waited, crouching, balanced on the balls of his feet. His heart rate dropped. His breathing slowed. He closed his eyes.

When his eyes opened again, the moon was high, and the sky was dark. He heard a muffled snapping of twigs and cracking of stone. She was here. A look to his wrist confirmed it. He gave the craft time to cycle through its environmental procedures, then jumped down into the bracken, a soft *thud* as he landed. He took the coat from its tree hook and returned to the centre of the clearing.

The cube materialised before him, and an opening appeared. A tall figure emerged. He studied her for a second: her smooth, almost featureless face, her elegant jawline flowing to the point of her chin, her large dark eyes, long black hair. Her clothes, practical, durable, and well suited for the warm forests in which she dwelt, were not ideal for England in December. She was hit by a sudden chill of the night air. "*Shedah rajah,*" she said, throwing her arms across her chest.

"English," he replied, handing her the coat.

"Of course." She accepted the coat and took in her surroundings. "This place is colder than I remember."

"It's getting warmer," he said, reaching into his jacket to retrieve a small white pen-like object. "Much faster than they realise." He held it out for her. "Welcome to Earth, Yanari."

"Bayen." She nodded, looking at the object with unease. "And is this as painful as I remember?"

His transformation was many years ago, but he still remembered the pain. The internal twisting, the feeling of being skinned and stitched back together, new teeth pushing out old. He would never forget it. He nodded.

Yanari took the object and frowned. "Have you ever wondered why the Makers, who seem capable of building anything, fail to build pain relief into these things?"

"I'll wait for you."

Yanari stepped back inside, the doorway disappearing, leaving no visible seam in the smooth wall of the cube.

Bayen returned to his tree and waited, a feeling of annoyance arising within. He was close to finding the Maker, and Kira Furlong would be the key. He felt it. He didn't need Yanari's help. Her presence would only complicate the hunt. But perhaps not. After all, she was sent from Giadeen himself, from the Great Tower. Which meant she'd been cleared by Grelik at the gates. Maybe she *would* be useful.

Three hours later, feeling fragile, Yanari was sitting in the van's passenger seat while Bayen drove at speed along the dark, twisty roads.

She was staring at her new alien reflection in the side

mirror, wondering how he'd harvested the DNA and whether her new appearance would be considered attractive. She doubted it. How could any human be considered attractive? She supposed they must find each other appealing, or they wouldn't exist in such vast numbers. But she questioned the necessity for such large nostrils? She couldn't even close them. She ran her finger over her fleshy lips then tongued her gums; they were sore. Her skin felt stretched and tender. Every bump in the road hurt, bruising her innards.

"Are we far from the Watcher?" she asked. Her throat burned.

"Not far," replied Bayen.

With heavy eyes, Yanari looked to the road as sleet fell from a sky beginning to lighten; it would soon be morning. She then took in the interior of her transport: the digital displays, the device with a full-colour screen mounted on the dashboard. "They are progressing quickly," she said.

"In some ways."

"I preferred their..." she searched for the correct name of the beast she had in mind, "...horse-drawn transports," she said, unsure if she was using the right words. "But maybe not on a night like this," she added, hovering a hand over a vent pumping warm air.

Bayen looked at her, then back to the road.

When the smooth road gave way to the sound of gravel, Yanari opened her eyes, unaware she had closed them. The van's lights swept across a dark old house in the middle of nowhere, picking out a small car covered in frozen leaves parked in front of a garage.

"Whose house?" she asked, eyeing the dark windows.

"Mine," he said with a sneer.

She made it inside with his help. The house was cold; they kept their coats on. The lights were off, and it smelt both dusty and damp. As they stepped over the pile of post littering the hallway, she heard flies and was then hit by another smell, more pungent. The flies were concentrated around a half-open door under the stairs. And the scent was one of death and decay.

Bayen guided her to a room and lowered her onto a sofa. He left, and she heard the door under the stairs being closed before he returned.

"I wouldn't go down there if I were you," he said.

Some flies had followed him, and she waved one from her face. Her eyes adjusted to the darkness; she saw more of them crawling over the flower-patterned walls.

Bayen walked to the window, pulled the curtain closed, then turned on a lamp in the corner, a cloth draped over its shade to dim it.

He disappeared from the room again, and she heard him clattering around in the kitchen. Moments later, he returned, handing her a glass of water before leaving her again. When he returned next, he had a bag of clothes in one hand and a rectangular grey device in the other. He dropped the bag next to Yanari on the sofa and placed the device on a desk, the contents of which had been swept away and now lay neglected on the floor beside it, photos of smiling humans in broken frames, their faces fractured by cracked glass.

She looked away from those faces, studied her alien hands, then looked to the Hunter sitting before his device, tapping at a panel of buttons positioned below a glowing screen. As she watched him, she picked at the blood under her soft fingernails. She felt a mess. She should bathe soon, but first, she wanted to talk.

"What is that?" She nodded towards the device.

He frowned. "When did you last pull from the Arkarnon?" he asked.

"Regarding this place? On my last visit."

"Then you should update your knowledge. Things change quickly here: technology, culture, language." He picked up the device and joined her on the sofa, placing it on the small coffee table, next to two china cups half full of mould, flies crawling around the rims. "This is a computer. Like the Arkarnon, it has access to information."

"What type of information?"

He angled the screen so she could see more clearly. It showed a picture of a woman.

"Who is she?"

"Kira. She is part Nim."

"Another descendant of the Maker?"

Bayen shook his head. "No. She is from the Watcher." Bayen looked at her. "What do you know of the descendent of the Maker?"

"Not much. Only that he's under heavy guard but free to roam our lands."

"Heavy guard? I heard a single Hunter watches over him."

"Yes. But a *Falcori* Hunter. And it's more for his protection; a human roaming our lands unprotected would not survive their first night. And Giadeen needs him alive."

"As bait," Bayen said under his breath.

Yanari nodded and looked back to the screen. "Is Kira aware of her heritage?"

"No. But there is one who is. A young boy who spends time with Rahiir. He seems to exhibit the Gifts of a Watcher."

She sighed and pulled over the bag of clothes to examine them. They looked comfortable. She would bathe tomorrow, she thought, and she stood and proceeded to undress. Bayen turned away sharply.

"How long have you been here?" she asked.

"In this house? Just a few months. Twenty years on Earth," he said, still looking away from the now naked Yanari.

She smiled. "Long enough to pick up their strange modesties." She finished dressing and sat. "I'm *decent* now."

Bayen looked back at his computer, continuing to stare at the image of Kira.

Yanari took in the young Hunter's appearance, short hair, square face, and broad, round shoulders. He was large — not as large or imposing as some Hunters she had encountered, but he had the same stiff manner and way of talking: short sentences, no wasted words. She tried to imagine his *real* appearance but struggled. "You don't look much like a Hunter," she said. "Your eyes don't quite have that cold, dead look about them."

Bayen's brow furrowed in annoyance. He closed the laptop, stood, then returned to the desk in the corner. "My Gift is new to me."

"You must be proud."

"Proud?"

"To be of the Gifted."

"I did nothing to earn it," he told her.

"Well, your parents must be proud."

"My parents died in the drought."

"You are from Pallon?"

Bayen nodded.

She made herself more comfortable on the sofa and downed her water, then eyed the glass with disgust. "How long has Rahiir been here?" she asked, turning the conversation back to the business at hand.

"Since his disappearance. Seventy-six years."

"Why did he stay?"

"If he's not with the Maker, I do not know."

"Do you think he is?"

"You are here to find that out. I just track them down."

"Answer the question."

"No. Rahiir does not seem the revolutionary type. Lives a simple life, works in a library, shops for his elderly neighbours, puts out their bins, sweeps down their paths."

"Not the behaviour of someone looking to overthrow Giadeen."

"And not behaviour you would expect from High Nim."

She raised her eyebrows.

"They didn't tell you?" He grinned.

"No."

"You are willing to take the life of an elder?"

"Yes. If it means saving Giadeen." She watched him place the computer into a large black bag on the floor. "How did you find him?" she asked.

"A Hunter's craft was destroyed as it left Earth's atmosphere. Its origin was traced to a clearing in the woods, not far from here."

"But how did you find the Watcher?"

Bayen reached back into the bag and pulled out an object similar to the small rectangular screen from the vehicle. The only difference seemed to be the deconstructed Nim technology secured to it.

"This," he said, holding up the device. "When someone passes, it scans them, records an image."

"What are you looking for in the scan? After transformation are we not identical to them?"

"Mostly. There are differences. Our higher bone density was the easiest for me to detect."

"Wait...for *you* to detect? *You* built that?" She raised her eyebrows in surprise. Bayen nodded almost imperceptibly, then placed the device back into the bag. Hunters could fashion deadly weapons and build traps, but that was it. She was impressed.

Bayen stood again, walked to the window, parted the curtains, and peered into the emerging dawn. "When you feel strong, I'll take you to him," he said. "While you interrogate him, I'll remain out of sight, ready to act if things turn sour."

"Turn sour?"

Bayen frowned. "If things *turn violent*. Please, pull from the Arkarnon tonight before you sleep. It will make communication between us much easier."

Or you could communicate without metaphor, she thought. Which, along with his surprising technical abilities, was another unusual trait for a Hunter.

Bayen returned to the open bag. She watched as he removed a dull black metal object and concealed it inside his coat. She recognised its form from her previous visit. It was less ornate than the ones she remembered, but its purpose was clear. "You use their weapons?" she asked.

"Whatever gets the job done," he replied, walking to the door. "I'll keep watch while you rest."

"Who are you watching for?"

He paused in the doorway and turned to face her, the dark hallway still buzzing with flies behind him. "If the Maker has followers, and Giadeen believes he does, we must stay alert. Assume that we too are being watched." He was about to turn away but added, "There is something you should know. Rahiir goes by the name of Ben. Some close to him call him Wren. Those who use that name know his true identity, not just the boy. When the time comes, we will need to deal with them, whether he's in league with Nabiim or not." Bayen narrowed his eyes. "Giadeen wishes it."

She felt him probing for a sign of weakness or lack of loyalty. For her, there was no reason for others to be hurt; she was only there to find and kill the Maker, but who was she to question the will of Giadeen. She nodded slowly and casually waved another fly from her face. "If Giadeen wishes it," she said, leaning back on the sofa. "Before I meet Rahiir," she added as Bayen turned to leave. "I want to watch him and these friends of his."

"Difficult, watching a Watcher," Bayen replied.

"Yet you have managed. He doesn't sense your presence?"

"They sense my presence when I want them to." He then merged into the darkness of the hallway. She listened after him, hearing nothing, no footsteps, until a moment later, there was a click from the door, and she felt a breeze briefly brush her ankles.

She was alone.

A large black fly looped across the room, landing on the wall by a photo of two humans, a male and a female. Unlike the other photos, this was black and white. It showed a young couple on a beach, looking happy, she thought. And although Yanari wasn't quite used to the unusual faces of humans, she saw herself in the female.

The fly left the wall and explored the inside of the lampshade in the corner, sending its giant shadow across the room. She lifted her legs onto the sofa and rested her head on the padded armrest. Then, with a slight gesture of her hand, the room fell into darkness. And Yanari, uncomfortable in her new skin, thought of her distant home, and the threat the Maker posed to it.

5

AN INVITE TO LONDON

Ellie and Isaac sat on the battered leather sofa, each wrestling a game controller while staring at the TV. Isaac's hands moved like manic spiders as he performed a multitude of combinations in quick succession. He leaned in, his body twisting and contorting as his on-screen avatar battled Ellie's. Ellie, in comparison, was reclined on the sofa, her eyes a picture of calm focus. Her hands, however, were just as rapid and spider-like.

"Yes. Yes. YES!" shouted Isaac on his way to sure victory.

Ellie paid him no mind as her thumbs, trained in the art of text messaging, refused to give up. Seconds later, Isaac's premature cries of triumph turned to cries of defeat.

"No. No. Noooo!" He dropped the controller to the floor and hung his head. "Remind me again, Max. Why do we let her hang out with us?"

"Yeah, right," Ellie laughed. "I let *you* hang out with *me*, and you know it."

"I remember now; it's because you're a geek."

"I'm no geek." She looked at him, eyes wide.

"Tell her she's a geek, Max," said Isaac, dodging her playful punch.

But Max wasn't paying attention; he was sitting at the desk in the corner using Isaac's laptop.

Isaac pushed himself up from the sofa and navigated around the magazines, snack wrappers, and video game boxes littering the floor. He stood beside Max, leaning in to look at the screen. "Anything new?"

"She added another cousin from her mum's side," Max said. "And a great aunt. But everyone descending from Wren is already here."

A series of names and connecting lines were on-screen representing the Furlong family tree. At the bottom was Max, a line leading from him to his mother, Dana Cannon, and his father, Jonathan Furlong. A line from his father went to Peter Furlong, Max's grandfather. From that point on, the tree became inaccurate, showing Peter to be the son of Betty Furlong. But Peter's mother was not Betty; it was Mary. And Peter's father was Wren.

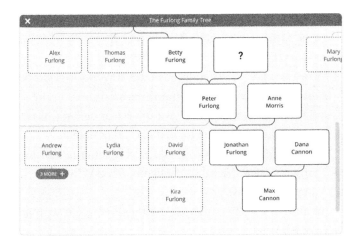

Isaac studied the screen. "You think any of these people suspect they're descended from an alien?" Isaac said, the word *alien* escaping quietly from the side of his mouth.

Max didn't like the word and had asked Isaac to stop using it. He still did, of course, but now he just mumbled it from the side of his mouth.

"How could they know?" said Ellie from the sofa.

Max clicked on the box representing his grandfather. A window opened, displaying more details and a photo showing him at a messy desk in front of an old computer. He wore a light blue jumper over a white, pointy-collared shirt. He looked happy but distracted. And he looked like Wren.

"Has Wren seen the photo?" asked Isaac.

Max shook his head. "He wants nothing to do with any of this."

"Really?" said Ellie. "That surprises me."

Max turned to face her. "He doesn't seem to care."

"You don't know that," said Ellie. "Maybe he's trying to protect them. In case Jenta or someone like him comes back one day to...I don't know..." She trailed off and shrugged. Then looked to Isaac for his thoughts.

"I reckon Max is right," he said. "Maybe he doesn't care. But that's not his fault. Might just be the way he's built." Isaac noticed Ellie's hard stare then quickly turned to Max with a smile. "He cares about you, though, mate."

"Thanks," said Max, trying hard not to return the smile but failing.

He looked back to the computer, closed the panel showing his grandfather, and clicked on his dad. There were two photos. One showed him graduating from university; in the other, he was standing in uniform next to an army helicopter.

He was never sad when he saw photos of his father; he'd died before Max was born, so he didn't know him to miss him. But there was a feeling of missing out, a longing for what could have been.

His dad had been the youngest of five, meaning all of Max's cousins were older than him, some in their thirties but most in their late twenties. As he looked at their names on the tree, he wondered — not for the first time — why none had ever been in touch. Maybe because his parents had never married, and the Furlong name hadn't made it to Max. Perhaps, without the name, they weren't seen as family.

"Two minutes to Kira time!" Ellie called from the couch.

Max closed the browser, looked at Isaac, and took a deep breath.

"Don't worry. Just be chill. It's no big deal," Isaac said.

"Feels like a big deal," replied Max.

"She's just your cousin," Isaac said. "Besides, you've seen her already in your dreams. So, technically, it won't be the first time you've met her."

"Probably don't mention that," Ellie suggested.

The call had been arranged over a week ago. Max had been worried about it ever since, visualising it going wrong in every possible way. As he was thinking of excuses not to go through with it, a tuneful melody issued from the computer, accompanied by the notification, *Kira Furlong is calling.*

"Good luck," Ellie said from the couch as Isaac slapped him on the back and joined her.

Max answered the call, praying the Wi-Fi would drop out or a power cut would strike the town. But a second later, Kira appeared on-screen, an abundance of thick black Nim hair taking up most of the frame, genes from elsewhere adding curls to the mix.

"Hey, Max," she said, her smile wide and bright. "It's so good to see you finally."

"Hey," he replied, his smile thin and self-conscious in comparison. "It's good to see you again...um...I mean, it's good to see you...too." *Three seconds in, and he already looked like an idiot.*

He glanced to his right, where his friends watched on with mild amusement on their faces. It felt rude not to introduce them, so he beckoned them with a nod. "These are my two friends, Ellie and Isaac."

They popped into the frame with a wave.

"We'll give you some privacy," said Ellie. "It was nice to have seen you." She dragged Isaac away, and they left the den with talk of finding snacks.

"They seem nice," said Kira, once they were alone. "It's funny, though...you said they are your *two friends*."

"Why's that funny?"

"You didn't say, *two of my friends*. You said, *my two friends*. Like they're your *only* friends. I thought it was funny."

"Oh," said Max, unsure how to respond.

"Sorry," she said, raising her hand to her head. "That sounds like I'm teasing you — I'm not. It's just a very Furlong thing to say. We're a family of loners. The fact you have *two* friends puts you at the more social end of the spectrum. I have many acquaintances and colleagues, but only a few *real* friends."

"Oh, I see." Max smiled again. "I have other friends, but they're...older."

"And *I* have Keith." She reached off-screen and brought in the cat Max had seen so many times before in his dreams. Keith didn't seem pleased about appearing on camera and tried to wander back out of shot. "He's the only friend I need," she said, pulling him back to nuzzle her face against his. "Isn't that right, Keith?" she said, using the voice reserved for small furry creatures and toddlers. "But, I think he's cheating on me with the old woman next door," she added as the cat finally managed to exit stage right. "He's spending more and more time over there. She's even installed a cat flap — and she doesn't have a cat of her own. Anyway, enough about my cat. It's lovely to see you finally." She smiled. "I haven't seen my other cousins for years."

"Why's that?"

"Most of them live or work abroad. Apart from Aunt Lydia. And what with my work, life's just a bit busy now."

"Oh," said Max. "Good job on the family tree, by the way. Did it take long?"

"No. No time at all. Aunt Lydia is a goldmine when it comes to family history. We sat down at her kitchen table with a bottle of wine and got most of it pegged down in a single evening. There's not much that woman doesn't know about our family. Apart from the dark secret, of course." She stroked her chin melodramatically.

Max swallowed.

Kira laughed. "It's probably not dark and not very secret. But still, I like to think it is."

"What is it?"

"Well, no one seems to know who Grandad's dad was. Betty, Grandad's mother, never married, which was unusual back then. I couldn't find any records that would help, not even Grandad's birth certificate. Our great-grandfather appears to be a man of mystery."

Max nodded as he listened. He knew precisely who his great-grandfather was, but he was not about to tell Kira.

"Anyway," she continued. "I'm sure it's nothing very juicy. Probably the postman or something. But it would be *great* to have a dark secret in the family, wouldn't it? Oh, there's something I wanted to ask you." She paused, then shook her head as if changing her mind, her thick, curly black hair bouncing side to side. "No, it's silly."

"What is it? You can ask."

She laughed to herself, then, tilting her head, she said, "I'm not sure how to put this...but are you—"

Max felt instantly hot in the cheeks as Kira searched for the right words.

"—good at anything?"

"Sorry?"

"I mean, is there something you *excel* at?"

Max hesitated. "Like...what?"

She shrugged. "Sport, science, medicine, art, languages? I don't know. It could be anything."

I'm good at seeing things very far away, and sometimes, when I concentrate, I can see through objects, is what he thought about saying. Instead, he said, "Not really. Why do you ask?"

"It's an odd family, a real mix of characters, and most of them seem a bit unstable if you ask me. But as we were putting this tree together, I was struck by how everyone on the Furlong side seemed to be high achievers, people at the top of their game in whatever career they chose. We have Olympians, Nobel Prize winners, top mathematicians, surgeons, inventors...." At this last example, she pointed to herself in mock arrogance and then laughed.

Max smiled. "No pressure then."

Kira laughed even louder. "I'm sure you'll be just as successful, and just as unstable, as all of them — us," she added with a roll of her eyes.

"Great," said Max, his smile turning into a grin.

As the call went on, Max became more relaxed. It was going better than he'd imagined; she was easy to talk to. She spoke of leaving Canada to study at Cambridge University and setting up the Artificial Architect Lab while attaining her PhD. She was passionate when she spoke of her work, like Isaac when he talked about space travel and engineering. She asked him what he wanted to do once he'd left school. And he felt ashamed for not having an answer; didn't everyone know what they wanted to do, what they wanted to be? Kira brushed it aside, saying she was confident he'd find the thing he was born to do. She said it with such conviction, he believed her.

Max's plan, before the call, was to find out if Kira thought of herself as *different*. He wanted to know if she felt like an outsider, as he once did and still did to some degree. He planned on asking questions that might lead to a profound discussion about loneliness and identity. A discussion that would confirm that she, too, was shaped by her unusual family history. In the end, he didn't know how to slip those questions in, and he wasn't sure he wanted or needed to. She didn't seem awkward like him or lacking in self-confidence. She was sharp, witty, funny, and engaging. All the things he wasn't. In a way, he was relieved.

One fear had been that she would be a lost soul, someone broken and detached from the rest of the world and the people in it. Hadn't she said that most of the family seemed *unstable*? He'd felt himself sliding in that direction once, slowly but inevitably. But that was before finding his friends and learning the truth about his unique heritage. With that knowledge came a sense of belonging he'd never had before. For him, growing up not knowing *why* he was different would have been a lot harder, he guessed. But Kira seemed to have life under control. She didn't need Max to tell her about the big family secret to make sense of it all. She was doing just fine. She was normal.

The time flew by, with neither of them struggling to find things to discuss. When it felt as though the conversation was naturally coming to an end, Isaac and Ellie re-entered the room, quietly placing themselves out of sight on the sofa, a tube of Pringles between them.

"You know what?" Kira said, suddenly hit by an idea. "You should come to my exhibition. It's in three weeks in London. I'll be staying with Aunt Lydia while I'm there.

She'd love to have you and your mum stay over for a few nights."

"Um…" Max wasn't sure what to say.

"He'd love to!" shouted Ellie from the sofa.

Kira laughed. "Bring your friends too. It's a *big* house. I'll give you a personal tour of the exhibit before it opens."

"Um…" repeated Max.

"See you in three weeks!" shouted Isaac.

Kira laughed again. "Listen, Max, think about it. Talk to your mum and let me know. It'd be great to meet you in person." Her eyes darted up and to the left, checking the time. "I've got to run," she said. "It's been great chatting. Let me know, OK?"

"OK," he said. "I'll think about it."

"Good. We'll speak soon. This was lovely." She ended the call.

"Bye," he said, but Kira was already gone.

Max slumped back in the chair and stared at the screen. For a second, he forgot about Isaac and Ellie but soon felt their eyes burning into the back of his head. He spun in the chair to face them.

"You better be going to her exhibition," Isaac said, with a mouth full of Pringles.

"I said I'll think about it."

Ellie looked at him and shook her head knowingly.

"Why are you holding back?" Ellie asked Max as they emerged onto a dark and foggy Church Lane.

"What do you mean?"

"You know what I mean. You're not going to accept Kira's invitation, are you?"

"No," he said. "I'm not."

"Why?" She stopped and pulled her scarf away from her mouth. "What are you afraid of? You wanted to find family, and now you have. She seems nice."

Max stopped and turned to her. "She does. But—" he sighed and glanced up to the church steeple, hidden behind the fog.

"You're afraid of what Wren will say?"

"No," said Max. "He doesn't seem to mind me getting to know them. He just has no interest in getting to know them himself."

"What about your mum? Would she not like the idea?"

"She'd love to meet them."

"So, what are you afraid of?"

"I'm afraid...I'll let something slip," he said as they began to walk again. "I'm afraid she'll find something out that gets Wren in trouble and half the Furlongs shipped off to a lab."

"You watch too much TV," said Ellie. "No, wait, you don't watch enough TV. But you spend a lot of time with Isaac, and he definitely watches too much. Look, I don't think you need to worry. Don't overthink it. You've just found a cool cousin you didn't know you had, and now she wants to meet you. Forget all the other stuff. See her. If you let something slip, she won't *believe* you. She'll just think you're a bit weird. Which is true."

Max smiled but said nothing. She was probably right; he was good at overthinking. But he still had no intention of meeting Kira in person. Not yet anyway.

"Isaac told me about training," said Ellie, changing the subject as they reached the neighbouring gates to their small front gardens. "About it being over."

"It's not over. It's just paused," he said. "Until the new year."

"What happened?"

"Just...stuff." He shrugged.

"Fair enough; you don't have to tell me."

"It's nothing — just a glitch. I'm probably just exhausted and need a break from it all. I started getting pains and... weird things."

Ellie frowned. "He's been training you too hard."

"No, it's not that—"

"I still don't understand why he's training you at all. It's not like you can put it on your CV."

Max smiled at her concern. "No. But it's a part of who I am."

She sighed. "I suppose." She opened the gate and walked up the path to her door. The smell of cooked food and the sound of a TV game show leaked out as she opened it. "Think about going to see her. Sleep on it. You might feel different in the morning." She stepped inside and closed the door.

Max pushed his gate open but didn't step through. He froze, allowing the gate to swing back with a squeak.

He was being watched.

It was now a familiar feeling, one he'd had many times. According to Wren, the ability to sense when you were being watched was an ability all Nim possessed, Gifted or not. It made sense on a world where you weren't at the top of the food chain. But here, on Earth, he'd found little use for it. If anything, it had become an annoyance.

He turned and looked up the lane.

Towards the town, soft glowing lights were shifting behind the heavy fog as cars turned the corner of Station Road. But the feeling was not coming from there. It was coming from the other end, where the cobbles turned into a dirt track, passing through a wooded area, leading to the fields.

Only the beginning of the track and the first few trees

were visible, caught in the glow of a single streetlight. Everything else was hidden in fog and shadow.

He took a few tentative steps back from the gate for a better look and saw footprints coming and going on the path, but they weren't fresh; the ground was too cold and hard for them to be recent.

The feeling of being watched was difficult to describe. To Max, it was like the world just suddenly narrowed around him, forming a cone, his senses pulled towards the pointy end where the danger lay. Usually, the feeling would fade after just a few seconds, but if anything, this was intensifying with each passing moment.

He considered turning back when a ginger cat appeared on the pavement beside him. Ignoring Max, like most conscious beings, it walked purposefully towards the trees as if on regular patrol. After a few steps down the path, it stopped. Its tail, which had been as upright as an antenna, fell until it was tucked between its legs. Its back then curved as it stared ahead into the darkness. It then hissed violently and bolted back the way it came, past Max, disappearing into one of the small gardens on the lane.

Rigid, his eyes remained fixed on the path. If his breathing were less erratic, he might be able to see further into the shadow. But when his breath did eventually even out, it became clear that whoever was watching was no longer there. The feeling was gone — and Max was alone.

6

FOLLOWED

The next day, Max didn't mention the whole being watched thing to his friends. Part of him now believed he'd imagined it, or if real, was probably nothing more than a curious fox.

The school day was uneventful. In the morning, he and Isaac spent a free period in the library revising, then met with Ellie at lunch, until her sixth form friends dragged her away with promises of freshly discovered scandal that she would not believe. As she left them, she looked back and rolled her eyes.

She rejoined them later at the school gates, heading home, lit by the beams of cars while thick flakes of snow fell around them.

"Mum said I can go to London," Isaac said, looking up from his phone, his voice barely escaping the small furry circle of anorak hood protecting him from the cold.

"You'll be going on your own," said Ellie. "He doesn't want to go."

Isaac tore off his hood to allow Max to see his disappointment. "What? Come on. We have to go. It'll be fun."

"I'll think about it," said Max.

"That just means he doesn't want to talk about it," said Ellie. "He's made his mind up."

"Well," said Max calmly. "It's my mind to make up."

Isaac's shoulders slumped as he raised his eyes to the sky. "But I've told my mum now. Anyway, why spend all that time looking for family if you're not going to visit them?"

"That's what I said," said Ellie. "He's worried he'll let something slip. About...well...you know...."

"So what?" said Isaac, moving closer and lowering his voice. "Let it slip. Tell her. I'd want to know if it were me. You can tell her about Wren without telling her about Ben. He doesn't need to be involved."

"You do know they're the same person, don't you?" said Max, glancing around at his fellow students, their heads bowed towards phones or jostling in noisy groups, too engrossed in their own lives to be concerned with his.

"My point is, they don't *have* to be. I can't see the problem here."

"Look," said Max. "Even if we went, there's no way I'd tell her anything. *A*, she wouldn't believe me, and *B*, what good would it do? It's not like she *needs* to know. She seems... really cool. If I told her, the news might break her. No," he added firmly. "She doesn't need to know. You'll just have to un-tell your mum. I'm not going."

"The news didn't break you, did it?" said Isaac quietly.

Max didn't answer.

On the high street, at the crossing, Max did the polite *thanks for stopping* nod to the vehicle to his right. As he stepped out into the beams of the bright headlights, he felt it again — someone was watching.

Once they'd crossed the road, he glanced over his shoulder. Away from the glare, he could see two silhouetted figures in a Land Rover. The eyes of the driver, lit by reflecting light from the rearview mirror, followed them as they walked.

Ellie and Isaac continued briskly, not noticing Max fall behind.

"Let's go this way tonight," Max said, catching them up. He steered them down a narrow street with a no entry sign.

Isaac started to protest. "This isn't the way—"

"Yes, it is," Max interrupted, hurrying them along.

"What's going on?" Ellie asked, looking back to see what had Max so spooked.

Max looked too, just in time to see the black Land Rover pausing at the entrance to the one-way street before revving its engine and speeding from view.

"We're being followed," said Max eventually.

"By who?" Isaac said, unconvinced and still seemingly annoyed with Max.

"Good question."

Max led them down another narrow turning, cobbled and closed to traffic. It was busy with shoppers admiring the Christmas displays of small boutique shops. They were halfway up the street when the Land Rover appeared again, stopping at the end of the road, its progress blocked by a line of concrete bollards. Max got low then dragged them into a small but packed toy shop.

"Is there a chance you're being paranoid?" asked Ellie as she followed Max, weaving his way through the customers to crouch by the festive window display. "There," he said, pointing to a woman wearing a long winter coat and bright orange woolly hat. She had just stepped from the passenger side of the vehicle and was now on tiptoes looking over the crowd of shoppers. With a look of frustration, she began to make her way down the middle of the street, her head bobbing and darting as she searched.

On seeing the woman's behaviour, Ellie and Isaac

needed no more convincing, and the three ducked as she passed the window. Crouching, they stared at the doorway, hoping she wouldn't enter. After a while, when she didn't, they stood and looked up the street but could no longer see her through the crowd.

The questions from Isaac and Ellie came fast: who were they? Why were they following them? Max answered the first one easily enough; he could see the GiaTek security sticker on the Land Rover still idling at the end of the road. It was too far for the others to see such a detail, and they took him at his word. As for why — Max didn't know.

When the Land Rover eventually sped off without the woman, they relaxed and left the shop, receiving curious glances from the customers and the shopkeeper, a plump man wearing a Rudolph Christmas jumper but bar humbug expression.

Outside, they took a narrow alley to a street running parallel to the one they'd just left. After a few more turns, Max felt it again, the feeling of being watched. This time it was as intense as the night before. He looked around, expecting to see the woman or perhaps the black Land Rover. But he saw nothing. Trying to bury the panic in his voice, he turned to Isaac and Ellie. "We need to split up. Go home. Go via the footpaths — they'll find it harder to follow."

"No. We should go to the library," Isaac said. "Wren could help."

Ellie nodded. "Yeah. I like that. I don't want these people knowing where I live. I mean, if they don't already."

Max protested but soon came around to the idea; anything to keep them moving.

Ten minutes later, using the most indirect route possible, they emerged onto Market Square from an alley beside a pub. Max scanned the busy square — no Land Rover, no orange woolly hat lady. All seemed clear. Even the sensation of being watched had passed. He looked to the library, then had second thoughts; the idea of possibly leading GiaTek anywhere near Wren suddenly seemed like a terrible one. He was about to tell the others when he realised they were already halfway across the square. Max sighed, then ran to join them.

Breathless, they burst through the library's automatic doors and were immediately caught by the disapproving stare of Mr Hall, the man most in town would guess to be an alien if they were told one lived there. They nodded politely as they passed him, his look far colder than the icy chill outside.

They found Wren pushing a trolley full of books down the centre aisle. He was wearing a light grey woollen jumper, black jeans, and a look of contentment on his face as he stopped to return a book to its rightful place on the shelf. His relaxed demeanour had a strong calming effect on the three as they approached, and Max almost forgot why they were there.

"Hey, Ben," said Isaac, his breath still heavy from the run. "What is it with you and this place?"

"Do we have to do this every time, Isaac?" Wren didn't look at them. He just smiled as he transferred another book from trolley to shelf, making the task look more like meditation than work.

"But I still don't get it," Isaac said, almost whispering. "A man with your...abilities shouldn't be working in a library. You could be making your fortune doing...something." He pursed his lips as he struggled to think of alternative professions for Wren, then looked to Max and Ellie for ideas. They both shrugged, Ellie uncomfortably flicking her eyes back to the entrance.

Max was about to mention their current situation, but Isaac, who seemed to have momentarily forgotten, said, "What about a professional poker player? You'd clean up in Vegas."

Wren's smile broadened. "No thanks, Isaac. I love my job. It's more interesting than my...previous job." He raised his dark eyes skyward.

The previous job Wren referred to involved watching Earth from orbit while in semi-hibernation for over a hundred years. Max, who'd happily spent hours people-watching from his tower block, had to admit, a hundred years of it was probably enough to make *librarian* seem like a great career move and a step-up in the excitement stakes.

"Anyway," said Wren, resting both hands on the trolley. "I sense you're here with a purpose other than criticising my life choices." He turned his gaze to Max, while Isaac and Ellie pretended to take a sudden interest in the books around them. Max looked sheepish and rubbed the back of his neck.

"OK," Wren said, "this doesn't look good."

"It's not," said Max. "We have a...situation."

"What kind of situation?" asked Wren, crossing his arms and tilting his head.

"The bad kind," said Max.

Wren looked at the three of them, then to the shelves on either side. "Now's not the time," he whispered, then nodded to a gap in the bookshelves, where, a second later, Max's mother appeared from the next aisle.

"Hey, honey," she said, surprised to see Max. A dent appeared in her brow as she seemed to sense the tension in the air. "Everything OK?" She looked to Wren then back to Max, concern growing.

Max forced a smile. "Yeah, of course," he said. "Just getting out of the cold."

"I know, it's *freezing* out there." She looked back to Wren, her expression softening. "I need your technical support." She pulled a stray lock of hair away from her face and tucked it behind her ear. "I think I've ordered a thousand copies of *Watership Down*. Every time I try to amend the order, the system crashes."

Wren chuckled. "It's a good book," he said. Max's mum laughed — a little too loudly.

Wren positioned the trolley into the centre of the aisle, then looked to Max. "I'll catch you later," he said with a nod, then departed with Max's mother.

"Max," said Ellie, once Wren was out of earshot, a broad smile on her face. "Are you aware your mum fancies your great-grandfather?"

"Very much aware, thank you," Max said, shoving Isaac to stop his laughing.

Isaac steadied himself and stopped laughing immediately, staring past Max, his eyes wide. Slowly, Max turned and saw the woman from GiaTek standing by the library's automatic doors.

7

A LIE DETECTED

The doors closed behind the woman in the bright orange woolly hat, then opened again as a bearded man joined her. He had a blue hat, furry flaps protecting his ears, and a puffy winter jacket. His lower half appeared unaware of the season, and he wore a pair of khaki shorts adorned with far too many pockets.

As Ellie dragged Max and Isaac down behind the trolley, the pair scanned the library.

"They followed us?" Isaac whispered in despair. "We were so careful."

"Not careful enough," said Ellie. She nudged Max. "Why didn't you spot them?"

"My eyes are good," said Max, "but they're in the front of my head, just like yours." However, he wondered why he hadn't sensed them when crossing the square. "We need to move," he said.

Using the trolley as a shield, they rolled it towards a gap in the shelves, then moved into the next aisle, one closed off at the end and not visible from reception.

Max looked up, and the others followed his gaze. The reflections in the angled windows set high on the four walls gave them a perfect bird's-eye view of the library below. They watched as the GiaTek pair split at the base of the ramp, entering the maze of bookshelves at different points.

"This way," whispered Max.

The three went from aisle to aisle, regularly checking the windows above to keep an eye on their pursuers, easy to spot in their bright orange and blue hats.

"Does this remind anyone else of Pac-Man?" whispered Isaac as they paused at a corner to avoid being seen by blue hat.

So far, orange hat and blue hat hadn't bothered looking up and continued to navigate the maze blindly and without hurry, allowing Max and his friends to remain one step ahead.

"We may have a problem," whispered Isaac, looking up to the windows. "If orange takes the next left, and if blue goes right, we're gonna get trapped."

Orange took the next left, so all eyes turned to blue as he approached the end of his aisle.

"Go left, go left..." urged Ellie under her breath.

Blue paused. He looked both ways, then undid his jacket. Then, after a few seconds, which felt longer to Max, he went left.

There was a trio of sighs.

It was a close call. One that convinced Max of the need to get out quickly; it was only a matter of time before they got caught. The problem was, they couldn't get to reception, not without passing one of them. The only option that remained was to hide out in one of the rooms at the back of the library. So, when the time was right, they made a run for it, breaking free of the book maze, rounding the long study desk — ignoring the disapproving looks from those who sat there — and ducked into the Local News and History room.

There was no one in the room. Max had hoped for a fire

escape or a *staff only* door — no such luck. So they hid behind a squat four-sided bookshelf in the far corner, to the right of the Hurstwick Incident display, a dusty and seldom looked upon exhibit, unknowingly dedicated to the arrival on Earth of Max's great-grandfather.

With their backs against the bookshelf, they waited in silence, Max closing his eyes and listening.

"Can you imagine," whispered Isaac after a while. "If your mum and Ben got married—"

There was a snort from Ellie as she stifled a laugh, and then a sound that was probably her elbow digging into Isaac's side to shut him up. "Now is not the time," she said. "What do they want?"

Max was about to tell them both to shut up when he heard a sound. It was the *HISS, HISS, HISS* of someone walking in a thick winter coat. It got louder and then stopped. Then a whisper. "One of us should have waited by the entrance." It was the woman.

"That would have been a great idea five minutes ago," said her companion. "I'll check the other rooms."

There was a moment of silence, but Max felt they were not alone. Slowly, he peered around the bookcase and saw her admiring the old map on the wall.

Her phone rang, startling Max, who quickly drew back his head.

"Zoe Durkin," she answered. There was a pause while the caller spoke. "Oh, hey, Dinesh," she replied. "How's life in the basement? Yeah, I bet. Uh-huh. Uh-huh. No, whatever you can do, I appreciate it.... No need for that. Right now, no one needs to know anything about this. Not yet anyway. I don't want to waste anyone's time over something that might be nothing. *No*, I'm aware your time's valuable too, I didn't mean...." There was a longer pause as the other party went on. "The *twenty-first*?" she said in a voice too loud for a library. Then, in a quieter tone, "Is it on a boat from China or something? Oh. Can't they put it on a plane? OK, OK, it is what it is. Thank you, Dinesh. Keep me updated, yeah?" There was a beep and a heavy sigh as she ended the call.

Max looked out again from behind the bookshelf. She was still there, standing with her back to them, still staring at the map of Hurstwick on the wall. Just then, Isaac shifted uncomfortably beside Max, the sound of his anorak enough to distract the woman, who turned to look in their direction. Max drew back in time but heard Zoe's approaching footsteps. He gestured wildly for them to move. As they scrambled around the bookcase, the rest of the room and the exit came into view. It would be a clear run. He glanced back to see Zoe's shadow growing across the floor behind them. It was now or never. Together, they ran to the door and were almost out, almost free, when Zoe's bearded shorts-wearing accomplice appeared, blocking their escape.

Isaac stopped sharply, causing Ellie and Max to crash into him.

"Woah there," the man said, hands out as if calming startled horses. "Where are we off to in such a hurry?"

"There you are," Zoe said, emerging from around the bookcase behind them. "I told you they were here, didn't I?"

"Yes, you did," replied the man. "She's always right," he whispered with a *what can you do* kind of shrug. He had a round, friendly face, but it was clear he wasn't going to move, his hands now resting on the thick walls either side of their exit.

"Let us go," said Ellie, moving past Isaac to stand before the man.

"Just a little chat," said Zoe. "That's all we want."

Ellie ignored her. "Stand aside," she said to the smiling man still blocking the doorway. "Or get a swift knee in the love spuds."

The man's smile faltered, and he suddenly looked less in control. He lowered his hands to cover the spuds in question.

"Oh, I like her," said Zoe. She let out an exaggerated sigh then said, "Let them go, Travis. I'll file my report without their side of the story. Just thought they might like to comment, that's all."

Travis stepped aside, looking almost relieved.

"But know this," Zoe continued. "This photo, along with fascinating video footage, will soon land in the inboxes of some very powerful people."

Max half-turned to see Zoe place a photo on the table. It was the drone selfie from the barn. He looked to Isaac. Isaac shrugged.

"But maybe this doesn't need to be a part of my report," she added, tapping the photo. "Maybe I didn't even find it."

Ellie and Isaac began to edge past Travis but stopped when they realised Max wasn't following.

"Come on," Ellie said, "We don't need to speak to them."

Max shook his head, then slowly walked to the table. Zoe smiled and sat down. Max sat opposite.

He remembered sitting in that same spot two summers ago, telling all to Mr Bartley, a man whose past was tormented by the crash landing of Wren. He told him about the diary, the key, the visions, the truth about the crash and the one who had survived it.

He wouldn't be sharing any of that today. Today he was there to listen. He *had* to know what this woman knew — or thought she knew.

Reluctantly, Ellie and Isaac sat on either side of Max and stared at the photo, a photo Max had forgotten existed. Of all the things that happened on that eventful day, the drone selfie barely registered in his memory.

Max looked at the woman opposite and waited for her to talk.

"I'm Zoe Durkin," she said. "And this is my colleague, Travis Wells. We're from—"

"GiaTek," said Isaac. "We know."

"That's right." She nodded, impressed. "So why did you feel the need to run from us?

"It's generally a good idea when you're being followed," Ellie said. She turned to Max. "Look, we don't need to talk to them. Let's go. If they don't leave us alone, we call the police."

"Please do," said Zoe. "We'll wait." She looked to Travis as he sat down next to her, then back to the three, who had made no move to leave or call the authorities. "No?" she said. "I didn't think so. Launching that drone from the no-fly zone was illegal; you'd be in a heap of trouble. No one wants that."

"Then what do you want?" Ellie asked.

"Just your take on what you saw that day."

"We didn't see anything," Isaac said firmly and quickly, crossing his arms.

"We have an interesting video that says otherwise."

"Shouldn't you be getting consent from our parents before talking to us?" Ellie said.

Zoe sighed. "More than happy to. Just give me their numbers, and we'll call them." Then, seeing no sign from the three to produce any numbers, she added, "I see. You don't want them involved either. That's fine. They don't need to be. This can be just between us."

The situation seemed hopeless. Isaac and Ellie slumped in their chairs, looking defeated. For a moment, Max had felt defeated too, but then he'd seen something his friends hadn't; something he wasn't looking for, but his attention had been drawn to it, like it was important. When Zoe mentioned having seen the video, her pupils had dilated, her pulse increased — evident by subtle vibrations on her temples — and there had been a slight flushing of her cheeks that quickly faded.

She was lying.

"We know what you saw," Zoe went on. "We watched the videos many times. We just want to hear your account in your words. Do that, and we'll keep your names and this photo out of the report."

More lies. They hadn't seen the videos. For some reason, all they had was that photo. But Max needed to be certain.

"OK," he said, deciding to put his theory to the test. "I'll tell you. But first, I want to make sure of a few things."

"Excellent." Zoe smiled and leaned forward, crossing her arms on the table.

Isaac and Ellie glared at Max. He ignored them, taking a deep breath, focusing entirely on Zoe's face. He took in every detail of her skin, the tiny blood vessels in her eyes, everything. It all became so clear so quickly.

"So, you're Zoe Durkin?" he said calmly.

"That's right." Her brow twitched. She looked slightly confused and amused by the question, but Max noted no dilation of the eyes, no flushing of the cheeks, no increased pulse.

"And you work for GiaTek?"

"Yes. I...think we established that already." Again, eyes normal, pulse normal, cheeks normal.

"And you want to know what we saw?"

"Yes." Tiny hairs on her neck quivered. Somehow, he knew this was frustration at his pointless questions and was not a lie. It was followed by a slight twitch at the edge of her forced smile that Max read as excitement.

He paused, allowing his breath to slow even more, then asked: "And you've seen the video?"

"Yes." She answered quickly and confidently with an underlying frustration still present, but this time the answer came with a wave of tiny signals that screamed *LIE!*

He felt a surge of excitement on discovering this new benefit to his enhanced vision. An ability Wren had failed to mention. He'd become a human lie detector. Well, mostly human.

"OK, I'll tell you what we saw," he said, feeling smug but trying not to show it. Zoe needed to believe what he was going to tell her.

"Great," said Zoe, retrieving her phone from her pocket. "Do you mind if I record you?"

Max shrugged, and when she was ready, he began. "As the drone cleared the hill, we saw the bypass," he said, wondering if his lie would be as transparent as hers. "There were lots of people there — helicopters, army, police. They were busy doing something; I don't know what. We hovered around for a bit, but nothing much was happening. Then we got a low battery warning. That's when we flew it back. But it didn't make it back."

"What happened?" Travis asked, leaning in.

"We lost it."

Travis's eyes narrowed. "What do you mean, *you lost it*?"

"Battery died, and it fell out of the sky. Somewhere in the woods."

"You try to recover it?"

"We looked for it," Isaac said, "But we couldn't find it. Oban Wood is pretty big."

Zoe stopped the recording. She sat back and smiled at Max. "I don't think you're being completely honest with me."

"Really," said Max. "But you saw the videos."

Presumably not used to seeing Zoe outfoxed, Travis leaned back in his chair and shook his head. Isaac and Ellie watched on intently.

"OK. You got me," said Zoe lightly, as if all just a game to her. "The SD card from the drone was damaged. We can access photos, but not video, for now. We've sent it away to be fixed. And soon we'll see everything you saw. So, is there nothing else you want to mention? Something you might have missed?"

"Like I said," Max said, "We didn't see anything."

"Look," Zoe said. "Whatever happened over there, it had nothing to do with you. You simply filmed it. You've got nothing to lose by telling us what you saw. If you're worried about getting into trouble, don't be; we'll keep your names out of it."

"Are you not listening?" Ellie said. "He told you what we saw."

"He did," replied Zoe. "It's just I don't believe him. I can understand the government having things to hide. But you guys have nothing to hide...." She trailed off with a look that suggested an idea was forming, which worried Max. "Wait...." She tilted her head. "Maybe you do have something to hide. Is that it?" She looked at the three of them in turn. "What are you hiding?"

Travis placed a hand on Zoe's arm. "I think we better leave."

"No." She pulled her arm away and stood.

Max said nothing. Ellie and Isaac crossed their arms with a look of defiance as Zoe began to pace.

"Look," Travis said, leaning towards Isaac. "It was your drone, wasn't it? We'll fix the SD card. Might take a few days; might even take a few weeks. But we *will* fix it. You could save us some time, though. You have the backups, right? You could earn yourself a few quid." He flicked his eyebrows. "New PlayStation? New bike? New drone?"

Max and Ellie glanced sideways at Isaac.

"There's no backup," Isaac said flatly, then he looked away.

Travis leant back in his chair, his gut protruding from his open coat. "There's always a backup."

Zoe Durkin had stopped pacing and was now standing by the glass cabinet containing the wreckage of the plane that never crashed in the woods. Max watched her intently. Her expression, reflected in the glass, was one of deep thought.

"You're free to go," she said, not looking at them.

The three stood and walked to the door. Max turned around. There was something he needed to know before he left. "If I see you outside my house again, I'll call the police."

She turned to face him with a frown. "Sorry, what?"

"I saw you. I saw you outside my house last night." He studied her closely, watching for the signs.

"Wasn't us," she said in a disinterested manner. "I have no idea where you live."

Max suddenly felt cold. She was telling the truth.

Zoe watched the teenagers leave.

"Something's not right," she said to Travis as she lost sight of them. "They're hiding something."

"Or maybe they're telling the truth, and they didn't see anything."

"They saw something. Did you not see how scared they were?"

"You can be quite scary—"

"They're not scared of me. They're scared of what I might find out."

"They're scared of getting in trouble for flying a drone where they shouldn't have."

"No. It's more than that. They're hiding something. I want to know what and why."

Travis slid a hand down his face and then threw his head back in exasperation. "You're getting way ahead of yourself. We won't know anything until Dinesh fixes the thing." He stood and tucked the chair under the table. "I'm going back to the hotel. I'm bushed. Harassing school children can be quite tiring."

As Travis left, Zoe picked up the photo from the table and glanced around the room, her eyes settling once more on the display, dusty and forgotten in the corner. Then, looking at the large map of Oban Wood on the wall beside it, she tilted her head and stepped closer, her eyes narrowing, taking in its familiar shape. Slowly, she reached out, placing her finger on the approximate location of Site of Interest 1, the epicentre of the giant energy spikes. "Huh," she said with a smile. Her finger, she noticed, was more or less in the centre of a faded circle. The label next to that circle read, *Crash Site*.

8

THE SPIRE

Max, Isaac, and Ellie left the library and made their way home, navigating the twists and turns of the town's back alleys. It was snowing heavily. The snowflakes were large and, in the absence of any wind, seemed to descend in slow motion. The three barely spoke; no one knew what to say.

At a split in the path, they parted ways with Isaac under a bright streetlight. With a bleak wave, he promised to delete the backup as soon as he got home. It was a backup neither Max nor Ellie knew existed. Learning of it annoyed Max, but he said nothing; he could see Isaac's guilt and didn't want to add to it.

"I'm gonna wait for Wren," Max told Ellie as they arrived on Church Lane. "He needs to know about this."

Ellie nodded, then hugged Max, leaving him by the covered gate of the churchyard. He watched as she walked home, passing between pools of warm light spilling from the windows of the cottages, his eyes flicking between her and the dark trees at the end of the lane.

When she disappeared from view, he entered the gates and took the path leading to the tower, the lights lining the path diffused by a fine fog hanging over the churchyard, like net curtains.

A mundane-looking door, not meant for churchgoers, was set deep into the tower's thick wall. Set so deep, the light on the wall above failed to reach the door itself, lighting only the two stone steps leading down to it. He descended the steps into shadow, slipped his school bag from his shoulders, then removed a key from the side pocket, the key given to him by Mr Walsh, Hurstwick's omnipresent handyman and one of Wren's oldest friends.

He opened the door and entered a dark space. Although it wasn't dark for him, nothing really was anymore.

It was a space used for storage. There were stacks of chairs and fold-up tables against the wall, a cluster of tea urns and a pile of crates, one with a cricket bat poking out. Max crossed the room and reached for the handle of another door. He opened it and stepped through into the grand interior of the church.

It was silent and cold.

He climbed the wooden spiral staircase to his left and emerged onto the mezzanine. He looked out over the nave with its rows of dark wooden benches, tinged orange from the lights outside, the wide centre aisle so clean it appeared wet. As he looked, he thought of the generations of Furlongs that had worshipped, celebrated, and mourned down there, and for a moment, felt a connection to them.

The distant sound of chimes from the church clock woke him from his daydream, and he turned away, heading to the room where the bell ropes dropped from the ceiling. In that room was the small black door, a door somehow invisible to those not "In the club," as Mr Walsh had once put it. He opened it and, in relative darkness, continued his climb.

He went through the tower, through the belfry with its

sleeping bells, and into the small space just below Wren's sanctuary, pausing among the cobwebs to catch his breath before climbing the short set of wooden steps leading to the hatch.

Every time he lifted that hatch, he remembered his first visit. He considered that moment to be the first time he really saw Wren. Of course, he'd seen Ben many times before, but Ben was a man-shaped blur, impossible to hold in memory, slippery to sight. But on that day, Ben had become Wren. He'd lowered his defences, allowing Max, and his friends, to *see* the real him.

Max dropped his heavy bag to the floor, causing a small cloud of dust to rise by his feet. He stretched his back and looked around the tall octagonal space. It'd been a while since he'd been up there, but nothing had changed. A single bulb hung from the ceiling — useless considering who occupied the space — and there was a low bed, a small mat, and a stack of books. Somewhere, hanging on the wall, hidden from view, was Wren's bag of tricks, his only link to the world he gave up.

Wren didn't live up here. It was too cold for that, and it lacked certain facilities. Instead, he rented a room at Mr Walsh's place, Rose Bank Cottage, a picturesque, thatched abode backing onto the churchyard. This spire — the spire he'd once destroyed — was his watchtower.

Wren's urge to climb and watch was strong, and he was unable to ignore his instincts — like a meerkat born in captivity, standing vigilant for eagles it would never see. For Wren, every moment not watching caused a slow build-up of tension that he could not dispel with breathing techniques or meditation. The only way for him to reset, purge that anxiety, was to climb and watch. Max felt that need, too, but to a much lesser degree.

He climbed the ladder in the centre of the room, the

walls narrowing as he passed through the rafters with their wraith-like cobwebs. When the ladder ended, he stepped off onto a small wooden platform, large enough for two to sit with some room to spare. Two portholes were cut into the stone spire: one looked out over the town, the other towards Oban and the fields. Against the wall between them sat an old record player, a row of a dozen records next to it. Max picked up "I'll be seeing you" by Billie Holiday — his great-grandmother's favourite, according to Wren. He carefully removed the record from its sleeve and placed it on the platter, flicking a switch to make it turn. Then he gently lowered the stylus. There was a lonely crackle for a moment, and then Billie Holiday's warm, rich voice filled the tiny space.

As it played, he picked up a framed photo of Mary from next to the player. She was on a bicycle, smiling at the camera while holding on to her hat as a breeze tried to take it.

He smiled back at her, then placed the photo back down as a chill breeze blew in through the porthole.

The portholes were windowless, with a fine wire mesh stretched across them. He unhooked the mesh from the one facing the town and pulled it away. He poked his head through and looked down to the dark churchyard below, the snow looking more plentiful from up here.

He gazed across to the town where the thin veil of fog softened the festive lights spanning High Street and Station Road.

Under the lights — blinking red, blue, white, and gold — the streets were busy with commuters and shoppers. The commuters powered along, heads down, trails of frosty breath behind them, while the shoppers leisurely took in the displays in the bright shop windows, no rush to be anywhere, enjoying another fine Christmas in Hurstwick.

Max took it all in.

And although he wasn't aware of it straight away, he was beginning to slow his breath in readiness to watch. It hadn't been his intention; he was supposed to be taking a break from watching. But before he knew it, his eyes were busy soaking up every detail they could. He could have stopped it, but it felt good. He felt a sense of joy at how easy this part of his Gift was becoming. After a few seconds, the town had revealed itself as a rich tapestry of colour and texture, its beauty enchanting him.

When in training, Wren had always given him a task, something on which to focus. Now, with no instructions to follow, he allowed his gaze to wander. He looked over the rooftops, at the pigeons huddled together under heating pipes and next to vents. He watched icicles hanging from gutters dripping water on the ledges below. He watched a man fling a bag of waste into a rubbish compactor behind the supermarket, the man's nose wrinkling as he took in the unpleasant smell. He then took his gaze up to the railway station, to the line of parked taxis waiting for the next commuter train from London. Some drivers stood in the cold around the second car in the rank, talking with hands buried in pockets, feet constantly moving to keep warm while exhaust fumes hung at their legs.

As his gaze went from place to place, lazily matching the rhythmical flow of Billie Holiday's soothing voice, he began to think about Zoe Durkin. He wondered what would happen once she saw the video. She would see the crumpled diggers and the excavator lifted into the air like a toy. And she would see Jenta's grey tattooed hand retrieve parts of the broken drone from the long grass in the clearing. She would see all that and then wonder why they hadn't shared it, posted it online for the world to see. People didn't keep videos like that hidden unless they themselves had something to hide. Zoe knew that.

While his mind was caught up in these thoughts, two things had changed. First, the song had finished, and a constant crackle now came from the small speaker. The second thing that changed was his gaze — he no longer had control over it. The town was now panning and zooming at an increasing rate before him. The feeling was dizzying, but he remained calm because a part of him knew exactly what was happening.

Wren had talked about this before, but Max had never experienced it. It was an automatic response, triggered by a feeling of danger. According to Wren, it was useful for picking out individual threats in chaotic situations. Max didn't know if it was something he could do, or even if it would ever be useful in a sleepy town like Hurstwick. But here he was, his focus systematically searching for someone — someone he perceived to be a threat. He had a good idea who.

His eyes jumped from face to face — long faces, round faces, faces creased with worry, carefree and bright faces, and faces vacant and pinched with cold. Despite the jerky, almost mechanical nature of being drawn to face after face, he felt calm and detached. Many were faces he recognised — it was a small town, and he'd spent a lot of time watching these people — but none were the *right* face. He was looking for someone specific. At the bottom end of High Street, near the level crossing just beyond the bend, he found her. Zoe Durkin. She was the *threat* his subconscious had been seeking.

Illuminated by car headlights, she crossed the wet and shiny zebra crossing, heading towards The Coach House, an old crooked-looking building, originally a pub, but in recent years extended at the back to become one of the town's larger hotels.

His calmness wavered as he realised she would soon

enter, and he would lose sight of her. As she got closer to the entrance, he saw that white, beautiful light, the same he'd seen when watching the crow from Windmill Hill. When the light faded, instead of seeing her, he saw what she saw; a hand in an orange glove, reaching out to the brass plate of a black wooden door. She pushed it open, and he saw the hotel lobby. There was a friendly nod from the large woman behind the desk, a busy bar, a hunched man with a potbelly standing at a slot machine with a pint in his hand. There was sound too — muffled, as if underwater. The bar disappeared, and he saw a flight of stairs covered in a garish flowery carpet. The orange-gloved hand again, this time as it reached for the stair handrail. As he watched this, a dull pain grew in his distant mind, an ache, slowly turning and sharpening to a point.

The floorboards creaked and popped as she moved down a narrow corridor, the same garish flowery carpet under her feet, pictures hanging on white walls with black beams. She stopped outside room 22 and slid a keycard into the electronic lock. There was a click, then a green light, and she pushed open the door. She didn't enter. Instead, he saw the corridor again as she moved back along it. She stopped by a picture on the wall. It was of a church, its spire exploding as a plane ripped through it. The image stayed in place, and for a moment, he thought the vision had frozen. But it hadn't; she was staring at it, unblinking. He saw her reflection in the glass. Max had no access to her thoughts, but he knew what she was thinking. She was making connections he hoped no one would: connections between events at the bypass and the Hurstwick Incident. Connections her superiors had most likely already made. But she had something they didn't, an extra piece to the puzzle — a photo of a boy directly linked to it all.

Suddenly, the brilliant flash of white light returned,

bringing a searing heat and a prolonged and unrelenting pain. He heard himself cry out again and again until the pain became unbearable.

Then there was darkness.

Consciousness returned to Max, but he dared not open his eyes. At first, he was aware of the side of his face feeling warm. This worried him. Then he heard the crackle of a fire, a gently ticking clock, and the feeling of a soft blanket under his fingers. And he knew where he was.

He opened his eyes.

He was lying on a sofa. He moved his head to take in the small, dimly lit, cosy room. There was an empty armchair by the fireplace, a newspaper folded over one of its arms. On a small table next to it was a mug and a half-eaten Jaffa Cake. Max craned his neck and saw a second empty armchair, this one with a footstool before it. Closer to hand, set just before the sofa, was a long, low coffee table. On it was an object he hadn't seen for over a year and a half — Wren's healing disc.

From another room came soft, familiar voices that soon became louder. Footsteps accompanied them.

"He lives," said Mr Walsh, entering the room with a bright smile, holding a glass of water. "You're all right. Nothing wrong with ya; don't look so worried."

Wren followed him in, ducking under the low door frame and again under the subsequent beams running across the ceiling. He was smiling too, but with concern just below the surface.

Max moved to sit up, but Mr Walsh insisted he stay put. "Give yourself a minute to come round," he said. "The big man gave you the once over with that thingamabob." He nodded to the healing disc. "You'll be just fine. You just need rest. And drink this."

With a wink, Mr Walsh set the glass of water down, using the healing disc — probably the most valuable object on the planet — as a humble coaster to protect a coffee table that had seen better days. Wren hadn't missed this, and as he sat, he subtly shook his head at Mr Walsh, who smiled innocently.

As Max reached for the glass, he heard the church clock begin to chime the hour and glanced at the carriage clock on the mantlepiece. It was 8 o'clock. He immediately swung his legs around to get to his feet. "Mum's expecting me home—"

"Don't worry," said Wren, holding up a hand. "I sent Dana a message from your phone. You're having dinner at Isaac's tonight."

"Thanks," Max said, relieved. He stayed sitting upright and wondered how Wren had unlocked his phone, then decided he didn't really care. "And I mean thanks for everything," he added. "For bringing me down, and...well...fixing me." He glanced at the healing coaster.

"How do you feel?" Wren asked.

"OK," Max said. And he did feel OK, which was surprising considering the pain he'd endured before blacking out. There was still pain, but it was dull, more the memory of pain.

Mr Walsh looked at him sympathetically. "You want to tell us what happened?"

"Not really," replied Max, forcing a smile through the discomfort.

But Max did tell them. He told them everything, starting with GiaTek and ending with his experience in the tower. By the end of it, Max saw the worry in Wren's eyes. It was subtle, but it was there. Mr Walsh seemed to sense it too; he shifted uncomfortably in his seat, frowning and looking at the fire from under his bushy white eyebrows.

A long silence followed, measured by the ticking of the clock and interrupted by the occasional pop from the fire. With a thoughtful look, Wren turned his attention to the flames. He placed his elbows upon the arms of the chair, interlocked his fingers across his chest, and stretched his long legs to bring his shoeless feet to rest on the footstool. After a while, Max followed his gaze and saw a black flameless log on the fire slowly rise, turn itself over, then settle and erupt with a new flame. Max couldn't help but smile. Mr Walsh had seen it too, and his frown immediately softened.

It was Mr Walsh that broke the silence. "Whatcha thinking, old man?" he said, leaning forward to reach for his half-eaten Jaffa Cake.

Wren's attention left the fire and turned to Max. "On Windmill Hill," he said. "When you saw the distant hills and the river, you said you saw them from above?"

Max nodded.

"Through the eyes of the crow?"

Max nodded again. "I think so."

"Now I've heard it all," mumbled Mr Walsh.

Wren stared back to the fire, a crease in his forehead. To Max, he seemed more interested in his new ability than in the pair from GiaTek.

"We should try to get the SD card back," proposed Max, steering the conversation back to what he felt was the more pressing concern.

"Is there any point?" Mr Walsh asked. "I'm no technical whiz kid — I can just about set the timer on my oven — but won't they have pulled off those files by now, backed 'em up or whatever it is they do?"

Max shook his head. "They said they need to fix it. She

spoke to someone on the phone who was waiting for a delivery, something that would help them fix it — it arrives on the twenty-first."

"The twenty-first is in three weeks." Mr Walsh said, stroking his chin. He then waved his hand dismissively. "So, they find out. What's the worst that could happen? They show the video to their superiors, slap you on the wrist for flying the drone in a no-fly zone, and threaten to take you to court if you tell anyone what you saw. I can't imagine it going further than that. Columbo and Mrs Marple couldn't link what happened down there to the two of you."

Wren sighed. "Peter's right," he said. "There's nothing to worry about here. I don't see this as a problem. But for peace of mind, I'll retrieve the SD card."

"It's not at the compound," Max said. "It sounded like it's been sent away to be fixed."

"If it's not at the compound, it could be anywhere," said Mr Walsh to Wren. "Even you'd struggle to find something so small without some hint to its general location. Unless you had a little help from young Max here. This new ability of his—"

"No," said Wren.

"Think about it; the young man seems to have abilities you don't. Combining his gifts with yours may get you closer to finding the dammed thing. Work together. He gets behind their eyes, finds out where they're keeping—"

"No," repeated Wren, firmly this time. "You saw the state of him. Just a few minutes of seeing through the eyes of another had all but killed him."

Mr Walsh drew his eyebrows together and finished the last of his Jaffa Cake.

Wren looked at Max, then spoke softly. "I do not know how to train you anymore. I thought I did. I thought you were just like me, but you're not. There is something different happening here, and I need time to understand it. The tiredness and the pains are normal; I remember them myself. But not to the level you've suffered." He pulled his legs from the footstool and leaned forwards. "I know we said we'd wait for the new year to restart your training, but now, I think we should wait longer. I don't want you trying this again—"

"I didn't try anything," said Max, attempting to remain calm but unable to overcome the tremble in his voice. "It just happened. I couldn't control it—"

"Because I pushed you too far too soon. You were not ready. You'll not use these Gifts again until I say you're ready." Wren managed to sound both sympathetic and authoritative at the same time. It was a tone that could not be argued with. Wren had made his decision.

But so had Max.

An hour later, after a bowl of hot soup and some warm bread, Max returned home, closing the door behind him and leaning heavily against it. There was dread in his bones. Deep down, he knew that failing to retrieve the SD card would mean trouble for him and his friends. He suspected Wren knew it too and was trying to protect him.

But Max didn't need protecting.

He would disobey Wren.

He had no choice. Mr Walsh was right; Wren wouldn't be able to find the card, not without Max's new ability to help him. If he could learn to control it, he was going to use it.

9

DOWNFALL

Sweden, June 1944

Joseph secured the rowboat to the jetty of the small tree-covered island and disembarked, fishing rod in one hand, two medium-sized perch in the other.

He paused to take in the early morning view. Like a mirror, the water reflected the hundreds of tree-covered islands fading into a hazy distance. The only sounds were distant bird song and the gentle slop of water under the jetty and against the small boat.

The peace and perfect reflections were soon shattered by the arrival of a pair of geese descending to skid across the water, their harsh calls signalling their presence to no one but him.

When the geese had said enough and the peace returned, he looked up briefly to the cloudless blue sky. He'd normally welcome such a sky, but now he felt threatened by it — too exposed. He left the jetty, lowered his rod and his catch into the long grass of the bank, and returned to the boat, where he untied it again. He dragged the boat along, then stopped, allowing it to drift past him to settle under a tree hanging out over the water. Once hidden and secured, he retrieved his fish and rod and made his way through the thick cover of trees, taking the overgrown path that led to his cabin just a short distance away.

Tall trees crowded the sturdy-looking cabin, leaving only a small circle of sky visible above. It was a cabin with red walls and white window frames, the paint in need of a refresh. The grass around it was long and reached the bottom of the windows, giving the place an abandoned feel. The only sign of life was the thread of smoke issuing from the brick chimney, smoke that was absorbed by the surrounding dense pine.

With his hands full, he pushed open the door with his foot and entered the one-room cabin. He hung his rod on two hooks set upon the wall and laid the fish on a stone slab by the deep sink.

"I'm back," he said in a low, gruff voice to a space that, to all appearances, seemed empty save for him. "Two fine fish today. Almost a pike, too, but it got away. As we say: with struggle comes balance."

He was answered by silence.

At the fireplace, he took two logs from a pile and threw them on the dying embers and within minutes, the fire was roaring. He knelt over it, warming his hands. June in these parts rarely got to a temperature that he found comfortable. He would use the glow-stone at night to keep warm, and the fire during the day.

"There, that's better, isn't it?" he said, looking to the darkest corner of the room with a smile, then waited for a second before responding to the silence with a nod.

For the next few hours, he went about his business, prepping the fish, splitting logs, repairing a small cupboard above the sink. As he worked, he mumbled to himself under his breath, a frown constantly across his brow. Sometimes he would look skyward, whether he could see the sky or not, and would then mutter indistinctly. Every so often, he would stop what he was doing and listen for any sound that didn't belong. If there were alarm calls from the birds, he would dart to the window and peer outside. If there were *no* alarm calls, he would dart to the window anyway, hoping to catch *them* out. He was constantly on edge.

When it was time to rest, he sat by the fire, over which hung an old copper kettle. Unaware of the local proverb, he watched it until the whistle blew, and its lid rattled, then poured the hot water into a cup containing dried mint and fennel. He then placed the kettle on the stone hearth and leaned back in his chair, closing his eyes, waiting for his drink to cool.

A minute or two later, his eyes opened and then narrowed. He had felt a subtle tap in his breast pocket. It was followed by the sound of a distant motor. On its own, the sound would have given him little concern, but paired with the tap in his pocket, it propelled him to the door, which he yanked open to stand alert on the porch. The quick *chug chug chug* of the engine grew louder, and he saw movement on the water, just visible in slices through the trees. It was a small boat.

He turned back into the house and walked quickly to his workbench. Under a window, on a shelf full of carved ornaments, was the wooden box with its silver thumb plate. He opened it. The hollowed impression that had once held the coal-like mass was empty, but the wooden ring and the milky-white sphere were still there. He removed the sphere and held it out, arm stretched. There was a crackle and fizz as blue discs of light expanded around his fist. Like before, one disc left the others to settle before him, forming a semi-transparent table of light, from which, a perfect 3D representation of his tree-covered island emerged.

As Joseph turned the sphere, the scene rotated, and he got a clear view of the approaching boat.

"Is it them?" he asked, glancing to the dark corner of the room. "Have they found us?" There was panic in his voice. But there was no answer to his question. He zoomed in for a closer look. A single-occupant piloted the vessel, standing at the bulkhead, both hands on the wheel, looking to the island through the side window of the wheelhouse.

At the point where Joseph expected the boat to cut its engine and drift toward the jetty, it changed course and curved around the north side of his island, its wake breaking on the tiny pebble beach under the overhanging trees. He listened for any change in pitch.

There was no sound from the visualisation, but he could hear the *chug chug chug* drifting through the open door. The sound was steady; it wasn't slowing down or speeding up. It simply continued heading west, where its destination would be the larger islands or perhaps even the mainland.

It wasn't them.

He let out a breath, the rings of light surrounding his fist disappearing as he dropped his arm to his side.

The visual of the island remained in place, and he continued to watch the small boat become even smaller, black smoke from its exhaust trailing behind it as it went.

He then felt the tap on his chest again.

"I know," he said, a trace of annoyance in his voice. "I saw it." He pointed to the tiny boat. "It wasn't them." He laughed suddenly and then smiled. "And they wouldn't use a boat. It's absurd." He scratched his head. "The Watcher has me paranoid — a prisoner on my little island."

Another tap on his chest.

Joseph's smile faded slightly, and he looked to the dark corner of the cabin once again.

Because the sound of the boat had followed the first tap,

he'd assumed it to be a proximity warning. But was it something else? He walked back over to the visualisation. Everything looked OK. The boat was leaving, almost out of sight now, and nothing else seemed amiss. He could see no danger.

The tap came again. He snapped his head back to the dark corner, his smile now gone. He pocketed the sphere, pulled down the neck of his woolly jumper, and reached in to retrieve the watch from his shirt pocket. He flicked open its black cover and studied the symbols around the clock's face. It hadn't been a warning. It was a recommendation for action. She had identified an opportunity.

Joseph walked towards the dark corner, floorboards creaking underfoot. He saw the tiny pinpricks of flashing light, like static discharge clustered together in an almost spherical shape. It was the most activity he'd seen in her. She was thinking. She was calculating.

"What is it?" he asked softly. "What have you found?"

He parted a curtain covering a small dirty window to allow himself to see her more clearly. Too large for the box, she no longer resembled a lump of coal; now, she looked like a mass of shiny black pebbles, melded together under intense heat and pressure. Over the last twenty years, five tendrils had begun to sprout from her, each one a twisting collection of nano-fibres.

She — for to him she had always been she — had been laid out on a table. It was a table that couldn't have looked more out of place in that rugged, rustic cabin. It was smooth, white, reflective, and was only two feet from the ground, its dainty-looking legs narrowing to fine needle-like points.

If someone were to visit, they would assume Joseph to be a deep-sea diver, and the specimen, spread out like a museum exhibit, to be a mysterious discovery from the abyss.

He looked at her with curiosity. "What are you trying to tell me?" He glanced to the watch and saw the markings change before his eyes. He saw the word. "Key."

In a hurry, he removed the key from his pocket and looked at it, expecting to see something, a change. But there was nothing unusual. The key was in its standby state, a thin blue line around its circumference. He frowned.

Then he noticed movement from one of her tendrils. The four larger tendrils, each sixty centimetres long, were spread out wide like a starfish; they were stationary. But the smallest tendril was moving towards him, twisting, unravelling.

"You want the key?" he said.

There was no answer.

"But...you're not ready," he said to the silence that had sounded like a yes to him.

Reluctantly, he bent down and held the key near to her, his smile growing as he watched his creation reach for it. The thin, unravelled strands caressed the key, like long boneless fingers, until finally, she gripped it tightly and took it from him. There was no disc of light as she took it. Instead, her tendrils quivered with a glow as a connection was made.

He detected a shift in the quality of light behind him, and he turned. The view of the island was changing. It was getting smaller as the viewpoint soared, and the surrounding islands became mere specks until he was looking upon the entire landmass of Northern Europe,

"What are you showing me?" he whispered as he walked

towards it. The image was sharp, with no distortions, but even so, he could not see what she was trying to show him.

"What am I not seeing?" he said to himself. He instructed her to enlarge the plane, not knowing if she could yet obey direct commands.

But she could, and the floating disc grew until he was wading waist-deep in the image, seeking what she wanted him to see. Suddenly, the point of view changed once again, zooming toward the northeastern tip of Germany. There were no borders visible, but he'd studied the local geography and knew it well. Fields and towns and forests rushed upwards at speed. His stomach turned as he was tricked into thinking he was falling. When the view came to a sudden halt, Joseph saw what she wanted to show him.

A lorry was moving slowly along a dirt track in a forest. Men in lab coats and army uniforms walked beside it as it rolled along. On the back of this lorry, horizontal, held in a metal cradle, was a rocket.

"Why are you showing me this? You said there was an opportunity. How is this an opportunity?"

Up until now, the image had been in full colour — a live feed from his ship, Larnik. Now it was changing. The colours were fading, the textures becoming less realistic. The landscape, people, and vehicles all took on a brown clay-like appearance. It was no longer a live feed. It was a prediction. And it was playing out at double speed.

People rushed around at a comical pace as the cranes manoeuvred the rocket into an upright position on its launch pad. Suddenly the viewpoint changed, zooming out to show all of Northern Europe once more. Joseph's eyes remained fixed to the spot in Germany, where a thin line was rising slowly. She was showing him the predicted trajectory of the rocket. It went straight up, curving only slightly.

At its peak, it arched back towards the Earth, eventually lost to the Baltic Sea.

He smiled. This was impressive indeed. She was evolving quickly, much quicker than he had thought possible. She was operating at a level he wasn't expecting for at least another decade.

Until now, she had only been capable of relaying information from the ship to Joseph via his timepiece. But this was something else. She could now process data collected by his craft and make predictions with it. The readings displayed on the clock face told him the prediction was almost certain to occur. "Ha!" He slapped his thigh and spun to face her.

Then a frown slowly crossed his features, not quite extinguishing his joy. "This is great progress," he said, turning back to the visualisation. "It is. You were made to spot patterns and make predictions. It is the reason you exist. But you said this was an opportunity. An opportunity for freedom? I do not see it. I do not see how this—"

He stopped mid-sentence.

He saw it.

The line of the rocket's trajectory was still visible, frozen in time. About ten inches from the point where the rocket reached its apex, he saw the tiny blinking light.

"The Watcher," he said flatly, the blood draining from his face.

He suddenly felt sick.

She had presented him with an opportunity of the worst kind, but not the complete solution. He estimated the Watcher was roughly twenty kilometres too high and ten kilometres too far south. The rocket would present no risk to the Watcher.

He stood there, his forgotten drink went cold, and the day outside grew dark, and the fire became a black pile of ash. From time to time, he muttered to himself, incoherently, shaking his head. In the first hour, he'd worked out how to move the Watcher into the path of the rocket. That had been easy. Now was the much tougher task of convincing himself that his actions were justified. That what he was planning was self-defence — and not murder.

10

A NEW TEACHER

Hurstwick, 2019

"Bad idea, Max," said Ellie. "If Wren says you need to stop, you should stop."

It was lunchtime. Snow had fallen all night and covered the school playground with enough ammunition for a decent snowball fight. The three of them sat and watched one in full swing from a cold bench outside the art block.

"I still can't believe you can do it," said Isaac. "So, you just look at someone, and then you can see what they see? Is that it?"

Max shrugged. "Something like that."

Isaac shook his head and looked to the sky. "And Wren can't do it?"

"No," said Max.

Isaac shook his head again, lost for words.

Mrs Collins, the art teacher, emerged from a door behind them. They watched as she tried to break up the snowball fight. Instead of calming the situation, she made herself the target and had to retreat towards the dining hall, her hands over her head, taking tiny quick steps so as not to slip and fall as a torrent of icy missiles honed in on her.

"Anyway," Ellie said. "How does this new talent of yours help get the card back?"

Max shrugged. He hadn't worked that out yet. Some ideas were floating around, half-formed, but he didn't fully understand his limits. He would need to find out fast.

"It's obvious, isn't it?" said Isaac.

"Enlighten us," said Ellie.

"Well, we know the card was sent to someone called Dinesh, who we can assume works at GiaTek. We find Dinesh. Max jumps in his head while he's at work and locates the SD card. We tell Wren where it is. Wren goes all invisible man to retrieve it. Then, feeling on top of the world, we all go to Kira's exhibition to celebrate."

"You make it sound easy," Ellie said. She looked at Max and raised a questioning eyebrow.

"It really isn't that easy," said Max. "I'm ninety-nine per cent sure it's going to be impossible. I just know I need to try. The first problem is, there are three GiaTek offices. Two in London, one in Stockholm. All large buildings with hundreds of employees. If he works in the Stockholm office, we have our second problem. For it to work, I have to see the person. They need to be in my direct line of sight."

"No, they don't," Isaac said.

"Ha!" Ellie laughed. "I think Max understands how this works more than you."

"Doesn't sound like it to me. He doesn't have to see the people he dreams about, does he?"

"No, I don't, but I can't control who I dream about."

"You better not dream about me," Ellie said with a smirk.

"Look," said Isaac, standing to face them. "This sounds a lot like *remote viewing*." He watched them for a reaction. On seeing no recognition of the term, he blinked hard. "You've not heard of remote viewing?"

They stared at him blankly.

Isaac sighed with frustration. "Really? Have you never watched *The X-Files*?" The blank looks continued. Isaac sighed again and began to pace up and down as he spoke, his hands dug deep into his anorak pockets. "Look, it was a big thing back in the sixties or seventies — remote viewing, not *The X-Files*. During the Cold War, the Americans and the Russians invested tons of money into research to see if people could look into government buildings to obtain secrets — *just by using their minds*. The programs were eventually shut down, but not before they spent millions trying to see if it could work."

"And...did it work?" Ellie asked.

"Of course it didn't," replied Isaac, laughing at the absurdity. "Humans can't do stuff like that. But an *alien*...."

Ellie looked at Max. "Apologies on behalf of my people," she said.

Max smiled. "I'll vaporise him with my mind beam later."

Ignoring them, Isaac continued. "If I remember correctly, they thought the subjects might perform better using sensory deprivation techniques. They would blindfold them and lock them in dark floatation tanks—"

"You just said it didn't work," said Max.

"Yeah, because they didn't have the right subjects. Wrong species. But the experiments and the ideas behind them might have been solid. If we could somehow deprive you of your senses, almost simulating sleep, without actually being asleep, you might be able to do it."

"Worth a try," Max said, lacking any better ideas.

"It's not worth a try," said Ellie, sounding annoyed. "You blacked out, remember; fainted. You were in pain—"

"Distance viewing used to hurt at first," said Max. "Now, I'm fine with it."

Ellie crossed her arms, pressed her lips tightly together, then looked away from them, bouncing her knees to keep warm.

Isaac sat back down, and they were silent for a while.

They watched as Mrs Collins returned to the fray with reinforcements. The snowballs now arched in on both her and Mr Erwin, the Deputy Head. He spun, pointing and barking names of those he recognised, but most wore their scarves high over their faces, hoping for anonymity as they continued the bombardment.

A snowball whizzed past Ellie, missing her by inches, leaving a pimple of snow on the brick wall behind them.

"Oi!" she shouted to a guilty-looking year-seven boy, who ran off to find safety in the herd.

Ellie looked at Max, her expression softening with concern. "Is it such a big deal if they see the video? They already know what happened; they had cameras set up everywhere that day. They saw more than we did."

"True," said Max, "but the two we met didn't know anything at all."

"Probably don't have the right security clearance," Isaac agreed. "Just a couple of low-level employees who stumbled across something interesting."

Max nodded.

"I still don't see why it's a problem," Ellie said.

"It's a problem," said Isaac, "because once they see the footage and take it to their superiors, they'll want to know why we didn't tell anyone. Think about it. What we saw is not the sort of thing people keep to themselves. Especially a bunch of teens with an internet connection. Unless—"

"Unless those teens had something to hide," finished Ellie. "Yeah, I get that bit. But it's a big leap to go from thinking we're hiding something to thinking we're directly involved."

"Think about this, then," Isaac said, standing again to face them both. "They had massive construction vehicles flying through the air, strange craters appearing overnight, huge meteor showers lighting up the sky, and who knows what else. Extra-terrestrials must be on their list of possible causes, right? When they see our video of Jenta in the clearing—"

"It was just his hand," interrupted Ellie.

"A hand that was clearly non-human," Isaac continued. "As I was saying, once they add all that together, an extra-terrestrial explanation will be the *only* theory worth taking seriously. Especially if they're aware of the crash in forty-four and the following cover-up."

Ellie did a half shrug, half nod, apparently unconvinced but coming around. "So, what's your point?" she asked.

"My point is, once they suspect E.T. is involved, and suspect we're hiding something, they might take a closer look at us."

"So?" Ellie said.

"So?" Isaac laughed in frustration, then turned to Max. "Hey, Max, not including all the fainting and the vomiting you get with those visions, tell Ellie how many times you've been sick in your life."

Max exhaled a cloud of warm breath. He knew where this was going. "Zero," he said flatly.

"And tell us, how many medical examinations have you had?"

"None."

"Blood tests?"

"Nope.'

"Appointments with an optician?"

Max shook his head.

"OK, OK, I get what you're saying," said Ellie. "But they're not gonna start doing tests on him."

"These secret government types can be sneaky," said Isaac. "They take you in for questioning, offer you a glass of water. Then they ship that glass to the lab for DNA testing, and boom! They've got you."

Ellie and Max turned to each other, a smile growing between them.

"Yeah, I know you're gonna say, *I watch too many movies*; you always say it. But I'm serious. Max might be completely indistinguishable from a boring human being, but, as no one's had a reason to take a close look, we just don't know."

The smiles faded, and the frowns returned to let Isaac know they were taking this all very seriously.

Isaac sat back down, scooping up a handful of snow and moulding it into a ball. "We can't let them think we're hiding something. We don't know where that could lead. That's all I'm saying. We need to get that card back."

Ellie put her arm around Isaac's shoulders. "I love how you care so much," she smiled.

Isaac shook his head. "I don't care," he scoffed.

"Yeah, you do," she replied. Her smile then evaporated, and she looked to Max. "Promise me you'll be careful," she said. "We won't have a healing disc to help us."

Max nodded. "Are you ready, Isaac?" he said.

Isaac looked at him, confused. "Ready for what?"

"Well, you seem to be the expert on all this remote viewing stuff. You're now my new teacher."

After school, through heavy snow, the three made their way to Max's house, stopping first at the library, where Isaac borrowed *Psychic Spies of the Cold War*.

"Did Wren see you?" Ellie asked. She had waited outside with Max in the cold.

"He wasn't there," Isaac replied. "Taken the week off, apparently. Did he mention he was going away?" He looked at Max, and Max shook his head.

On the cover of *Psychic Spies of the Cold War* was a typical representation of a spy: a fedora, worn at a jaunty angle, a rain mac with the collar raised, and a pair of dark glasses. The only departure from the classical spy look was the third eye in the middle of the man's forehead. To Max, the image cast doubt over the book's usefulness.

"It says here we need a target," said Isaac, the book now open on his lap as he sat against the wall in Max's bedroom. "We have just over two weeks before Dinesh takes delivery of the item that lets him fix the card. We need to find him before that. But we also need to make sure you can do this thing without seeing the target. So we should try someone closer to home first. A test before the real thing."

"Who do you have in mind?" asked Ellie. She was sitting at the foot of Max's bed, looking uneasy. Several times on the walk home, she'd repeated her concerns over Max's health. And he'd assured her he would take it slow and steady.

"How about my brother?" offered Isaac.

"No," said Max.

"Why?"

"He's always with his girlfriend—"

"Yeah, good point." Isaac shuddered at the thought. "Your mum?"

"No way." Max screwed up his face. "She might be on the toilet or something."

A smile grew across Isaac's face. "Or with Wren—"

"Behave, Isaac," Ellie said, holding up a finger while a smile played at the edges of her serious-looking mouth.

"OK," said Isaac, both hands held up in apology. "Then it needs to be one of us. And as I'm the instructor here," his hands went to his chest, "that just leaves—"

"No," Ellie said firmly. "I'm not having anyone poking around in my head. I'm just here to make sure you don't break Max."

"Oh, come on," Isaac said, "it's science."

"It's an invasion of privacy, is what it is."

"No, it's perfect," Isaac continued. "We need a place close by that one of us knows well, one Max is not familiar with. If you go next door and sit in your room, Max can...do his thing, then tell us what he saw. Maybe...*maybe*...he can tell us what posters you have on your wall?"

"So as well as poking around in my head, you also want a tour of my room?"

"It's perfect. It's close, you know it *very* well, and Max has never been in there. Wait, have you?"

"No, he hasn't," Ellie said, her voice rising several octaves. She'd once made Max promise, on danger of death, that he would never, *ever*, look into her room. In her words, *even if I'm screaming, and you smell burning.* She made him swear on Isaac's life.

"Pretty please?" Isaac said, trying to look like an abandoned puppy.

There was a long pause. Eventually, Ellie caved. "How will it work?" she said, looking somewhere just above their heads.

"According to this," he slapped the book, "Max should either be submerged in a sensory deprivation tank, or sit quietly and stare at a photo. As we don't have a sensory deprivation tank..." He quickly raised his phone and took a photo of Ellie. She narrowed her eyes and shook her head, still clearly unhappy with the experiment.

"It probably won't work!" Max called to Ellie as she walked to the door.

"I'll bang on the wall when I'm ready," she said, then left the room.

Max went to the corner and sat cross-legged.

"No," Isaac said. "Try the closet. It's no deprivation tank, but the darkness might help."

The closet was built into the wall and large enough for Max to sit inside. He took in some cushions and placed Isaac's phone upright on a shoebox before him. The photo of Ellie looked back at him, unimpressed, an expression that said, *I can't believe I'm letting them do this.* Once Max was settled, Isaac retreated to the desk chair, and they waited for the bang on the wall.

"Thought any more about the exhibition?" Isaac asked as he reclined and looked to the ceiling, slowly spinning in the chair.

"Still not going."

"Not even a little tempted?"

"It's best I don't. Especially now. I'd prefer not to get Kira caught up in any of this."

"Shame. It looks interesting. I've been reading up on her work; she's definitely operating on another level...." He sighed and looked at his watch. "What's taking her so long?"

"Bet she's tidying up," said Max.

"Yeah." Isaac smiled. "Or taking her pony posters down."

They both laughed, stopping as three slow knocks, barely audible, came from the other side of the thick wall.

"Let's roll." Isaac went to the closet and closed the door on Max.

Max turned the phone's brightness down to its lowest setting and got comfortable. He began to breathe slow and deep, focusing on the image of Ellie until he felt a stillness.

In his calm state, time lost all meaning. But he knew this was taking longer than before. He suspected it wasn't going to work, and now his eyes were feeling dry and beginning to sting from staring at the screen.

So, he tried a different approach.

He turned off the screen and closed his eyes, trying to visualise Ellie, imagining her sitting on her bed as she stared at her bedroom wall. He pictured her shoulder-length dark hair, with the faded red streak that started by her right temple that she would sometimes tuck behind her ear. Wait, was it red? Or did she change it? Was it purple now? He felt his focus slipping, so he tried to remember what she was wearing: a dark red woollen jumper, jeans, winter walking boots. No, she was indoors; she would have taken the boots off. He stopped. Knowing what she was wearing was not going to help.

His mind went to her face: her olive-coloured skin, the dimples beside her smile, her small nose, slightly upturned at the end, the freckles that spread across it from cheek to cheek. As he built this image of her, he thought he saw dull patches of light trying to form — blues, browns, yellows. Something was happening. Or maybe it wasn't. He wasn't sure. The shapes refused to develop into anything detailed, and they eventually faded until all was dark again. He opened his eyes and sighed.

He pushed open the door, squinting in the bedroom's bright light. Isaac looked back expectantly then shrunk in the chair as Max shook his head.

"Try again," he said with a shrug.

He tried two more times with no progress.

On his third attempt, he tried to imagine her room but found he couldn't. He imagined his room instead, but with more feminine decor, frilly bed covers, pink wallpaper. He was annoyed at the image and his lack of imagination. There was nothing pink or frilly about Ellie.

He tried again, this time visualising the extreme opposite of his first attempt, black and harsh and sharp and gritty, blood-red curtains, death metal poster. Rubbish. That wasn't Ellie, either. This was useless. He had nothing, and now he was struggling to stay awake.

"We'll try again tomorrow," said Isaac, walking down the short path to Max's gate.

Max stood at the door. "Yeah, OK," he said. "But I think we might be wasting our time."

Ellie emerged from her door and leaned on the wall. "You boys giving up then?"

"For tonight," Isaac replied.

She turned to Max. "And I can trust that you won't try again without giving me some warning?"

"Of course," Max said.

Isaac crossed the road, heading to the footpath running between two cottages that would eventually take him to his side of the town.

"Go via High Street," Max heard himself saying.

Isaac stopped and turned. "Why?"

"Safer," said Max.

"This is Hurstwick" He laughed, then disappeared down the footpath.

"You OK, Max?" Ellie said. She was starting to shiver from the cold.

"Yeah," he said. But he wasn't. Hurstwick felt different. It didn't feel safe anymore.

" Get some rest," she said. "You look knackered."

After one more reminder for Max to stay out of her head, she returned inside.

Alone, Max lingered, watching the dark, deserted lane until his mother called from inside, telling him to shut the door.

He stepped inside and closed it.

The lane was quiet. Snow fell on the cobbled road, the cars, and the neatly trimmed hedges. And across from Max's cottage, on the roof, snow fell on a dark figure crouched by a chimney.

In the days that followed, they tried everything: sitting down, lying down, photo, no photo, facing her general direction, soft music, scented candles. He even tried lying in the bath with the lights off. Nothing worked.

"We need a floatation tank," said Isaac, fighting a yawn. He was sitting at the desk, flicking through his book, while Ellie sat on the bed looking at her phone. Max lay stretched out on the floor, looking at the ceiling. It was the sixth day of trying.

"We don't need a floatation tank," said Max. "We tried the bath. It didn't work."

"A bath is different," said Isaac. "A floatation tank is—"

"We need to call it a day," Ellie said, bored. "We tried everything. It's been a week. I can't believe we lasted this long before giving up."

"*Some subjects would remain suspended in dark chambers,*" read Isaac, ignoring them. "*Often floating in water with white noise playing over loudspeakers. Using these techniques, some volunteers claimed to have seen places and heard conversations taking place over a thousand miles away.*"

"Maybe it was a one-off," said Ellie. "An accident."

It wasn't an accident, thought Max. It was a development — the development of a Gift he didn't really want. As well as being painful and possibly dangerous, it was also, as Ellie had once put it, *a violation of privacy*. It felt wrong.

"Wait!" Max sat bolt upright, pointing to the book, flapping his hand impatiently. "Go back," he said. "What was that bit about white noise?"

"Um," Isaac frowned, flipped back a page, then reread the passage.

"That's it." Max stood up and began to pace. "On the hill, just before I saw through the eyes of the crow, there was a helicopter. I was aware of the sound. To begin with, I thought it would distract me. But now...I wonder if it helped."

"What about in the spire?" asked Isaac.

Max tried to think. "I don't know. I can't remember."

"Any traffic noise, or—"

"The record," blurted Max. "I was playing one of Wren's records. When it stopped, there was this crackling sound that just went on and on. I remember. As it played, I felt...different."

"Different how?" asked Ellie, looking up from her phone.

"It felt like I'd...gone deeper. Like in a trance." He looked at them both. He knew this was it.

"One more go?" Ellie said, looking slightly less fed up than a second ago.

Max nodded. Ellie returned to her room while Isaac downloaded a white noise audio file. Max climbed back into the closet, this time with the white noise quietly playing through his headphones.

After a few minutes of getting his breath under control, he began to picture Ellie's face again. As the crackle in his ears slowed, becoming a deep rumble, the image of her face was pushed away, as if it wasn't needed. His subconscious was taking over. Like before, in the spire, a part of him knew exactly what to do. He felt his awareness widen with each breath, breaking the boundary of his skull and reaching outwards. Like ripples in a still lake, his consciousness expanded, colliding with other minds, which sent back smaller ripples of their own. As these reached him, he got a sense of them. He felt an emotion that wasn't his; it was a sense of excitement. It was Isaac. It faded as he left Isaac behind to find another. Soon he found a more complex set of emotions, all in conflict with each other. There was excitement again, but also nervousness, apprehension, and fear. As soon as the realisation came that this was Ellie, the bright and beautiful white light appeared before quickly fading to black.

Max heard her.

She sighed.

Seconds later, he heard a ping from her phone, followed by a soft tap tap tap of her fingers on glass as she typed a message in reply. Then he saw her, small and distant as if seen from the wrong end of a telescope. Her back to the wall, her arms hugging her raised knees, she was looking ahead. He drifted closer.

He then felt something. A feeling like a knuckle that needed to pop. Or like two magnets just beyond the point of attraction. It was a feeling of inevitability, then a snap. The knuckle popped, the magnets came together. There was a second bright flash of light, and suddenly, he was there, looking out through Ellie's eyes, her focus on the wall ahead. Where, pinned above a chest of drawers, was a single poster.

Then came the pain.

As he forced his eyes open, he felt a sensation of being dragged backwards through a tunnel, away from the light.

He elbowed open the closet door and rolled into the room, pulling out half the contents of the closet.

Isaac rushed to him. "Are you OK? Did it work?"

Max laid on his back, arms spread out. "You were right," he said, breathless, closing his eyes again, trying to ignore the pain. "She *is* a geek."

"So, you're a Marvel fan," Isaac said gleefully to Ellie as she entered the room.

"It worked?" she said, her hand covering her mouth, eyes wide with shock. "I don't believe it." She was looking at Max, who was still on the floor but had managed to prop himself up on his elbows. He smiled at her through the pain.

"I can't believe you're into comics," Isaac laughed.

"What?" She looked offended. "Can we focus on what's important here? Max was in my head, looking out through my eyes. Anyway, I'm not into comics. It's a Loki poster; I'm into Tom Hiddleston." She began pacing the room. "I can't believe...you can do that," she said, almost to herself.

Isaac slumped down onto the bed and stared into space.

Ellie stopped pacing, looked at Max again, then sat down next to Isaac. "You're not going to vomit, are you?" she said to Max.

Max shook his head and closed his eyes. He wasn't going to vomit. He just needed a moment to adjust to being back in his own head. He crawled to the wall and sat with his back to it, head dipped, eyes closed. When he next looked at his friends, Isaac was grinning in wonder, but Ellie looked uncomfortable.

He felt a brief sadness in that moment. Every change that had happened to Max over the last year and a half made him less like his friends; another thing they would never have in common, something that pushed them further apart. It made him sad. Knowing he was becoming more like Wren had always been a comfort, but now he was becoming less like him, too.

"Did you feel anything?" Isaac asked, turning to Ellie. "When he was, you know..." He tapped her forehead, and she pushed his hand away. "Did you feel different?"

She paused and considered her answer. "I don't think so. No. I wasn't aware of anything feeling different." She looked at Max. "Could you do anything else apart from seeing what I saw? Could you...read my mind? Or—"

"No," Max replied quickly. "Nothing like that."

Ellie seemed to relax, her look of unease changing to one of curiosity. "So, what next? Now we know you can do it; what's the plan?"

"We find Dinesh," Isaac said. He reached for his phone, but it was dead. Ellie gave him hers. "*Dinesh... GiaTek,*" he said as he typed. There was a moment of silence as Isaac repeatedly swiped and flicked his thumb across the screen. "Two people called Dinesh working at GiaTek," he said. "Dinesh Sharma, Senior Systems Engineer, and Dinesh Kumar, Pilates Instructor. My money's on the first one." After a few more taps and swipes, he turned the phone around to show them a photo of a bald Asian man. He was in his late twenties or early thirties, sporting a very well-groomed goatee. "That was too easy," said Isaac.

"Listen," said Max. "I don't have the energy for this now." A wave of exhaustion had washed over him, and it wasn't going away. "Send me the photo. I'll try later. If not, we'll go again tomorrow."

Disappointed, Isaac nodded with understanding, looking back to the phone.

"It's late," said Ellie. "And it's Sunday. He won't be at work now. Get some rest."

She stood to leave, her hand outstretched for her phone. But Isaac was still staring at it, his brow creased while he chewed at his fingernail. "What is it?" she asked.

He hesitated. "According to this, GiaTek is a part of FossCorp."

"Is that supposed to mean something to us?" said Ellie.

"FossCorp is sponsoring Kira's exhibition — and funding all her research."

Max's head still hurt. He rubbed his temples and stared at his feet while processing Isaac's words.

Ellie shrugged. "Coincidence?"

"Maybe," said Isaac. "Bit odd, though, don't you think? A week ago, I'd never heard of GiaTek — not exactly a household name. Now they're looking into the events at the bypass, giving us grief, *and* funding your cousin's research at the same time."

"Ellie's right," Max said. "Coincidence."

"Maybe," said Isaac again. "It'd be interesting to know how she got funding from FossCorp. Did she approach them, or did they approach her?"

"Max could ask," suggested Ellie.

"Not an easy question to slip into conversation," Max said. "Anyway, she'll be too busy with the exhibition. It's only two weeks away."

"If *only* she'd invited us to stay for the weekend," said Isaac with sarcasm. "We could have teased the information out of her."

"I told you. We're not going to London," said Max.

"What does it mean if it's not a coincidence?" asked Ellie.

Isaac pondered for a moment. "I guess It means they've somehow linked her to whatever they discovered at the bypass and are keeping a close eye on her. Maybe even funding her research in the hope she delivers some super-alien-tech that can change the world and earn them billions?" Isaac shrugged then looked to Max. "Look, I don't know. But are you not curious to find out if it *is* a coincidence?"

"I am curious," he admitted. "But not enough to go to London. Not while all this is happening."

There was a knock on the door, and Max's mum poked her head into the room. "Isaac, your mum called; she's been trying to reach you — wants you back home to do your revision."

Isaac groaned and handed the phone back to Ellie, then stood.

His mother looked down at Max, still sitting against the wall next to the door. "Oh, and she mentioned a trip to London? Were you ever going to get around to telling me about it? The timing's perfect. Julie and Sharon want to meet that weekend. And I'd love to meet Lydia and Kira. It'll be fun." She looked back at Isaac, who was now scratching his nose to hide his growing smile. "Anyway, you better get off. Nothing more important than revision." She then closed the door, and Max heard her go downstairs. Moments later, the *clink* and *clank* of her emptying the dishwasher drifted up through the floorboards. Max sighed heavily, then looked at them both. "I'll let Kira know we're coming."

11

THE HUNT FOR DINESH

Zoe stepped out of Hut 4 and was blasted by the cold wind rushing up the bypass. She looked across to Hut 1, then looked at her watch.

"Coming through," said Travis.

She stepped aside as he passed, carrying a heavy-looking box to a van waiting with its rear doors wide open. "Don't let Duncan waffle on about nothing, will you!" he called over his shoulder, raising his voice over the wind. "I need you back. I'm not doing this all by myself."

She watched him load the box into the van, then looked back to Hut 1. With a deep breath, she pushed her shoulders back and strode off towards it.

Every Monday at eleven, she met with Duncan, the head of the Oban Task Force, for her weekly kick-off. She would brief him on her plan for the upcoming week and make requests for any equipment she might need. Each meeting was short, and the format never changed. In the beginning, she used the opportunity to try to tease out details about the wider project. But she never got anywhere, so she quickly gave up trying.

As she neared Hut 1, concern grew that the meeting

hadn't been cancelled. With it being the final day on site, she'd assumed it would be unnecessary. And Duncan hated unnecessary meetings — unusual for a government man. She wondered if this would be a meeting of a different kind, and she mentally prepared herself for trouble.

"Ahh, Zoe." Duncan smiled and spread his arms to welcome her as she entered the Hut. He was never this warm. Usually, he would barely make eye contact, and she'd never seen him smile. But it took Zoe only a second to realise why he was behaving so differently.

Hut 1 was one of the largest on the compound. It consisted of four small glass-walled offices and a large open space, home to a long boardroom table. At one end of the table, mounted on the wall, was a big screen, where Greta Nilsson, CEO of GiaTek and Zoe's boss, was sat looking down at them both. Duncan's warmth was a show for Greta.

"Greta and I have just finished our catch-up, and I've asked her to stick around and join ours. I hope you don't mind?"

"Of course." Zoe smiled at Greta nervously as she took her usual seat at the table. Greta smiled in return; hers was a perfect Scandinavian smile of understated confidence.

"I've already gone over your final report," Duncan said as he filled two glasses of water from a jug. "Very thorough as usual. So we don't need to go over any of that. Instead, I'd like to discuss something else."

"Of course," Zoe replied, accepting the glass from Duncan and taking a sip.

Duncan leaned back and crossed his legs. "I understand you've recently taken an interest in local history?"

"You mean the Hurstwick Incident?" Zoe said. She glanced to Greta, whose eyes narrowed slightly as she tilted her head.

"So you admit it?" Duncan said, his blond eyebrows flicking upwards.

"I admit, I've been looking into the incident, yes. Was I not supposed to?"

Duncan was about to answer when Greta spoke.

"Is there a problem, Duncan?" she said. "I don't know what this Hurstwick Incident is, but I'm assuming it's public knowledge if it's considered local history?"

"It is," Zoe answered for him. "There's an exhibit at the local library; I was just—" She stopped as Duncan raised his hand.

"It's not a problem," he smiled. *A crocodile's smile*, thought Zoe. "I'm just curious, that's all. I've seen no mention of this *Hurstwick Incident* in any of your reports. Yet you've been looking into it during work hours, isn't that right? Had you been asked to look into it by your superiors at GiaTek?" He glanced at Greta, then back to Zoe. "If so, I should have been made aware of any new lines of enquiry."

"No," said Zoe, realising Duncan was challenging Greta as much as her. Greta seemed unintimidated. If anything, she looked as if she had more important things to be doing. "I was looking into it by myself," Zoe continued. "I didn't put anything in my report because I didn't find anything compelling."

"But you were looking at the incident in relation to our work here?"

Zoe nodded.

"Is there a point to this conversation, Mr Clark?" Greta asked. "If there is, I suggest you reach it quickly."

If Zoe wasn't so nervous, she would have smiled at the comment. She had never seen Greta and Duncan in conversation before, but she would have assumed Duncan to be the dominant of the pair. After all, Duncan had hired GiaTek to join the task force; he was the client.

Duncan smiled another fake smile. "The point, Ms Nilsson, is that when GiaTek was invited to work with this task force, your predecessor, Mr Foss, assured me that your work here would be one hundred per cent transparent to government oversight. I am the government in this relationship, and I had to learn second-hand of this *unusual* line of enquiry. There should be no secrets kept from me."

"I'm aware of the agreement, Duncan," Greta said, her tone flat. "I was working closely with Richard Foss when it was drawn up. I assure you that there has been no violation. It sounds like Zoe had an idea, looked into it, and found nothing worth reporting. Ideas arise and are discarded all the time, a consequence of hiring smart, curious people. And we only employ smart, curious people."

Duncan paused, then turned to Zoe. "What led to this idea of yours?"

"If I may enquire," Greta interrupted, "what is the Hurstwick Incident, anyway?"

Duncan gestured for Zoe to explain.

"During the Second World War," Zoe began, "a German plane came down in Oban Wood. On the way down, it destroyed the steeple of St Mary's Church. Every pub, restaurant, and hotel has a depiction of it on a wall somewhere."

Greta nodded. "And you thought it interesting because...."

"Well, I noticed the area in which the alleged plane came down corresponded to the location of the energy spikes."

"Alleged plane?" Duncan said.

"Sorry?"

"You said *alleged* plane. Do you think it was not a plane?"

"Did I? Well, I have no reason to believe it was anything else."

Duncan sighed. There was a long pause. "What led you to form a link between the two? What led you to the Hurstwick Incident?"

"I stumbled across an old display in the library."

"And what led you to the library—"

"Is this relevant, Duncan?" asked Greta, and Zoe imagined herself a witness in a courtroom drama. "It seems to me you are making a big deal over nothing. Unless you're saying there *is* a link between the two, which might have been helpful for us to know about?"

Duncan paused again. Eventually, he smiled, dismissing the suggestion with a scoff and a hand wave. "Of course not," he said as he stood. "Well, ladies, I'd like to say it's been a pleasure working with you both. Just one more thing before we wrap up. I should remind you that GiaTek and its employees are bound by the Official Secrets Act, and any breach will be treated seriously. Talking to anyone outside the task force about matters, or *ideas*, relating to our work here will be considered a breach of that act." He looked to Zoe and widened his eyes, waiting for a response.

"Of course," she said.

Duncan looked to Greta.

"Are we done here?" she asked.

Duncan nodded.

"Excellent," said Greta. "Thank you for all your hard work, Zoe. I'll see you when you're back in London." She smiled and ended the call.

Duncan walked to the door and opened it. Zoe stood and followed.

"I understand you're taking time off?" he said as she stepped out into the cold. "Going anywhere nice?"

"Just...staying here for a while."

"Hurstwick?"

"Yes."

"Thought you'd be dying to get away from the place?"

"It's growing on me."

"This is your pack," said Isaac, as he slid a brown folder across the table to Max. It was lunchtime, and they were in the school library.

"Pack?" Max raised an eyebrow and lifted the flap of the folder.

"It's what spies call the file containing everything they know about their target."

"*Do* they call it that, or did you make it up?"

"I made it up." He smiled.

"You're loving this, aren't you," Max said, placing the *pack* in his bag, looking around to see if anyone was watching, and for a split second, he felt like a spy.

Alone that evening, in the warm glow of his bedside lamp, Max stared lazily at the file's contents, spread out on the bed before him. There were three photos of Dinesh, presumably from various online profiles, and several photos of the two London GiaTek offices. One office was in the centre of London, a building of glass and stone on a busy-looking street, while the other, on the outskirts of the city, was a large low squat building on an industrial estate. Both were circled on maps of varying detail, one map showing the entire southeast of England.

It was probably far too late for Dinesh to be at work, and Ellie had warned him not to try anything while alone — *in case you fry your brain and no-one's there to help.* But the urge to try to connect to Dinesh was too great. It would just be a quick test, he told himself. Just to see if it was even possible to connect with someone so far away. If successful, he'd come straight back out, no hanging around.

Max adjusted the angle of the bedside lamp, made himself more comfortable with his legs crossed, then donned his headphones. The white noise surrounded him as his eyes moved over the photos and maps. His breathing slowed. After a few minutes, his eyes closed, and he felt himself drop into a calm trance-like state. The white noise deepened. It ebbed and flowed like waves around him. Then, without warning, the waves crashed over him, taking him deeper and deeper until the sound was so deep he could only feel it.

His mind wandered. No. *Wander* suggests a lack of purpose, but there was purpose here. His mind was doing its thing, while Max just sat and watched. It was different from when he was seeking out Ellie's mind. Then it had been like ripples expanding to find her. This was like surging through a network of connected tunnels, heading to a specific location. There was nothing visual to support this feeling until he saw a bright light ahead hurtling towards him. The shock of its brightness and the speed of its approach threw him from his trance. He was once again in his room, his back pressed against the wall, the white noise hissing in his ears, his heart thumping wildly.

He waited for the pain to arrive, but it didn't. He felt OK.

So he tried again.

This time knowing what to expect, he held firm as the light rushed towards him. He held on tightly, focusing on the light as it grew and eventually surrounded him. It was that same white light he had seen in every waking vision since the crow on the hill. It was more than just a light, but he had no words to describe it.

When it faded, he saw Dinesh.

Just like with Ellie, he was looking down at him through the wrong end of a telescope. The image wasn't crisp; everything was slightly blurry, but he could see he was standing on a light grey floor before a wall of colour. The image sharpened, the wall resolving into a set of shelves, full of boxes and tins of various shapes, colours, and sizes. He was in a supermarket. There was a second bright flash, and the view changed again. He was now looking through the man's eyes, seeing what he saw, watching a hand extend towards the shelf and grab a pack of chocolate Hobnobs, while Wham's "Last Christmas" played over the supermarket speakers.

It worked. He couldn't believe it.

And it was *easy*.

There was no point hanging about; knowing Dinesh had great taste in biscuits wasn't helpful to Max, and he forced himself to open his eyes.

He gasped for air as he felt, somewhere, a connection being severed. An intense pain grew behind his eyes. The lamp seemed too bright, and he leaned over to switch it off. But he fell from the bed, and the lamp followed him to the floor.

He stayed there as the room spun, and the pain throbbed.

He breathed. He breathed some more. With each long breath, the room slowed until it stopped spinning altogether.

The pain was still there, but it was manageable. Max cleared away the photos and maps and then clambered into bed. He slept deeply.

"I can't believe it worked," said Isaac as the three walked to school. "I'm taking all the credit, you know. I'm a genius."

Max smiled, then looked to Ellie. She'd informed Max, just moments ago, that she wasn't talking to him right now, and he was foolish for attempting it without anyone there for support.

"So we just need to find somewhere private," Isaac went on. "Somewhere you won't be disturbed. Lunchtime would be ideal. Dinesh will probably go out for lunch, at which point you'll be able to see which building he works in."

Max nodded. It made sense.

"Where's good?" Isaac pondered. "Music room?" He looked to Ellie, but she looked away unhelpfully.

"No," said Max. "They have a music club at lunch. What about backstage in the main hall?"

"No," said Isaac, "It's too open; anyone can walk in—"

"The Plantation," Ellie said, seemingly reluctant to offer assistance. "The garage is secure. You can do it there."

Isaac and Max exchanged a look, then nodded.

No one knew why it was called the Plantation. Students had handed down the name over the years, and it just stuck. It was a wooded area at the edge of the playing field, out of bounds to students, and was home to the garage, where the groundskeeper kept his tools and a small tractor with a mower attached.

People usually only ventured into the Plantation to retrieve stray footballs — although occasionally the younger kids would enter when playing hide and seek, and older kids for other things that required privacy. Today though, with temperatures hovering just south of zero, the Plantation was deserted.

"See anyone, Max?" Ellie asked; It was lunchtime, and she was now talking to him again.

"Looks empty," he replied as they walked around the edge of the playing field.

They avoided the main entrance to the Plantation — a track worn by the coming and going of the lawnmower — and instead entered from the side, fighting their way through thick and brittle bushes.

Once through, Max looked around. At this time of year, a lot of the undergrowth had died away, allowing them to see much of the school building.

"It's still too exposed," Max said.

"It's alright," said Ellie. "We're going inside." She walked to the garage door and knelt by the padlock, one of those with the numbered dials.

"You know the combination?" Isaac asked, looking around warily while Ellie worked the lock.

"Everyone does," she said as the lock clicked open. "The groundskeeper is Becky Perera's dad." She stood and pulled open the doors. "The combination is Becky's birthday." She smiled then gestured with a dramatic curtsy for them to enter. She followed them in, closed the doors behind them, and turned on the light.

The garage was packed with tools and gardening equipment, all neatly arranged on the walls. Most of the floor space was taken up by the tractor, covered in a grease-stained sheet.

Max, wasting no time, took the folder from his bag and sat on the floor, spreading out the photos and the maps. He then put on his headphones and selected the white noise track.

Isaac looked at his watch. "Thirty minutes before the next lesson."

Max nodded and began to control his breathing.

Ellie climbed onto the stool at the workbench while Isaac removed the tractor's cover and sat in its spring-loaded seat. He turned the wheel, pretending to drive it and smiled at Ellie. Ellie shook her head and blinked slowly.

It took Max a few minutes to get comfortable on the cold concrete floor. Once he was, he found it easy to slip into the right mental state, and it wasn't long before the sensation of rushing down tunnels began. He started to enjoy the feeling. It was like a rollercoaster in the darkness. It took him in all directions, faster and faster, never slowing, sharp turns that would have crumpled his body but could be handled easily by the mind.

But something wasn't right. It was taking too long. Last night there had been a light at the end of these tunnels. Now it was just turn after turn in the darkness. He waited. Still no light. Was he doing it wrong? What was different? The tunnels went on and on until, eventually, he felt a tap on his shoulder, and the rollercoaster slowed to a stop. Had it really been thirty minutes?

He opened his eyes and saw Ellie crouching before him.

"Anything?" she asked.

"Nothing," he replied.

They persisted. After school, from Isaac's den, they tried a second time. Max tried on his own the following morning from his closet, only to be disturbed by his mother, who had clean school shirts to hang up. She had a fright when she found him.

They continued to visit the Plantation every lunchtime, but the results were the same; endless tunnels in the darkness. No light. No Dinesh. No SD card. Just failure after failure.

There wasn't even any pain. Evidently, the pain came from seeing through the other person's eyes, not from the search itself, so these failures were less demanding on Max's health. However, instead of pain and dizziness, it was tiredness and insomnia that took their toll. These effects were less visible to his friends, so after another failed attempt, on the fourth day at the Plantation, there was no one near to catch Max when the fatigue hit. Ellie was sitting on the stool and Isaac on the tractor. They both watched helplessly as Max stood and then dropped, his head hitting the cold, hard concrete with a dull thud.

12

TESTS AND DREAMS

Consciousness returned, but he kept his eyes closed.

A dream was fading from his mind, slipping away into a fog, until all that remained was an image of a fire spreading across a cloudless sky. But even that was soon forgotten.

Then there were voices — lots of them. Max tried to work out what they were saying, but there were too many. The voices echoed and made him think he must be in a large space. It certainly wasn't the cosy living room at Rose Bank.

What did he remember?

He was in the garage, in the Plantation. There was another failed attempt to find Dinesh, and then he'd stood up to go to his next class. What class? History? He'd never missed a class before. Was he still at school? Had he fallen asleep at his desk?

He felt his breathing start to quicken, but with a thought, he slowed it.

His eyes were still closed. He would have to open them sooner or later.

"Can I get you anything, dear?" said an unfamiliar voice close by.

He wondered if the question was for him, but then a very familiar voice answered. It was a soft, gentle voice. "No, thank you."

It was his mother.

Max opened his eyes. He was on a bed in a semi-upright position, his head to one side. He saw a machine, all screen and wires. It was switched off. Behind it was a green curtain, and there were two empty chairs next to him. They looked like school chairs, but this was not school.

He turned his head. His mother was standing by a window, looking out at a grey concrete town, her hand resting on the back of a more comfortable-looking chair. Max recognised the view; he'd seen it from Windmill Hill many times before. It was Denbridge. He was in the hospital.

"Mum," he said. His throat was dry, and the word failed to rise above the din of the place. So he called again. This time she heard him and turned, relief on her face as she rushed towards him and smothered him with a hug.

"I —"

"Don't talk," she said, gripping his hand while taking her seat. "You had a fall, a bang on the head, but you're OK. No permanent damage. Let me get you a drink."

As she poured him some water from a jug, he raised his hand to touch the side of his head. There was a lump. It felt bruised.

"They did scans and tests, and everything came back looking normal," she said, passing him water in a plastic cup.

The water tasted like the cup, but his dry throat welcomed it.

"What kind of tests?"

"Sorry, my love?"

"The tests...what were they?"

"Oh, I don't know. Brain scan, I think; blood test, probably. I was too panicked to pay attention. The important thing is, you're fine."

He closed his eyes and sighed heavily. *Tests*.

"You just missed Ellie and Isaac; they'll come back tomorrow."

"I'm staying here?"

"You were unconscious, and they want to keep an eye on you. They gave you something for the pain; you'll feel groggy for a while." She patted his hand. "Just rest."

He felt soft and fuzzy, as if someone had sanded all his edges and corners into smooth curves. He felt a kiss on his forehead as he closed his eyes again.

The next time he opened his eyes, it was dark, and his mother was gone. There were two figures at the end of the bed. One wearing a white coat, the other, a square-faced man, wore a dark suit. When they saw Max was awake, they hooked a clipboard to the bed frame and moved off, talking in hushed tones, their footfalls echoing down the ward.

After that, his night was restless, a mixture of visions and dreams. He saw Kira in what at first felt like a vision, but its strangeness quickly convinced him it must be a dream. With her long black curly hair, she sat cross-legged before a giant, motionless spider. She was tending to one of its legs, which Max somehow knew to be injured.

The image eventually dissolved and became a familiar sight, a vision he'd had many times; a man at a workbench, carving intricate wooden ornaments. He was holding what looked like a deer, using a small curved blade to work its fine details. As he looked closer, he noticed something he'd never seen before: the man wore a ring made of wood. Before he could make anything of it, the vision faded, replaced by a vision he'd only ever experienced once before — a tall Nim woman in blue robes standing upon a platform of a giant tree. "*Ta kaah*," she said. He remembered the translation from before: *Save him.*

But Max *had* saved him. Max had saved Wren. He had done what he was supposed to do. Yet the words kept coming; "*Ta kaah.*" Then Max realised this was not a vision, merely the memory of one. Somehow, he knew it was playing again to show him something he'd missed. He studied the scene, looking for the previously unseen detail.

Then he saw it.

On the index finger of her left hand was another wooden ring. It was identical to that worn by the man carving the deer. *Ta kaah. Save him.* Max suddenly knew those words had never referred to Wren. The words that had once driven Max to save Wren were words pleading for the safety of another.

Max was suddenly distracted by something that had never been in his original vision. This was something new, presumably added by his unconscious mind, extras, courtesy of his painkillers. The clouds behind the woman were being pushed away by an unseen force, leaving a clear blue sky. It was not clear for long. Moments later, it was torn apart by what looked like a fiery whip slowly striking from the heavens. The forest shuddered from a silent shockwave, and birds took flight. Then everything was on fire.

"How are you feeling this morning, Max?"

Max nodded as a young male doctor shone a light in each eye, then asked him to follow his finger as it moved across his field of vision. "Read the bottom line of the chart over there for me?" He stepped aside and pointed to an eye test chart on the wall.

"F - R - T - K and..." he paused so as not to make it look

too easy. "P? or D? D, I think." He thought about reading the tiny *printed in Pakistan* in the bottom corner, but now was not the time for showing off.

"Excellent." The doctor placed his penlight into his shirt pocket and studied the notes on the clipboard. "All your vitals look fine. We originally suspected a fracture to your skull, but you seem to be built of solid stuff, Mr Cannon. Just a mild concussion. You're all good to leave this morning."

Max heard his mother sigh with relief next to him, and the doctor scribbled on his chart while advising Max to rest for a few days.

He'd spent two nights in the hospital and returned home on Saturday morning, where Ellie and Isaac were at his door waiting.

"I have to get to work," said his mother as she opened the door. She leaned in and kissed Max on the forehead. "If you need anything, call me. I'll have my phone switched on. Mr Hall won't like it, but who cares." She kissed him again.

"I'll be fine, Mum."

She waved to Isaac and Ellie, then turned and left.

"How you feeling?" Ellie asked as the three walked along the hallway.

"Fine," Max said, entering the kitchen and taking a seat at the small table.

"Did they ask you any...odd questions?" asked Isaac, leaning against the kitchen counter. Max noticed his eyes flick momentarily to the biscuit jar.

"Help yourself," Max said, nodding towards it. "They didn't ask me much at all. They might have spoken to my mum."

"Oh, I nearly forgot," said Ellie, quickly standing and positioning herself behind Max. "Wren insisted I give you the once over with this." She held out the healing disc and proceeded to move it slowly over his head. "Been a while since I've done this," she added.

Max felt his scalp tingle pleasantly. "So I guess he knows about our little side project?"

Isaac nodded. "He seemed more concerned than mad."

"He's not mad," said Ellie. "He invited us to a birthday party. Father Elliot's a hundred on Thursday. They're having a few people over at Rose Bank."

"Don't expect anything wild," said Isaac. "Mr Walsh said these things rarely make it past eight o'clock."

Max smiled. "What happened at school? How much trouble are we in?

"We both got detention and a few behaviour points," said Ellie. "And they changed the combination on the lock, which hasn't helped us with popularity points. I think you've been let off the hook, though. But you had to eat hospital food, so I suppose we're even."

Max removed the plaster from inside his elbow, expecting to see a pin-prick from his blood test, but it had already healed. Preoccupied with thoughts of what other tests they might have done, he massaged his upper arm, where it felt bruised.

"We were there when they took your blood," Isaac said.

"It's OK," Max said, sensing guilt in Isaac's tone. "Would have looked strange if you had tried to wrestle them to the ground and break me out."

"The thought did cross my mind." Isaac took another biscuit from the jar.

"There," said Ellie, pocketing the disc and sitting down opposite Max. "All fixed."

"Thanks, doc." Max raised his hand to his head. The lump was gone, as was the tenderness. "I'm not going to try again," he said after a pause. "If they fix the card, they fix it.

I'm never doing it again. Wren was right. It's dangerous." He looked first to Isaac and then to Ellie.

"Good," said Ellie. "It's not worth hurting yourself over. Plus, you've just been in hospital, had all sorts of tests and scans, yet here you are, safe in your kitchen, not some deep underground lab being poked around."

"Yeah," said Max, massaging the discomfort in his upper arm once more.

13

A CARD FROM THE QUEEN

There were five more days of school left before the Christmas break, but Max didn't go in for any of them. Instead, his mother, insisting he make a *complete recovery*, arranged with the school to have work sent home. Apart from feeling slightly more tired than usual and the mild discomfort in his arm, he was back to normal. And when Thursday arrived, the day of Father Elliot's party, his mother raised no objection when Max said he was meeting his friends and would probably eat out.

He met Isaac and Ellie, who had both come straight from school, at the corner of Bramfield Park, near the small lane leading to Rose Bank Cottage. Isaac was first to the door, white Christmas lights running around its frame and over its small crooked porch. He pressed the bell. Moments later, the door creaked open and a familiar face greeted them.

"George!" they cried in unison.

"Well, look who it is," George said, stepping aside to allow them in. "So good to see you. Come in, come in...."

George was the first person to have met Wren on Earth; he had been a young boy, an evacuee. Their friendship was the reason Wren had stayed, and Max hadn't seen him for over a year. Seeing him now filled him with happiness. They exchanged pleasantries — *isn't it cold, when did you arrive,* and so on — while they hung their coats on hooks already bulging with winter coats.

"Now, don't let me forget," said George, suddenly serious, "there are some here not in on the old *secret*." He tapped his nose. "So I have to be careful. Give me a nudge if you find me being indiscreet; I've had a glass of sherry, so...."

Max nodded with a smile. "We will. It's great to see you again," he added.

George brought him in for a hug. "You too, young Max. Wren's been keeping me informed of all your progress. Sounds like you're developing some remarkable talents."

"Did he tell you anything else?" Isaac asked.

"If you are referring to the incident with the drone and the selfie, and the man currently trying to fix the whatchamacallit —oh, and Max's trip to the hospital, then no, he didn't tell me anything."

Max gave a tight-lipped, embarrassed smile as George ushered them through to the sitting room.

Mr Walsh's cottage reminded Max of a Hobbit hole; everything was small: low-beamed ceilings, small windows that hardly let in any light during the day, tiny doorways that, in a year or two, even Max would need to duck under, or risk being knocked out.

They found the sitting room full of warm, friendly smiles. Most they recognised; some they didn't. Many chairs lined the walls, commandeered from the neighbouring houses. Guests, more than the little house had probably ever seen, spilt out into the kitchen and into the small rustic conservatory beyond. Music from the forties, or maybe the fifties, filled the air, along with the low-level hum of conversation. Laughter sprung from one corner of the room, and

Max spotted Father Elliot, birthday balloons tied to the handles of his wheelchair. A crowd had gathered around him as he read aloud from a white card edged with gold and silver. Just behind them, standing alone, was Wren. He was watching the group with a comfortable smile on his face, one that broadened when he saw Max and his friends approach.

"What's going on here?" Isaac asked George as they passed Father Elliot and his captivated audience.

"Oh, that?" George said. "The Queen sends a card to anyone who manages to hang on to a hundred. He's been reading his to anyone who'll listen. Only now, he seems to be adding his own interpretation of the text."

Father Elliot, noticing the three of them, looked up with a mischievous glint in his eye, then he carried on reading aloud, "*...and I came so close to giving up my crown,*" he continued in his best Queen's English. "*For I desired nothing more than a quiet life in Hurstwick with you, tending to your prize-winning brassicas.*" Mr Bartley, standing beside Father Elliot, ejected drink from his nose as laughter erupted once again from the group.

"I found these youngsters loitering outside," George said as he guided them through to join Wren.

"How many cards from the queen do you have?" Isaac said quietly to Wren, shielding the words with the back of his hand.

"She owes him quite a few, I reckon," George said, leaning into Isaac. "And if you ever squeeze out of him just how many, you let me know. He never told me." He smiled at Wren as he slapped Isaac on the back. Wren blinked slowly and shook his head. He was about to say something when the lights in the room dimmed and the music faded.

They turned to see Mr Walsh enter the room. He was pushing a trolley, upon which stood a giant, beautifully decorated birthday cake in the shape of the church. *Happy birthday* was sung as it was rolled towards Father Elliot, a few members of the church choir putting everyone else to shame. When the song reached its climax, the old man leaned forward and blew out the single golden candle. Applause filled the room, then quickly turned to silence and then to laughter as Father Elliot gripped his arm and faked a heart attack. He was on form, thought Max.

Mrs Waldron, the owner of the antiques shop on the high street, cut the cake into slices as the guests crowded around. Mr Walsh plated up and handed them out.

"Stay back," Father Elliot said, looking at Wren and holding up his hands defensively. "You'll destroy the entire church this time." Everyone who heard it laughed, including Wren, but only a few in the room got the joke.

As the party went on, Max found himself standing alone with Wren. While the others mingled and talked and picked from the buffet, they were ignored. Neither of them minded.

Being ignored was one of the benefits of being a Watcher. A part of the *deception* Gift, which usually developed long after the Gift of perception. But the seeds of the Gift were there in Max. It was the reason he'd grown up being ignored by everyone, save his mother; he was used to it now. Especially when he'd discovered that it was something he could, one day, learn to control. Wren had told him that with time and practice, he'd be able to vary the amount by which others would perceive him. Not just him, but also the physical environment around him. When it came to Max's physical presence, the default level was a mild awareness, like distant road noise or the hum of a bathroom extractor fan. With practice, he'd be able to dial up that presence so that he could not be ignored, like the crash of a cymbal. With centuries of practice, a Watcher could fade from perception altogether, disappearing entirely from the minds of those around them. Max knew he'd never reach that level. He'd seen the family tree; the descendants of Wren may have inherited some traits of the Nim, but extended lifespan didn't seem to be one of them.

"So within two minutes," said Wren quietly with a smile, "we had one joke about my age and one reference to me destroying the church. At this rate, I'll be questioned by strange people in black before the night is out, and halfway to Area 51 by morning."

"I'm sorry," Max said.

"That was me doing funny," said Wren with a straight face.

"No. I mean, I'm sorry about...you know, not listening to you."

Wren looked down to Max and smiled. "Listen. I'm not always right. Occasionally I do the wrong thing, and I say the wrong thing." He looked back out into the room. "I'm only human, after all."

Max smiled and looked down to his feet, relieved that Wren wasn't mad, but he was still ashamed for disobeying him.

"What I'm trying to say," Wren continued, "Is that I was wrong to try and stop you from exploring your new Gifts. Our Gifts are important to us; they define us. I should have supported you. I should have helped you. I sometimes forget how scary it can be when we learn new things about ourselves. So for that, *I'm* sorry."

At that moment, Mr Walsh appeared with two plates, each containing large slices of cake. "He insisted you have a piece of the steeple," he said, rolling his eyes and handing the first plate to Wren. He gave the second plate to Max before disappearing back into the crowd.

Max looked at the portion of the church steeple on Wren's plate. "I believe Area 51 is nice this time of year."

Wren laughed, and Max suddenly felt lighter than he had in weeks.

Someone decided it was time for dancing, and the volume of the music was cranked up. For the first few songs, Mrs Waldron danced with Mr Walsh, then scanned the room looking for her next partner. Wren must have dialled down their presence because her eyes slipped past them several times. And Max noticed a subtle darkening of the light around them. The music too changed, becoming softer and slightly muffled.

She gave a knowing look in their general direction before dragging up Isaac instead, giving him a crash course in the jitterbug. Ellie watched, laughing hysterically but stopped when Mr Walsh bowed before her with an outstretched hand.

"That was close," said Wren as they watched. "She dances well for the second oldest person in the room, don't you think?"

Max's eyes went from Mrs Waldron, to Father Elliot, to Wren, and then back to Mrs Waldron. "She's older than Father Elliot?"

Wren nodded.

Max wondered how much of her youthfulness was genetics and healthy lifestyle and how much was down to being best friends with a man in possession of a seemingly magical healing disc.

"They're like family to you, aren't they," Max said, watching Mr Walsh and Mrs Waldron dance, while Father Elliot continued to have those around him in hysterics.

Wren turned to Max. "Is this your way of moving the conversation towards the Furlongs?"

"Was it that obvious?" Max finished the last crumbs of his cake and placed the plate on a nearby sideboard. "Why do you not want to know about them? Is it to protect them? In case Jenta one day—"

"No," Wren interrupted. "Jenta will not be returning." Wren put his plate down next to Max's and looked back out to the party in full swing, the music still muffled as Wren's privacy barrier remained in place.

"If I'm protecting anyone," he continued. "I'm protecting myself. Watchers are built for being alone. We often do our job in complete isolation. Sometimes many years pass without any physical interaction with others. Food and supplies are left at the foot of our towers by those we protect. But it is often Hunters that leave that food. And they are not interested in conversation.

"As I became a Watcher, I was aware of my attachment to others slowly dissolving — a necessary change. Hunters grow cold and singular in their focus, enabling them to kill effectively. Watchers become emotionally distant so they can leave their loved ones to survive a life of seclusion without loneliness to distract them. That part of me doesn't exist anymore. It died when I met George. Something in his genetic makeup changed me, and I desired company and friends. But my friends pass on too soon. The pain of them passing feels unbearable at times, an emotion I'm still not used to. On this world, I exist outside the natural order of things, so I fear I'll never get used to it."

"I understand," said Max. And he did. He wondered if he would become emotionally distant as his Gifts developed. He was going to ask but decided he'd rather not know.

"Be patient with me," said Wren with a smile and a firm hand on Max's shoulder. "Maybe one day I'll want to know more about them."

Max nodded.

"In the meantime," Wren added. "Tell me more about your new Gifts."

With still no one paying them any attention, they continued to talk. Max spoke of what he'd learned of his new ability, about white noise and the beautiful light he would see before slipping behind someone's eyes. Wren asked questions, and Max did his best to answer. When the conversation turned to his stay in the hospital, Max was reminded of the dreams he'd had, and, in particular, one specific detail.

"Are wooden rings common? On Nimar, I mean."

"Not common," Wren said after a pause. "But there is a specific group who wear them—"

"Makers?"

"Yes," Wren said, almost a whisper. "The wooden ring is often the first thing they make as part of their formal training. Some keep them as reminders."

"I saw one. Well, two, actually," said Max. "The man I sometimes see carving wooden figures...I always thought he was a descendant of yours. But, if he's had formal training, then he can't be, right?" Max then remembered the dream that followed. "There's also the woman on Nimar. I only ever saw her once in a vision when Kelha was here. I sometimes remember her in my dreams. I think she wears a wooden ring, too."

Wren said nothing for a while. Instead, he turned his attention to the dark window overlooking the garden. "I never believed the Maker, the one Jenta was sent to look for, was here," he said eventually, turning back to face Max. "Jenta seemed to believe it but offered no evidence. You see, there are a tiny fraction of worlds that can support the Nim. And only a tiny fraction of those are home to species similar enough to hide among, with some alterations. But the universe is a big place, Max, and those tiny fractions still equate to many worlds for the Maker to choose from — thousands upon thousands."

"But now you think he's here?"

"After what you've just told me, I think it's very likely."

It was seven-thirty when the party came to an end, half an hour before Mr Walsh had predicted. Dark skies and full bellies made it feel much later. Father Elliot had been last to leave, escorted by Mr Bartley and Mrs Waldron. George, who was staying at the cottage for the night, started clearing plates from tables and windowsills. Max, Isaac, and Ellie were about to separate themselves from the comfortable sofa to help, when Mr Walsh ordered everyone to sit, saying the mess could wait for the morning and there was plenty more cake to get through.

Max declined the offer of more cake, and he let his head fall back to the soft upholstery. His mind drifted as conversations went on around him. Soon he wasn't listening at all, just watching the red flicker of flame through his closed eyelids. Then a change in tone, and the mention of the name Dinesh, quickly brought his attention back.

"I also searched for Dinesh," Wren had said. He looked at Max, noticing his awareness return. "Unlike Max, I had to leave the house and venture into the cold." He smiled briefly. "I watched both GiaTek buildings for two days straight, in case he kept irregular hours. I never saw him. However, I could have easily missed him; there are many employees, and both buildings are large, with more than one entrance. I couldn't cover them all."

"Maybe you got unlucky," Mr Walsh said as he stretched his legs and rolled his shoulders. "Maybe the fella was on holiday."

Irregular hours, thought Max. Those two simple words from Wren had suddenly made sense of everything. He leant forward and looked at Isaac and then at Ellie. "What if Dinesh works nights and sleeps in the day? Maybe I can't connect to people when they sleep?"

He looked to Wren, who nodded thoughtfully.

"The one time it did work was at the supermarket," said Ellie with a shrug. "That was in the evening."

"Then maybe that's it," said Max, somehow knowing it was. "I thought I was doing it wrong; the first time had been so easy — surprisingly easy."

The room went silent.

Max noticed a look between Mr Walsh and Wren. Mr Walsh raised an eyebrow in question, and Wren returned a dismissive slow blink.

"What is it?" asked Max.

Wren looked away to the fire while Mr Walsh took an interest in the cake crumbs on his plate.

"You want me to try again," said Max. "Don't you?"

"NO!" Ellie said. "You're not doing it again. They don't want that, do you?" She frowned at Wren.

George, sitting on a wicker chair brought in from the conservatory, looked back and forth between Wren and Mr Walsh. "Do you want him to try?" he asked. "Because I'm not sure that's a great idea."

"It's a terrible idea," said Ellie. "Anyway, Max, you said you don't care if they fix it. So why take the risk?"

Max didn't answer. Instead, he looked to Wren. "Do you want me to try?"

There was a long pause. Then Wren spoke. "I think there is a safer way for you to continue to develop this new Gift of yours. But doing so now, so soon after your visit to the hospital, is irresponsible."

"Safer, how?" Max asked.

"Using the healing disc as you enter your trance state may prolong the amount of time you can spend *in* that state, without feeling pain. However, there is a possibility the disc could disturb your trance and bring you out prematurely. It's all just theory."

Noticing a sigh from Ellie beside him, Max looked at the clock on the mantel. It was nearly eight-thirty. He had seen Dinesh in the supermarket at around eight before. If he'd been on his way to work, the timing might be perfect. He turned it over in his mind. The possibility of using the Gift without pain excited him.

"Listen," Wren added. "This is not something you need to consider now. You said he's relying on a delivery to complete the repair. You said the twenty-first. That's this Saturday. I've observed deliveries at both locations. I know where to go to retrieve—"

"If you succeed," said Max. "You're just delaying things. You take it, and he orders another. You need to know exactly where he works to find that SD card."

"Tracking the delivery will tell us what building he works in."

"But the buildings are big—"

"Yes," conceded Wren. "The central London office is the smaller of the two, but even that is seven floors, and each floor over three thousand square metres. A lot of ground to cover for something so small."

"But we know he works in the basement," said Isaac.

"We do?" Ellie said.

"Yeah. The woman from GiaTek; she asked him how life was in the basement. I assumed that meant he...worked in the basement?"

"Do both offices have basements?" Max asked Wren.

Wren nodded. "Still, it narrows the search greatly."

"Not as narrow as I could make it," Max said.

"I can't believe you're going to do this," said Ellie.

Isaac was getting to his feet. "The pack's in my bag. Headphones too."

Max looked at Wren, feeling a mix of excitement and nervousness.

"The choice is yours, Max. No one can make you do this. Like I said, it's just a theory."

"A theory we should test," Max said.

Minutes later, Max was kneeling by the fire, Ellie sitting beside him, the healing disc in her hand.

"Clear on what to do?" Wren asked Ellie as he stooped in the doorway.

She nodded. "Run the disc over him every minute. If it lights up, I focus on those areas until the light fades."

"Good. We'll be in the kitchen." With a look of concern he closed the door, leaving them alone in the glow of the fire.

Max grabbed the headphones that were now around his neck. He paused before putting them on. "Thank you," he said to Ellie, "I know you didn't want me to do this."

"Shut up and get on with it," she said. "Some of us have school in the morning." There was a hint of a smile at the edge of her lips, but he could see she was afraid.

Max placed the headphones on, the white noise already playing. The folder lay open before him on the rug. He looked briefly at the photos of Dinesh — he knew the face well now — then looked at the maps and the street view images, and his breathing started to slow. He glanced once more at Ellie, who was trying her best to look calm, but Max noticed the racing pulse in her neck.

He closed his eyes.

He fell into the trance with ease. The white noise

lowered almost immediately to a deep rumbling vibration that ebbed and flowed with his breath as before.

In the darkness, he was soon moving through the tunnels at speed. Unlike his previous attempts, there was a feeling of purpose; he was no longer frantically searching without hope. There was a destination, and he was moving rapidly towards it.

A turn and a dive and a climb, and then he saw it: the beautiful white light ahead of him, growing quickly until, suddenly, it engulfed him.

The white light, which felt somehow cleansing, faded to show Dinesh — small and distant. He was riding an electric scooter over a black road, wet and shiny, snow at the edges and on the pavements, splashing through puddles, dodging potholes. He wore a helmet and a neck scarf covering half his face. No wonder Wren struggled to recognise him, he thought. Then came the second white light, and he was in the man's head looking out at the world.

He was approaching a junction, red lights facing him, a pub to his left, people milling around outside talking and smoking. Everything else — the coffee shops, the sandwich bars, the newsagents, the bank — was closed. He slowed for the red light, allowing a bus to cross the junction, but he didn't stop. Instead, he mounted the pavement, turning into a street Max recognised from the photos. He was close to the central London office. The timing *was* perfect.

A dull pain developed. As it worsened, his vision blurred and wobbled. It felt as though someone was reaching into his skull and squeezing his brain, trying to pull him out. He was just about to lose Dinesh when the pain went away. Ellie was using the disc, and it was working.

The pain came and went one more time before Dinesh reached the office. Ahead, he saw the glass wall of the foyer with its rotating doors. Max expected him to slow and dismount, but he continued past at speed, entering the building via a side entrance and a ramp leading down to a secure underground car park, which he accessed with a keycard. In a dim concrete room, home to a handful of bicycles under a flickering strip light, he locked up his scooter, then made for a door leading to a stairwell. After climbing two flights of stairs, he exited into the ample, plush open space of the main foyer, the rotating doors to his right.

He passed a cluster of black, leather sofas and armchairs and a chest-high reception desk. A woman sat behind it, only her head visible, her hair in a tight bun and eyebrows in a constant state of surprise.

When she looked at him, Max felt a sense of panic, a feeling that the game was up. But they exchanged pleasantries without drama, and Dinesh continued onwards, where he said good evening to a security guard standing next to a bank of turnstiles, a large man who wouldn't look out of place on the door of a rough nightclub, thought Max.

Dinesh stopped to chat with the man, but Max didn't catch any of it. The headache had returned. This time it seemed to fade even quicker than before. Ellie was getting better at dealing with them. By the time it cleared, he was past the turnstile and heading to the lifts.

Above the lifts, set on a black marble wall, was the large chrome company logo of GiaTek. In smaller text underneath: *A division of FossCorp.*

One lift was open, spreading its cone of light across the polished floor. He stepped inside and selected *B2* from a bank of buttons. Max committed it to memory. *Central London office, Level B2.*

As the lift descended, he examined his reflection in the mirrored back wall, moving his head from side to side. Spotting a rogue hair protruding from his left nostril, he removed one of his woollen gloves, and with his thumb and forefinger, yanked it out. His vision went momentarily blurry as his eyes watered but then cleared after a few blinks.

When the door opened with a *ping*, Dinesh spun on his heels and exited the lift, turning left, and then immediately left again into a small kitchen, which lit up as he entered. He removed a Tupperware box from his backpack, his name written on the lid, and placed it in the fridge. Then he left the kitchen, continuing along the corridor, removing his other glove, his hat, and his scarf as he went.

On either side of him, glass-walled meeting rooms sat dark and empty. After the meeting rooms, the walls became white, with grey doors distributed evenly on both sides. Max started to count them before noticing they were numbered.

Dinesh didn't continue for long. He stopped after about twenty feet, opening door number fourteen on his right.

Max added it to the list. *Central London office, Level B2. Left out of the lift. Past the kitchen. Past the meeting rooms, door number fourteen.*

As he entered the room, bright strip lighting flickered to life and filled the room with a uniform brightness that seemed to offend Dinesh; with a groan, he quickly reached for the switches on the wall and clumsily flicked them off.

The only light now came from the computer screens occupying a long desk running down the centre of the room. Beyond this desk, partially hidden in darkness, was a storage area with several rows of metal shelves and racks containing electrical and computer equipment. The furthest shelves were hidden entirely from Dinesh's eyes, in a darkness that Max hadn't experienced for some time.

Dinesh planted himself before one of the computers, and with a heavy sigh, flicked on a desk lamp. He then pulled a flask from his bag and placed it next to a small wobbly-headed figure of Iron Man.

Max was adding Iron Man to his list when the pain returned. He held on as long as he could, hoping to discover the SD card's location, but after a few minutes of watching Dinesh delete emails, he decided it was time to leave. The goal had been to find out where he worked, and he'd done that.

He opened his eyes to see Ellie before him. Her hand held the disc to his forehead between thumb and forefinger. She lowered the disc with a relieved smile, looking at him expectantly.

He smiled back at her. "We got him," he said.

14

A VISIT TO CHURCH

In the snow-covered garden, Wren stood at the open back door, a shaft of light reaching for Max, Isaac, and Ellie as they made for the gate opening into the churchyard.

Wren smiled as Isaac scooped a handful of snow from the lawn and hurled it at Max, hitting him square in the back.

As a snowball fight began, Wren took his gaze to the dark trees of the churchyard, just beyond the garden fence, where he noticed two fat woodpigeons huddling together for warmth on the branch of the large chestnut tree. His eyes lingered upon them for a short while, then continued upwards to the snow-heavy sky. He forced a shift in the light to see past the cloud to the stars beyond. They appeared as a spray of sharp blue and purple points, a thick band of Milky Way framed by the black trees surrounding the cottage garden.

A feeling that something was out of place, cut short his appreciation of the view and brought his gaze back to the pigeons perched on the branch. He was familiar with these two birds. They were a breeding pair that would typically spend cold nights in a cavity in the old tree. Tonight *was* a cold night. He looked to the cavity, set deep into the trunk, expecting to see the reason for their eviction, maybe a rook or magpies. But it seemed empty, and, judging from the subtle white glow within, was warmer than the exposed branch.

Suddenly, there came a scream. The birds stood with alertness, ready for flight. At the same time, adrenaline pumped into Wren's limbs but quickly dissipated as he looked to his young friends. He smiled with relief. Isaac was now running through the open gate while Ellie wriggled and shook the snow from her neck and shoulder, squirming as ice ran down her back. She called after Isaac, grabbed a handful of snow, and gave chase. Wren had no doubt she'd get her revenge.

Max followed, and as he turned to close the garden gate a snowball exploded on the side of his head. Wren chuckled and listened to their battle cries diminish as the fight continued through the churchyard.

He was about to close the door and return to the comfort of the sitting room when movement caught his eye. It was the pigeons. High in the tree, they were now ambling back to their warm spot.

With still no sign of what forced them into the cold, a feeling of unease grew within Wren. He stepped outside into the snow, closed the door, then pulled up the zip of his winter fleece. As his eyes moved from tree to tree, he crossed the garden. He could usually see or sense the reason for a disturbed bird — normally a cat or another bird, but this seemed to be neither. He felt a stillness in the air, like a held breath. He looked at the fence, and it faded to show Isaac sprinting around the north side of the church, Ellie in pursuit, while Max circled the south side to head him off.

He opened the gate and stepped into the churchyard. There were many tracks in the snow, most from guests leaving the party, taking the back way home. There were others too. Some were older, shallower, lined with fresh snowfall, others were new tracks that didn't originate from the gate. Some belonged to dog walkers and kept close to the line of trees, patches of yellow snow clearly visible at intervals. But one set caught Wren's attention. It ran near to the garden fence, paused just feet from Mr Walsh's gate, then made towards the church in long determined strides.

With the line of trees between him and the church, Wren moved south, parallel to the gardens. He saw Isaac reappear from behind the church, scrambling and slipping. Ellie followed him, poised with a snowball ready to launch.

Wren knelt by a tree, his hand resting against its twisted old trunk. He watched everything apart from his friends, paying most attention to the shadows, which, under his stare, quickly surrendered their secret — a woman. She was standing still in the corner where the porch joined the main church building. As Isaac and Ellie ran past her, she stepped back, further into shadow.

More shouts erupted as Isaac realised he'd run into a trap, Max appearing from behind a headstone, launching a barrage of snowy projectiles, Isaac ducking and swerving to avoid them.

Aware of the ongoing battle in his peripheral vision, he kept his focus on the woman. He'd never seen Zoe Durkin from GiaTek before but suspected this was her. He looked around for her companion, but there was no sign.

As a breeze disturbed snow in the tree above him, bringing flakes down to settle on his shoulders, Wren's attention briefly turned to Isaac. He was now at a safe distance from Ellie and Max, bent forward, his hands on his knees, taking deep breaths. "I think we're even!" he shouted breathlessly.

"I don't think so!" called Ellie, arming herself with more

missiles, cradling them across her chest in preparation for the next assault.

Max was standing silent, looking back towards the church, his head moving from side to side in small motions, like an owl. *He senses her,* thought Wren, *but he can't yet see her.*

Isaac increased the distance between them, and at the gate, he called his goodbyes and left the churchyard. Ellie yelled threats of vengeance, then dropped her ammunition and joined Max. Together they walked to the gate, Max occasionally glancing back towards the shadows.

When they reached Church Lane, the woman emerged from her hiding place and followed them. Wren faded and crossed the open churchyard, arriving at the gate just a few strides behind her.

She stopped and leaned out into the lane, watching the pair as they made their way home.

Wren studied the woman, wondering what she hoped to gain by following them. She brought her head back sharply as if Max had once again turned towards her.

A few seconds later, he heard the distant sound of the two front doors closing, one after the other, and the woman turned away. Instead of heading to the hotel, as Wren had expected, she went back through the gate. He stepped aside quickly, allowing her to pass.

She wandered the churchyard aimlessly as Wren followed, masking his footprints, as they left the path and walked among the graves.

Something wasn't right. With a growing sense of dread, it became clear that her wandering was not aimless at all. She approached a small grouping of graves at the western edge, under the large oak. Every step closer to those graves increased Wren's caution, and he considered her with different eyes as she stopped before a grave that Wren had stood by countless times before. If this woman knew of Mary, what else did she know?

"I think now is a good time for us to talk," said the woman.

Wren raised an eyebrow in surprise. She was looking at the grave as she spoke.

"I wonder, Rahiir," she continued. "Who was she to you?"

Wren said nothing to the woman who was not Zoe Durkin.

"She must have been important," she added, looking in his direction, her eyes not finding him. "You do not need to tell me." She took a few steps closer to him, scanning the ground for his footprints. Seeing none but her own, she closed her eyes and took a deep breath. When she opened them a second later, she studied the ground again. "There you are," she said, her eyes resting on where he stood.

He was impressed. She had cleared the weak deception of his footprints with ease. The more potent form, the one keeping him hidden, remained, although there was no point in maintaining it now.

He allowed himself to be seen.

"I have never seen a fade before. An impressive skill." She bowed low.

Wren dipped his head, but he said nothing, just looking at her, deciding whether he should be afraid. She was no Hunter. *But was she alone?* Remembering the displaced pigeons, he looked around again, this time to the trees.

"It is just us," she said.

He knew that was a lie.

"You do not talk much, Watcher," she said. "But talk we must. Can we go somewhere warm?"

He looked her up and down, and she smiled as she

realised what he was doing. She turned around, her arms wide.

"As you can see, I am concealing no weapons. I've not been sent here to kill you."

There was a subtle emphasis on the word *you* that caught Wren in the chest. He noticed her bracelet, which was most likely fitted with a pulse weapon, but they were slow and easily avoided if one was ready. And he would be ready.

She stopped her turn, facing him once more with raised eyebrows. "So, can we talk?"

"Follow me," he said.

It was warmer inside the church, but only just.

Wren leading the way, they made their way down between the pews. He sat on the third row from the front, while the woman sat opposite, across the aisle.

He watched her as she took in her surroundings, wondering if her dark eyes and hair were remnants of her true appearance or introduced by her guest DNA. She looked up to the church ceiling, lit by the lamps lining the path outside; their orange light transformed to greens and reds by the stained glass windows. She turned to him. "I am here," she began, "to find the Maker known as Nabiim. And the weapon he calls his *prototype*."

"Then you are wasting your time with me," he said.

"You were reported as dead by the Hunter known as Jenta. Yet here you are, alive and well, showing no intention of returning home, making a new home on a world believed to be a hideout of Nimar's most dangerous fugitive. This does not look good for you."

"I am not concerned about how things look to you."

"Why so defensive, Rahiir?" She tilted her head.

"My name is Ben now."

"But there are some who call you Wren. Is that right? A select few. They must be very special to you."

He fell silent for a moment. The threat was clear in her words, if not her tone.

"I am Yanari Coldim, of Nakrite," she said softly. "Your birthplace I believe."

So the dark hair and eyes were hers, he thought. He tried to assess her Gift. Too articulate to be a Hunter, her face was kind; perhaps a Healer. Most likely she was not Gifted at all. But there was a confidence about her, a sharpness in her eyes. He couldn't forget the ease with which she had uncovered his tracks. She had a strong mind. She was not to be messed with.

"The search for Nabiim has been ongoing for many years," she continued, "It's why you were sent here."

"I was sent to observe—"

"You were sent to look for signs of Nabiim," she interrupted. "Giadeen identified this world as one where he could be hiding. And as Makers are unable to remain idle, you were sent to look for signs of his inventiveness, technological advancements outside normal parameters for a species such as those that you have chosen to live with — and to breed with."

He allowed no emotion to reach his face.

"Yes," she went on. "We know of Max."

"I can't help you," said Wren. "I don't know where he is. There are over seven billion people on this planet. Seven billion. Nimar has a population that could barely fill a handful of their cities. Unless you have a lead, you stand no chance, and I can be of little help."

"You are the lead."

"Then you need to find another."

She smiled and nodded. "You are High Nim. I cannot order you to assist us." She narrowed her eyes. "But I notice you haven't asked *why* we are looking for Nabiim."

"It is of no concern of mine."

"If there is anyone you love on Nimar, then it *should* be of *great* concern to you."

Wren had to admit he was curious. Nabiim was a common name, but he knew of only one that was Gifted, only one with any level of fame. "This Nabiim, he is one of the five?"

Yanari nodded.

"Another reason for me not to help. Nabiim saved our world. I won't help you hunt him down and do him harm."

"I do not mean to *just* do him harm, Rahiir. Once I have his weapon, his prototype, I mean to kill him. He may have once been the saviour of life on our world, but now he is the greatest threat to it. He wishes to destroy Giadeen."

Wren's emotion finally made it to the surface in the form of a frown. What she was saying was absurd.

"Your eyes can see the truth, Rahiir. Giadeen believes Nabiim is forming a rebellion to remove him from his tower. He has become consumed with hatred towards our protector. He must be stopped. If Giadeen dies, Nimar dies with him. It would not be the murder of one, but countless life forms. You understand that. You know life could not continue on our world without him. Yet you sit here unwilling to help."

He studied her face intently. She seemed to believe she was telling the truth.

"Many Nim are unaccounted for," she went on. "You are one of those. All that are missing are assumed to be in league with Nabiim; until it can be proven otherwise."

"Do you think I am with him?" Wren asked.

"I do not know."

"I'm not."

She looked at him for a long time. Then she asked, "Are you loyal to Giadeen?"

Wren laughed. "Things have indeed changed on Nimar that such a question should be asked of anyone. You may as well ask if I'm loyal to the air I breathe."

"I'll take that as a *yes*." She looked past Wren, raising her hand as she did so.

He turned to see a young man on the seat behind him. He smiled at Wren as he slipped a silenced gun into the front pocket of his tracksuit. Wren recognised the man. He had managed to get close once before on Windmill Hill.

"It has been an honour to meet you, Watcher of the High Nim," Yanari said as she stood and bowed. "May you find balance in your struggle."

"And you, in yours," he responded, surprised at how instinctively the words came after so many years. He stood as they left, Yanari walking ahead with the young man, clearly a Hunter, a few strides behind. They passed from sight. He heard the heavy doors of the porch close, the echo crashing around him and lingering in the pipes of the church organ. He sat back down and looked to the cold stone floor. He was afraid.

15

WATCHING THE WATCHER

Hurstwick, 1947

Joseph sat on a bench under a large oak tree in Bramfield Park as the last of the spring sunlight caught the decapitated church tower. He watched the men at work on the scaffolding surrounding it, steel and wood from the ground passing from man to man then secured into place. As he watched, he was reminded of a time he'd been involved in the construction of a much larger project. The method and materials had been different, but the spirit of teamwork was familiar.

According to the local paper, the restoration would take eight years to complete due to the intricate stonework required. Yet the men worked fast, as if the deadline was just days away, slowing only when the light diminished.

For the last four evenings, Joseph had sat there. On the first, he'd been resting, occasionally glancing up to the scaffolding, lazily watching it as it slowly rose to the height of the absent spire. He had been tired, his body aching from a long day walking in the woods. Now, on this fourth evening, he watched with interest, captivated by what he saw.

He hadn't come to Hurstwick to find the Watcher. There was no hope that anyone could have survived such a violent impact. He was there to pay his respects. But the Watcher had survived. Joseph had found his ship. It was buried deep underground, in a wood the locals called Oban. If the Watcher had been killed in the crash or died sometime after, the sentinel ship would have destroyed itself or fled if it was able. But it was still there — intentionally hidden. Not only that, but his scans revealed the ship to be in good working order, waiting for its master to return.

After finding the ship, Joseph had wandered into town. Inside a small tavern by the railway, swathed with floral hanging baskets, he'd learned of the crash and destruction of the church spire. To his relief, no one had been hurt, just a few scrapes to the groundskeeper. It was good news.

Bringing down the Watcher had been his darkest hour, and the regret he'd been living with for the last three years had been unbearable at times. But after that first day in town, his guilt was forgotten, overtaken by his curiosity. If the ship was ready and waiting, why hadn't the Watcher returned?

As he sat now watching the men clamber over their scaffolding, he still didn't have his answer. But he had found his Watcher.

By pure chance, he had found him on that first evening while observing these men at work. As they clambered down under a reddening sky, Joseph had stood, intending to catch his train to London. But he paused, noticing one man not descending with the others. As they went down, he went up, climbing to the highest point, where he sat looking out over the town. Joseph sat too. And he watched his Watcher.

The next evening, as bird-song filled the air, Joseph returned to the park to a bench much further back, avoiding the Watcher's enhanced awareness. But even from this distance, the Watcher was easy to spot among them. All the men looked comfortable navigating the framework, but only one was born to it. The ease with which he moved from level to level was breathtaking. There was no showing off, no acrobatics, nothing to draw attention, just fluidity and grace that spoke to a lifetime of climbing and someone used to far greater heights. He was fearless.

Joseph, who had no head for heights, cast his mind back to childhood. On a stormy night, to ease his fear, his father had pointed their antique optical telescope to the watch tree on the horizon, to the Watcher standing guard, protecting them. He remembered her stillness and dignity as the storm whipped at her hair and robes. While others cowered from the storm, she stood alert, oblivious to the elements, her eyes scanning the foothills for the lethal shirkon, and the skies for arak birds — able to fly in all but the deadliest of weather. With the memory came a surge of anger towards Giadeen, who was now using these selfless protectors to hunt him down. He wondered what lies this Watcher had been told, if he'd been told anything at all.

During the working day, the men of the spire would interact with the Watcher as if he were one of them, but as the sun fell closer to the horizon, they took less notice, leaving him to climb while they descended.

As Joseph watched now in the fading light, the men were preparing to leave for the day. He expected the Watcher to climb higher, as was usual. But tonight, he followed the others.

Intrigued, Joseph stood and crossed the park, passing the bandstand, walking under the hissing trees, towards the cobbled lane where the men would soon emerge from the churchyard.

There was a tap on his chest, and he opened his pocket

watch. It was a reminder not to get too close. She was concerned.

He returned the watch to his pocket and observed a group of men leaving Church Lane, heading towards the high street with tired smiles, caps held in hands, hair damp with sweat. The caps that remained in place soon came off as they passed a young woman waiting under the weeping willow. She smiled at them pleasantly, then looked towards the covered gate in anticipation.

Two men soon appeared. One was short, with blond hair poking out from under his cap. The other was tall. He wore no cap and had jet black hair and dark eyes. He looked unaffected by the day's work. There was no sweat or look of exhaustion like the others. He wore a white shirt with his sleeves rolled up, his jacket hanging over his shoulder, hooked onto a long finger, reminding Joseph of one of those American actors he'd seen on movie posters.

The small blond man spied the woman and doffed his cap. "Good day to you, Mary," he said cheerfully.

"Peter," she nodded with a friendly smile before turning her eyes to the tall man with black hair.

Peter looked between his tall friend and Mary. Both were silently gazing at each other with subtle smiles.

"Well," said Peter. "Don't I feel like a third chopstick. I'll guess I'll be off then." He waited for one of them to say something. When they didn't, Peter spoke on their behalf. "See ya tomorrow, Peter. Grand work today, Peter. Boy, am I glad to have a friend like you, Peter. And to think, you keep all my secrets, and they're not bloody small secrets either—"

The tall man suddenly laughed as he was pulled from his trance. He gripped his friend on the shoulder. "Sorry. I'll see you tomorrow."

Peter winked at him, then jogged to catch the other men, probably heading for a well-earned pint.

Joseph had crossed the street and had watched the exchange in the reflection of a corner shop window. He had to be careful. He was closer to the Watcher than he felt comfortable. If it weren't for the distraction of the young woman, he would no doubt be aware of Joseph's presence.

He watched as the tall man approached the woman. She walked away before he could reach her, turning to him and smiling playfully. When they came to the blossom-covered grass of the park, she ran, laughing while he gave chase.

Joseph turned from the window to continue watching. They ran further into the darkening park, where she let him catch her under a broad chestnut tree. She flung her arms up and around his neck. He dropped his jacket, and they kissed.

Joseph turned back to the window. Knowing, finally, why the Watcher had stayed.

Days later, on a bright, sunny afternoon, Wren and Mary walked together through the long grass of the meadow. Wren was barefoot, one hand in his pocket, the other holding his shoes. He turned to Mary. She was a few paces behind, lazily admiring the wildflowers, humming a tune.

"We should go on holiday," he said. It was a concept he wasn't entirely sure he understood, but he liked the sound of it. "We should get away for a while. Maybe a couple of months travelling."

"But my work..." said Mary.

"OK. Two weeks. That's what people do, right?"

She laughed. "It is what people do, yes."

"So?"

"How about a weekend?" She walked to him and wrapped her arms around his waist.

"Come on. A week is my final offer." He tickled her.

"OK, OK, a week, a week," she cried, wriggling and then collapsing into a sitting position in the grass. "I can't be taking too much time off," she added. "I've only just started this job. And you know what, I really love it. Yes, it was exciting at the War Office — I enjoyed it. But *this,* I think I'll be happy working there for the rest of my days."

"Really?"

"Yes, *really.*" She picked a clump of grass and threw it at him.

"What?" he protested. "I didn't say anything."

"You didn't need to, spaceman. I can read you like a book."

"A *library* book?" He sat beside her with a smile.

"Shut up," she said, with an expression of mock sadness. "It's a good job. I like it." She put her arm through his and rested her head on his shoulder, looking out over the field towards Moore's Farm.

"So, where are you taking me?" she asked. "To your planet? Meet the folks?"

"I couldn't decide between my planet or Norfolk."

"Ooh, let's do Norfolk."

"Norfolk it is." His smile broadened. "Spaceship or train?"

"Train," she said, squeezing his arm. "Separate trains, though." Suddenly all business-like, almost as if she'd already considered this trip. "A day apart. You go first. I can meet you there. I'll say I'm meeting some old War Office friends."

"Very cloak and dagger. Are you sure you weren't a spy during the war?"

"Well, if I told you," she looked up to him, "I'd have to kiss you."

She kissed him anyway.

The train whistle blew, and a second later, a jolt threw Mary back into her seat. She watched Hurstwick Station roll by. She waved to her father, who, despite his worsening leg, had insisted on accompanying her to the station. He leaned on his walking stick and waved back. She blew him a kiss.

He slid from view, and she turned her head to keep sight of him but soon lost him to a cloud of steam hanging at the head of the platform. When it cleared, she saw the north edge of Hurstwick roll by and eventually recede. The allotments, the park, the River Den.

As the town turned into fields and the sun warmed her face, she became aware of the compartment door sliding open, then closing again. When she turned away from the window moments later, a gentleman had taken a seat adjacent to her. He was tall and smartly dressed and was studying a shiny black pocket watch.

He closed the watch, slipped it into his pocket, then removed his hat. "I need to talk to you, Mary," he said. His voice was low and soft, with a hint of a French accent. "This won't be easy to hear. But you *need* to hear it."

16

THE SPIDER

Somerset House, a former government building turned event space and centre for the arts, was a grand, regal affair in the centre of London. At its heart was a courtyard, which at this time of year was alive with tourists and Londoners enjoying the outdoor ice skating.

With a coffee in one hand and a phone in the other, Kira Furlong powered past the ice rink and through the crowds, her gravity-defying black curls bouncing as she went.

"Pick up, pick up, pick up..." she murmured as she rounded a forty-foot Christmas tree.

"Olá, this is Jose. Please leave—"

"Damn it, Jose." She ended the call and selected another number.

"This is Petra. Leave a message, and I'll—"

With frustration, she hung up and slid the phone into her pocket.

Leaving the crowds behind, she entered the west wing of the building. She flashed her exhibitor pass to a security guard, then walked down a dimly lit corridor, her footsteps echoing off the stone walls and high vaulted ceiling, from which hung the banners announcing the imminent opening of her exhibition. They were a painful reminder that with less than twelve hours to go, she was not ready.

She let out a long breath, and, before the thick walls of the building rendered her phone useless, she checked to see if anyone had tried to call back. They hadn't. Catching sight of the time on the home screen, she quickened her pace and turned off the main corridor into an ample dark space, which lit up as she entered.

For the next three months, this was her space. Her chance to show a wider audience her dream and the dreams of the people she worked with: a vision of a new way of building.

Dotted around the hall were a selection of abstract and curvaceous objects. Some were presented on waist-high plinths, with the larger items sitting directly on the dark wooden floor. These objects could easily have been mistaken for priceless pieces of art, but there were no velvet ropes or glass barriers here to protect them from the masses. Kira wanted the public to touch them, to *feel* them. If any became damaged, then, in her mind, they were not good enough in the first place. They were designed to be solid and durable, built from what she believed would be the building materials of the future.

As impressive as these items were — to her, anyway — they were not the main attraction. People were coming to see the artist and not the art. The Spider, the creator of these objects, dominated the room, a massive machine that would have looked at home in any state-of-the-art car factory.

Called the Spider on account of its eight robotic limbs, it was far more elegant than its factory dwelling cousins. Some thought it beautiful. Kira was one of them. Some called it The Dead Spider, as it resembled a spider on its back, its legs curled into its centre. She didn't like the comparison, but right now, on the eve of the big opening, it was an accurate one.

People were coming to watch it weave its weird and wonderful sculptures, its legs moving at speed as if wrapping a captured fly. However, as things stood, it wouldn't be building anything. A small heat pump at the base of one of its legs was currently displaying a red light, and red lights were bad. Without a working heat pump, the resin used to make the sculptures would be the wrong temperature, resulting in the Spider making nothing more than a sloppy mess on the floor.

She squatted at the base of the leg next to an open panel revealing the offending red light and a thick tangle of multicoloured wires. She sighed and placed the coffee next to her on the floor.

Before going for that coffee, she had been staring at those wires for over an hour. There were three hundred of them, and at least two of them were in the wrong place, or not securely connected. She hadn't designed this part of the machine. If she had, there would have been an elegant order to the complexity, and the problem would have been quick to identify and fix. And it probably wouldn't have failed in the first place.

Jose and Petra were more familiar with the faulty module. One of them should be here, but both were undoubtedly enjoying pre-open-day drinks in some swanky bar on The Strand.

She blew a stray black curl away from her face and tried not to get angry. Anger would fog her mind, and she needed to focus.

She made herself comfortable. And with her long nimble fingers, she parted the wires, picking through them like files in a filing cabinet, checking each one against the blueprints laid out beside her.

She sat for almost an hour, her neglected coffee going cold, but could find no fault. She was about to give up when the room suddenly went dark.

Suspecting she'd been sitting motionless for too long, she waved her arm in the air to trigger the sensors. But the room remained dark. The only light was a shifting yellow and red from the spotlights outside, entering through the three large windows on the far wall. She stood and waved her arm again. When the lights failed to come on, she jumped in the air. Nothing.

With lighting controlled centrally, and no switches to flick, Kira marched to the Spider's control unit, a large computer mounted on a waist-high trolley. Via its keyboard, she enabled the Spider's perimeter lights. The room was still dark, but now there were eight pools of purple light surrounding the machine, enough for her to work with.

"This is all very impressive," came a deep but soft voice from behind. Kira spun to see a young man in dark clothing step forward into the light. "What does it do?" he asked, his eyes following the thick cables running from the control unit to the Spider's base.

"You startled me," she said, studying the man. People often roamed about while she worked: usually a security guard or a cleaner; sometimes a lost visitor looking for the bathroom. This man didn't look like any of those. "Can I help you?" she asked politely.

"It's some kind of 3D printer, isn't it?" said the man, ignoring her question. He glanced at the blueprint on the floor, then slowly circled the huge machine. He walked casually with his hands in his pockets, passing between light and shadow. When he'd made a complete circuit of the Spider, he stopped just a few feet from Kira, his smile wide and warm, purple light reflecting in his small dark eyes. "Am I right?" he asked.

"It's similar to a 3D printer," she said. "But not quite."

"What makes it different?"

Kira had no time to explain; there was much to do, and she still had to meet Max at the station. But she was also polite. She glanced at her watch. "Well," she began, deciding to give the stranger a well-rehearsed pitch that needed little thought to deliver, while at the same time, tapping at the keyboard, composing an angry email to Jose and Petra. "It uses a material we developed; a biopolymer augmented with renewable materials. It lasts just as long as existing building materials such as concrete but with far less impact on the environment. Instead of putting our material down in layers, like 3D printers, this," she nodded to the Spider as she typed, "weaves strands of it together to form much stronger structures."

"Interesting..."

"I think so," she said, looking up from her screen with a half-smile that appeared only briefly. "Look, I'm very sorry, but I need to get on. Do you know your way around? I can point you to the reception hall if you'd like?" She clicked send on the email.

"I'm fine," said the young man, moving to a large painting on the wall, partially lit by the purple lights of the Spider.

Kira had commissioned the piece for the exhibition. It showed a city of the future surrounded by lush forest. It was a future she had imagined since childhood, a city that was a part of nature, not a scar upon it.

"Is this how you see your future?"

She narrowed her eyes at the phrasing of the question. "It's how I see *our* future — yes. Um, excuse me, but who are you? Do you work here?"

"My name is Bayen," he replied. "And...I do not work here, Kira."

Kira shifted uncomfortably as he turned to face her. His smile was still there, but she was chilled by it. It was the smile of a crocodile.

"Is there something I can help you with?" She swallowed and took a deep breath, but the air in the room was suddenly thin. She had never felt so vulnerable.

"There *is* something you can help me with." He began to circle the Spider once more, admiring the machine. "I understand the Foss Corporation funds your work?"

"FossCorp. That's right," Kira replied. She didn't feel like answering, but this was public knowledge.

"Have you met Richard Foss?"

"No," she said. For a moment, she wondered if this man was Foss. There were very few photos of him, but she quickly dismissed the idea as absurd; this man was far too young.

He stopped, then seemed to examine the air around her before continuing his circuit. "Have you ever seen him? Spoken to him?"

"No."

"A man provides you with money — *lots* of money — to create such spectacular things," he gestured to the machine, "yet you have never met him or even spoken to him. Do you not think it strange?"

"Not strange at all." As she spoke, she found herself opening another email window, an urge to write something down, a call for help, a note. But then she closed it. She was being paranoid. This man had done nothing obvious to cause this feeling of threat. It was most likely her anxiety and stress taking their toll, but she wanted him gone. "He funds many projects," she continued. "Hundreds of them. I don't expect a dinner invite anytime soon. So if you don't mind—"

"And you don't expect him to attend the opening tomorrow?" He was now in shadow again, on the far side of the Spider. She couldn't see him but could somehow feel him watching her.

"I very much doubt it. We're tiny compared to the rest of his portfolio. If he did turn up, it would be...unexpected. And, if I can't fix this thing tonight, my chances of ever meeting the man himself go from slim to none." She peered into the darkness, still unable to make him out. "I'm sorry, but...why do you want to know all this?"

There was no answer, just a quiet metallic click.

She stepped aside from the computer, trying to see him. She narrowed her eyes, attempting to penetrate the darkness. "Hello?"

Another *click* sound.

"What are you doing back there?" Still no reply. She took a few more steps, then began to circle the Spider until she was almost jogging around it. She made an entire circuit then spun on her heels to take in the rest of the room. The man had gone.

Slowly she backed away from the purple pools of light and went to the door. The long dim hallway was empty, with no echo of footsteps.

Back inside, she stared at the Spider, which now felt like a menace looming before her. She walked towards it, realising she was shaking. Her hand went to her forehead and came away with a layer of sweat. She paused, noticing the access panel on the faulty leg was now closed. Certain she had not closed it, she approached and pried it open. It opened with a metallic click.

With confusion, she stepped back and looked down at

her coffee and the spread of blueprints on the floor. It was the correct leg. So why was the indicator now green?

She hurried to the computer to run diagnostics. As she waited for the verdict, she scanned the darkened room, impatiently drumming her fingers on the trolley. A gentle ping came from the computer, bringing her attention back to the screen. She raised her eyebrows as she scrutinised the results. According to the diagnostics, all eight heat pumps were now working perfectly.

Just then, the lights in the room came back on. Startled, a hand on her chest, she looked around — she was still alone.

She blew out a long sigh, then, remembering her plans, checked the time. She was going to be late for Max.

17

FURLONG TOWERS

Max stepped off the warm train and onto the bitter cold platform of Kings Cross Station. Isaac was close behind, followed by Ellie and then his mother.

During the forty-minute journey, the four had sat around a table in an almost empty carriage, Max in silence for most of it, watching the dark countryside rush past, the darkness occasionally interrupted by snow-dusted towns and villages.

While the others had talked, his mind lingered on an earlier conversation with Wren, where he'd told Max of the two visitors he'd met after the party. Max's blood turned cold on hearing one was a Hunter. Wren had tried to comfort him. *They're here only for the Maker*, he'd said, *the Maker and no one else*. But Max couldn't help be afraid. If Wren honestly thought there was no danger, he would have said nothing. He was warning Max to stay alert. If this new Hunter was anything like Jenta, no one was safe. After talking to Wren, he remembered that night on Church Lane — that feeling of being watched. It all made sense to him now.

"So," Isaac said, leaning into Max as they crunched

along the salt-covered platform, jostled by the crowd of oncoming commuters. "Two days to find a link between Kira and FossCorp."

"If there is one," said Max, looking over his shoulder, making sure his mother was out of earshot. She was on the phone, organising where to meet old work friends tomorrow.

"If there isn't, we still get two days out in London."

"Yeah," Max said. He hadn't yet found the right time to mention the new arrivals to Isaac or Ellie. He was hoping he wouldn't need to.

Outside the station, they weaved through a crowd of commuters. It was Max's first visit to London since his senses had been supercharged, and the experience was overwhelming. There was too much to process: the people, the traffic, the sounds. He was slowly being crushed under the weight of it all. But as they made the short walk to their meeting point, not far from the station, he gained control of his breath, and the world around him stepped back, giving him space to exist.

They had arranged to meet at The Birdcage, a large, illuminated structure, its bars wide enough to walk through to access a single swing at its centre. Max scanned the area for Kira. She wasn't there.

"She's probably just running late," said his mother, noticing his look of concern. "She'll be here."

They waited, Max and his mum sitting on a nearby curved wooden bench, watching Ellie push Isaac dangerously high on the swing. As the swing returned to her, Ellie jumped to reach it, forcing it down, driving Isaac higher each time, the chains becoming slack as he reached the highest point. Tourists and commuters watched on, amused by his high-pitched shouts of protest, but Ellie was having far too much fun to stop.

Unsurprisingly, it was Max who spotted Kira first. She emerged from the underground station, her thick black hair contained under her woolly hat. She looked flustered — distracted as she glanced over her shoulder at the masses of commuters behind her. It was a look that disappeared once she noticed Max. She apologised for keeping them waiting, blaming technical issues with the exhibit. Introductions followed, comprising awkward handshakes and half hugs, before taking a taxi on a winding journey through the back roads of North London to Aunt Lydia's house.

Conversation in the taxi covered the weather, the trip down from Hurstwick, and how unprepared they all were for Christmas. When the car stopped, and the interior light came on, Kira leaned across and tapped her card on the payment terminal.

"Let me get this," Max's mother protested, reaching into her handbag.

The machine beeped as the payment went through. "That's very kind, Dana," Kira said, opening the door and stepping onto the snow-covered pavement, "But everything's covered by Richard Foss."

"Who's Richard Foss?" Isaac jumped in, keen to not miss his chance.

Kira turned to Isaac, "He sponsors the exhibition and funds our research," she said. "Best of all, he covers all my expenses, including taxi rides."

The taxi pulled away.

"Is he married?" asked Max's mother with a thin smile and side glance to Max.

Kira laughed as she pulled a bunch of keys from her bag. Max blinked slowly and shook his head, then turned to Isaac, waiting for his follow-up Foss-related question. But Isaac had been distracted, thrown off the scent by the big house that loomed over them. He stood looking up to it, his jaw slack.

It was a large, detached Victorian house set on the corner of an affluent square. Four wide steps rose to meet a shiny black door set deep into a porch. Max counted a ground floor, a first floor, and a second floor, then noticed the quarter-sized windows of the basement and the attic. He expected to see a panel of buzzers for the individual flats it must have been converted to, but saw a single doorbell instead.

"Welcome to Furlong Towers," Kira said to Max. "Former home of our grandfather, where your dad and my dad grew up, and now home to Aunt Lydia."

"Nice digs," said Ellie as Kira climbed the steps, followed by Max's mother.

"Very nice," Isaac agreed, watching Kira open the door, then gesture for them to follow. He leaned into Max. "See what happens when your lot decide to *not* work in a library."

They stepped off the welcome mat onto the black and white tiles of a large hallway. Ahead, a broad staircase climbed up and back on itself before meeting the first floor. There were several doors around them and a fireplace, which, instead of a fire, was home to a vase full of peacock feathers. A grandfather clock faced them from the back of the hallway, next to a door that Max guessed led to the basement.

The smell of cooking and the sound of Christmas songs drifted from the kitchen. The place felt homely.

As they dropped their bags and hung up their coats, Aunt Lydia appeared, backlit by the kitchen's bright light, drying her hands with a tea towel. "Perfect timing," she said with a smile. "Hope you all like shepherd's pie."

After another round of introductions, they sat for dinner.

Max kept glancing at Aunt Lydia throughout the meal, finding it strange to be in the company of someone else who once knew his father. According to the family tree, which Max had committed to memory, she was almost ten years older than his dad, which put her around forty-nine, but she looked younger. There was the familiar thick black hair, the same as his own, the same as his father's — and, of course, the same as Wren's. She was tall and upright with sharp but friendly features. Max had only seen a few photos of his father, but the resemblance was there.

Aunt Lydia wanted to know everything about everyone, and she showed a genuine interest as she listened. When the conversation turned to her, they learned she was a surgeon, recently divorced, and had no children. A twin of Kira's father, she rarely saw her other siblings, none of whom lived in the UK anymore.

"We moved here in seventy-four," she said, answering a question from Max's mother, who now had a large photo album on her lap, as the conversation continued in the living room around a roaring fire. "I was three...four; Jon wasn't yet born. We grew up loving this house. I was sad to leave it. I moved back after Dad died to look after the place."

"What did your dad do?" Ellie asked.

"He was an engineer and mathematician." She glanced up at a photo of him on the mantlepiece. "He worked with the government back in Canada; I don't know what he did exactly. But in the early seventies, he came here to work for a small private company. They worked on all manner of things, and his name ended up being tied to over a hundred inventions in the end. Mundane, small things, most of them,

but they all added up. Enough for him to afford this place."
She sighed and looked around the room. "The plan is to sell
the house eventually," she continued. "Once we work out
what to do with all his stuff. He was a bit of a hoarder. I
sometimes feel like I'm living in a museum. It's far too big
for just me."

"I'll move in," said Isaac as he rifled through a tin of
Quality Streets, avoiding the toffees.

Lydia turned to him and laughed. "So, what are you
going to do when you leave school, young man? How do you
propose to pay your way?"

"Engineer," Isaac answered, unwrapping a coconut
éclair.

"Maybe you could work for Kira?"

"More aerospace really. Rockets, satellites. That type of
thing."

"And you, Ellie?" Lydia asked.

Ellie was mid-yawn, the back of her hand covering her
mouth. "I want to study zoology at university," she said.
"Maybe get into conservation after."

This was news to Max and Isaac, who exchanged a look
and a shrug. He felt bad for not knowing what Ellie wanted
to do after six-form. Maybe he was too caught up in his own
life, his own problems. He needed to pay more attention, be
a better friend.

The room got darker as the fire became less enthusiastic.
"It's getting late," said Lydia as she stood. "And tomorrow's
the big opening." She smiled proudly at Kira and then
began to place empty mugs onto a tray.

Before turning in for the night, they were given a tour of
the house. They began with the library on the ground floor,
then the basement for a quick look at the games room with
its snooker table and dartboard. On the first floor, Lydia
showed them their rooms. Max was sharing with Isaac,

Ellie was next door, and his mother was across the hall. After dropping off their bags, they were taken up to the second floor with instructions to bring a warm jumper or coat.

"Let me show you what I really love about this place," Lydia said, walking to a door, wood-panelled like all the others but slightly narrower. She opened it, reached inside, and flicked a switch to reveal a set of spiral stairs, light cascading down from a space above. Max was reminded of the stairs in the church tower, but instead of leading into a belfry, these led into a dim, spacious loft full of neatly stacked and labelled storage boxes, piles of dusty books, and sheets covering large items — probably old furniture. He caught a glimpse of a wooden high-chair in the corner and an ancient-looking pram beside it, both old enough to belong to his father.

They followed Lydia as she ducked under rafters, heading towards another door, this one with a round window at head height.

She opened it, and a chill breeze blew in.

Seconds later, they were outside, hurriedly putting on their coats, standing on a narrow paved terrace between two peaked roofs. It was a modest space: just a circular iron table with two chairs covered in snow and a handful of plant pots, their spindly black twigs poking through snowy domes. But it was the view that made it special.

It looked over a square full of mature trees enclosed by tall black railings, and across to the snow-covered rooftops of the surrounding houses, with their twinkling Christmas lights and columns of drifting chimney smoke.

"This is the real reason I'm finding it hard to say goodbye to this place," admitted Lydia, nodding to the view. "Just look at it." She inhaled as she pulled up the collar on her cardigan, then crossed her arms as protection against the chill. "You can imagine Mary Poppins descending any minute," she said.

Max agreed. It was a view of London he'd only ever seen in Disney movies. Nothing like the view from his tower block in his part of the city.

"Your dad loved it up here," Lydia said, looking down to Max. "He was always up here. Especially in the summer." She looked away.

He sensed her loss, which, like his mother's, was different to his. They had both lost someone they had known and loved, while he'd lost something he'd never had. But it was still loss.

Ellie and Isaac moved to the rear of the roof, and Max followed. Beyond the back garden was an alleyway and then the gardens belonging to the houses on the next street. The neighbourhood must have been on a hill because the view was far-reaching in all directions. To the south, he could see the towers of the city: The Shard, The Gherkin, and The Cheesegrater, along with the cranes steadily adding new landmarks to the skyline. He looked east, and after a few moments, identified a distant cluster of much smaller towers that made up the Manor Fields Estate, his home for fourteen years. To his surprise, he felt no attachment to them. They were just buildings.

It was getting cold, and the view became less appealing than the idea of a warm bed. With Isaac and Ellie following, he made his way back to his mum and the others.

"...well, there's one guy at work," his mum was saying quietly to Lydia and Kira, huddled together, arms crossed, shoulders raised. "But, dating someone from work can be... well, awkward."

Blood rushing to his cheeks, Max made his exit quickly, ducking under the low door to re-enter the loft, hoping, without any real hope, that Mr Hall or even Mr Walsh was "the guy from work". *Awkward?* She had no idea. He'd have to talk to Wren, get him to fade from his mother's attention or something.

He waited on the landing below. When his friends appeared, Isaac's mouth was a thin line, as if glued shut by Ellie. Kira, Lydia and his mum followed shortly after, their cheeks rosy from the cold.

"Well, there we have it," Lydia said, turning off the loft light and closing the door. She was about to lead them down the stairs when a thought seemed to stop her. She turned to Max with narrowing eyes. "Would you like to see your grandfather's office?" She didn't wait for an answer, just beckoned him with a nod, heading to another door. She opened it, switched on the light and stood aside.

Max peered into the room, unsure if he was supposed to enter or admire from the doorway. He felt Isaac and Ellie looking over his shoulder.

The office of the son of Wren was a small room. It contained a leather sofa and a thick-set mahogany desk, home to an old-looking computer and stacks of papers. Against one wall were two full-size metal filing cabinets surrounded by floor-to-ceiling shelving, every inch packed with books, videotapes, ornaments, folders, cardboard tubes, and box files. The opposite wall was just as busy, but with photos, mostly taken in the seventies and eighties, judging from the clothing and hairstyles.

Looking into the room felt like seeing the man himself, a mind that had been archived into physical form. Max imagined he could spend the whole day there and come out feeling as if he knew the man.

"Dad spent a lot of time in here," Lydia said, looking around the room. "Often with a colleague or two. As a child, I'd fall asleep on that sofa, listening to them talk into the small hours, then wake up in bed, no memory of how I got there."

Max was not listening. Instead, his attention had been entirely captured by what he saw on the shelves. He blinked hard, believing his tiredness to be playing tricks on him. But they were there. Dotted around in various spaces were small, intricately carved wooden animals. He'd seen them before — in his visions, carved by the man with the wooden ring.

Max lay in bed, his eyes closed.

In a deep state of awareness, he knew only Kira remained awake. He could hear her tapping on her laptop, probably some last-minute task for tomorrow's exhibition.

He waited for her to sleep, mindful not to drift off himself. But there was little danger of that; he wouldn't be able to rest until he took a closer look at that office.

He opened his eyes.

The light from outside cast shadows of the window frame across the ceiling. Max turned his head slightly to the right and saw flakes of peeling paint above Isaac's bed, forming shadows like long sharp teeth.

As his eyes drifted back to the smooth ceiling directly above his bed, the sound of a tap drawing water reached him through the walls. The click of a light switch followed. Once again, he closed his eyes and took his awareness to Kira's room, where he heard the twang of a bedspring and a soft rustle of bedcovers, then, minutes later, her deep, slow breathing.

Silently, he swung his legs out of bed, pulled on his jeans, and went barefoot to the door. It let out a creak as it opened. Isaac snorted and rolled onto his back. Max hesitated, then stepped out onto the dark landing, gently pulling the door closed. He listened briefly at the door, then walked towards the staircase, wishing he had Wren's ability to mask sounds as the floorboards announced his every step.

On reaching the stairs, he peered down over the bannister to the dark hallway below, to the black and white tiled floor and the grandfather clock, with its deep rhythmic *clunk*.

With as much stealth as he could manage, he climbed the stairs slowly. At the top, he paused and listened before moving to the office door. It opened without a sound, and he stepped inside.

He went straight to the wooden figures. He picked one up. Its likeness was that of a deer, but the proportions were unusual, more like a stylised representation of a deer. It had a beauty to it — a simplicity. The others were of a similar size and style and clearly made by the same hand, each with intricate fur, feathers or scales. One resembled a lion; another, a horse. There was also a bird and coiled snake, which he hadn't been able to see from the doorway. He examined each in detail, looking for a name or a signature from the artist, but there wasn't one.

Max found the figures to be both excellent and disappointing at the same time. Makers were responsible for Nim technology; the key to Kelha and the healing disc, and Kelha herself, for that matter, were pieces of technology that were magical to him. But these figures, although beautifully crafted, could have been created by human hands. He was expecting more from them, but perhaps there was something he was missing. Or maybe they were just simple trinkets, built to keep idle hands busy.

His attention was grabbed by the wall of photos behind him, his eyes picking out a picture of his dad as a young boy. He was standing in school uniform before the street door —

the same door Max had passed through several hours ago. He looked to be about twelve, and Max guessed it was his first day of secondary school. There was a similar photo of Max on the wall back at home.

There were photos of his dad at Max's age. They affected him in a way other photos hadn't, filling him with sadness. He knew nothing about the boy who looked like him. And for a moment, he wished he could talk to him, ask him what it was like for him growing up. Did he feel like an outsider? If so, did he have good friends like he did, looking out for him?

Feeling his eyes begin to sting, he turned back to the wooden figures and took a deep, wavering breath.

"Why are you here?" he whispered, leaning into a creature that couldn't decide if it was a crab or a scorpion. "How did you get here?"

The figure didn't respond, but as Max scanned the room, he felt the answer was here.

He went to the wall he hadn't seen from outside, the wall behind the door. It contained more photos and seemed to be dedicated to his grandfather's professional life. One showed him addressing a crowded lecture hall, a blackboard full of equations behind him. Another showed him in discussion with a man sitting with his back to the camera in a low seventies-style chair. The man was gesturing with enthusiasm while his grandfather leant against a desk, listening with mild amusement. A group of men stood together in another; they were arranged in a line, dressed in smart attire, some holding small medals in velvet-lined boxes. Something was wrong with this picture. One man, at the end of the line, was standing just out of shot, only his shoulder and arm visible. But there was plenty of space on the other side, so there was room for him. He'd been intentionally cut out.

As Max moved from photo to photo, he began to see the man everywhere. In each image, his face was somehow obscured. Sometimes it was a dipped hat, the glare from the sun, a blemish on the paper. The clearest shot of this camera-shy man could be seen in a photo of a cricket team celebrating a win. In the centre of the picture, his grandfather held up a trophy that conveniently blocked the man's face just beside him.

Max took a closer look.

He was tall, slim, and broad-shouldered. What hair he could see looked light brown. When Max looked down at the man's hand, he saw precisely what he expected to see: a dark wooden ring on his index finger.

No longer feeling tired, Max dashed from photo to photo. In each one where the man's hands could be seen, the ring was present.

Finally, he went back to the photo of his grandfather in discussion with the man in the chair. He saw now that the room in the picture was *this* room, and the man his grandfather was listening to, wearing a ring of wood, was the Maker.

18

THE EXHIBITION

"It's *Saturday* morning, Zoe," Travis said, looking both unimpressed and confused. He stood in his doorway wearing a T-shirt and a pair of baggy shorts, one side of his head still convinced it was lying in bed. "Why am I seeing you at"—he glanced at his watch—"five forty-seven in the morning on a Saturday? Are we dating now? Because I don't—"

"I need your car." She cut him off.

"What for?"

"Surveillance. A stake-out."

"Of course. Silly question," he mumbled.

"So, can I have it?"

"No."

"Why not?"

"Are you following those kids still?"

"Maybe. Look, I know you think it's a waste of time, but there's something huge going on. Duncan more or less ordered me not to look into a link to the Hurstwick incident; he made it very clear. After the meeting, I get an email from boss lady Greta, telling me the same thing. Then—"

"Then maybe you shouldn't?"

"What?" She looked at him as if he'd lost his mind. "No way I'm stopping now. I've been busy. You wouldn't believe what I found—"

Before she could tell him, he turned and walked back down the hall. "Coffee?" he shouted over his shoulder.

"I'd prefer car keys." She stepped inside, closed the door, and followed him into the kitchen.

"I'm not giving you my car keys—"

"But—"

Travis held up his hand. "*But*, if you convince me that whatever it is, is worth losing your job over, and possibly mine, I'll be your driver for the day." He clicked on the kettle and spooned instant coffee into two semi-clean-looking mugs.

Zoe agreed and sat herself down at the small kitchen table. "So," she began as Travis moved a pizza box out of her way and flung it in the fridge. "I started with local papers from the time of the incident, thankfully all digitised and searchable. I read all the accounts, but it was pretty much a wasted effort, apart from one interesting find. There were a few mentions of a long scar in the woods, a huge amount of damage, which I hadn't heard about before." She pulled an iPad from her bag, looked for a clean spot on the table to place it down, then gave up and held it instead. "Anyway, there wasn't much else, so I started to go through the files on the Task Force shared drive. Mostly low-level stuff: aerial and satellite photos. Remember the cool 3D map of the area?"

"Yeah, er...satellite elevation data?" Travis placed Zoe's coffee on the table, then took a swig from his.

"Well, I found the raw data used to generate that map. I reran it, changing the resolution settings to show a more detailed image. The original had a resolution of five metres. I knocked it down to two metres."

"And your laptop survived?"

"It got a bit hot. Anyway, the result was this." She handed him the iPad. It showed a 3D image of the softly undulating land to the north of Hurstwick. There was no detail — no roads, paths or trees — just elevations marked by a grid of contour lines. "It turns out," she continued, "that *Point of Interest 1* is located in a shallow dip—"

"We knew that."

"We *did* know that. But we didn't know the dip was just a small part of a very long trench." She took the iPad back and changed the angle of the image to show it more clearly. "Interestingly, Point of Interest 1 is located right at the *end* of that very long trench."

"How long is this trench?" Travis leaned in and squinted.

"Around six hundred metres."

"Holy crap."

"It's pretty shallow. If you went for a walk in the woods, you might even miss it with all the undergrowth. But that's not all." She brought up another image, almost identical to the first but overlaid with two points connected by a dashed line.

"What am I looking at?"

She pointed at the first dot near the bottom of the screen. "That's the church." She ran her finger along the line, passing over the field and then along the trench, stopping at the end and the second dot. "And that's Point of Interest 1."

"You got a theory?"

"Only one. Whatever smashed through that church tower carved a huge channel through the woods. It remained quiet, underground, until just over a year ago, when it let out a huge burst of energy and disappeared."

"But it was a plane," said Travis. "Every bloody pub in

that town has a picture of a plane smashing through the church."

Zoe snorted and sat back in her chair. "You think a plane can carve out a trench that long?"

There was a long silence, then Travis sat down. "Wait," he said, his brow creasing. "It doesn't make sense. Even at five metres resolution, the trench should have been visible on the original image."

"Exactly what I thought," she said with a smile. "So I ran it again at the original resolution. And," she swiped to the next image then flipped the iPad around to show him. "The trench *is* visible. Not as defined as the two-metre image, but clear as day."

"Then the original was rendered using different data?"

"*Manipulated* data. Someone didn't want us linking the Hurstwick Incident with the energy burst, so they adjusted the data and removed the trench."

"And whoever was smart enough to do that wasn't smart enough to delete the original data set?" Travis crossed his arms, looking sceptical.

"People make mistakes."

There was another long pause as Travis looked thoughtfully at nothing in particular. His eyes then met hers, and he sighed. "OK. So I'm almost in the car with you but not quite. What do the kids have to do with this? Why follow them?"

"Because Duncan Clark is also following them. Not in person, obviously. But they are being followed."

Travis unfolded his arms and clicked each of his knuckles, one by one. His eyes flicked to the iPad and back to her. Then he stood, the chair squeaking on the lino floor. "I need my morning poo first."

"You share too much."

Travis used a handful of Burger King napkins to wipe condensation from the window of the old Saab. It was still dark out, and a few of the lights in the big house had recently been switched on. "And you have no idea who lives here?" he asked.

"I told you. No idea." Zoe rubbed her eyes with her gloved fingers and shifted uncomfortably in the seat. "They met a woman at Kings Cross, jumped into a taxi. I followed in another."

"Did you say, *follow that taxi*?"

She turned to him slowly. "Yeah, I did." She smiled a little.

"Cool." Travis opened a can of Red Bull. He took a swig then checked his mirrors. "Funny how neither of us has said it."

"Said what?"

"You know...what it means if your theory's correct."

"Do we need to say it?"

"No. Suppose not." There was a silence. Travis brushed some imaginary dust from the top of the steering wheel then glanced at her sideways. "I'm just saying; something comes down in the woods, remains buried deep underground for over seventy years, then lets off a massive energy pulse, then, *POOF,* disappears. I can only think of one explanation."

"Me too."

"Yet you still don't want to say it?"

"I'd rather not."

"Fair enough." Travis yawned and then rechecked the mirrors. "Should we be looking out for Duncan's men?"

"By all means, keep an eye out," she shrugged, "but I've not seen them for days. Last time was at the hospital."

"Maybe they decided it was a waste of time."

"Maybe it is," Zoe replied, her eyes fixed on the house. "But what if it's not? Duncan's hiding something big, and those kids are a part of it—" She sat up, alert, as a black cab rolled past then slowed to a stop. "This could be it."

The porch light came on, and the three teenagers emerged, wearing winter coats and backpacks. They paused on the pavement, waited for the two women to appear from the house, then all five got in the taxi.

The taxi pulled away, and Travis followed closely, too close for Zoe. She told him to slow and hold back. He kept a few cars between them, still checking his mirrors for anyone following.

To begin with, the traffic heading south was flowing, only getting heavy as they neared the centre, but when they got to Holborn, they found themselves crawling, stop-start.

"Any word from Dinesh?" Zoe asked, her cheek against the cold passenger window, watching the taxi at a standstill three cars in front.

"His gadget arrived a day early," he answered, drumming the wheel with his fingers as he stared ahead. "He was working on it last night. He'd have called if he'd found anything."

"Can you convince him to work on the weekend?"

"It's Saturday morning, and I'm out in the car with you. So, anything's possible."

"Thanks."

They were on the move again, and Travis shifted through the gears, picking up speed. Just as they were in their stride, a man in a high-vis jacket stepped into their path, turning his bright reflective sign from *GO* to *STOP*.

"Go, go, go!" Zoe urged, watching the gap between them and the taxi widen. "Don't you dare stop." She gripped the dashboard, and the engine revved. Travis swerved to avoid the man with the sign, who staggered back, waving a gesture popular with football fans disputing a ref's decision. He then swerved again, veering into a bus lane to avoid a motorbike emerging from a side street. Receiving the gesture for a second time, he mumbled apologies as he worked his way up the gears, clearing a set of lights before slamming on the brakes.

They caught up with the taxi. There were now four cars between them. Travis took a deep breath and shook his head. When they started to move again, the taxi turned onto Aldwych and then The Strand, where it pulled up before the entrance of Somerset House.

Travis passed them, stopping a little further down the road. "I can't park here," he said.

Zoe watched the taxi from the side mirror and released the seatbelt over her shoulder. "You go," she said. "Call me once you've talked to Dinesh."

"Will do."

Zoe got out, removed her bright orange woolly hat — not the best look for covert surveillance — and made her way towards her five targets as they passed under the arch of the north wing of Somerset House. Not wanting to lose sight of them for too long, she began a stiff-legged jog through a light smattering of early-bird Londoners and tourists, her hands dug deep into her coat pockets as the chill morning air went through her.

Passing under the arch, she stopped suddenly, turning away, looking up and around, pretending to admire the architecture, while her quarry took selfies in front of a large banner.

Once they'd moved off into the courtyard, she resumed her pursuit. She glanced at the banner advertising *The Artifi-*

cial Architect, noticing the familiar logo of GiaTek's parent company, FossCorp, wondering briefly if this was a piece of the puzzle or just a coincidence.

If anything, Max was relieved to see Zoe Durkin following them. In the taxi, he'd convinced himself it was the Hunter he had sensed outside the house that morning. Now, as he crossed the courtyard, he could see her and the entire scene behind him, reflected in a silver bauble of the giant Christmas tree.

He didn't say anything to his friends. Instead, he added it to the growing list of things he really should mention. The discovery that his grandfather probably knew the Maker was high on that list.

As he thought of the Maker, he remembered the woman in the tree with the wooden ring. And as he passed the Christmas tree, he could almost hear her voice in the wind as it hissed through the ribbons and tinsel. Her pleading whisper: *Ta kaah — save him.*

"You OK?" Ellie placed a hand on his shoulder. "You seem...distant."

He took a short breath and nodded, then glanced at his mother. "I'll tell you later," he whispered.

She looked at him, thoughtful, then looked past him, her face lighting up as she spotted the ice rink. What looked like a small road-sweeper was currently crawling across it, its spinning brushes sending glittering frost clouds into the air. "We're definitely going on that later," she said. Isaac and Max looked doubtful.

Kira collected four visitor passes at reception then led them down the long corridor to the exhibition hall.

"Nice," said Isaac as they pushed through the heavy

door. He went straight to the Spider, ignoring the handful of people hurriedly preparing for the opening. "It's bigger than I imagined," he called back over his shoulder, pulling out his phone to take a picture.

Kira smiled at his enthusiasm.

As they were being introduced to a few nearby colleagues, most too busy to talk, a woman in a long bright red coat and Doc Martens boots exploded through the door. She looked dishevelled and in need of sleep.

"I'm so sorry," the woman said as she stormed past them. "I just got your message. My phone died, which of course, meant my alarm didn't go off. Then the stupid tube..." she continued with more excuses as she strode towards the Spider.

"Petra, it's fine. It's fixed," Kira said, walking after her. "She just needs warming up."

Petra spun and scanned the room, noticing her guests for the first time. She then looked to Kira with confusion. "Is Jose here?"

"No."

"Then who fixed it; you?"

"Maybe?"

"Impressive." A smile appeared, then the confused look returned. "Maybe?"

Kira shrugged. "I don't know. Look, we'll talk later. Let's just wake the big girl up."

Petra nodded and went to the computer. A few moments later, each leg of the giant spider stretched up then dipped gracefully, and with subtle mechanical whirls, it proceeded to rotate each of its joints, resembling a group of ballerinas stretching before their big performance.

"This is nuts," said Isaac, holding up his phone to film the spectacle.

"So what does it do, exactly?" asked Max's mum, mesmerised by the machine's movements.

"Let me show you," Kira said, slipping into tour guide mode. "These beautiful objects you see around you are all designed and built by the Spider—"

"Designed by it, too?" Isaac interrupted.

"Yes," replied Kira, welcoming the interruption, "with a tiny nudge from us. We get it started by showing it a simple sketch, and it translates that sketch into these." She gestured around the room.

"What's the purpose?" asked Ellie. "I mean, they're lovely, but...."

"It's *learning* how to design," said Kira. "You see, right now, everything around us in the physical world, comes from nature or the minds of humans. The Spider is influenced by both, but it's my hope that eventually, it will build things we can't even dream of; structures stronger and more elegant than those conceived by nature or us. Let me show you." She walked to a nearby exhibit. Looking like a large breeze block, it was about one foot high and two feet wide. "This is one of our biggest wins to date."

"It's a brick," said Isaac, unimpressed. "A large brick, but a brick."

Kira laughed. "It *is* a brick, Isaac. Gold star for you." Isaac took a bow. "Now stand on it," Kira said.

Isaac stood on it.

"Jump up and down."

He jumped a few times. Then, with an unimpressed shrug, he looked at Kira.

Kira raised an eyebrow. "Now pick it up."

He stepped off and picked it up. "Woah!" he said, lifting the brick with unexpected ease, holding it before him like an empty cardboard box.

Kira laughed. "Impressed now?"

"It's light as a feather." He held it above his head, then threw it to Max, who flinched as he caught it.

"Not quite," Kira said, "but lighter than, say, a sponge or a block of polystyrene of the same size." She turned to Max. "So what you're holding there is what we hope to be the building material of the future. Its internal structure was designed by the Spider and is, weight for weight, stronger than anything being used in the construction industry today. As a bonus, it's made from one hundred per cent renewable material. The only problem is the cost of production. It costs about a thousand times more than any standard building material of the same size, and it takes about a week to make a single brick. So don't expect to be living in a house made of these just yet. Give it ten years, hopefully."

Max ran his hand over its surface and examined its texture. "Looks like coral."

"You have...incredibly sharp eyes," said Kira with disbelief.

"Oh, I think I saw a close-up photo...erm, on your website?" To change the subject, he threw the brick to Ellie — who caught it without flinching — then pointed to something behind Kira. "What's that?" he asked.

Kira turned to look. "Ahh, you're going to love this," she said, leading them towards another exhibit. Max, Ellie, and Isaac exchanged looks of relief, then followed.

"All this must have taken quite a bit of investment," Isaac said after Kira had shown them a few more of the Spider's creations.

"You could say that. The cost of just the hardware is in the millions." She nodded to the Spider, "When you include research and development, salaries, rent, it all adds up."

"And taxis," added Max's mum, who was holding an exhibit that looked like a fruit bowl.

"And it all comes from this Mr Foss guy?" said Isaac, trying to sound casual as he looked around.

"The lion's share of it, yes. We were fortunate. Normally it's a long, drawn-out process trying to secure funding, especially for a research project that won't be making any money for a long time to come. But Richard Foss saw the potential and believed in the dream. He stepped in and gave us what we needed."

Isaac nodded. "How did he learn about you? I mean, the project."

She hesitated. "I can't remember."

As she answered, a flicker of discomfort passed across her face. It lasted only a fraction of a second, but time somehow slowed for Max, allowing him to see it. There was a brief softening of her gaze, telling him the discomfort was related to memory. A barely perceptible movement of her eyes towards the Spider and then to the door told him the memory was linked to this place. He then saw a flash of his own memory, of when he'd seen Kira exit the underground station at Kings Cross, glancing back over her shoulder, looking disturbed.

In the library, Max had detected Zoe Durkin's lies by observing subtle changes to her pulse, eyes, and the flushing of her cheeks. Those signals had been clear and distinct; these were far more subtle and harder for Max to pin down. But they told him a story he had no reason to believe but found he could not doubt. Someone here, last night, had been asking Kira about Richard Foss, and that person had made her feel afraid.

The doors to the exhibition opened on time at ten o'clock, and the visitors began to trickle in shortly after. They presented their tickets, were offered the program guide, then walked around the hall, most heading straight to the Spider, which had started to build its next masterpiece. By eleven, the number of visitors had grown significantly, so they left Kira to it, arranging to return at seven-thirty for celebratory nibbles before going out for dinner.

After saying goodbye to Max's mother, who went to meet her friends for lunch, the three made plans for the day in the courtyard. They were discussing heading towards Leicester Square when Ellie dragged them towards the ice rink. They both protested, Max claiming his arm was still hurting from the hospital visit, but the pitiful excuse fell on deaf ears, and after a promise from Ellie not to laugh at how terrible they might be, they paid for their tickets and ventured out onto the ice.

Ellie, of course, laughed the entire time as both boys gripped the barrier for dear life, their legs constantly trying to escape from under them. Eventually, they started to get the hang of it, so Ellie instead found enjoyment in buzzing past them at speed.

They left the courtyard with some new bruises, turning west to spend the next few hours as tourists. After sightseeing, they went to Nando's for lunch, then watched *Star Wars Episode Nine* at the cinema. It was dark when they returned east along the embankment, the cold, grey River Thames crawling beside them like a giant grey serpent.

Over the course of the day, Max had plenty of chances to mention the visitors from Nimar, the photos in his grandfather's office, and the unease he had sensed in Kira, but he didn't. He didn't even mention that the woman from GiaTek had been following them all day. They were having fun, and he wanted the fun to last. Because with everything that was happening, he sensed their fun coming to an end.

There was a loud POP as they stepped into the exhibition hall. Max jumped, and Isaac laughed. It was followed by a light round of applause from the small group gathered by the Spider. Petra poured the foaming champagne into an assortment of mugs and glasses while Kira stepped down from the super-strong brick at the centre of the group, having just given a speech.

As Max looked for his mother in the group, his eyes landed on someone he hadn't seen before, a tall man, slim and upright, with a smooth dome of a head and an impeccably groomed beard. He wore a long black coat over a dark suit and black roll-neck jumper.

The man reeked of money.

With a casually commanding presence, he stood with one hand holding a walking cane — Max guessed for style rather than support — and the other in his pocket. Max noticed everyone's eyes flicking to the man as he listened intently to one of Kira's colleagues, and knew instantly that this *had* to be Richard Foss. And when the man's hand left his pocket to accept a glass of champagne, Max knew, without doubt, that Richard Foss was the Maker.

19

THE HEIST

Through a star-field of falling snow, Daphne Waldron's Citroën 2CV pitched and rolled through the almost deserted back streets of the city. Mr Walsh, sitting in the passenger seat with a dog-eared *London A to Z* on his lap, barked directions, punctuated with pleads for caution, his right foot pressed to an imaginary brake pedal.

With his final instruction, Daphne pulled up in a narrow side street outside a sleeping launderette. She killed the lights but left the engine running, providing a little heat on a cold night.

Wren leaned forward from the back seat. As the wipers squeaked weakly to and fro, he eyed the offices of GiaTek on the main road, light from its glass box foyer spreading across the wet shiny tarmac, a security guard inside, chatting with a bored-looking receptionist. From the ground floor up, the building went from glass to concrete, thin windows glowing like arrow slits in the thick walls of a castle, the surrounding buildings fragile against its brutal appearance.

"What's the plan?" asked Mrs Waldron, half turning to face Wren.

"I go in, destroy the SD card; we head back to Rose Bank and open that bottle of Glenfiddich whisky you've got me for Christmas."

She sighed. "Honestly, I don't know why I bother wrapping your gifts."

"Standard stuff, I reckon," said Mr Walsh, his mind focused on the job. "We distract the guard, take his security pass, then leave the easy bit to you, old man."

"Why do you need the pass? Can't you just fade, walk in, do your thing, then walk out again?"

"Preservation of energy for one," said Wren. "And electronic locks make things trickier nowadays."

"So, how do you want to do this?" Mrs Waldron looked out at the building. "Australian Embassy 1972?"

Mr Walsh scoffed. "No offence, Daphne, but I doubt you have that kind of flexibility anymore."

"Don't be so sure, Peter," she replied with a stern look.

Wren placed a hand on each of their shoulders. "We just need a distraction and Peter's light fingers. Can you handle that?"

Daphne turned fully to face him. "When have we ever let you down?"

"Australian Embassy 1972," Wren said with a flat smile, pulling up the collar of his black winter coat.

"That was Margaret," she replied as the three exited the car at the same time. "Remember? She'd had one too many martinis and got distracted by that handsome diplomat." She locked the car then looked at them both. "Ready?"

Wren gestured towards the main road. "Lead on."

Peter Walsh and Daphne Waldron walked arm in arm, passing through conical beams of street light filled with swirling snow. Wren held back, watching them, allowing the gap to widen.

He could have done this alone, but when they insisted

on helping, he couldn't protest. He could see their keenness for one last adventure, and he always enjoyed their company.

When a large enough gap had formed between them, Wren followed, keeping to the shadows as the pair neared the building. They were now close, illuminated by the light spilling from the glass foyer. When directly outside the entrance, Daphne Waldron, in better shape than many half her age, fell to the ground.

Wren winced; the fall had looked convincing.

As if knowing he'd be watching from afar and likely concerned, she winked in his direction before morphing her expression into one of agony as she played her part as *poor old woman in distress*. Mr Walsh did an equally convincing job of someone too drunk to help his partner effectively. But with assistance from the security guard, who had been quick on the scene, they got the *poor old woman* back to her feet. Mr Walsh thanked the young gentleman profusely, hugging him, wishing him a Merry Christmas. A tall dark-haired stranger arrived offering further assistance. None was needed. But the old man, grateful for the offer, shook the man's hand, passing along a credit-card-sized piece of plastic as he did so. "Merry Christmas," he said with a wink.

Wren returned the season's greetings, looked to the guard, now receiving Daphne Waldron's thanks, and merged with the slowly revolving doors.

The receptionist barely noticed him breeze towards the barriers with long, purposeful strides, her attention and concern with the old couple outside.

With help from his newly acquired security card, the barriers opened, and Wren strode towards the lifts. Not wanting to wait, he triggered the call button from afar, and a lift door slid open with a gentle ping as he arrived. Without needing to adjust his pace, he entered, finding a young woman inside, hugging a laptop to her chest. She stepped aside to make room, her eyes never once landing on him. Wren pressed the button labelled B2, with his finger this time, and stepped back into the corner.

At B1, the woman stepped out. There was no polite tight-lipped smile, the type you might expect from someone also working the late shift on a Saturday night. Instead, she left with a glazed look on her face, as if exiting an empty lift.

On B2, Wren got out and turned left, as Max had instructed, glancing into the dim, empty kitchen before he continued onwards.

A man pulling on his coat joined the corridor ahead. They passed each other without acknowledgement, Wren hearing the light of the kitchen flick on in hope, but the soft ping told him the man had gone straight for the lift. He heard the doors open and close and the distant whirl as it travelled up the shaft.

Once Wren had passed the glass-walled meeting rooms, all empty and dark, he reached out with his awareness and found a handful of minds nearby, all of which were a mix of busy and bored.

He stopped at door number fourteen and looked through it. The wood turned to glass, and he saw the shelves of equipment and boxes that Max had described, the desks, the workbench — and unexpectedly — Dinesh.

He was sat on a high stool, bent over, working under intense lamplight in an otherwise dark room.

Wren considered his next move: stealth or brute force. He chose stealth.

With a calm gaze, he looked up and down the corridor for cameras — there was only one, and it was facing the lift.

He took a long deep breath. The door and the section of the corridor around him darkened, becoming less defined, obscured to nearby minds. As he reached for the door handle, he paused. A slowing whine of distant motors came to him, followed by the now familiar soft ping. Travis exited the lift and turned into the kitchen. There were two beeps and the sound of the vending machine dropping a snack. A second later, Travis was out and walking towards him, wholly engrossed by his phone.

Wren faded and cleared the deception around the door, and when Travis entered room fourteen, he stepped in behind him.

"Hey, man," Travis said, hanging his coat on the back of a chair. "Thanks for this. You're doing us a massive favour."

Dinesh didn't turn around or look up. He just raised a hand in a gesture that could be interpreted as either *hi* or *get lost*.

Wren waited for Travis to take a seat before moving further into the room. Then, with his hands casually behind his back, he leaned over the shoulder of Dinesh and, in the lamplight, saw the SD card. Secured in place, its innards were exposed to a dozen needle-like rods, held by a circle of small metallic cylinders, standing like robot surgeons around the tiny patient.

It was all linked to a laptop, its screen divided into four black windows; the white text of three of them scrolling in stops and starts, while the fourth was a constant stream of information, too fast for human, or Nim, eyes to read.

Wren looked to Dinesh and then to Travis, then slowly took in the details of the room.

He counted four ways to proceed.

The first was the simplest; he would reach out and apply pressure to the card until his invisible finger crushed it. But that was clumsy, inelegant, and would just give these people more reason to believe something strange was afoot.

The second option — activating the fire alarm and stealing the chip when Dinesh and Travis left — was also easy, but, again, would cause suspicion. And there was no guarantee they would leave the card behind.

The third option was to deceive Dinesh into thinking the SD card was burning. In his haste to save the card, he might damage it further. But there were too many uncertainties with this approach.

So he opted for a fourth, more energy-expensive, option that was far from easy and would probably take several attempts. It involved causing a subtle fluctuation in the volume of space currently occupied by the card. This would cause the card to momentarily exist in a larger volume of space, and in doing so, tear itself apart at the molecular level. The adjustment would be tiny and last barely a nanosecond, appearing to Dinesh as nothing more than a flash of static. If the chip were examined, post-mortem, say, under a powerful microscope, the damage would be invisible — but more importantly, irreversible.

The drawback was the energy required. He would need to unfade and rest before attempting it. He moved away from the pair, to the darkness of the storage area at the back of the room. There he unfaded and waited.

"How far along are we?" Travis asked as he swivelled in his chair behind Dinesh.

"We?" said Dinesh, still not looking up from his delicate task. "There is no *we* here. I'm doing all the work. Did you know I've spent eleven hours of my own time on this already? Did I mention that?"

"Once or twice." Travis unwrapped his chocolate bar.

"Well, I'm telling you again. You know as well as I do, they won't pay me overtime for this."

Travis shrugged. "Depends what we find. How much longer?"

"Twenty minutes tops."

Travis groaned.

"Oh, I'm sorry, twenty minutes too long for you?" Dinesh said with seething sarcasm, looking at Travis for the first time. "Did you know, as well as repairing this thing, I had to modify the repair tool because it came with the wrong configuration."

"OK, OK, I'm sorry. Your efforts are appreciated. Twenty minutes is perfect. Take twenty-five." He took a bite of his Snickers bar. "If Zoe's right about this thing," he added, with a mouth full of chocolate and nuts, "all your suffering will be worth it."

"Where is Zoe?" Dinesh enquired, suddenly light and friendly. "I thought she would want to be here for this?"

"She would," said Travis, still chewing. "But...she has...a thing."

Dinesh turned back to his work. "This better not be some elaborate prank. If all this work results in a video of Rick Astley singing that stupid song, I'm going to kill someone. Probably you."

Travis scratched his beard and snorted at the idea.

In the darkness behind them, on the other side of a metal shelving unit, Wren was ready. He'd nudged a box slightly to the side for a better view of the workbench. At first, the SD card was obscured within the circle of metal cylinders, but a quick shift in the light fixed that. He was calm. His heart was barely beating. His eyes were entirely black as his forefinger and thumb on both hands came together to aid the mind in feeling out the fabric of space connecting everything around him. He could feel the workbench, the equipment. Now came the cylinders holding the rods. He was close. He needed to narrow his focus just a little more. But before he could get any closer, the door swung open, flooding the workbench and Dinesh with light from the hallway. Wren released his target, and he faded instantly, dipping his head to see the new arrival.

A woman stood in the doorway, the bright hallway behind her. As she stepped into the room, her eyes moved from Travis to Dinesh, then penetrated the darkness where Wren stood. For a moment, he imagined she had seen him, but then her eyes returned to Travis. "Working late, Travis?"

"You know me," he said, smiling nervously.

"I do know you. That's why I sounded surprised." She looked back to Dinesh. Her eyes narrowed. "Dinesh, isn't it?"

He nodded. "Ms Nilsson."

"Please, I'm not your teacher. Greta will be sufficient."

"Sorry...Ms...Greta," he mumbled, then fiddled with his sleeve.

She sighed, looking from one uncomfortable face to the other, waiting for someone to speak.

"Um, how are you?" offered Travis.

She looked at him as if he were something stuck to something else that was stuck to the bottom of her shoe. Then she addressed Dinesh, holding out her hand. "Give it to me."

Dinesh swallowed. "Sorry?"

"You have something you shouldn't." She glanced at the laptop screen, still displaying a wall of text scrolling at impossible speed. For a moment, Wren thought he saw tiny movements in her eyes, almost as if she were reading.

Dinesh looked to Travis for support, just as Travis took a sudden interest in the ceiling.

"I'm not here to play games." She took a step towards the workbench, raised her chin, and leaned in to see what Dinesh was working on. "I'm here for that. Please give it to me." Her hand remained open in front of her. Dinesh again looked nervously to Travis. "You don't need his approval. I'm CEO of this company. And that should have been declared and handed over as soon as it was found. Taking it from the site was a breach of our contract with the government and the Official Secrets Act. The consequences could be jail time for you."

Anger, directed at Travis, flashed across the face of Dinesh, who clearly hadn't been made aware of this. He unscrewed a clamp, reached in, delicately removed the card, and dropped it into Greta's open hand.

"Thank you," she said in a pleasant tone, carefully closing her hand around it. "Who else knows of this?"

"Just us," Travis replied.

"And Zoe?" she asked with a tilt of her head.

Travis confirmed with a guilty schoolboy nod.

"We'll all have a chat about this on Monday, shall we?"

Travis nodded again, and Greta turned and left the room.

Almost as soon as the door had closed, Travis's phone lit up and vibrated across the desk. "Great timing," he groaned. He reached over and put Zoe on speakerphone.

"Hey, we got a problem. We just had—"

"Shut up," Zoe said. "Just listen."

Wren, about to pursue the SD card, stopped on hearing the stress in Zoe's voice.

Travis held the phone. "Are you OK?"

"Remember I said others were following those kids?" she shouted over the traffic noise, breathless as if she'd been running.

"Yeah."

"I don't think they're Duncan's people. I don't like the look of them. Something's about to go down. I've just turned into Arundel Street, off The Strand, ten minutes from the office. Can you get here—"

She was cut short by a revving engine and a screech of tires, followed by shouting. Someone screamed in the distance.

"Zoe? Are you OK?"

"I need to go." She was now running. "I have to film this. Track my phone, get here now...Arundel Street..."

The line went dead. Travis didn't hesitate. He grabbed his coat, causing the chair to spin wildly as he launched himself from the room.

Still hidden from the minds of those around him, Wren followed, keeping pace with long strides as Travis jogged. Before reaching the lifts, he slowed ever so slightly, noticing Greta in one of the dark meeting rooms. She approached the glass as Travis thundered down the corridor. In one hand, she held a phone to her ear. Her other hand was down by her side in a tightly balled fist, strong tendons in her forearm flexing, her knuckles white. When she opened her hand, what remained of the SD card fell to the ground and was finished off by the heel of her shoe.

A moment later, Wren was in the lift, standing next to an agitated Travis. Wren was calm in most situations but felt disturbed by what he'd just seen. Greta crushing the SD card had raised questions in his mind, but it wasn't that. What bothered him was that after watching Travis pass her by, Greta had turned her intense blue eyes to Wren. She had looked straight at him.

The gentle ping of the lift doors opening brought his mind back to his immediate concern: Max. He had to get to Max.

20

A DINNER INTERRUPTED

"Max, Ellie, Isaac, this is Mr Foss. The reason *this* is all possible." Kira gestured wide to encompass everything in the hall.

"Please, Kira," he said, humbly bowing his dome of a head, "It's Richard, I told you. And this—" he mimicked her gesture "—is down to you and your very talented team. I'm just glad I could be of help." He smiled at the newcomers, a smile that faltered ever so slightly as he noticed Max staring at the ring on his hand. "Tell me." He tilted his head. "Are you three also part of the team? Interns, perhaps?"

"No," Kira answered for them. "Max is my cousin. These are his friends. They're all staying with me for the weekend."

"Oh, I see. Excellent." He straightened slightly, a movement Max read as surprise. "And Max," Foss continued. "Are you also an engineering genius, like your cousin?" He tilted his head the opposite way as he waited for Max to answer.

Max was slow in replying. "Can't even wire a plug," he admitted, holding his gaze.

"Well, I'm sure you have...other gifts?"

Max shrugged, noticing Isaac and Ellie exchange a

glance at the edge of his vision. Foss had seen it too, and he nodded to Max with a narrowing of his eyes.

Suddenly feeling uncomfortable, Max looked around the hall. "Is my mother here yet?" he asked Kira.

"She tried to call you; she's running late, going to meet us at the restaurant." She then turned to Richard Foss. "Are you *sure* you won't join us? It'll be just the four of us and Max's mother."

"You know what," he said, flicking his eyes to Max and then back to Kira, "I think I've changed my mind. It'd be a pleasure, if it's not too much trouble? And you must allow me to pay, of course." He held out his glass.

Kira clinked it with her mug. "No trouble at all. And you would have paid anyway. I'm expensing *everything*."

They both laughed. Then Richard Foss turned and lifted his glass to Max. "Well, this will be nice."

They left Petra and the rest of Kira's colleagues at the gates of Somerset House. The group of twenty-somethings were heading west to Covent Garden with talk of sourdough pizza and cocktails while Kira, walking slightly ahead with Foss, led Max and his friends east to the restaurant, along the wet snow-edged pavements.

"I bet it's a fancy restaurant," Ellie said over the noise of the Saturday night traffic. "If Foss is paying, I'm ordering the most expensive thing on the menu."

"I don't like it," said Isaac.

"Don't like what?" Ellie said. "Free food?"

"No, I love free food. I just don't think it's a good idea to be having dinner with Foss."

"Why?" Ellie asked. "He seems nice."

"If he suspects Kira might be, well, different and linked

to all the weirdness at the bypass, he's gonna be sure of it when he learns her cousin lives just a few miles from there. Before you know it, FossCorp will be all over Max, too."

"He knows exactly who Kira is," said Max. "And me too." He kept his voice low, not taking his eyes off Foss, who in his long black coat, tweed cap, and walking cane, which flicked out as he walked, looked every part the gentleman about town.

Kira, walking beside Foss, checked back over her shoulder with a wave, ensuring she didn't lose them as they turned the corner. Max waved back before she disappeared from view.

"How would he know?" Ellie asked, sidestepping a large man in a grey tracksuit crossing their path.

"Because Richard Foss is the Maker," Max answered flatly.

"What are you talking about?" said Isaac, throwing his head back as if the statement was absurd. "You mean the one Jenta was looking for?"

Max nodded. "Not just Jenta," he said, unsure where to start. "Look, there are lots of things I need to tell you. Things I should have told you already."

They turned the corner onto Arundel Street.

"Tell us now," said Isaac, looking ahead, squinting through his glasses at Foss. "Why do you think he's the Maker?"

Max puffed out his cheeks, then gripped the straps of his backpack. "In my visions," he began, as Isaac and Ellie moved in closer to hear him, "I see a man who wears a wooden ring. According to Wren, Makers wear wooden rings: a reminder of their early training, apparently. Richard Foss wears one." Max looked at them both. Neither seemed convinced. "There's more. I think he knew my grandfather. In his study, I found photos of a man who was also wearing a wooden ring. I can't be a hundred per cent sure because I couldn't see his face, but I think it's him." He nodded towards Foss. "In one photo, he was at the house, in the study, talking to my grandfather. He's known about the Furlongs for a long time."

"If you're right," said Isaac, "then this is *good* news. Foss-Corp aren't looking into Kira; they're looking after her."

Max nodded. "Maybe."

"OK," said Ellie. "He might be *a* Maker, but *the* Maker? The one Jenta was looking for?"

He opened his mouth to tell them about the two visiting Nim when he felt eyes on him. The feeling was intense, like it had been that night on Church Lane. Fearing the worst, he looked over his shoulder and was relieved to find it was Zoe. She was on the other side of the road, speaking into her phone. But his relief was short-lived. She was not looking at him at all. Her attention was captured by something or someone behind them. He turned his head fully and saw the eyes that had been burning into him. They belonged to a woman who had only just turned into their street and was about fifty or sixty metres behind. Max could see her clearly. She was tall with long, dark hair, black and glossy like Wren's. He glanced around, looking for her partner. He couldn't see him but knew he'd be close.

He turned back to Kira and Foss, now far ahead of them, his heart racing.

"You OK, Max?" Ellie asked, looking behind but seeing nothing unusual.

When Max looked again, the woman stepped into the road and crossed oncoming traffic, heading towards a slowing van which she entered via the sliding side door.

Then, unsure if it was real or a manifestation of his guilt for possibly leading these Nim to the Maker, he heard the pleading tones of the voice. *Ta kaah.* Real or not, it urged him to quicken his pace.

As he looked ahead to Foss and Kira, a screech of tires came from behind, followed by the increasing pitch of the engine as the van picked up speed. It weaved through the traffic. A woman carrying a small dog in a handbag, about to cross the road, screamed and jumped back out of its way. Soon it was level with Max and still accelerating. Ellie and Isaac were now also aware of the van, and all three watched as cars swerved out of its way, sounding their horns, flashing their lights. Suddenly its wheels locked, and it skidded, mounting the curb, coming to a halt just before Kira and Foss.

Before he knew it, without any thought for himself, and with *Ta kaah* repeating in his ears, Max was running. He pushed through pedestrians who were now standing still and watching the drama unfold. There was still some distance to cover, but he saw the van's side door slide open and the woman leap onto the pavement, bearing down on Foss at speed. The driver joined her, a thick-set man Max had seen before.

Foss stepped in front of Kira, holding his cane towards his aggressors, but the woman snatched it at lightning speed as her companion grabbed Foss by the back of his neck and bundled him into the vehicle.

"You!" Kira shouted, pointing at the large man with a look of recognition. "It's you!" She stepped forward, but the woman pushed her to the ground before joining Foss in the van. The man slid the door shut behind her and, without a glance to Kira or the crowd of stunned onlookers, casually climbed back behind the wheel, as if he'd just been shopping.

The whole thing was over in seconds, and by the time Max arrived, the van was reversing back into the road. Isaac and Ellie appeared seconds later, helping Kira from the cold ground. Max watched the van battle its way through traffic, nudging cars from its path. Then, as he turned to check on Kira, he was thrown off balance by a powerful force surging through him, taking his breath away. He stumbled but remained on his feet as a blanket of silence and darkness dropped around him. The street lights and the lights of the surrounding offices were dead. Cars silently rolled to a stop, some gently colliding with others.

As Max looked to the van, it too was rolling.

And soon, nothing moved.

The whole street seemed to hold its breath.

Then, as people began to step from their dead vehicles, exchanging shrugs and looks of confusion, Foss burst from the van's rear doors. Without even a glance to Kira or Max, he sprinted down a narrow side street, his cane back in his possession but his tweed cap now absent. In a second, he was gone, and the street held another long breath and looked to the van.

Max was just wondering if the blast had killed them when the driver's door slowly opened. The Hunter stumbled out, falling to his knees, holding his head. Whatever that pulse was, he had taken the full force of it.

One concerned onlooker walked towards him but quickly backed away after seeing the anger in his small dark eyes. The Hunter got to his feet and then sniffed the air. Slowly turning full circle, he took a huge breath that seemed almost to double his size, his neck muscles straining, veins in his temples bulging. On exhalation, his head snapped towards the dark alley where Foss had escaped. He then followed at an unnatural speed, on icy ground most people struggled to walk on.

All eyes went back to the van as noises came from within. The woman looked out from the rear doors, reached for the handles, and pulled them shut. Max saw her climbing from the back into the driver seat, where she stretched out to close the door. She sat for a second, her attention directed to something on her wrist. Then the lights of the van came back on, and the engine sputtered to life. She pulled away, swerving side to side, bouncing off stationary cars still dead on the road, taking off doors that had been left open. She was not a good driver.

Max turned to his friends, his words coming faster than he could think. "Get back to the house," he said. "Get word to Wren. Tell him they have the Maker."

Kira, Ellie and Isaac all spoke at once. Isaac was the loudest and stepped closer to Max. "What are you on about? You don't have to go," he said. "None of this is our business. Who the hell were they?"

"Stay with Kira," said Max.

Kira was pleading for someone to tell her what was going on, but Max didn't have time, and Ellie and Isaac were too busy telling Max he was being stupid. He left them, running as fast as he could down the same alley Foss had seconds before, his friends still calling after him, telling him he wasn't thinking, that he was going to get himself killed.

Max had been too slow.

The side street was a dead end, with no sign of the Maker or the Hunter. The way was blocked by high wooden gates to a construction site. Above the gates, he saw an old building in a state of restoration, glass missing from its windows, their plastic membranes flapping in the cold breeze. Next to the gate, against the wall, was a covered skip.

As he looked around, he could see no obvious route they could have taken. The wooden gates, plastered with warning signs, were fastened with bolts that were still intact. The buildings on either side had no doors or windows to access, and the glassless windows thirty feet above looked too high even for a Hunter, and definitely Foss.

He went to the skip against the wall and lifted the plastic covering, coated in a layer of frost and snow. Rigid from the cold, it cracked and loosened, but the skip was empty, save for a few bricks and paint tins. It was then he noticed the skip wasn't flush with the wall; there was a gap. When he squeezed through, he found a narrow staircase descending into shadow. He stood on the top step, looking down. At the foot of the stairs was a heavy-looking door hanging off its hinges, a dark space beyond it.

"Lost them?"

Max spun to see Ellie squeezing through the gap behind him. "I told you not to follow."

"Sorry, Max, but you don't get to tell me what to do," she said, catching her breath while peering around him at the dark staircase.

Max knew it was pointless arguing. "And Isaac?" He glanced behind her.

"I told him not to follow." She shrugged at her own double standards. "He's going back with Kira. Hopefully, he'll convince her not to call the police." As she said this, the sounds of distant sirens came to them.

"I don't think you should come," he said, turning back to the door.

"And I don't think you should go."

"It might not be safe."

"Max, it's definitely not safe. I'm assuming those were Nim?" Ellie swallowed, but she was trying to look brave.

Max nodded.

"And that was one of the other things you meant to tell us?"

He nodded again.

"Why go after him?"

It was a good question. Max didn't want to follow; there was no sense in it, no logical reason to risk his life. Plus, what could *he* do? Max was no match for a Hunter. He'd come out on top with Jenta because there was a plan, and he had support from Kelha and his friends. This was different. There was no plan, and Kelha was light-years away. Still, he felt drawn to follow. No, not drawn, *pushed*. Something was pushing him forwards. Perhaps the memory of the woman in the tree, the pleading of her tone, or the fire erupting from the clear blue sky behind her. All of it was propelling him to action. Yet none of it made any sense. He wanted to tell all of this to Ellie, who was now looking at him in the gloom, waiting for a sensible answer. But he didn't have one.

He looked back down to the dark doorway. "It feels important." It was all he could manage, but it seemed good enough for her. She replied with a single nod, narrowing her eyes to follow his gaze.

Max took a step down then hesitated, waiting for a change of heart from Ellie or himself.

Looking for a last chance to avoid going forward, he asked himself if it felt important enough to risk Ellie's life, because he knew she wouldn't leave him. To his shame and disgust, the answer — whether it came from within or some outside source — was, yes, it was worth the risk.

21

GOING UNDERGROUND

Standing before the dark void of the doorway, Max could see the freshly splintered wooden frame and the wet footprints on dry concrete that crossed the threshold. Beside him, Ellie tried the light on her phone. It was dead. "Foss owes me a new iPhone," she said, returning it to her pocket. Max's phone had died after the cinema, and he could see fine without it.

They stepped inside.

"I can barely see you," Ellie said. There was a quiver in her voice.

"Then you should go back," he said, trying one last time to go it alone. He briefly considered running and leaving her blind, unable to follow. But that wouldn't stop her. She'd end up following anyway and fall down some hole.

She reached out with her gloved hand to find him, then gripped his hand tightly. "There," she said. "Problem solved. And don't get any funny ideas; this is just for practical reasons. Lead the way."

"Really?"

"Go!"

Max sighed and moved through the door into a long

narrow passageway, the end of which even his eyes couldn't penetrate. Cables ran along straight walls of white brick that were stained and cracked. He could see strip lights along the arched ceiling but no switch to turn them on.

"Ready?" asked Max. "It's a long corridor, straight. We'll move quickly; there's nothing to bump into."

She nodded in the dark. "Let's do it."

They began to walk, gradually picking up speed, hearing nothing but a low distant hum of traffic and a rhythmic *drip drip drip* somewhere up ahead. As they went, Max saw the bright eyes of rats looking back, scuttling away as they approached. He didn't know if Ellie was squeamish when it came to rodents and decided not to mention them.

The floor was sloping downwards, and soon they came to a steep flight of stairs. Max instructed Ellie to take the metal handrail and then guided her slowly down.

At the bottom, they walked through a stagnant puddle and came to a T-junction.

"Where are we?" whispered Ellie, her voice amplified by the long tunnels stretching in both directions.

At first, Max shrugged, forgetting she couldn't see him. "I don't know," he then said. "Might be part of the Underground. Not a station, though. Maintenance tunnels?"

"Why have we stopped?" she whispered, even quieter this time.

"Deciding which way to go." Both directions looked identical, long narrow passageways leading into nothingness, but on the ground to the right were a single set of wet footprints. He looked back to the puddle behind him.

There was something there.

He blinked hard and shook his head, his breath caught in his throat.

Whatever it was, it was ghostlike, shimmering in the darkness, growing brighter until it formed an image of Foss leaping over the puddle and sprinting off along the tunnel, the tails of his long coat flapping behind him. A moment later, the shimmer appeared again. This time it was the Hunter. Instead of leaping the puddle as Foss had, he splashed through it, stopping right next to Max, his ghostly bulk enveloping Ellie, who was oblivious to the apparition. The Hunter inhaled, looked both ways, then sped after his prey, his phantom feet silently received by his awaiting footprints. Max wasn't sure if this was his imagination at work or something more — another Gift on the growing list of Gifts he had never asked for. A visual echo, perhaps. At least this one didn't bring any pain with it.

"This way."

After a minute of more running, the view ahead changed. The rats, which had been constant companions, were now gone, and the tunnel opened into a large, cavernous area crossed by a metal walkway.

They slowed as they met it.

On either side, large pipes rose from below, climbing high above them, where a diagonal shaft of light cut through the blackness, disappearing and reappearing with a lazy regularity, interrupted by the blades of an unseen ventilation fan. It provided enough light for Ellie to see, but she continued to grip his hand.

Apart from their footsteps on the metal walkway, the *voom, voom, voom* of the distant fan was the only sound. There was no road noise; even the multitude of pipes were silent. Like the tunnels that brought them here, they were redundant pieces of hidden London, the dead roots of a living city.

They moved with caution as the walkway became more rickety.

The slower pace gave Max time to think and question, once again, his decision to pursue the Maker, his paranoia now imagining the Hunter lurking around every bend, hiding in every dark recess. Maybe he'd already dispatched Foss and was on his way back to deal with them. He wondered if he'd be able to hear a Hunter approach, then remembered the jogger on Windmill Hill with a sinking feeling — it was him. If Wren could be caught by surprise, what chance did he have?

Max found his heart beginning to race, his breath struggling to control it. He wasn't yet in full panic mode, but it wouldn't be long before he was.

"We can go back if you want," said Ellie as they ducked under a pipe that crossed the walkway. "You came this far. You tried to help."

Five minutes ago, he couldn't imagine not following the Maker—the pull to action at been so strong. Now, in this dark, cold, dangerous place, his rational mind seemed to be winning the arguments: turning back was beginning to sound like a great idea.

He was about to say so when the sound of someone running came to them. At first, it was hard to tell the direction, but it was soon clear it was behind them.

"If that's the other one," said Ellie, pushing Max onward. "I'd rather she didn't find us here."

As they ran, the clangs of the metal walkway echoing around them, he tried not to think they might be running straight into the arms of the Hunter.

Under their feet, the floor returned to solid concrete, dappled with more stagnant puddles, and it was once again pitch black for Ellie. The air was warm and stale. A light appeared ahead, flickering behind a half-open sliding metal grille. Once on the other side, they found themselves in a larger passageway that felt more like a tube station, albeit a neglected one. A corroded sign below the light gave them two choices: left for *Trains*, right for *Street*. With the footsteps behind growing louder, the decision to head for the street was an easy one. They soon came to a short flight of stairs climbing to a door set into a brick wall, cobwebs clinging to it, dancing in a breeze.

When Max opened the door, his spirits lifted briefly. They were at the surface. There was traffic noise again, and the air was cool. But the place was dark and empty and, judging by the old posters on the wall, had been abandoned many years ago.

They ran towards a dim light coming from around the bend, passing an entrance to a wide spiral staircase descending into a darkness they had no desire to return to.

The space opened up before them. They could make out the closed metal shutters of the station's exit ahead, an arched window set above letting in street light from outside. A door slammed somewhere far behind them, presumably the one they'd recently come through. The pair looked for a place to hide and found cover behind a wide square pillar of glazed tiles adorned with posters, torn and water-stained.

Footsteps approached.

They waited, listening as they grew ever closer. This person had a light that had somehow survived the energy blast, and Max could see the ground brighten as it neared. He nudged Ellie, and they shuffled around the pillar to avoid being seen as they passed.

The footsteps continued towards the exit, where they heard the shutters being rattled, followed by a disappointed groan.

Ellie was about to lean out to look, but Max pulled her back. If it *was* the Nim woman, she'd feel her eyes on her.

After another rattle of the shutters, the footsteps returned, and Max and Ellie once more moved around the pillar to avoid them, grateful for the hum of traffic masking the sound of their clothing and shuffling feet. Soon, the footsteps were retreating down the spiral staircase, heading for the platforms far below.

As the echoes of footsteps faded, a roar of an engine came from outside as a vehicle approached, sending splinters of light through the gaps of the shutters. Shadows swept across the ticket hall. Max braced himself, expecting something to come crashing through. But nothing did. Instead, the engine was killed, and the light died.

With no time to prepare himself to look *through* the shutters, Max rushed to them and placed his eye to the thin gap between metal and brick, feeling the heavenly cold bite from outside. "It's her," he said, watching the tall Nim woman exit the van. He turned to Ellie. "She's coming. We need to move now."

They checked the nearby doors dotted around the ticket hall. All were locked. Even the door they'd just come through refused to open, requiring a key from this side.

They heard the shutters sliding open, out of sight around the bend. On hearing the metallic clang of them being slammed closed, they exchanged a frightened nod and dashed towards the stairwell.

Round and round they went, descending the broad iron-edged steps into darkness. They moved quickly but as quietly as possible, each with a hand on the cold metal handrail, Max leading the way, listening, trying to reach backwards with his awareness, but all he could hear was Ellie close behind.

There was a dank warm breeze, and soon a flickering light from below gave form to the steps, giving Ellie confidence to move quicker.

When they finally reached the bottom of the stairs, they

sprinted along a curved passageway, surprised to find part of it lit by fluorescent lighting. They went from light to shadow, hoping to find a place to hide, somewhere they could wait for the woman to pass them, allowing them to double back and return to the surface. But there was nowhere to hide. And the thought of having to climb those stairs again was hard to bear. His legs were already burning and shaking.

He glanced back, not yet feeling watched, but he knew she was close.

Eventually, the stairs behind curved from view, and they came to a point where multiple passageways converged. Water had collected in several large puddles, and Max slowed to look for tracks while Ellie looked back, concerned, keen to keep moving.

The Hunter had run through another puddle, his wet footprints continuing straight ahead. Max perceived another echo of him sprinting under the flickering lights, not as clear as the first, but he saw it.

"This way," Max whispered, guiding Ellie away from the route taken by the Hunter, around the puddles and down a dark passageway that took a tight curve into shadow. They were just a few metres in when Max heard the woman approaching the junction they'd just left. After a pause, she was on the move again, her footsteps receding in pursuit of her companion.

"What now?" whispered Ellie, after a moment of silence.

"We go back." Max's desire to save the Maker was now completely gone. Fear had bolstered self-preservation, and he wanted nothing more than to step outside into the cold winter night and be free of the damp, suffocating underworld.

"If that was the Nim woman — who was the other one?" Ellie said. "The one behind us before?"

Max hadn't stopped to think. "You don't reckon it was Isaac, do you?"

Ellie scoffed. "Isaac is many things. Brave is not one of them. Besides, he would have called after us. It wouldn't be Kira either; she was too shaken up. And if she did follow, brave or not, Isaac would have gone with her. We'd have heard two of them."

Max nodded. She was right.

They stood in the darkness, listening for movement and waiting for their legs to stop shaking, readying themselves for the return climb. A steady drip was close by, and an occasional low rumble at the edge of hearing that Max guessed were trains hurtling through parts of the labyrinth still in use. There was also a constant low-level buzz that he felt as much as heard. Max imagined it to be something big and electrical. And he wondered if some parts of this place were not abandoned. Perhaps they gave tours down here. That would explain the few working lights.

"We should go now," Ellie said after a while. "Before she comes back."

They returned to the junction, pausing under a flickering light, where Max peered into every converging passageway, feeling no pull in any direction other than towards the stairs.

"Come on." Ellie tugged on his arm.

As they stepped forward, what few lights were on suddenly died. Ellie gasped. Max, momentarily blinded by the sudden change, found her hand.

"What happened?" Ellie whispered.

Before he could answer, one of the lights flicked on and then off again. It was followed by the light next to it, on and then off. Then the light next to that did the same. Then the next one. As the cycle repeated, the effect was clear; like landing lights on a runway, these were meant to be followed, and when distant voices came from behind, Max didn't question the lights — he did as they asked.

"What's going on?" Ellie asked as she went with him.

"I don't know," he answered. "But let's go with it."

The lights seemed to be leading them back to the stairs. He could see them now, dimly in the distance. But when the light nearest the stairs flicked off, another appeared to their right, illuminating a once dark recess, revealing a half-open door that, in their panic, they had missed on the way down.

As they squeezed through the opening, the light above them went off, and once again, only Max could see.

They were in a short tunnel, about ten metres long, the walls derelict and crumbling, lacking the brickwork present in the main passageways. Max looked around for a way out. But it was a dead end. If there was something here he was supposed to see, he couldn't see it. They were in trouble.

"Stay here," he whispered, leaving Ellie and returning to the door. Through the gap, he saw the two Nim approaching down the now dark passageway. The man was sniffing the air while the woman walked behind, studying a device on her wrist that lit up her face in the darkness.

Max thought about closing the door, but the noise would only draw them faster. There was a chance this space had already been searched, and the pair would head straight for the stairs, but he knew the Hunter would *see* their scent.

He turned to Ellie. She was staring into the blackness, unaware of the threat coming their way. Unable to see anything, she held out her hand for Max. He grabbed it and backed away from the door, taking her with him. "I'm sorry," he whispered. "I've messed up. They're coming this way."

He felt her squeeze his hand as their backs made contact with the far wall.

"It's not your fault," whispered Ellie.

Max said nothing. He'd noticed his coat sticking to the wall behind him. He turned to touch it. It was warm as well as sticky.

"What is it, Max?"

"I don't know. It's the wall. It's...." He trailed off as he ran his hands over it. It looked different from any other surface down there. Old and pimpled like the wall of a cave. And it was clean, lacking in the stains and cobwebs he'd seen elsewhere. It was out of place.

The texture was now changing under his touch, losing definition, becoming smooth. It then seemed to lose its hardness, feeling soft like sand. Max pulled his hand back in shock. It now looked like sand too, only sand with a million worms just below the surface, twisting and writhing. A hissing sound followed, and Max feared it would attract the Hunter. But it quickly stopped.

Ellie had heard it too. "What was that?"

Max didn't know what to say. He reached out to touch the constantly shifting surface again. And as he did, a hand from the other side reached through and grabbed him firmly, pulling them both through the once-solid wall.

22

SAVE THE MAKER

Max held his breath as the hand pulled him through the wall but had no time to warn Ellie to do the same. He heard her muffled scream, followed by coughing and spitting, and finally a long desperate gasp for air as they both fell to the ground.

Ellie scrambled around, looking for him. He reached out and grabbed her. "I'm here," he whispered. He tried to sound reassuring, but he was terrified.

"Where is here?"

Max looked for the owner of the hand and saw Richard Foss. His back was to them, his arms wide, his hands claw-like to the wall as it shifted from liquid, to sand, then finally to stone.

After a few silent seconds, Foss turned and collapsed to the ground, his back against the wall of his making, his forearms resting on his raised knees. Max's eyes, sensitive to heat, saw the subtle glow dying from the man's fingertips, then noticed something stranger: a thousand tiny tendrils, finer than hair, retracting into the skin of his fingers and his palms. Some didn't retract. Turning brittle, they came free as Foss brushed his hands together.

Max was stunned. He'd assumed Makers were just master craftspeople — brilliant engineers, individuals who were good with their hands. But Foss had just shown a complete mastery of matter that Max could not begin to understand. He'd seen Wren make objects float, move things without the need to touch them, which in itself was beyond explanation, but this was something else.

"Max?" whispered Ellie. "You really need to tell me what's going on."

"I'm...um." Max was unable to find the words.

There was a sniff in the darkness behind him. He turned to see Zoe Durkin huddled in a corner behind what looked like an oil drum, her smashed phone on the ground before her. She was moving her eyes around in the darkness, trying to catch something, but it was clearly in vain.

Max looked back to Foss. His eyes were closed, his breathing heavy and slow.

"Talk to me, Max," Ellie said. "I can hear people. You can see them, can't you?"

"Yes," said Max softly. "We're safe...for the moment. We're with Mr Foss."

"I hear someone else," Ellie said.

"That would be Ms Zoe Durkin," said Foss, his voice weak with a hint of bitterness. "Her inability to mind her own business almost got us both killed. But I suspect it was the two of you she followed down here. So I have you to thank for our current predicament."

Zoe looked stunned, as though she'd seen things she couldn't explain. It was a look Max was familiar with. He suddenly felt sorry for her, and a sense of responsibility for her situation.

"I'm sorry, Mr Foss," Max said after a pause. "I thought I might be able to help—"

"Shhh." Foss raised a hand and then stood. With a

frown, he pushed his ear against the wall and removed a pocket watch from inside his coat. Max watched him, then turned his attention to the wall and was surprised by how easy it was for him to see through.

Two figures stood on the other side. Both were tall, one slim, one heavily built. The heavy built Hunter crouched and held his open hand an inch above the ground, something Max had once seen Jenta do. When he stood, he was eyeing the wall with curiosity and was about to touch it when something, maybe a sound, caused both their heads to snap towards the door. The woman quickly left to investigate, but the Hunter lingered, his hand dropping to his side, forgetting his curiosity. He moved away from the wall, scanning the ground as he made his way through the door to follow his companion.

Max exhaled. "They've gone," he whispered, then immediately regretted it.

Foss turned to him while pocketing his watch. "It's clear you have good eyes for seeing in the dark, as I do. But I'm guessing yours are better than mine?" A smile was beginning to push his frown away, but the frown fought back and once again dominated the man's face.

Max nodded slowly, aware that Zoe was probably listening to everything.

Foss took his frown to the centre of the confined space and removed an object from his pocket. It resembled Wren's glow-stone, only smaller. He placed it on the ground, where it gave off a soft yellow light. Both Ellie and Zoe shifted where they sat, taking in their grim surroundings for the first time while Foss returned to sit by the wall.

Zoe was squinting, her eyes darting between Max, Foss and Ellie. Then, seemingly deciding none were a threat, she shuffled out from her corner, studying the space with an increasing sense of panic. Max realised she was looking for an exit, and not finding one was causing confusion and fear.

Ellie must have realised too; she stood and walked to her. "It's OK," she said, reaching out tentatively to touch her on the shoulder. "It's OK…"

"It's not OK," Zoe replied, her voice breaking into a panic. "How is any of this OK?"

"You're right," replied Ellie. "But it's going to get a lot less OK if you don't calm down."

"Don't tell me to—"

"I'm not telling you to do anything," Ellie continued calmly. "I'm just saying it's best for all of us if we stay quiet. By all means, have a panic attack, freak out if you want. But you need to do it quietly—"

"Or we die," added Foss unhelpfully.

"Please," said Ellie, now holding Zoe by both shoulders. "Please…"

Despite the threat of death, Zoe's panic seemed to subside. She nodded and looked down at the girl a head shorter than her. Max thought he saw a flicker of admiration from the woman. She then raised her chin subtly as her professionalism and confidence began to trickle back. "Sorry," she said quietly, adjusting her hair and straightening herself. She opened her mouth to say something to Foss but decided against it and moved back to the corner. This time she stood, arms crossed, eyeing them with suspicious curiosity.

Ellie turned to Foss. "How long are you planning on staying in here?"

Foss chuckled and shook his head. "I hadn't planned on any of this. I had a plan. It was going well until you all showed up needing rescue." He looked at each of them in turn, then closed his eyes and sunk his chin towards his chest. "Once I have rested, I'll lead you out."

Max, still in the place where he'd fallen, looked around for a better place to sit. He spotted a stack of concrete slabs and took a seat there.

Ellie joined him. "Is it worth seeing where they are?" she whispered to him, out of earshot of Zoe, but a slight movement from Foss suggested he had caught it.

Max shook his head.

He sat silent for a while, watching Foss as he rested, listening for any sounds from the other side of the wall, but heard nothing suspicious against the background electrical hum that seemed to be ever-present.

"I have a question," Zoe whispered. She'd stepped forwards from the shadows again. She eyed the stone on the floor, then looked at Foss, his head still dipped as he sat against the wall. "How the hell did we get into a room with no door?"

"That question will have to go unanswered, I'm afraid," Foss replied without looking up. "So please, sit and be quiet."

She bristled. Understandably, she wasn't keen on his tone and was about to respond and tell him so, but a glance at Ellie seemed to calm her once more. She retreated to her corner, looking downtrodden but somehow determined at the same time.

Duncan Clark marched down the long wood-panelled corridor, plush maroon carpet underfoot. "When was it recorded?" he asked the young man walking beside him.

The man glanced at his iPad. "Seven forty-six, sir."

"And identical to the O.E.S?"

"It shares many characteristics with the spike at Oban.

Its signature is just as baffling but much smaller. About a thousand times smaller."

"The effects?"

"Damaging. Thirty per cent of all cellular networks in a one-mile radius are still down. Some cars nearby were temporarily affected."

"CCTV?"

"Back online now, but we were blind for about twenty minutes. Slocombe and his team are going over the footage we have up until the spike."

"Eyewitness reports? Social media?"

"Lots. All conflicting and confused. A couple of stories about an attempted kidnapping that seem to align. Interviews are happening now."

As they neared the situation room, Duncan noticed a large square-faced man sitting comfortably on one of two leather chairs, set into a tall bay window of the corridor. A brown folder was on his lap.

"Mr Clark!" the man called as Duncan neared. "May I have a minute of your time?"

Duncan recalled the man's name as Brian McCarthy, someone he'd rarely had dealings with but had been present at the various oversight committees during the set-up of the Oban Task Force. He was higher in the food chain than Duncan, so he nodded respectfully and turned to his young colleague. "Thank you, Steven. I'll be along shortly."

As Steven entered the room, Duncan caught a glimpse of the swarm of activity inside and then walked to the man in the leather chair.

"Good evening, Duncan." Brian McCarthy stood, and they shook hands. "Working on a Saturday? Must be important." He nodded to the now closed door.

"Isn't everything," Duncan said as they both sat.

"Indeed. So I won't keep you for long. I've been informed

that your little investigation and my little investigation have tonight become one big investigation."

"I don't follow."

"Well, here's an overview of mine." He handed Duncan the brown folder. "Project Desert Man. The desert man it refers to was a patient from a refugee camp hospital in northern Iraq in the early two thousands. His blood results were unusual, showing anomalies that would normally have been dismissed as sampling errors, had the patient not displayed some fascinating characteristics to go with them." He removed his glasses and polished them on his tie. "It's detailed in there." He nodded to the folder still closed in Duncan's hands. "Anyway, mistakes were made, things were overlooked, and the patient slipped off the radar. Since then, almost every blood sampling piece of equipment in the world now ships with a piece of dormant code. Anytime these strange anomalies are recorded, we get an alert.

"Two weeks ago, we got our first result, and we've been tracking the subject, a fifteen-year-old boy named Max Cannon, ever since. Young Cannon lives in Hurstwick, not far from the Oban Energy Spike. His last known location and the location of *tonight's* energy spike, are the same."

Duncan leaned back and eyed the folder. "Do you have any working theories?"

"We can discuss theories all night, but I don't think that will get us anywhere. My team has already gone over the footage from tonight's incident, which involves some surprising guest appearances. As well as our fifteen-year-old boy, we have billionaire recluse Richard Foss, who I believe you've had dealings with when setting up the Oban Task Force. There was also an employee of GiaTek on the scene."

Duncan sighed. "Let me guess: Zoe Durkin?"

"Good guess. We also have some unsavoury characters that we might need *special* help with."

"By special, you mean special forces?"

Brian McCarthy nodded.

"Is that not overkill?"

"You've seen the footage from the bypass, and you've read the Crinklaw report. Do you really think special forces is overkill?"

Duncan didn't answer. He looked thoughtfully at a spot on the carpet between them.

"For now," Brian continued as he got to his feet, "This is just a surveillance operation, with teeth. Everything you need to know is in the file, including profiles of those at the scene of this new energy spike, and the location of a house we suspect they'll be returning to. It's under surveillance. We need a clear picture of what's going on, Duncan. We need these people found and contained."

In the dim space behind the newly constructed wall, Foss got to his feet. "We are leaving," he said, picking up his walking cane and the glow-stone.

"Wait," Max said, "What if they're still out there?"

"Then we have a problem," Foss replied. "But, I have places to be, and as wonderful as it is spending time with you all, I must be going."

Max stood and walked to Foss. "What if I look first," he suggested in a whisper, for only Foss to hear.

Foss sighed. After a moment's hesitation, he gestured to the wall. "Be my guest, young Watcher," he whispered.

Max glanced in the direction of Zoe, then to the light in Mr Foss's hand. "I'll need privacy."

Foss nodded, then extinguished the light. "Just a few minutes longer, Ms Durkin, and we'll be on our way."

Foss raised an eyebrow as Max unexpectedly returned to

sit cross-legged on the pile of slabs. Without his phone for white noise, he'd need to focus on the low-level hum that continued to form part of the audible background. And he would need to be quick; there was no healing disc this time — unless Foss had one.

Closing his eyes, he took a deep breath of stale air. He began to visualise his target; his wide grin, his small eyes, his thick neck, and sloping shoulders. After a short time, he felt control being handed to his subconscious.

Ripples of awareness expanded outwards, like when he'd first searched for Ellie. The part of his mind he could still control pondered on the two methods at his disposal: expanding ripples for people nearby and speeding down tunnels for those more distant.

As the first tentative ripples were sent out, Max briefly felt the fear, intrigue and confusion of the minds directly around him. Then, another — more wave than ripple — was propelled with enough force to reach a mind further away. Here he felt a sense of deep purpose blended with a complex set of emotions: loyalty, deception, anticipation, excitement. And something else. A feeling of being on a knife-edge. An overwhelming sense of duty and responsibility. It was a mind obsessed with a mission.

It was the mind of a Hunter.

The beautiful bright light appeared. When it faded, he saw a figure jogging along a train track, balancing perfectly on a single rail. Then the second flash came, and Max was behind the Hunter's eyes.

It had been over a year and a half since he'd seen through the eyes of Jenta, the Hunter bent on killing his friends and destroying his town, but he remembered those visions vividly. Thousands of colourful strands of scent, intertwined, semi-permanent, almost living. He didn't see that now; this Hunter was different from Jenta. The strands of scent were there but were weak in comparison. They were fuzzy, cloudy. Maybe this Hunter was less developed, or perhaps their Gifts were weakened when in human form; Jenta hadn't bothered with a disguise; that wasn't his style.

This Hunter was not following any particular scent. The ones he could see were low to the ground and from much smaller prey. Most importantly, he was not nearby, so as Max became aware of a dull pain developing, he ended the vision by opening his eyes, closing them immediately to focus on his second target — the woman.

It was harder now. He sent out the ripples of awareness, but even the minds of those around him barely registered, and the pain was increasing every second. He gave up.

When he opened his eyes again, Foss stood close by, leaning on his walking cane, with an expression of interest.

"He's in one of the train tunnels below," whispered Max. "He didn't...feel close."

Foss frowned and studied Max intently. "The female?" he asked eventually.

Max shook his head. "I couldn't find her."

"Let's hope she's not waiting for us around the corner."

Foss turned to face the wall and placed a hand on its rough surface. After a few seconds of not much happening, it suddenly turned to a fine ash that fell to the floor, a cloud of it rising in small eddies against the tunnel's curved walls.

Max was stunned for a second time. He looked to the others and was surprised by their flat expressions. Of course: in the complete darkness, only he had seen it.

"We'll take the stairs, straight up," Foss whispered as he offered the now bright glow-stone to Ellie. "You'll need this. Once on the stairs, there will be no talking. Not even a whisper; the slightest sound will carry to the top. Do you understand? Do not touch the handrail either. That is very important."

Ellie nodded as she accepted the glow-stone, and Foss walked to the metal door.

Max followed, looking back at Ellie and then to Zoe at the rear. She was eying the door with confusion as they passed through it, presumably wondering where it was a few moments earlier.

Once through, they rounded the corner, immediately coming face to face with a woman descending the steps. Zoe yelped with fright, and Max backed into Ellie while Foss swung his cane at the woman. She caught it with ease, yanking it from his grip.

"Really, Richard," she said. "This is the welcome I get?"

"Greta?" he said in a panicked whisper. "You...but...you shouldn't be here. Why did you come?"

"Shut up, Richard," she said sharply, throwing the cane back to him while studying Max and the others with wariness.

At this point, Zoe stepped forward, snatching the glow-stone from Ellie. She held it up between Foss and Greta. A crazed smile formed on her face, like someone realising they were in a strange dream. "Greta?" She then looked at Foss. "She called you Richard. And...they called you Foss. You're Richard Foss?"

"Well done, Zoe," he said with a bitter hiss. "Great deduction. I'm so pleased GiaTek are still hiring the smartest people in the business—"

"We don't have time for this," Greta said, matter-of-factly.

Foss took a step closer to Greta. "Coming here was irresponsible," he said. "You are too important."

"Tell me," she replied, tilting her head. "Just how important am I if you're dead?" She raised her perfect eyebrows and waited for an answer. When none came, she nodded triumphantly. "Exactly," she said, then turned to look up the dark spiral stairwell. "That way seems to be clear — for now. Any idea who they are?"

Foss sighed. "He called her Yanari in the van. I didn't get his name. But I don't intend to send them Christmas cards, so can we go before they return?"

Greta led the way. Like Max and Foss, she didn't need extra light to see. Max noticed she was barefoot and that she stopped on occasion to gently touch the iron handrail, feeling for vibrations. He wondered if she was Nim, or part Nim.

Slowly and quietly, they progressed, Ellie and Zoe staying tight to the inside of the stairwell, their light barely reaching a metre beyond them, while Foss, Greta, and Max, kept slightly ahead, staying close to the outside wall.

Max felt they must be near the top now. He could make out the traffic noise. He was imagining the cold night air when a deep thud went through him.

He stumbled back and held the handrail, then looked to Foss who was on his knees his head resting on the step, Greta at his side. She was shouting something, but all Max could hear was a high-pitched ringing in his ears. Above them, was Yanari. She had been casually sitting on the top step waiting for them, her hand outstretched, a bright glow fading from within the sleeve of her coat. Her mouth moved as she spoke but again Max could hear nothing. As he backed away, moving towards Ellie, Greta exploded up the stairs, almost too quick to see, slamming into Yanari as she stood to deploy another blast from her hidden weapon.

Yanari fell back, shock on her face at the speed and violence of her attacker. Greta was on her, striking her viciously. Some blows landed, but most were blocked.

Another pulse erupted, and Greta was flung back down the stairs. She rolled and rolled, disappearing into shadow.

Yanari got to her feet. She reached out towards Ellie and Zoe. There was another powerful pulse. Ellie was knocked sideways. Zoe, taking the full force of the blast, twisted through the air, hitting the ceiling as it sloped down behind them and landed in a crumpled mess on the steps.

Max froze as Yanari descended the stairs taking aim at him, but Foss kicked out as she passed, causing her to stumble and miss her target. A section of wall next to Max imploded, tiles turning to dust around him, the metal handrail embedding itself into the brickwork.

The woman quickly steadied herself, grabbed Foss by the shoulder and threw him down the steps, where he landed across the unmoving figure of Zoe.

Yanari, emotionless, a picture of calm, took aim again, this time at Ellie, who was behind Max, coughing from the dust. As the glow from Yanari's sleeve intensified, Max rushed forwards. But he was too slow. The pulse fired. He felt a sharp pain in his cheek and something heavy landing on his shoulder as more tiles and masonry rained down upon him.

He fell to his knees and looked back to Ellie. She was still there. She was on her feet, gripping the handrail while wiping the dust from her eyes.

Above him, through the cloud of thick dust, illuminated by the glow-stone, which lay half-buried on the steps behind him, he saw Yanari. Her arm was pointing to the ceiling, where there was now an impact crater. Her cold, calm expression replaced with a twisted look of anger as she struggled with an unseen force. Suddenly, her feet left the ground, and she was slammed into the wall as if hit by an invisible car. She was pinned there. Her once black hair, now white with tile dust, was smeared across her face.

Unable to move, trying to speak, she squeezed out a single word: *"traitor."*

Wren appeared. "We'll see," he growled, his face an inch from hers. He then turned to Max, who remained frozen to the spot. "Get him out of here," Wren said through gritted teeth, nodding towards Foss. "Both of you. Take him and go."

Yanari writhed and kicked and almost worked herself free from his grip. But Wren threw her to the steps, then spun her, expertly securing her face-down with his knee between her shoulder blades.

Ellie, glow-stone in hand, had responded to Wren's request without hesitation and was now helping Foss to his feet. She herded him up the stairs. "Wake up, Max," she said as they passed him. "It's time to go." She dragged him to his feet, and he followed.

Foss paused next to Wren to offer help, but Wren shook his head. "Go."

"Why are you...helping him?" Yanari said as she struggled under his weight. "You heard what he's trying to do."

"I heard," said Wren. "I just didn't believe."

Foss climbed over the debris now strewn across the steps while Ellie looked back to Zoe Durkin, caked in a layer of white dust. She hadn't moved since she came to rest there. Max feared it was too late for her.

"I'll see to Zoe," said Wren, sensing their reluctance to leave. "Get away from here."

Ellie nodded sharply and climbed with Foss, Max hanging back, still reluctant to leave.

"I can't do this with you here," Wren said, tightening his grip on Yanari. Max felt a chill from the coldness in his voice.

Just then, they both sensed a quick movement in the darkness below. It was the Hunter. He was sprinting towards them, full pelt, purposeful and calm, dust swirling in his wake. Before Max could react to protect himself, the Hunter, defying gravity, took several steps along the curving wall to pass them, his focus entirely on Foss, who was now almost beyond sight around the bend.

Wren stretched his free arm to grab his ankle as he passed, bringing him to the ground. But the Hunter was not down for long. He pushed himself up and backwards, slamming into Wren. The two of them rolled down the stairs together, freeing Yanari, who turned to watch them disappear through darkness and dust. She stood. She rubbed her bruised throat, coughing between deep breaths. Ignoring Max, she snapped her head up to where Ellie and the Maker had made their escape. She ran.

Fearing for Ellie, Max followed, stumbling and tripping as he went. As he neared the top of the stairs, he heard someone behind him. It was Greta. She was moving at a pace equivalent to that of the Hunter. She quickly passed Max, leaving him on the top step, listening to Wren and the Hunter fighting below the dark; the grunts, the swish of clothing, the cracking of stone, or was it bone. He was about to turn back when he heard Ellie shouting.

He ran to her.

Dazed and in pain, he ran. And at the end of the long ticket hall, he saw Foss slumped against the closed shutters of the exit, bathed in the dull light of the arched window above. Ellie was crouched next to him, watching Greta and Yanari fight before them.

Yanari's weapon fired twice in quick succession. Both times Greta skilfully twisted out of harm's way, the sounds of exploding tiles and masonry following each blast. Before she could let off a third, Greta struck her in the chest with a kick, slamming her against the wall. As Yanari slowly slid to the ground, Greta moved in, grabbing her by the shoulders, throwing her into the pillar as if she weighed nothing. Yanari yelled in pain. As she moved to get up, Greta was upon her, sitting across her torso, her knees pinning Yanari's arms to her side, striking blow after powerful blow. The violence was shocking to Max, and he found himself calling for her to stop.

Greta did stop.

She turned her head towards Max, looking straight at him, anger mixed with fear in her eyes. In a fluid movement, she rolled off Yanari into a crouching stance, like a coiled spring. Before Max knew it, she was bearing down on him, grimacing. Max recoiled, then realised Greta's target was not him, but someone behind him; he spun to see the Hunter's large bulk emerge from the dusty stairwell, his once grey tracksuit now white with dust. There was red too, lots of red. Max's stomach turned as he wondered what that amount of red could mean for Wren.

The Hunter stopped and stood ready, his arms relaxed by his sides, legs slightly bent.

Greta launched herself at him, but she didn't stand a chance. He dropped a shoulder, she passed him, he spun with a strike so violent, so quick, Max could barely see it. He dismissed her as a mere annoyance, and she fell, still and lifeless to the floor. All that aggression, that anger, that life, suddenly extinguished. The Hunter waited in readiness for her to get back to her feet. But she didn't. He thought he saw disappointment in the man's small dark eyes.

Max froze as the Hunter approached. If Greta, an unexpected force of nature, had been dispatched with such ease, what chance did he have? He waited for his fate to be delivered, but the Hunter passed him by, ignoring him, his eyes fixed on Foss alone.

Max glanced back to the stairwell, yearning to see Wren emerge from it. But there was a stillness there, the dust hanging low to the ground, like mist in a graveyard.

Tears stung at his eyes, but he had no time to mourn. The Hunter was approaching Foss, as Yanari slowly got to her feet. Death was now a certainty for Foss, as it was for Ellie and himself.

He looked at Ellie.

None of this was worth risking her life. His mind hadn't been his own when he had decided to pursue Foss. He should have gone back with her, not brought her into this: a fight he didn't understand and had no business being part of.

He forced himself to follow the Hunter, step after step, one foot in front of the other. He passed the discarded glow-stone on the ground and edged slowly along the wall, moving closer to Ellie all the time. He didn't want her to be alone when the end came.

Yanari, a bloody mess, was now standing over Foss. He tried to stand but had no fight left in him and slid back down. Ellie, unlike Max, had not accepted her fate. Huddled next to Foss, her eyes were alternating between scowling at Yanari and looking for something big to hit her with.

Yanari held out her arm, the glow of her weapon building in intensity once again. "You are Nabiim, the Maker?" she asked.

Foss said nothing, just stared back at her, blinking brick dust from his eyes.

"Giadeen wants this quick and painless," she said. "But first, you must confirm who you are. Or this will be slow and painful."

Foss, his hand shaking, reached into his pocket. Yanari quickly knelt and grabbed his wrist and reached in herself.

"Is this the weapon?" she said, retrieving something Max couldn't quite see. "Is this the prototype?"

"There is no weapon," he said.

She discarded the item. It was small and black and sounded metallic as it slid across the ground. "Tell me your name, and I will end this quickly for you."

"I don't know what lies you have been told—"

"Your name!"

The Hunter arrived, taking his place beside the crouching Yanari. On seeing him, Ellie scrambled away to the closest corner. Yanari seemed to notice her for the first time. She stood and aimed at Ellie just as Max joined her. But the Hunter placed a hand on Yanari's arm, lowered it, and then looked at Foss. "Confirm you are Nabiim, and this will be quick for you. And we will spare the children." His eyes flicked quickly to Yanari and back to Foss.

The Hunter's words gave no hope to Max. He had seen it was a lie.

Foss frowned with a slight tilt of the head. "I am Nabiim Fenakor of Karath," he said. "But kill me, and Nimar will be no more." And then, almost a whisper, "Do what you must do."

Yanari hesitated, narrowing her eyes as she seemed to consider his words. "And the weapon?"

"There is no weapon."

She took a step back, raising her hand towards him, the glow from her sleeve building slowly.

Max looked away, and a heavy pulse thundered through him as the air buzzed with static. It was followed a second later by the sound of a body slumping to the ground.

After a long stillness — paired with the now constant

ringing in his ears — Max braved a look and was confused by what he saw.

Yanari was on the ground.

She was not moving.

The Hunter knelt before Foss, his hand resting gently on the man's shoulder. Foss looked back at him, uncertainty in his eyes.

"I can't believe it is you," said the Hunter.

23

RETURN TO FURLONG TOWERS

Foss looked down at his hands and touched his chest, confused as to why he was still alive. He then saw the woman who should have killed him, motionless on the floor.

"Why?" he said, looking back to the Hunter kneeling before him. "Who are you?"

"I am Bayen," he said after a pause. A look of weariness and relief on his face. "I am the grandson of Lamiir. We've been looking for you for a very long time. How I wished we could have found you sooner." His jaw flexed and Max thought he could see the beginning of tears in the Hunter's eyes.

Foss looked back to the woman. "And her?"

"Yanari. Sent by Giadeen. There will be time for more questions. Right now, I have to get you somewhere safe. The prototype. Tell me you still have it."

Foss looked past Bayen and nodded to the dark shadow on the ground that was Greta.

Bayen followed his gaze. He looked back at Foss with confusion. Then he understood. "She was the prototype."

Foss nodded. "She *is* the prototype," he said, his voice weak.

"But she is dead."

Foss laughed, then stopped and held his side in pain. "*You* could not kill her."

As Max watched this exchange, he was dimly aware of Ellie getting to her feet. He was slightly more aware as she approached the still crouching Hunter. Then completely aware as she delivered a hard kick to the Hunter's meaty shoulder.

"You bastard!" she screamed as she followed the kick with another, this time to his back as he retreated. "What did you do to Wren?"

Max sprung to his feet, unsure if he was going to pull her away or join in. Before he could decide, the Hunter had put distance between them, holding out his dusty white hands.

"The blood is mine," the Hunter said as he stepped sideways to avoid another kick. "Look." He reached up behind his ear. When his hand came down, it was wet with fresh blood. "Your friend is in better shape than I am. He's tending to the woman." He inhaled deeply, and Max could now see he was in much pain, but hiding it well. "The blood is mine," he said again. He suddenly looked faint, and his eyes went back to Greta. He walked to her and knelt beside her, looking like a man who had lost everything.

Ellie pointed at Bayen to say something, her chest rising and falling quickly, her lips tightly pursed, her eyes like gun barrels. But she didn't say another word. She picked up the glow-stone from the ground and then bolted towards the stairwell. Max followed, rounding Greta, still motionless on the floor.

At the dark entrance of the staircase, they heard footsteps over rubble and a heavy, laboured breath.

Wren appeared carrying Zoe in his arms, her hair matted with dust and blood.

They stepped back, making room for him, watching as he laid her gently to the ground.

"She's alive?" Ellie asked as Wren removed his jacket and placed it under her head.

"Only just." Wren took the healing disc from his pocket and handed it to Ellie. "You know what to do," he said. He pointed to places on Zoe's head. "Here, and here. It will see to the fracture of her skull and any damage to her brain, but it won't fix this." He moved down to her leg, where a clean white bone was jutting from her dark trousers. Max tore his eyes away, feeling queasy as he noticed her foot pointing in the wrong direction.

"So, the Hunter kept his word," Wren said over the sound of ripping fabric.

"What word?" Ellie asked as she worked the disc with a frown of concentration.

"That he must save the Maker. And would save you too."

Max looked back towards the exit, to Bayen and Foss approaching the still form of Greta. "But I don't get it."

"You took a risk on trusting him," Ellie said. "He could have killed us."

"A calculated risk," said Wren. He turned to them. "You are not hurt?"

They both shook their head.

But Max was in pain, an all over pain that was dull and undefined. When he heard a wet crunch coming from Zoe's leg, he turned away. He saw Foss kneeling over Greta, stroking her cheek while whispering close to her ear. A minute later, her eyes snapped open, and she smiled at Foss. When she became aware of the Hunter behind him, she sprang to her feet, ready to continue the fight. But the simple act of Foss raising his hand between them instantly put her at ease, no explanation necessary. She turned her attention back to Foss, examining the wounds on his face.

Max found her behaviour odd, to say the least. His earlier assumption that she must be Nim no longer felt right. She wasn't human either; he knew that. She was something else entirely.

He braved a look back towards Wren, whose eyes were now black as he looked over every inch of his patient. He instructed Ellie to move the disc to Zoe's shin which was now wrapped in Wren's jumper, her foot pointing in the right direction once more.

"She'll make a good recovery," Wren said, examining her head closely. "We just need to get her to a hospital."

"No." It was Bayen. He was approaching. Foss, supported by Greta, was a few steps behind.

"No?" said Wren, turning to them. "When she wakes, she'll need—"

"No hospital," said Bayen firmly. But Max saw a slight bow of the Hunter's head, a lowering of the eyes, which Max read as apologetic or respectful.

Wren stood toe to toe with Bayen. "Then what do you suggest? Leave her here?"

"Bayen is right," said Foss. His voice, still weak, carried authority. "We can't take her to the hospital. Not yet anyway. But we shouldn't leave her." He grimaced in pain as the sound of sirens drifted in from the world outside. "We have to get away now." He looked to Greta. "How long do we have?"

"Your party trick from earlier has been detected and already matched to the Oban Energy Spike. This area will be in lockdown within thirty minutes." She turned to Wren. "We have to go."

Wren eyed Greta with suspicion. "And her?" He gestured to Zoe.

"We take her to your granddaughter's house," Foss answered. "A fine doctor, I believe."

"Lydia?" said Max.

"Yes," Foss replied, then turned to Bayen, who nodded his approval as a police car sped past outside, sending blue light streaming through the windows above the doors. "Then it's settled." Foss smiled at Wren. "I, too, need somewhere to recover. Are you ready for a family reunion?"

Half an hour later, Max and Ellie were in the back of Mrs Waldron's car, following the battered van through the streets of North London.

It was late, the roads were empty, and the snow fell heavily. Ellie had fallen asleep on Max's shoulder during the journey, but she woke to the harsh crank of the handbrake.

A few doors down from the house, they waited in silence. The square was still. A couple of street lights were on, as was the porch light of Aunt Lydia's house, but all else was dark at this late hour.

"Ready?" asked Mr Walsh, turning in his seat to face them.

Max nodded, then he and Ellie exited the old Citroën, and the two crossed the street together.

"I hope Isaac hasn't told them everything," said Ellie as they climbed the steps to the front door.

Max said nothing. He hoped he had. It would save him the job. He'd hated keeping secrets from his mother, but tonight she would finally learn the truth about him *and* his father.

He glanced back down the street towards the van, then stepped into the porch just as the front door opened. It was

Isaac. "About bloody time," he said, looking relieved as he stepped out. "I thought you were dead."

"So did we a couple of times," said Ellie, brushing herself down under the light of the porch. "Is everyone still up?"

"In the kitchen," replied Isaac, looking at his watch. "I convinced them not to call the police until midnight. So, perfect timing." He looked them up and down, taking in their dishevelled appearance. "I missed all the fun then?" he said as he stood aside and pushed open the door.

"The fun's far from over," said Max. Before he entered, he leaned out from the porch and signalled to the van with a wave.

Once inside, the dark hallway brightened as the kitchen door opened and Max's mum appeared, followed by Kira, then Aunt Lydia.

"Told you they'd be back," said Isaac with a smile, trying to lighten the mood.

Max walked to his mum while she ran to him. She hugged him tightly, burying her cheek into his messy hair.

"I'm OK. We're both OK," he assured her.

"What happened? They said you ran off chasing someone...."

"I'll explain everything, promise," said Max, breaking from the hug to look at Aunt Lydia. "But first, we're going to need your help."

Lydia nodded. "Anything."

Max thanked her and then opened the street door, and the light outside flickered then died. They stood staring out to a darkness that seemed almost too dark. Then, after a few moments of nothing happening, shadows seemed to spill into the hallway.

"We can't take her to the hospital," said Max, as Wren

broke from the shadow, Zoe in his arms. "We were hoping she could recover here. She just needs rest."

Those in the hallway moved back to make room for those following Wren. Lydia knew none of these people, and Kira knew only Foss. She recognised the thick-set man, of course, and was surprised to see him there. But not as surprised as Max's mum to see Ben and Mr Walsh and the woman from the antique shop on High Street.

"I'll explain later," Max said, closing the door while avoiding her questioning gaze.

Lydia gestured for Wren to place Zoe on the thick rug at the foot of the stairs. She then switched on the lights, illuminating every cut, graze, and blood splatter on her newly arrived guests. As Wren placed her gently down, everyone looked on with concern — everyone but Isaac, who kept his eyes locked on the blood-soaked Hunter.

"What happened to her?" Lydia asked as she knelt and began to unravel the jumper binding Zoe's leg.

"Broken leg, and head injury," answered Ellie, a distant glazed look in her eyes.

"Then she should've been taken to the hospital."

"No," Bayen growled.

Lydia spun to look at him disapprovingly. "No?" she said. "She's unconscious. She's had a head injury. She might not wake from this."

"She'll soon wake," said Wren calmly. "She just needs somewhere safe to rest. Somewhere to recover."

Lydia, paying Wren no attention, moved Zoe's head to the side and saw the dried blood on her collar and in her hair. "She's had *severe* head trauma," she said as she stood. "I'm calling for an ambulance."

"Please don't," said Ellie before Bayen had the chance to protest again. "She'll be alright."

Lydia spun back to face everyone. "I can't believe what

I'm hearing. She will not be alright." Determined, she walked off to find a phone, but Foss stepped into her path.

"You're going to hear a lot tonight that you will find difficult to believe, Little Lidi Bear," he said.

She stopped with her mouth open, staring at the man before her. "What...did you call me?"

"Has it been so long that you do not remember me?"

She stepped back and looked him up and down with a frown, then tilted her head with recognition. Her gaze travelled from his face to the hand resting on the head of his cane, her eyes narrowing as they took in the man's wooden ring. "I don't understand," she said. "How can...you—"

"All will be clear before morning arrives, I promise you. First, you have a patient to attend to," he whispered.

Lydia sighed and glanced disapprovingly at Bayen, who hung back from the rest, staring at her with no hint of emotion. To Lydia, he must have looked like a boxer, back from a training session at an abattoir. She looked at Foss and down to the ring once more. With a shake of her head, she walked back to Zoe and knelt.

She fingered the torn fabric of Zoe's trousers, then examined closely the dried blood covering her shin. "No," she said quietly. "A broken bone needs specialist attention. If it's not properly dealt with, she'll suffer—."

"The break was clean. And it's been fixed." Wren interrupted with a tone meant to be reassuring but seemed to infuriate Lydia.

"Oh, that's your professional opinion, is it?" she said with no attempt to hide her sarcasm. "You fixed it then? Aligned the bone? Did you use screws or plates? Or did you simply wrap your jumper around her leg to make it all better? I assume you checked your handiwork with an X-ray machine? You have an X-ray machine, right?"

Wren looked to Max and then to Max's mother. And

Max squeezed his mother's hand, knowing what was coming.

"Well?" Lydia said, waiting for a response.

"I have two." Wren said.

Lydia, about to stand, stopped and looked at Wren with a frown. "You have two?" she said with a bewildered look.

Wren closed his eyes. When he reopened them, Lydia was staring into two shiny black stones. She scrambled to her feet, stumbling backwards in panic as Max felt his mother recoil. Kira raised her hand to her mouth in shock. When it looked as though Lydia was going to run, Ellie moved and stood beside her, placing a hand on her back. "She'll be fine," she said. "He fixed her. Please, she just needs rest."

Wren carried Zoe up the stairs, one arm around her back, the other under her knees. Cradled within his large frame, she looked like a sleeping child. Lydia, carrying a bowl of warm soapy water and some towels, followed with Kira. Max went, too, with Ellie beside him. He didn't need to follow, but he wasn't yet ready to speak to his mother, who, with a look of stunned confusion, had been guided into the living room by Mr Walsh.

"Look after our guests," Lydia said to Kira as Wren lowered Zoe to the bed in a spare room on the second floor. "I'll clean up her leg — make sure she's comfortable." She pulled on a pair of latex gloves, then turned to dismiss Wren, but paused when she saw him kneeling beside Zoe. His eyes were black once more, reflecting the dim bedside lamp and the glowing healing disc that he held over the side of her head. Lydia looked back to Kira. "We'll both be down shortly," she said. Then seeing the concern in Kira's eyes,

"I'll call if I need you." She stepped back, and then closed the door. Kira stared at it blankly, then, ignoring Max and Ellie, she turned and went back downstairs. Max started to follow but stopped. He looked down over the dark polished wooden bannister to the hallway below.

"You don't have to tell her," Ellie said.

He sat on the step. "How can I not tell her? I should have told her a long time ago."

"Why didn't you?" Ellie asked, sitting next to him.

"I don't know. I guess I thought I'd never need to." He removed a piece of white rubble lodged between the laces of his trainers and held it between his finger and thumb. "That's not true," he admitted. "I knew I'd have to one day. I've just been putting it off. I don't want her to...look at me differently."

"She won't look at you differently. You're her son, and she loves you. And you're the same person you've always been."

"I'm not, though, am I? You and Isaac look at me differently. Ever since that day I saw through your eyes."

"Are you surprised?"

"No."

"Good. Because you *are* different, Max. Not in a *we're all different* kind of way. I mean *really* different. Scary different, if I'm honest. But we're still your friends, and you know we'd do anything for you. Didn't we prove that tonight?"

Max nodded. Then he grinned. "Isaac didn't. I can't believe he didn't come and help."

"Yeah. What a crap friend." Ellie laughed and nudged him. "Look," she said, serious again. "You're right. Your mum probably won't look at you the same way once you tell her. But she'll still love you. That won't change."

Max turned and looked through the door at Lydia and Wren. They were on opposite sides of the bed, Wren still holding the disc next to the side of Zoe's head, while Lydia cleaned dried blood from her leg. The scene gave Max hope. It seemed people could adapt quickly to new realities. Five minutes ago, someone able to see through living tissue was not part of Lydia's reality. Now she was in a room, caring for a patient, with a man who could do just that. He wondered how quickly she'd adjust to the reality that the living X-ray machine was also her grandfather.

He stood and took a deep breath. "Let's get this over with."

24

FAMILY SECRETS

Max and Ellie entered the dim living room. The Christmas lights were off, the fire just a pile of glowing embers. Close to the fireplace, in an armchair, was Foss, the chair opposite him empty. On the sofa was Max's mum, bookended by Mr Walsh and Mrs Waldron.

Isaac, who had been looking out the window, turned as they entered. "Everything OK?" he asked.

Max nodded in reply but was looking at his mother.

"The big guy's walking back to the van," Isaac said, turning back to look outside.

"Good," said Ellie. "I don't like him."

"Me neither," said Kira, entering the room behind them. "I don't trust him." She walked to the window and looked out with a frown. "What's he doing out there?"

"He'll be looking after the prisoner with Greta," Foss said quietly. He stirred uncomfortably in his seat, still in pain, thought Max.

"Prisoner?" Max's mum said, her eyes moving from one face to the next. "Can someone, *anyone*, please tell me what's going on? My boy goes missing. I'm told I can't call the police. When he does show up, it's in the middle of the night with two of my work colleagues and the woman from the antique shop on the high street." She turned to face Mrs Waldron, switching momentarily to a calmer, more polite tone. "I'm sorry, I don't know your name." Mrs Waldron smiled and shook her head, indicating it wasn't important right now. "And then there's the other two," his mum went on, "one looking like he's been beaten senseless," she looked to Foss when she said this, "and the other looking like he's been doing the beating. And now I hear there's a *prisoner* in the van?" She stopped. She was almost hyperventilating. Max knelt before her and placed a hand on her knee. "And..." she continued, now in a small voice with an expression of someone questioning their sanity, "...Ben."

Max's heart sank. "It's OK, Mum."

"Ben..." she repeated, looking at a space somewhere between Max and herself, "...his eyes. Did I imagine that?"

Max shook his head slowly.

"Then, can someone tell me what's going on?"

Max glanced at Kira. She had moved away from the window and was now sitting on the arm of the sofa. He then looked to Foss, who nodded subtly before looking to the embers of the fire — no one seeming to notice them suddenly brighten and return to flame.

"I'll tell you everything." Max held his mother's hand. "Things that'll sound unbelievable. But you must believe me because it's all true."

Max thought it would be difficult to talk in front of everyone. He thought he'd be embarrassed. But as he began to speak, he became blind to the others. To him, she was the only person in the room. Still, he found he was censoring himself, withholding, for now, details about Jenta and near-

258

death struggles. He kept to the parts she needed to know. He told her about finding the diary and about George, the boy who'd once lived in their cottage on Church Lane. Then he spoke of the man George had discovered in the barn after the Hurstwick Incident. That it wasn't really a man but something else. Max didn't say alien. He said his name was Wren, and he wasn't from Earth. And that Wren was still alive today.

At times, his mother smiled as if on the receiving end of an elaborate joke. But her smile would quickly fade on seeing the seriousness of those around her.

"Ben is Wren?" she said slowly at one point, during a lengthy pause in Max's retelling.

Max nodded.

"Explains the eye thing..." She trailed off as her scepticism returned. "No. He's too young. He's Ben. He's just Ben." She shook her head. "Why are you saying all this? Someone has filled your mind with fantasy. It's not real."

"I've known Ben since I was nineteen," Mr Walsh said softly. He smiled. "It's real, Dana."

Max had paused because he was getting to the hard bit. The bit he feared would change his relationship with his mother forever. Ellie was right, of course; she'd always love him, he knew that. She'd do her best to treat him just the same, but she wouldn't be able to help how she felt. She might try to hide it, but his eyes would see every minuscule difference.

"There's something else." Max looked at Kira now. This concerned her, too.

Picking up on this, Mr Walsh moved to the empty seat opposite Foss, and Kira took the space next to Max's mum.

Max stood, went to the mantelpiece, and picked up a small photo of his grandfather as a young man. He stood silent, his back to them.

"Max?" Kira said. "Are you OK?"

Looking at the photo, he continued. "Remember the dark family secret you joked about? About our great-grandfather?"

"Yeah," she said as Max walked towards them with the photo in his hand. "No one knew who he was."

Max handed the photo to his mother. "Until now."

Max had thought the resemblance between his father and Wren was close, but his grandfather and Wren looked almost identical.

His mother held the photo in her trembling hands. "He looks like Ben," she said, her voice small again.

He pointed to the photo in the small gold frame. "That is Ben's son, Peter," he looked to Kira. "Ben is our great-grandfather."

"Wait," said Kira. "No. This makes no sense." She leaned back on the sofa and looked to the ceiling. "Apart from Ben being in his mid-thirties, Great Granny Betty didn't visit England until Grandad was about two or three."

"Betty was not Peter's mother," Max said. "Peter's mother was Mary Furlong. Betty's cousin. She died when Peter was very young, and Betty raised him as her own."

"So that's Ben...upstairs...with Aunt Lydia?" Kira laughed. "Is that what you're saying? She's up there now with her grandfather, who is—"

"An alien." Max's mother dropped the photo onto the rug. Her head fell into her hands. "I can't...this is too much."

"It's OK, Mum."

"Please stop saying it's OK." She looked up and touched him tenderly on the cheek. "Because it isn't." She stood and then went to the door. Not looking back, she said, "I need to be alone." And she left the room.

Mr Walsh and Mrs Waldron left the room shortly after, asking if anyone wanted a cuppa. No-one did.

Foss seemed to be meditating. His eyes were closed, hands resting on his thighs, walking cane propped up against his chair. Half asleep, Ellie and Isaac sat at the small table in the dim corner, a pile of board games stacked between them.

Kira remained on the sofa, now by herself. She'd retrieved the photo from the rug and was staring at it. In the short time Max had known her, she'd never looked so small.

"I'm sorry," Max said after a while. Kira blinked as she was pulled from her thoughts, but she said nothing. "I shouldn't have contacted you. I shouldn't have come here."

"Why did you come?"

"I wanted to see if you were like me."

"And what are you like, Max?"

"Different. In many ways, I'm like Ben."

"How?"

"We share certain gifts."

She looked at him thoughtfully. "The eye thing?"

Max nodded.

"Well, I'm not like you."

"I know." He nodded in Foss's direction. "I think you're more like him."

She glanced at Foss — who was still unmoving — then pinched the bridge of her nose, closing her eyes tightly as she shook her head with disbelief.

After a while, she looked back at the photo in her hand. "What's Ben like?"

"He's great," said Isaac from the table behind her. He got

to his feet, then walked to the sofa and sat on the arm of it. Max saw Kira smile for the first time since they got back.

"What makes him great, Isaac?" she asked.

"He just is." He shrugged and smiled.

Ellie joined Kira on the sofa. "You'll like him," she said, nodding. "He can be quite funny sometimes."

Kira's smile widened when she saw their obvious affection for Wren. Then her frown returned. "I've seen some strange things tonight. But still, I'm finding it all hard to believe."

"We did, too," Ellie said. "It's to be expected."

"It's just...he looks so—"

"Normal?" offered Isaac.

"Yes. And young. *Too* young. How old is he?" Kira asked Max.

"I don't know," he replied.

"I asked him once," said Isaac. "He said younger than mountains, older than trees. Which isn't very helpful, I know, but it gives you an idea."

Kira flicked her eyebrows and shook her head. "So, old then."

As they continued to talk, Max's attention was drawn to the window. Unnoticed by everyone, he stood and walked to it. Pulling the curtain aside, he looked out to the snowy street, where he could see the van parked in the shadow between two pools of street light.

Behind the frost-covered windscreen, he could see Bayen shivering. Yanari was in the back of the van but was now awake, her arms and feet bound. Greta watched over her, alert and unaffected by the cold.

"How is she?" The question came from Ellie, and Max turned to see Wren and Lydia enter the room.

Aunt Lydia massaged the back of her neck and rotated her head. "Amazingly, by the morning, she'll probably be walking around as though nothing happened. Thanks to *Wren* and an amazing gadget I'd love to get my hands on."

Kira got to her feet. "So, you know?"

"We talked." Lydia went to Kira. "Explains quite a bit about our dysfunctional family, doesn't it?" she said as she took Kira by the hands.

Kira nodded again, and they embraced. "I suppose it does." She then held her aunt at arm's length. "Wait. So, you're telling me you believe this? Lydia Furlong, Fellow of the Royal College of Physicians, believes that this man," she nodded towards Wren, "is...well—"

"After what I've just seen," Lydia interrupted. "There can be no doubt. The amount of bruising and blood on that woman suggested huge trauma. But her wounds have all but completely healed. Some of them before my eyes. So yes, I believe it."

Kira puffed out her cheeks, interlocked her fingers and placed her hands on her head. "OK. I was relying on you to bring us all back to Earth."

"Well, I'm sorry." Lydia smiled and turned to present Kira to Wren, who had been standing silently by the door, still and calm, his default state.

Kira dug her hands into her pockets. "I'm told you're my great-grandfather," she said, studying him intently, a single eyebrow raised in suspicion. "I still don't know if I believe that, of course. But I'll play along, for now."

"Of course." Wren nodded, then extended a hand. She took it. "It's a pleasure to meet you, Kira Furlong."

"Likewise. I think."

"Right!" The word was bright and sharp, and in total contrast to the mood of the room. It was Foss, his eyes now open and alert. "Happy families," he said with a smile, glancing at his pocket watch. "Now, if everyone's caught up and bonded, we need to think about what happens next.

Time is ticking and things outside of this room are in motion. Before I leave, I have questions for our two friends outside and would like to invite them in." He looked to Lydia for approval.

"Both of them?" asked Ellie. "That woman almost killed us. She's a maniac. And I still don't trust that...pit bull."

"That pit bull saved my life," Foss replied. "Albeit at the very last minute after I'd taken quite a beating, which I'm not best pleased about. And *that woman* is misguided — and needs educating."

Lydia didn't know what to say. She turned to Wren, looking for him to decide.

"If it's OK with you," Wren said, "I think we all need educating. I too have questions."

25

BAYEN'S RESISTANCE

"Will you two be OK?" Wren asked as he stood with Peter Walsh and Daphne Waldron on the porch.

"Don't worry about us," said Daphne. "This is a family affair now. We'd just get in the way."

"You are family to me. And Lydia said you are welcome to stay. There's ample room."

Peter did up the buttons on his coat. "You still have a lot to talk about, and George has offered his spare room and sofa. We'll be fine. He's expecting us now. He's not far from here."

"Say...hello, for me, won't you?"

Mr Walsh nodded and swallowed hard.

"When will we see you?" Daphne asked.

"Soon. I hope."

Mr Walsh took a sharp intake of breath, his eyes suddenly shiny. "Well. It better be soon," he said with a slight nod of the head. "Good night, old man."

Wren watched them cross the road to the car. Suspecting the night to hold more surprises, he knew he might not see them again, so he held them in his gaze for as long as he could until they were gone.

From the window, Max watched the old Citroën pull away, then took a seat at the games table with a tired-looking Isaac and Ellie. From there, he watched Aunt Lydia as she rebuilt the fire that would soon be roaring, ready to burn through a long night.

Foss hadn't moved from the armchair. He looked concerned. Every few minutes, he would inspect his pocket watch with a frown, then sigh heavily. He also looked to be in pain. Wren had offered the use of the healing disc, but he'd declined with a look of distrust. Max guessed the trust issue was with the disc and not with Wren.

Opposite Foss was the matching armchair and a smaller wooden chair next to it, moved from the writing bureau in the corner. Both chairs were empty, in readiness for Bayen and Yanari.

The door creaked, and all eyes turned to it as it swung open. Kira entered, followed by Max's mother, who looked tired, her woolly cardigan buttoned up, her arms crossed, her shoulders hunched. She looked at Max and smiled, holding out her hand for him to join them as they made their way to the empty sofa.

Earlier, believing Max couldn't hear, Foss had asked Kira to convince his mother to join them, saying it was important for her to be there for Max. Max didn't like the sound of that, but was glad she was there.

Lydia set the fireguard before the fire and joined Isaac and Ellie at the table. By two o'clock, the room was full, the guests from the van now warming by the fire, the air heavy with a tense silence, a silence broken as a knot from a log popped on the fire, acting as a starting pistol.

"So," said Foss, looking to Bayen. "You've found me. What now?"

"We return to Nimar," he said, the wing-back armchair barely containing him. He had cleaned himself up, his injuries fixed by his own healing disc, but the night's violence still stained his clothes.

"Why should I go anywhere with you?"

Bayen looked at Yanari sitting beside him. She was secured by a thin silver rope and watched over by Greta, standing in shadow a few feet behind them.

"You must return," he said, a hint of pleading in his tone.

"Why must he?" Wren asked. He was standing beside Foss, towering over all in the room, almost as tall as the Christmas tree behind him, its gold and silver baubles reflecting the shifting firelight.

Bayen looked first at Max's mother and then at Ellie and Isaac.

"Don't be shy," said Wren, almost playfully. "You can speak freely here. Max, Kira and Lydia are Nim. They are your people. Dana is Max's mother; she has been kept in the dark for too long. No more secrets." Wren nodded toward Isaac and Ellie. "And good luck trying to put distance between Max and his friends. They come as a package, inseparable. So tell us, Bayen. Why does Nabiim have to return with you?"

"Please," said Foss. "I prefer Foss, now."

Wren nodded, then looked to Bayen to answer.

But Bayen was silent for some time, and Max didn't think he was going to answer. Wren and Foss seemed comfortable with the long pause, as if typical for a conversation among Nim.

"We need you to end the rule of Giadeen," Bayen said eventually.

"Giadeen does not *rule*," said Wren, his tone less playful now, almost offended. "Giadeen *protects*."

Bayen scoffed at Wren's statement. "For a Watcher, you don't *see* much, do you? Giadeen rules over Nimar. He has for some time."

On the sofa, Kira gave Max a sideways glance. Max shrugged. He'd never heard the name Giadeen before and tried to think back to when Kelha had filled his mind with the knowledge of Nim culture, language, and technology. He couldn't remember Giadeen or any type of ruler being a part of it.

"Look, who's Giadeen?" asked Kira, addressing both Foss and Wren. "If we're going to be here during this conversation, I can't just sit and listen without asking questions."

Foss nodded. "Agreed. And it's a reasonable question," he said. "Giadeen was once my friend. A Maker, like me. Together with four others, we built the heart of the Mesh." He held up a finger to pre-empt Kira's next question. "The Mesh," he continued, "protects Nimar. It is the single greatest structure of our age. And one of the largest artificial structures in the galaxy. It surrounds our world, protecting it against our fierce sun. Without it, Nimar would now be a dead world — beaten, burnt and barren, like our once lush moon."

"And you wish to destroy it." All eyes turned to Yanari, her face still bruised and bloodied. She scowled at Foss as she spoke. "The one thing that keeps us safe and united as a people, and you wish to destroy it."

"I wish nothing of the sort," replied Foss, calmly surprised by her statement. "But there was a time I wanted to make it better." He looked back to Kira and Max. "Although our sun is temperamental, it is also predictable. Its tantrums can be predicted with great accuracy. There is a period of calm, lasting just over a thousand years, followed by four hundred years of extreme violence. With each period of violence more destructive than the last. We were three hundred years into the peaceful period, still recovering from a particularly vicious stellar onslaught, when Giadeen emerged as our greatest Maker, with Gifts unsurpassed by any in our long history. He united Makers from all over the planet with his vision of the Mesh. It was ambitious, to say the least; nothing like it had been attempted before.

"Work progressed quickly, with thousands of Makers working night and day. But no matter how fast we worked, the sheer scale of the project meant there was not enough time to do everything we planned. With over six hundred years of hard labour behind us, we were almost ready, but not quite.

"While Giadeen oversaw the construction of the Mesh itself, I led a small team of Makers tasked with building the core intelligence that would control the Mesh from its central tower. This intelligence would need to make trillions of minor adjustments to the Mesh every microsecond, allowing it to withstand the intense forces of our sun. Without that intelligence, the Mesh would crumble under its first assault.

"As I was the most experienced at building intelligent organisms, it fell to me to design it. I had completed most of my work, but time was running out; our thousand-year window was coming to an end, and I would not be ready in time.

"It was then that Giadeen suggested a shortcut: we could build an interface to merge our unfinished intelligent organism with a living mind. The two would work together as one to control the Mesh.

"I objected to the idea, strongly at first, but Giadeen's logic was infallible. Simulations showed us it would work.

We were a mere ten years away from our sun's next onslaught, which many believed would be the last any Nim would witness. And this was the only way to complete the project on time.

"We believed the procedure would be irreversible, so I offered myself as a sacrifice. I was willing to do it, but Giadeen was on hand with more of his logical arguments. It was clear it should be his mind that we connect to our half-finished intelligence. He was the brightest of us all, his mind the most robust, and not by a short measure. So, as I had designed the intelligence, I would need to be the one to oversee the melding of the two minds.

"With only two years to spare, we did it. The Mesh was working as designed. Nimar had been saved. Giadeen had saved us. Nimar thrived under the Mesh, and our time on that world had been extended." Foss sighed and turned to Kira. "That is Giadeen. He is the creator and controller of the Mesh. We worship no gods on Nimar, apart from Nimar herself. But Giadeen, in the Great Tower, forever linked to the Mesh, is the closest thing we have ever had to a god. He was our saviour."

Kira said nothing at first, just sank back into the sofa, gazing at the fire. "Suddenly, every project I've ever heard of or read about feels...small." She looked at Bayen. "And you want to get rid of it?"

"No," said Bayen. "Not the Mesh. We would not survive without it. Just Giadeen as controller. He is no longer effective."

"You said you wanted to make improvements to the Mesh?" Wren asked Foss.

"I did. But I was foolish to think it. I had stumbled across a way to harmlessly disengage Giadeen from the Mesh. A way to free him without killing him. If I could also build a replacement intelligence to take Giadeen's place, I could get my friend back, and Nimar would get back the greatest Maker it had ever known.

"Unsure of my chances of success, I kept this to myself at first, and began work on a new prototype intelligence, one that didn't need to connect to a living mind. I worked at a slow pace, on my own in the bowels of the Great Tower. When the time came, when I needed help, I approached my fellow Makers. Together we made great progress, and it seemed feasible that this new intelligence could replace Giadeen effectively. It was an exciting time." He smiled at the memory, but the smile soon faded. "Then news of what we had been working on reached Giadeen. We thought he would be supportive of our project. We thought he wanted to be free from the Mesh. He did not want that freedom. Angry, he sent us away from the tower, never to return. So, I went to my home in the mountains. Years later, I heard the news that two of the Makers who had worked with me, Ranoos and Shadeen, were found dead. I tried to contact Natter and Lamiir for more news, but they were missing. Shortly after, I heard rumours that a stranger had been seen in the foothills — a Falcori Hunter. It was then I fled."

"When did you arrive here?" asked Wren.

"I've been here since 1822." He looked up to Wren beside him. "Probably about the time you were sent to keep watch."

Wren nodded. "I wasn't told why I was sent here."

Foss smiled and nodded. "I guessed that." He turned his attention to Bayen. "You said, *we* need you to end the rule of Giadeen. Others think like you?"

"Many."

"Why? What has he done to lose the loyalty of so many?"

"We suffer under his rule. He asks the tribes to send their Gifted to the tower. Mostly Hunters, but Watchers too."

"And they comply?"

"They have no choice. Those who refuse experience forest fires, flooding...drought. Giadeen doesn't claim responsibility for these events, but everyone knows they are caused by the Mesh. He uses it as a weapon. The great north wind now sweeps as low as Nara and Nacta. Nara is now uninhabitable.

"Those who obey Giadeen suffer without their Watchers to watch the borderlands and Hunters to lead the hunts. The fragile balance is at risk. Without Hunters, some regions have reverted to the old ways — farming and agriculture; they use technology to tip the scales in their favour. Those who refuse to give up the way of the Struggle die in great numbers."

"The Struggle?" Kira asked.

"Our way of life," said Bayen. "We realised a long time ago that to survive on our world, life had to be hard. A struggle. An easy life leads to imbalance, and ultimately death for all."

Foss looked thoughtfully at Bayen. "Although it wasn't designed for it, it's true the Mesh can affect the climate. But why? Why does Giadeen require the Gifted in the first place?"

"For protection," answered Bayen.

"From?"

"You."

"Ha! Absurd."

"He believes you're leading an uprising against him. That you have completed your prototype and are ready to replace him with it. He does not openly talk of the prototype. Instead, he refers to a weapon that he claims you are planning to use against him."

"And the people believe that?"

Bayen glanced at Yanari. "Many. But if they knew the

truth, that you had built something able to replace him and restore balance...."

Foss pinched at the tip of his beard thoughtfully. "I gave up on my prototype and my goal of replacing Giadeen the day he made it clear that was not what he wanted."

"Then why is she standing in this room, completed?"

"I could not leave her incomplete. It would have been cruel."

"I'm sorry, Foss, but I don't believe you. Earlier, you warned Yanari that Nimar would perish without you. I think you still want her to replace him. And I think you should be doing everything you can to make sure she *does*." Bayen looked away from Foss, regretful of his tone, but maybe not his words. "He will never give up looking for you or Lamiir."

"Lamiir still lives?" Foss asked with a solemn smile. "And she is your grandmother?"

Bayen nodded. "And the leader of the Vohin, our resistance."

"Does Lamiir have a plan? What was she expecting to happen once I had been found? You have six years before the Fire Skies. Six years to remove Giadeen from the Mesh. That is not a lot of time."

"They are working on many possibilities."

"So, there is no plan."

Bayen said nothing. He just lowered his eyes to the rug before him.

After a short silence, laughter erupted from Yanari. "You don't stand a chance of getting near Giadeen," she said. "You'd have to pass unseen under the eyes of a hundred Watchers. Then defend yourselves against even more Hunters. All in a place where your technology and weapons will not work. You'll be dead before his tower makes it onto your horizon."

Bayen turned to face her. "You've seen the tower with its

Watchers and its Hunters — Watchers and Hunters who have been torn from their tribes — and you are still loyal to him."

"They are for his protection, willingly donated."

"You still believe this after what you've heard?" Bayen growled.

"Ignore her, Bayen," ordered Foss. "She is a fanatic, a zealot. She won't be convinced."

"No," said Bayen. "She is not a fanatic. If she were, she would have been killed on the steps of the Great Tower."

Yanari shifted next to him, a flicker of a question in her eyes.

"Go on," said Wren. "Explain."

Bayen flexed his jaw and turned away from Yanari. "A Hunter by the name of Grelik guards the gates to the tower. Giadeen believes he is there to allow only the loyal through to meet him. It is in fact the opposite. If Grelik allowed her to pass, it was because he sensed doubt in Yanari or a willingness to think for herself."

Yanari snapped her eyes away from Bayen and stared into the fire. Max watched as her anger spiked and then diminished. The scowl remained but softened.

"I have a question," Max heard himself saying during a long pause in the conversation. He was reluctant to ask, for it felt like such a small thing after everything he'd just heard. The things they had talked about seemed far off and unreal, at a scale impossible to comprehend, in a world he'd seen only briefly in visions. But there were things closer to home that he wanted to understand.

Foss nodded for him to proceed.

"It was no accident you were sponsoring Kira's research, was it?" he asked. "And Lydia knew you...from before; there are photos of you upstairs in Peter's study, and—"

"Yes, Max. It was no accident. I've known about the

descendants of Wren for some time." He suddenly looked grave and sorrowful. "I've watched the family grow with interest. I mostly keep my distance, but sometimes, when I hear of a particularly talented individual, my curiosity gets the better of me." He sighed and smiled at Kira. "It was foolish of me to get close to the family. I knew one day it would get me into trouble. But I couldn't help but watch over them. I felt it was...my duty."

"Your duty?" asked Wren beside him.

"My duty." Foss nodded slowly, and with some effort, rose to his feet. Using his cane for support, he walked to the fire, dimming the room further, then turned to face Wren. "You see," he continued, "If it weren't for me, they wouldn't be here." He straightened himself and looked sternly at Wren. "Do you really think it was a coincidence that the first man-made object to enter space just happened to hit your craft and bring you down?" Agitated, he scoffed and looked around the room, then hit the rug with the tip of his cane. "I couldn't even begin to calculate the probability of such an event. And I'm very good at calculating probability. That V2 rocket brought you down because I wanted it to. I wanted you dead."

Wren remained impressively calm; so much so that Max wondered if it was news to him at all.

But there was a growing tension in the room. Max was aware of Isaac and Ellie stirring at the table behind him.

"Well," demanded Foss, "are you going to say something?"

"What is there to say?"

Foss shook his head, annoyed. "You Watchers are all the same. Emotionless. Soulless." He was now shouting. "Are you really not going to react?" He rolled on the balls of his feet. "OK. What about if I told you that after the war, I went to Hurstwick to find you — to see if you'd somehow survived. And I found you. Oh yes. I found you, and I found Mary, too." He paused and let out a breath. When he spoke again, his voice was softer, and his eyes had lost their intensity. "I found you both," he said. "And...and I warned her off. I told her to run from you. She loved you. It was not easy to convince her, so I had to lie. I put the fear into her, and she ran away. She left you because of me, Wren. Because of me. I didn't kill her, but I might as well have."

Foss held his head up and pushed out his chest, waiting for a response. Wren took a step forward, and Max sensed Greta move ever so slightly in the shadows. Wren's brow creased, his jaw flexed. Greta began to slowly move closer, a look of readiness about her. But with a slight hand movement from Foss, she stopped.

Wren took another step forward and placed his hand on Foss's shoulder. Foss flinched, expecting contact of a more violent nature.

"This feels like something to discuss another time," Wren said slowly, his voice flat, devoid of forgiveness or anger. But Max could see he was fighting to control his emotions, and the grip on Foss's shoulder was not gentle.

Foss shrugged the hand away, then massaged his shoulder, seemingly disappointed at Wren's measured response, hoping for violence. Max guessed he'd been living with the guilt for a long time and wanted desperately to be punished.

As Wren turned and went to the window, Foss looked down to Max sitting in between his mother and his cousin. "I'm sorry, Max. I didn't mean to say those things. Watchers are not heartless machines. If anything, you descend from a Watcher with too much heart. A Watcher unlike any I have come across. And although I have only been aware of your existence for less than a day, I can see you are unlike any..." He trailed off as a thought seemed to interrupt him. Then he looked at Max with such intensity, Max had to look away.

Foss turned back to the fire, muttering under his breath while questioning looks and shrugs circulated the room.

Then, with all eyes on him, Foss spun to announce enthusiastically, "Greta and I will travel to Nimar, *if* Max comes with us."

It was two-thirty when Travis pulled up opposite the house. He checked his phone to see if Zoe had returned his messages. She hadn't.

He looked around. The street was quiet. A few of the houses nearby blinked with Christmas lights, forgetfully left on while the residents slept.

The big house on the corner seemed to be awake. Its porch light was off, the hallway light too, but from behind a drawn ground-floor curtain came the warm shifting glow of a fire within. Not a dying fire, but the flicker and dance of a fire at its peak.

He stepped out of the car and onto the narrow pavement alongside the shiny black railings of the square's central garden. He began to walk a slow circuit of the square, keeping close to the bars, watching the vehicles for anyone observing the house. On completing his circuit, he stopped and leaned with his back against the railing. He blew his warm breath into his cupped, gloveless hands and rubbed them together. Then he dug in his pocket for his phone. Still no messages from Zoe. He returned the phone, then readied himself. If anyone knew where Zoe was, it would be those kids. He could wait until morning, or he could ask them now. They seemed to be awake, so why wait?

He pushed himself away from the railing to step into the road. As he did, he found his movement restricted. At first, he thought his hood had snagged on something, but then he felt hands grabbing at his shoulders and arms. With growing panic, he looked down to see black-clad arms holding his legs, pulling him back to the railings from the other side. A gloved hand roughly covered his mouth as he was about to shout for help. He struggled, but it was useless; the arms were powerful. He was pinned to the railings, unable to move. Then a van rolled up, blocking the view of the house. For a second, Travis felt relief that someone was here to help, but then the side door opened, and three men wearing SWAT-like uniforms silently exited and moved towards him. His exchange from one group to the other was carried out with well-trained fluidity. Within seconds, he was in the van, zip-tied and gagged and wishing he'd never met Zoe Durkin.

"What?" Ellie shot up from her chair, hitting her leg on the table.

Foss turned to her. "I said—"

"We heard what you said," said Isaac, now wide awake. "We want to know why you said it?"

"Then you should have asked *why*, not *what*," replied Foss.

"We're asking now," said Max's mother, a protective arm around her son.

Wren, no longer at the window, gestured to Isaac and Ellie to remain calm. "Max isn't going anywhere," he said. "The suggestion is absurd."

"Absurd," Ellie repeated as she retook her seat.

Bayen, noticing Foss's enthusiasm slipping away, stood and approached him. "If it's because Max is a Watcher, we have Watchers."

"But Max isn't a Watcher," said Foss. "Is he, Wren?"

Max's chest tightened, and he turned to look at Wren, confused.

Wren looked at Max. "No," he said after a pause. "I don't think he is."

"This young man," said Foss as he stared at Max, "is probably the most interesting being I have ever met, and I include Giadeen in that statement. What I saw Max do in those tunnels, no Watcher could do. If I were a betting man, and I am, I would say that Max is well on his way to becoming a Seer. I saw him *see* through the eyes of Bayen. And he did it with ease."

"You can *do* that?" said his mother. She looked frightened, her face full of a hundred more questions trying to get out.

"He can," Foss answered for him. "Only a few in our history could do what I saw Max do tonight. All of them existed before my time." Foss returned to his armchair. "If his skills continue to develop, he'll be able to do more than look through the eyes of others. A *lot* more. But just that ability alone would prove useful for anyone wishing to enter the Great Tower unnoticed."

"A Seer," Bayen said, almost too quietly to be heard.

"A Seer," Foss repeated with a slow nod.

"He's not going anywhere, Bayen." Wren still looked a picture of calm, but Max could hear a slight tremble in his voice.

"Then I stay also," said Foss. He leaned back in his chair and rested both hands on the spherical handle of his cane.

"Your people are suffering," said Bayen. "They are *dying*. You can save them."

"Be patient," said Foss. "Another opportunity will arise for your resistance. Wren is right. Max cannot go — he should not go. He is a child. I was unwise to propose it. But, until a way into the tower can be guaranteed, I won't risk

Greta's life on a half-baked plan. You were right, Bayen. I still want Greta to fulfil the role for which she was built, but there'll be only one chance to replace Giadeen. We have time on our side. We might only have six more years before the Fire Skies, but when it begins, Giadeen will be preoccupied with the Mesh, giving us four hundred years to plan his removal. During that time, the High Nim may be able to convince the guilds to return to their tribes, leaving the tower unprotected and allowing us to enter when the Fire Skies finally cease. We can act then."

"You won't live that long," said Bayen. "Giadeen might be preoccupied during the Fire Skies, but his agents will not be. They are hunting you. They are closing in on you now. I found you. If they hadn't sent Yanari to me, tonight's meeting would still have happened. It would have been a lot less violent, but we would have met. After tonight's events, they'll know you're in London. They will find you."

Foss sighed heavily and grimaced as if in pain. "There are other places I can go. I need to rest now. You all need to rest. The morning will soon be here. We can talk again then."

"But even after we talk, you will not return with me."

"No."

"Not even for family?" Bayen said slowly. He seemed ashamed of his words, his eyes falling to the rug as they came.

"Family?" Foss replied with a perplexed look.

Bayen frowned.

Foss tilted his head. "What are you not telling me, Bayen?"

Bayen returned to his seat. "Giadeen has a prisoner. A descendant of yours."

"Not possible. Having a family is not something that simply slips one's mind."

Bayen sighed with frustration. "You may not have had family on Nimar," he said. "But here?"

"No." Foss leaned forward in his chair, suddenly looking concerned. "Why are you saying this?"

Bayen was silent.

"I think you need to start talking," said Wren.

Max looked at his mother. Even in the fire's glow, her face looked white and drawn as she watched Bayen intently.

Bayen raised his head, his eyes searching for the right place to start. "As part of the search for Nabiim," he began, "Giadeen's agents monitor communications across the planet. About fifteen years ago, they intercepted a message originating from a refugee camp in northern Iraq."

Max felt his mother's hand tighten around his. He looked at her, her eyes still locked onto Bayen, a flutter in her neck as her heart rate increased.

"The message," continued Bayen, "concerned a man who had wandered into the camp from the desert; he was badly burnt. Naked. His clothing scorched from his body. He had sustained terrible injuries. The fact he was walking with such injuries was a miracle. He was not expected to last the night. However, after a week of treatment, he made a strong recovery — an *impossible* recovery. The doctors were stunned. One took blood samples and sent them to a lab for testing. The results that came back were interesting enough for that doctor to send messages to several leading scientists, sharing the results and details of the patient's story.

"Specialists were sent to the camp to meet the patient, but the agents of Giadeen arrived first." He paused and looked at Foss, who nodded for him to continue. "At first, they thought they'd finally found you, but scans of the young man revealed he was only part Nim. Assuming he was a descendant of yours, they took him to Nimar, hoping his memory would recover and lead them to you, or for you to get word of his capture and return to rescue him."

His mother's breathing was shallow again. He felt her hands sweating. "Fifteen years ago?" she whispered. "Iraq?" Bayen nodded as she stood and paced the room, her eyes wide and unblinking, her hand to her chest. "Why are you all doing this to me? It's too much. It's too much." She then bolted from the room. Before Max could follow, she was back, digging through her handbag, pulling out piles of receipts, her house keys, a rolled-up shopping bag, a hair-brush, all dropping to the floor by the fire. As she fell to her knees and tipped the rest of the bag's contents onto the rug, Lydia went to her and knelt beside her. From the pile, Max's mother removed a small square photo Max had seen many times, a photo of his mother and father cheek to cheek, with matching grins.

She held it out at arm's length in front of Bayen's face. "Is this him?" she demanded.

Bayen hardly looked at it. "I do not know."

"Look at it!"

"I'm sorry," he said. "I wasn't there. I didn't see him."

The hand with the outstretched photo fell to her side. She looked broken. Max went to her and held her.

"Fifteen years ago," she said again in a whimper. "Iraq."

26

GONE

Max opened his eyes to see the room was dark and the fire almost dead. The carriage clock upon the mantel told him it was five forty-five. His mother was curled up beside him on the sofa under a blanket. She was asleep, her heavy breathing interrupted every so often by whimpers and half words.

Max moved his head. Wren was at the window, the curtains closed, his hands behind his back. He wondered how long he had been standing there like that, unmoving.

When footsteps approached from the hallway, Max closed his eyes and pretended to sleep. Moments later, he heard the hushed tones of Foss.

"Anything?"

"The police are here," replied Wren.

"Oh yes. I see them."

"You don't sound concerned."

"Should I be?"

"They are watching the house."

"I'm sure with our combined abilities and the resources at my disposal, they'll not pose too much of a problem. Relax. Trust me."

There was a pause.

"Where are Bayen and Yanari?" Wren enquired.

"In the library across the hall. Greta is checking on Ms Durkin."

There was a *longer* pause.

"We must never leave Bayen and Max together alone," said Wren.

"You fear he'll attempt to abduct him, to lure me to Nimar?"

"He is desperate. I sense he's done many desperate things in his search for you. The thought of taking Max would have crossed his mind."

"I'm sorry," Foss said. "I'm sorry for many things. I'm sorry for bringing you down here. I had no right. But I was frustrated by your constant watch."

"I understand."

"I'm afraid you don't. Having you constantly overhead made this world feel like a prison to me. Before you arrived, I was leading an interesting life, spending time with fascinating individuals. Of all the species we know of, they are the most like us. But also very different."

"In good ways," said Wren.

"Yes," Foss replied. "But in some ways, they are not like us at all. They are a species of Makers, but they make too much. Part of being a Maker is knowing when to make and when to make do. They try to solve every problem by making a thing, even when they are drowning in things. But"—he lowered his voice even more—"some of those things, Wren, are beautiful. Art."

"In all those years," Wren said. "Why did you not reveal yourself to me, tell me that I had family?"

"I suspected you would have done me no harm," said Foss, pondering the question, "But I couldn't be sure. You might have been playing the long game, waiting for me to stop by for a cup of tea before striking me down. After all, no one has patience like a Watcher."

Max heard a short hiss of breath that must have been Wren's laugh.

"Anyway," added Foss. "You seemed to be getting on just fine. You fit in rather well in that quaint little town."

"How did you do it?"

"Bring you down?"

"Yes," said Wren. "Just before impact, Kelha moved to avoid a meteor shower—"

"There was no meteor shower," Foss confided. "I'm not proud of what I did. Well, I was for a while.... Very clever, don't you think? Get you to move away from a meteor shower that didn't exist, into the path of the first human object to enter space?"

"Very clever," said Wren. "Well done."

"Like I said," said Foss, detecting Wren's sarcasm. "I'm not proud of it."

As they continued to speak in hushed tones, Max's mind drifted. He thought about his father and wondered if it *was* him taken to Nimar. If it was, was he still alive? At one point, he thought his mother would ask Wren to bring him home. He wished she had, but at the same time, was glad she didn't. The thought of Wren leaving was too much to bear. But the idea of his father alive and alone on a strange world hurt him deeply.

He pictured his father's face, wondering if he'd be able to find him like he'd found Dinesh. But it was useless; he had no sense of space, no sense of where to send his mind. Or maybe Nimar was too far.

Tiredness soon dragged Max into a sleep full of dreams. In one, he was in the room upstairs, lying on his bed as the morning light entered from a gap in the curtain, catching the peeled paint on the ceiling, casting teeth-like shadows

— shadows that filled him with a sense of unease. In the dream, he closed his eyes. When he opened them again, he was staring into the face of Bayen.

He woke with a start, now alone on the sofa, looking around for his mother.

"Bad dream, Seer?" Foss was in the armchair. The fire was now out altogether, and his glow-stone hovered a few feet before him. "Your mother didn't want to wake you. She's in the kitchen."

Still not fully awake, Max stood. He stretched, then massaged the dull pain that had returned to his upper arm.

"Your abilities are a credit to Wren. He has trained you well. But he can't help you anymore. He doesn't understand your Gifts. No one alive does."

Max stood before him, not knowing what to say.

"However," Foss continued. "The knowledge of the Seers lives on. They left stories and teachings. They exist in our Arkarnon. Do you know what that is, Max?"

Max shook his head.

"The Arkarnon is our shared consciousness. Think of it as a library that you can access with just a thought." Foss smiled. "I can see this conversation is making you uncomfortable. And I apologise. Go find your mother; have some breakfast."

Max left the room, feeling Foss watching him. In the dim hallway, a dusty shaft of morning light entered the small window above the street door. He remembered Wren telling Foss the police were out there. And despite their relaxed reaction to the situation, Max felt his stomach tighten at the thought of them watching the house. He listened to the lazy clunk of the grandfather clock, then heard the faint voice of his mother coming from the kitchen. He moved to go to her but stopped when he heard Wren. They were talking. Giving them time to talk alone, he turned to climb the stairs.

As he climbed the first few steps, he remembered the uneasy feeling from his dream, which hadn't faded after waking. He told himself it was just a dream; Bayen hadn't tried to take him; he was still here, and as far as he knew, he couldn't see the future, unless that too was a Gift of a Seer. But the feeling of unease grew with each step. Unable to shake it, he stopped halfway up the staircase, looking over his shoulder at the wide-open hallway and to the closed door of the library, where Bayen and Yanari would be resting. He stared at the wall. It faded with ease. He was getting better at this.

The library was dark, its walls lined floor to ceiling with books. There was a studded leather couch, a writing desk, but no sign of Bayen or Yanari — they were gone.

"Bayen has Isaac!" shouted Max to the empty hallway as he turned and bounded up the stairs, panic causing him to stumble. He recovered quickly, and on the landing, ran to the door, almost falling into the room to find Isaac's bed empty, the duvet draped along the floor. Max glanced up to the ceiling, noticing the flaky paint above Isaac's bed but not his own. Without knowing it, he had seen through Isaac's eyes.

"Max?" Wren was standing in the doorway.

"Bayen has Isaac," Max repeated breathlessly as his mother, Kira and Aunt Lydia appeared behind Wren. "I thought it was a dream, but it was a vision. I saw—" He suddenly stopped. Even with all the commotion, Ellie had still not left her room across the hall. His heart sank. Max's mother had the same thought and pushed open Ellie's door. But Max, stepping out onto the landing, knew she was gone.

"Search the house," Aunt Lydia said in a panic as Greta arrived from upstairs. "They have to be here still."

Wren's eyes were already black, his head moving in all

directions, coming to rest upon the ceiling. "They're gone," he said, the black in his eyes dissolving from the inside out.

Foss was climbing the stairs, leaning heavily on his cane. In his outstretched hand, he held a scrap of paper. "They left this," he said, handing it to Wren.

Wren read it, then handed it to Max with a heavy sigh.

"No harm will come to them. They will return the instant Nabiim and Max set foot on Nimar. Be ready on the roof. Say your goodbyes."

Max dropped the note and fell to his knees. Kira crouched next to him and placed her arm around his shoulders.

"This is my fault," said Wren. "*Max and his friends come as a package, inseparable.* Remember? I gave him the idea." He looked down at Max. "I'm sorry."

"Wait!" said Dana. "Are you telling me that Isaac and Ellie, who were in my care this weekend, are now on another planet?"

"Only one way to find out," said Foss. He turned to Max. "Can you find them?"

"I'll try."

Moments later, Max was rushing through the black tunnels once more. They had decided to focus on Bayen, as it was likely Isaac and Ellie were sedated during their abduction.

After several long minutes, he was shown the bright, beautiful light. As it faded, he heard crows, and wind, and footsteps crunching in the snow. And he felt hope; these were earthly sounds. He then saw Bayen, small and distant, walking head down along a worn track through the snow.

After the second bright flash, he was behind Bayen's eyes, looking out as a man came towards him, tall and lean and red-faced from the cold, a hazy thread of scent trailing behind him. The man carried a long black bag and had come from the direction of a large remote house, surrounded by fields and hedgerows. They said nothing as they passed on the path.

When Bayen reached the house, he entered via the back door. In the kitchen, he saw another man carrying a bag like the one before. Bayen stepped aside, allowing him to pass.

Inside, he continued towards an open door set under the stairs, from which a black mist poured like coal dust into the dim hallway. But it wasn't coal dust. It was the smell of rot and decay as it rose from the cellar, the smell of death.

He descended the narrow steps, batting a large fly from his face, and found himself in a tiny basement lit by a single naked bulb, where the smell of rot was so intense, he could feel it sting the back of his throat. In one dark corner, he saw the source: a cardboard box full of old rotten meat and vegetables, crawling with maggots and flies. He had expected much worse.

Bayen paid it no attention and walked towards the brick wall, passing straight through it. He was now in a basement several times larger than the one he'd initially perceived. Two others were there, a man and a woman. The man was tall and dark-skinned with long greying hair in a tight pony-tail. He was larger than Bayen, with a kind face. The woman, also tall, looked South-East Asian, with short black hair and dark lipstick. Neither acknowledged him as he entered, just busily and efficiently packed away weapons into bags. The weapons were familiar to Max, human weapons — assault rifles, sniper rifles, handguns, grenades. Enough for a small army.

Bayen walked to a nearby table, neatly laid out with

objects next to an open bag. Most items were similar to those he'd seen in Wren's bag of tricks, with some being a hybrid of technologies from both worlds.

He packed away all but one object: a small, milky white pyramid. He turned this upright, so it balanced impossibly on its point, and he stepped back as it threw up a cone of white light.

A few moments passed, and a face appeared in the light. Max recognised her instantly as the woman in his vision and dreams, her large dark alien eyes reflecting sunlight from another world. She bowed, momentarily showing the palms of her hands, giving Max a glimpse of the wooden ring.

"I will be with you soon," Bayen said. The language was not English, but Max understood.

"And Nabiim?"

"He will follow, perhaps with others."

She closed her eyes and smiled in what was an unmistakable expression of relief and joy.

"However, he does not follow willingly," Bayen added.

Her smile faltered. "You have not hurt anyone?"

"No."

"Good. I will recall all Vohin to Nimar. You, too, must come quickly. Word will reach Giadeen, and they will be coming for you. I am proud of you Bayen. Your parents would have been proud, too." Her smile returned as she bowed, and the image of her withdrew into the upside-down pyramid.

As Bayen tossed the device into the bag, Max felt a pain grow and then diminish as Wren worked the healing disc. He wanted to end the vision now, to tell Wren they were still on Earth. But until he had a location, that information was useless. How he would *get* a location, he didn't know, but when Bayen left the basement and returned to the hallway, he spotted a pile of mail by the front door. He willed Bayen to walk to it, hoping to glimpse an address. Even a partial address might be helpful. For a second, it looked to be working; he was making his way towards the door. But hopes were soon dashed as he peeled off to enter another room where an elderly couple was sitting on a sofa, bolt upright, eyes wide open, staring into space. Standing behind them were two identical men with the whitest of skin and reddish-blond hair. They were removing small silver discs from the temples and foreheads of the old couple.

"We need to hurry this up," Bayen said to the pair.

The two glanced at each other and nodded in unison. Then looked to Bayen. "We're done," they said in a single voice.

As they left the room, Max desperately tried to take his gaze toward the letters on the floor. As he fought to steer his host, he felt a disconnecting *pop* and a feeling he was free from Bayen. He was left floating, and the skull that had once contained him disappeared down the hallway. Max tried to turn his attention back to the door, to the pile of letters. But turning your head when you don't have a head is no easy task.

The two from the basement appeared, large bags over their shoulders and another in each hand. They followed the others into the snowy garden, the door closing behind them.

Max was stuck, untethered in the hallway. He was just wondering if they would ever return when he started to drift towards the kitchen, feeling himself being drawn back to Bayen. He glided through the house and was outside again, just in time to see the last person disappear through what looked like an opening in the fabric of reality, but which he knew was a doorway to an awaiting ship. The door closed, and seconds later, a flurry of snow rose in twisting eddies as they departed.

Isaac and Ellie were gone.

Rootless and alone, he remained in the snowy garden, listening to the crows. He was in no hurry to return. This place was peaceful. Aunt Lydia's house was full of tears and fear. But he had to go back — someone was calling him. It was Wren.

Max opened his eyes.

"We have to move," Wren said. "We have company."

27

FLIGHT

Max followed Wren from the room and found himself staring at a house on the landing. At first, he thought he was looking at a doll's house, but it wasn't. The tiny pigeon settling on one of its snow-topped chimneys gave it away: it was an actual house — a live projection of *Furlong Towers*, set on a floating disc of light.

"I seem to remember there being a sizeable attic?" Foss was saying. Of everyone there, he seemed the most calm. He was standing close to the projection with his hand outstretched, gripping an object Max recognised as a key, similar to one that had lived under his floorboards for all those years.

"Yes, we have an attic," answered Lydia, in a panicked voice as the image zoomed out to encompass the square and the surrounding houses.

"Then I suggest we hold out up there," Foss said.

Greta guided them towards the stairs. As Max followed, he saw the cause of Lydia's panic. Black-clad figures were moving towards the miniature house. They advanced in single file, their legs bent, their motion fluid, weapons at the ready. The view then changed, showing the alley behind the house, where another group, smaller than the first, moved in the same purposeful way, one carrying a ladder, which was placed against the garden fence. They didn't climb it. Instead, they crouched, seemingly waiting for orders.

With a flick of his wrist, Foss ended the light show and reattached the key to the head of his walking cane.

Max climbed the stairs, following his mother, Lydia, and Kira, but stopped when he noticed Wren and Foss heading down to the ground floor.

Before he could ask what was happening, Greta's hand was on his shoulder. "Upstairs, Max," she said. "They'll be along shortly."

On the way to the attic, Greta made a detour to collect the still unconscious Zoe. Max watched as she lifted her with ease and carried her up the narrow, winding staircase, laying her down carefully on a fold-out camp bed aunt Lydia had hastily set against the exposed brick of the chimney breast.

After covering Zoe with a thick blanket, Lydia busied herself clearing space for them all to sit. They were soon facing each other on cushions and boxes in the dusty light that poured through the half-sized windows.

No one spoke, just the odd sniff and worried sigh from his mother. She was sitting next to Max, her arm tightly around his waist, so Foss couldn't take him.

But Foss was nowhere to be seen; he and Wren were still absent. Now and then, they would hear one of them call something indiscernible to the other. Then it was as if the house itself would respond to their calls with a groan and creak.

"What are they doing?" asked Kira as she watched ribbons of dust fall from the ceiling as the house complained, deep sounds like the cry of a whale.

"Giving us more time," answered Greta.

Max looked to the door that led to the roof terrace. Snow had formed a crescent moon in its circular window. On its polished wooden doorstep were beads of moisture where flakes of snow had recently melted. So Bayen had taken his friends this way, Max thought. He wondered if they were conscious when they left, whether they were afraid. He closed his eyes to stop tears from coming, then opened them on hearing approaching footsteps.

Wren appeared first, followed by Foss, who turned immediately, dropping to one knee. One hand held his cane for support, while the fingertips of his other rested on the wooden floorboard by the top step. Suddenly, the wood around his fingers rippled like a thick liquid, before sending a dark sand-like material spreading upwards. In just a few quick seconds, the entrance to the stairway was blocked by a strong-looking wall, fibrous and muscular.

An abrupt laugh erupted from Kira, which she caught quickly by cupping both hands over her mouth.

Foss turned to them, sweat beads glistening on his bald head. "I do hope you don't mind, Lidi, but I made a few temporary adjustments to the layout of the ground floor... and the first floor...and um...the attic." He nodded towards his latest piece of DIY.

"It's fine," Lydia said, her face trying a few expressions before settling on a polite smile.

Foss then turned to Max. "Well?" he said. "Did you see your friends?"

"I was too late."

"You tried," Foss replied.

Max felt his mother's hold on him tighten.

"You're not taking my Max," she said. "The note said to meet on the roof, and here we are. But he's not going anywhere." She put herself between Max and Foss and tried not to look afraid. "He stays with me. It's your fault he took them. You get them back. But Max isn't leaving me like his father."

Foss held up his hand as he sat on a large wooden crate. "I won't be taking Max anywhere against his will — I promise you. Right now, we've more pressing matters to contend with." Foss detached the key from the end of his cane and fired up its blue glowing rings. Soon the house was on show again, in miniature form, on the suspended disc of light.

There was a gasp from the shadows.

Zoe was now awake and sitting on her camp bed. "What is that?" she said, her voice croaky. She stood, gingerly, and stepped forward into the blue light, one hand grabbing a beam for support, the other pointing to the house, her outstretched finger shaking. "How are you doing that? Who are you people? How did I get here?" She asked, leaving no room for answers.

Greta stepped into her line of sight. "Glad to see you on your feet, Zoe, but you should be resting. Come, sit."

"Greta?" she said, shock turning into a smile and then confusion. "So it was you...it was you in those tunnels—"

"Yes. But we're out now. Come—"

"Am I fired?"

"Shhh, come sit." Greta led her back to her camp bed, and all eyes returned to the view of the house.

The team in the alley was no longer preparing to mount the fence. They looked lost. No longer poised for action, they stood around like actors between takes. The group at the front of the house seemed even more bewildered. They had passed the front door and found themselves at the corner of the street with no idea where to go next.

"What's going on?" Kira whispered. "They're not coming in?"

Foss briefly glanced at Wren. "They are currently experiencing some confusion. It'll buy us *some* time, but not much."

"How much time?" Max asked.

"Depends on how determined they are," said Wren.

Max continued to watch the men as they tried to figure out what they were supposed to be doing. He wondered if deception like this was a Gift of a Seer or exclusive to Watchers. But now wasn't the time to ask.

"Greta, how did they find us?" Foss asked in a manner that reminded Max of Isaac speaking to his Alexa device. Her response was not that different either.

"One of us is likely being tracked," Greta said. She was sitting next to Zoe on the camp bed, still trying to calm her.

"Explain," said Foss.

She stood and rejoined them. "We were not followed. CCTV in the area was compromised by the energy blast, and Larnik took out what was left en route, and other areas to avoid them following the outages. To find us would have taken at least a day. According to Larnik, they arrived here shortly after we did. They used another way to follow: a tracking device." She looked at Max.

Max nodded. "I think it's me," he said, his hand reaching for his upper arm, which had been uncomfortable since his hospital visit. "Can you look?" he said to Wren.

Wren stepped forward, his eyes turning black once more. Max rolled up the sleeve of his T-shirt, which he knew was probably unnecessary.

"I see it," said Wren. He removed the healing disc from his pocket and instead of holding it *near* the skin, he pressed it on his arm. "This might hurt."

Max looked away.

There was a heat, followed by a sensation of someone pinching at his skin. Seconds later, a sharp scratch.

"Awesome," said Kira, looking over Wren's shoulder. "I

think that's the first time I've used that word and actually meant it." She looked to Foss, then pointed to his wall. "That's awesome too, by the way."

Max examined his arm, wiping away a bead of blood to reveal unbroken skin beneath. He looked at the tiny pill-like device in Wren's open hand. "They must have done it when I was in the hospital."

"So, they know more than I gave them credit for," Foss said. He looked back to the visualisation of the house.

The group in the alley were now hunkered down, waiting for orders. The team at the front had regrouped in the square. They stood in a semi-circle on the snow-covered grass, assault rifles held across their chests, while a heavy-set man gave them a severe dressing down. Standing next to the group were two uniformed police officers and two men in civilian clothes.

"Duncan," said Greta quietly to Foss. Foss nodded, then adjusted the view, zooming out to show more of the square.

Roads leading into the square were cordoned off, a crowd of onlookers starting to grow. Unmarked vans and SUVs were parked down the centre of one of the side roads. Overhead, Max heard a helicopter.

Foss sighed. "They'll have another attempt before long." With a snap of his wrist, the image disappeared, and the attic returned to its dull half-light.

"I'm going to need your craft," Wren said to Foss, pocketing the disc and crushing the tracker under his shoe.

"Don't tell me you intend to go after them yourself?"

"I do."

"Well, Larnik will be of no use. It will not support three on the return trip. Not that you could find them without Max's abilities.

"I *will* find them," Wren said, his tone firm, his dark eyes bearing down on Foss.

"I do not doubt that you would eventually find them, but it could take you years."

Wren continued to look at Foss silently for a while. "You are glad about this," he said eventually. "You see this as an opportunity."

"It is a *great* opportunity," Foss replied without hesitation. "But I'm not glad. I would prefer Max to come on his own accord, willingly, as an adult. After all, as Nim, he is entitled to walk under Nimarian skies. It's unfortunate timing, I admit, but the opportunity is huge. If Bayen's story is true, Giadeen has become a risk to the balance of our world and will eventually destroy the people he was supposed to save." He looked at Wren, who held his gaze, unblinking. Foss blinked first and turned to Max. "Would you be willing to go? We can't force you."

"I've already told you," said his mother, with a white heat in her tone that caused Foss to recoil. "Max is staying here." She pulled him back to her.

"Then he will probably never see his friends again," said Foss. "And what about his father? Are you not curious to know if it's him?"

Without a word, fighting back tears, his mother walked to Foss and slapped him across the face.

Foss rubbed his cheek and glanced at Greta, who had made no move to protect him.

"You deserved that," Greta said.

"You're probably right," he answered. Looking defeated, he stood and removed the key once again from the cane. This time, the rings that sprung from it were familiar to Max. They were control rings for a ship. "I am sorry to leave you in this situation, but—"

"If *you* go back," Kira interrupted. "Even without Max, won't they still return his friends? It's *you* they want."

"Yes. I imagine they would. But like I said, I'm not going

back without Max. It's too much of a risk. Greta and I are more important than Max's friends—"

"How could you say that?" Max's mother replied in disgust. "They're children."

"I apologise if that insults your sensibilities," Foss said. "But it's a fact. Millions of lives depend on the two of us surviving. So I cannot return to Nimar without, at least, the hope of a plan. And for any plan to work, we need to know how to enter the Great Tower safely. A plan without that knowledge is doomed to failure. So until there is a way of gaining that knowledge, Greta and I will remain in hiding." He flicked his wrist, then brought the key to his chest. A moment later, Max saw a flurry of snow rush past the small window, blowing away its crescent moon.

Foss walked to the door. With a sorrowful frown, Greta followed.

"If you want a ship," Foss said, looking back to Wren. "You shall have one. It's only a matter of time before Bayen's resistance shows up, offering you a free ride to Nimar. They'll be hoping for my attendance, but will have to make do with yours. But when you are gone, blindly looking for Max's friends, ask yourself who will look after Max? Not only to protect him from those people outside, but also Bayen's resistance. He has a valuable Gift, and because he is Nim, many will say he has a responsibility to help. And what will Giadeen do when he learns of a child with such a Gift?"

Max's mother broke down, sobbing into her hands, and Foss looked away uncomfortably as Wren glared at him.

"There must be a way to get them back," said Kira.

"There is only one way," said Foss, now looking out the small window to the roof. "Max—"

"No," said Max's mother firmly. "Think of another way to get them back. One that doesn't involve Max leaving me. Aren't you supposed to be some kind of genius?"

Greta left Foss's side and walked towards Max and his mother. "I'm sorry," she said with kindness in her voice. "Foss originally built me for one purpose: predicting outcomes. I exist to predict the path a solar storm will take as it travels through space, allowing me to redirect energy through the Mesh to keep his world safe. I taught myself some other tricks along the way, but predictions are what I do best. There are only two choices you have, Max: stay or go. Each choice gives rise to countless outcomes, all based on what happens *after* that simple decision. The outcomes where your friends return to Earth, *all* of them begin with you choosing to go." She looked to his mother with a sorrowful look, then back to Max. "*If* you choose to go, Foss and I will follow. And I'll make sure your friends return here the instant you step foot on Nimar. I can be quite persuasive."

"And you can't go without Max?" Lydia asked.

"No," said Greta. "Richard can be a complete git sometimes, but he's often right. Without Max, we have no hope. To risk going to Nimar without hope is risking the lives of millions. So, we'll go into hiding and wait for another opportunity to arise. But that doesn't help Max's friends."

"Come on, Greta," said Foss. "We need to go."

"Can't he make something?" asked Kira desperately, as Greta was about to turn away. "Something that could do what Max does? He made you, for god's sake."

"I am just a glorified computer. A computer that can run a successful company and enjoys yoga and painting. But still, I am a machine. What Max can do cannot be made. Not by Foss."

"Then what about some kind of device that—"

"There is a field around the tower," said Foss impatiently. He was looking out onto the roof through the small circular window. "No outside tech can get near it. Even

Greta cannot approach until the field is down. Taking down the field is another almost impossible task made possible by the eyes of a Seer." Foss then looked at Max. "The journey between our worlds takes no time." He was talking quickly now, keen to get moving. "Your friends will be back home before the day is done. You will be back once we have intelligence on the tower and its defences. I don't know how long that will take. It might be an hour, a day, a week—"

"A month," added his mother. She wasn't angry anymore, just distant and ghost-like. "A year. Fifteen years..."

There was a stillness as everyone chose something different in the attic to stare at. It was a silence eventually broken by a thudding sound from somewhere deep below. Foss and Wren exchanged looks but didn't seem concerned.

Max, trying to ignore the sound, looked at Greta. He could not read her like he could read other people. But he believed her, and he trusted her — more than he trusted Foss, who he'd suspected had known Bayen would take his friends. But then Greta, predictor of outcomes, must have seen this coming too.

Max knew his path led to Nimar. He knew before he had seen the note from Bayen. Surprisingly, the idea of leaving Earth didn't scare him. Mainly because, as a concept, it was too big to comprehend. What scared him was the thought of never seeing his friends again, and the thought of his mother being held responsible for their disappearance. None of this was her fault.

He looked at his mum, and she shook her head as a tear ran down her cheek. She then closed her eyes, and the shake of her head slowly became a nod, accompanied by more silent tears. She was crying for him, for his father, and for Isaac and Ellie. And the only way to ease her pain was to leave her.

Max turned to Foss. "I'll go," he said. "I'll go with you to Nimar."

The thudding from downstairs had stopped, and the only sounds for the last hour had been distant sirens and the helicopter high overhead.

Max was sat with his mother on the floor against a thick wooden post. She was behind with her arms around him, her chin buried in his mop of hair — a position they had often assumed for movie nights in the flat when he was much younger.

He'd changed his mind several times about leaving, but each period of doubt hadn't lasted long. He had to go. Not for the millions of lives at stake that Foss had talked of; he hated to admit it, but those lives meant nothing to him. It was hard to feel anything for people thousands of light-years away — people he didn't know. Like going to another planet, it wasn't real to him — a concept too big to stir any kind of emotion. Even the thought of his father alone on a strange, alien world wasn't enough to pull him away from his mother. But Isaac and Ellie? He would go for them.

Foss's ship, Larnik, was now back in orbit. At regular intervals, he would use it to observe the activity outside.

At one point, they had seen police evacuating nearby houses and moving the crowds of onlookers further back. Several news vans had also arrived and were clogging up the neighbouring streets. The men with guns were no longer visible; Max guessed they were now in one of the armoured vans parked off the square, or in the house somewhere below them.

He preferred it when he could see them.

With the live feed from Larnik currently switched off,

Max's gaze wandered around the attic, which seemed smaller than it once had.

In one corner, Wren was sitting with Aunt Lydia. They talked quietly together, sometimes smiling as they spoke, which surprised Max considering the circumstances. At one point, Lydia stood and wandered from view, rummaging in boxes in the shadowy places behind them. She returned holding what looked like a small photo. She handed it to Wren who looked at it for a long time. When he handed it back, she pushed his hand away, insisting he keep it. He nodded his thanks and continued to hold it.

Kira had been pacing for much of the time, sometimes pausing by the brand-new wall blocking their exit, to run her hand over it or prod it. Max even caught her sniffing it once. He could see her mind working hard to figure out its mysteries. Later, she was sat with her back against it, writing on a scrap of paper while deep in thought.

To his right, Zoe and Greta were sat on the camp bed, beneath quivering cobwebs covering the exposed brick behind them. Greta seemed to be instructing her on what to say and do once this was all over, and Zoe listened intently. She seemed calmer now — and in good shape, considering she'd almost died the night before. The fact that she could now stand was a miracle.

After sitting still for so long, Max felt the need to stretch his legs, setting off a brief panic in his mother. "Just stretching my legs." He calmed her with a kiss to her forehead.

He walked the length of the attic a few times, then stopped by the door and gazed out its small round window, his cold hands dug deep into his pockets.

"I'm sorry."

Max half-turned to see Zoe standing behind him, her

arms crossed and shoulders hunched. "What are you sorry for?"

She looked to the floor. "If I hadn't found the SD card, you might not be in this situation."

"Maybe."

"So, I'm sorry. I really am."

He turned to her fully. "The SD card played a part in all this. Trying to get it back led us to Mr Foss. But something like this would have happened sooner or later. Other things were happening, too."

"Greta told me some of it, not all of it. Look, I didn't understand much of what I heard earlier," she said, lowering her voice. "But I know what you're doing is brave, and you're probably worried about what happens to your mum after you're gone. If there's anything I can say to the police, or your friends' parents, anything that takes the heat away from your mother, I'll say it. I know that's not much, but—"

"No," said Max. "It's a lot. If I'm gone for a long time, and if my friends are gone for a long time, I don't want people thinking it's her fault. So, thank you."

Zoe narrowed her eyes. "They said your friends will be right back."

"Yeah." Max nodded. "But Greta also said there were countless outcomes."

Later, when he was sitting with his mother again, they heard a phone ringing somewhere in the house below them. It was his mum's ringtone. He looked at his watch. It was four o'clock, and they were due back home over an hour ago. It would be Isaac's parents, or Ellie's, wondering where they were. It stopped, then rang a few more times. When it eventually stopped for good, Max felt his mother's body shake as she began to cry. He put his arm around her and tried not to cry himself.

It was dark outside when a loud thud came from the roof. It was followed by a sliding sound and then another thud on the terrace. Everyone got to their feet in readiness.

"It's a phone," said Greta. She was looking out the small round window of the door.

Foss relaxed and nodded. "No harm in talking, I suppose."

Greta stepped outside and returned a few seconds later, holding a padded canvas bag, bright orange, with the word *phone* written across it in big black letters. She threw it to Foss.

Shortly after it was unpacked, it rang, and Foss put the call on speaker.

"This is Duncan Clark," said the caller. "Who am I speaking to?"

"Hello, Duncan," replied Foss. He looked to Greta and raised an eyebrow. There was a pause on the other end.

"Am I speaking to Richard Foss?"

"You are."

"Mr Foss. Are you OK? Are your captors near you? Can they hear you?"

Foss looked around the attic, a mischievous look upon his face. "Yes, they can hear you."

"Is anyone hurt?"

"We're fine. They're treating us well." He shrugged to Greta, who rolled her eyes.

"Can we speak to your captors?"

"They wish me to do the talking."

"Very well. Who are they, and what do they want?"

"They said you know who they are. Is that right?"

There was a second pause, and then, "We have an idea, but we don't know what they want."

"They want to go home, and they want you to fall back. They're getting nervous and would hate to have to hurt you. Which I have been assured they could do quite easily."

"I'll see what I can do. I can't promise anything. If they'd be willing to release hostages — say, perhaps the children — maybe I could get them to move back as a gesture of goodwill."

"Are you pretending not to be the one in charge out there, Duncan?"

There was another pause, this one much longer, as if they had muted themselves and were discussing a reply. Then, "Are you pretending not to be the one in charge in there, Richard? Come on. Tell us what's going on, will you?"

"This will soon be over, Duncan. Just don't get in the way."

"It doesn't have to be like this, Richard. This could be... a...special moment. A moment of historical importance."

"Agreed. Not the type of moment you bring weapons to."

"*We* didn't let off an energy weapon in the centre of London. We didn't destroy those construction vehicles, crushing them like toys. And, if you'd allow me to go back further, we didn't destroy a beautiful village church and acres of woodland. The weapons are for our protection, Richard. If you allow us to enter, we'll show you the utmost respect, but we need assurances from you."

Foss frowned, then removed the pocket watch from inside his jacket. He glanced to Greta then nodded sharply. "I think this conversation is coming to a close, Duncan."

"Please, don't hang up."

He didn't hang up, but the phone did go dead, as did the light in the attic. Max stood and went to the window over-looking the square and saw that lights were out for the whole neighbourhood. Movement caught his eye. The armed men were back and were sprinting towards the house, crossing the snowy street. A second later, there was an explosion from below.

The house shook, and dust and plaster rained down around them, lit by the glow-stone now bright in Greta's hand. Then came the distant sound of a chainsaw as they tried to penetrate Foss's modifications to the lower floors. Or perhaps they found it easier to go around them and cut through the original walls of the house. Whatever their technique, they were getting closer.

"They're here," Foss said, returning the watch to his pocket.

At first, Max thought he meant the people downstairs with guns. But then, with a flurry of snow and cold air, the door to the roof opened, and a tall figure stooped to peer inside. Max recognised the kind-faced man from the basement in his vision, the man packing weapons into bags before leaving with Bayen. He stepped inside, barely fitting through the door, his eyes scanning the group, finally settling on Foss, who was now holding the glow-stone.

"Nabiim," the large man said with a bow of his head and a hand on his chest. "Bayen sent me. My name is Tarin." He moved aside and gestured to the rooftop. "Do you have the prototype?" He suddenly stiffened and stepped forward. The door closed. And Max saw Greta behind him, holding something against his back.

"That'll be me," she said. "But you can call me Greta."

Tarin turned his head slightly.

"Move another muscle and die in agony," she said. "How do we know Bayen sent you? You could have intercepted his messages."

"You will have to trust me."

"And you'll have to do better than that."

"I've seen him with Bayen!" Max shouted over the sound of the chainsaw, which was getting louder each time it was used.

Greta released the man, and he turned to face her. His frown turned to a smile when he saw she had been holding nothing but the handle of a paint-stained brush to his back. He turned to Max. "And you must be Max."

Max nodded.

"Haven't changed your mind, have you?" Foss asked.

"No," Max said, as his mother's hand tightened around his.

"No one can make you go, Max," said Wren, startling Tarin, who hadn't seen him.

"I'm ready," said Max.

He hugged his mother. As he stepped away, Kira and Lydia went in to comfort her.

"Wren will look after him," Aunt Lydia said. "He'll be with family."

"Maybe his cousin could go with him?" Kira said, turning to Foss as she said it. "There's so much I want to know." Her eyes went to the structure blocking the entrance to the attic, and then to Tarin.

"You are Nim?" Tarin asked.

"Twelve and a half per cent," she said.

"Then you are Nim." Tarin bowed. "And there is room for you."

"I knew it," Lydia said. With one arm still around the shoulders of Max's mother, she grabbed Kira by the hand. "Are you sure about this?"

Kira nodded. "I'm sure of it. Give this to my dad." She handed Lydia a piece of folded paper. "I'll return when Max does."

The sound of the chainsaw was now loud and very close. Ignoring Foss's barricades, they were cutting a hole in the ceiling from below. Max could see the cloud of sawdust growing from the far end of the attic. When the chainsaw stopped, a canister leaking white smoke was tossed through the new opening. Wren calmly retrieved it and threw it back the way it came. Then, with a wave of his hand, a mass migration of heavy boxes and old furniture went from one side of the loft to the other, converging at speed to the spot where the men were trying to enter. There were shouts from below as the items disappeared through the floor to meet them.

"This is our cue to leave!" shouted Foss over the noise.

Max returned quickly to his mother and hugged her again, telling her he loved her. She held him tightly. He didn't want to let go. In the end, she released him and pushed him towards Wren, who took him to the door.

He glanced at Zoe, alone and scared in the shadows. She braved a smile and nodded to him. It was a nod that restated her earlier promise: she would do and say the things that would best serve his mother. He nodded his thanks in return.

Tarin was first out, followed by Foss and Greta. Kira went next and then Max, with Wren close behind.

A blizzard was waiting for them as a helicopter slowly descended from above. Disoriented by the noise and swirling snow, Max had lost everyone but soon felt a hand on his shoulder that guided him the right way. As he was moved along, two lengths of black rope fell from above. He slowed to look, but the guiding hands moved him onwards. There was shouting; he didn't recognise the voices. Everything was happening so quickly — a snowy, windswept blur. Vaguely aware of Wren behind him and Kira to his side, her hair lashing at his face, he continued on. He sensed a struggle ahead, black-clad figures converging around Foss or perhaps Greta. More shouting, barely audible over the spinning rotors above them. Blue flashes lit up the roof, coming from somewhere ahead, then, a moment later, he was stepping over men in black on the ground, curled up in foetal positions, bound by fizzing blue electric light. He came to the low wall at the edge of the roof. Helping hands with no bodies pulled him up until he was standing on the edge looking down to the garden below him, where he saw a bird table blow over as waves of snow rippled across the lawn. The hands pulled him forwards. Then all was black. The wind had stopped. Flakes of trapped snow drifted slowly before his eyes. No more noise from the helicopter, just the sound of breathing around him.

Soon, the hands were guiding him along a dark narrow passageway into a confined space, where he stood packed tight with the others, unable to move. He felt nauseous, as though his insides were twisting, his body warping. There was a SNAP; he couldn't tell if he had heard it or thought it.

Then a whisper in his ear.

It was Wren. "We're here."

28

THE LIGHT IN THE SKY

Standing in the darkness, Max felt heavy, as though his limbs were filled with wet sand. With his heart thumping slowly in his chest, he looked around, but moving his head required too much effort. Soon, even his eyes in their sockets felt sluggish. The others were feeling it too. Kira was bent over, her hands on her thighs as she drew in deep breaths. Her hair, normally springy and full of life, was hanging limp, framing a face that was drawn and anxious. Even Foss and Wren looked uncomfortable, both frowning as they adjusted to this new feeling. Only Greta seemed to be taking it in her stride as she stood by Foss to support him.

Max looked for somewhere to sit, but there was no seat or bench. Just four walls, dark and patterned with tessellating triangles, each triangle with a tiny pinprick of cold blue light at its centre. No longer able to take his weight, his legs gave up, and he folded to the floor. A second later, Kira fell next to him. He wanted to call out to Wren to ask him if this was normal, but he found it too difficult to talk.

After a while, he noticed the colour of the light slowly changing from cold blue to warm orange. With this change came an easing of his discomfort, not complete relief but enough for him to sit upright.

As the room went from orange to red, two men entered. They were identical in appearance, and although the light had coloured them red, Max remembered their porcelain-white skin and blond hair from his vision earlier that day.

Without a word, one walked to Wren, the other to Foss. Knowing what to expect, they rolled up their sleeves and received an injection into their forearm. Once done, they approached Max and Kira. His heart rate doubled; he hated needles; Without conscious thought, he heaved his arms away.

"It's OK, Max," said Wren. "It's to help your body cope with your new environment, not least this increased gravity."

"You'll die without it," added the blond man as he knelt beside him.

With great effort, Max rolled up his sleeve and offered him his heavy arm and watched as the white pen-like device was pressed against his skin just above his wrist. To his relief, there was no needle to observe. The end was rounded and looked utterly harmless. Still, he felt a sharp prick on contact, but nothing he couldn't handle.

Almost instantly, his arm felt hot, and the heat soon spread to the rest of his body. At first, it was not unpleasant, but as the heat increased, so did his fear. He remembered George's account of Wren's transformation in the barn, and feared he was about to undergo a similar experience. But the heat passed, and his limbs began to feel normal again. He looked to Kira. Apart from her limp hair, she looked a lot more like herself.

The man then approached Greta.

"She won't need that," Foss said.

He turned to look at Foss, confused, then looked back at

Greta, still seemingly unaffected by her new environment. He nodded. With their work complete, they left the room.

In the following silence, Max had time to think. Despite having just received an injection to cope with increased *gravity*, he was finding it difficult to believe he was no longer on Earth, that he was now an unimaginable distance from his mother and everything he'd ever known. He wondered how far he'd travelled, then remembered conversations with Isaac about space travel and relativity and the speed of light. Wasn't he supposed to get older faster than those he left on Earth? Or was it that people on Earth got old quicker while he aged at a standard rate? It was probably that one. He wished he'd paid more attention to those conversations. But Wren would have said something if either of those scenarios had been true.

"What now?" Kira asked as she got to her feet and helped Max to his.

"We wait," said Foss, who still seemed to be in discomfort. "We wait for the injection to do its thing and for the air in here to change, then we step outside." He smiled as he spoke, but Max could see he was nervous.

"What about contamination?" Kira asked as she hovered her hand over a nearby wall, looking at the pinpricks of light hitting her skin. "Are they not worried about us bringing any nasty bugs along?"

"Those lights you seem fascinated with are dealing with that problem as we speak."

"Wow," she said. "Really? I thought they were just setting the mood." She was about to ask another question but was prevented by a yawn.

Max yawned, too, though he was not tired. Something was happening to the air. They were all yawning, even Greta.

"Your lungs have undergone a few changes and are...

recalibrating," said Foss, between yawns. "As a side effect you might cough a little, and taste a little blood. It's quite normal."

Max noticed a change in the quality of the air. The once cold air that had followed them from the roof became warm and humid. And breathing came with a strange sensation that his lungs were expanding more than usual, as if this new air was finding parts never reached before. Where he would typically expect his lungs to fill and then begin to empty, they just kept going. The feeling, not unpleasant, was dizzying, and he laughed involuntarily. He looked to Kira, who was laughing, too.

"Nimarian air," said Foss, looking at Wren. "It's what I've missed the most."

Wren smiled politely at Foss, but his underlying expression was of subtle impatience — not a look Max was used to seeing in him.

"Worry not, Max," said Foss turning to him, rotating his shoulders, and arching his back. "You'll see your friends soon, I'm sure. And they'll be back before the day is out."

The light coming from the walls faded, quickly replaced by light spilling into the room from the corridor. Max felt a rush of air against his skin — somewhere, a door had opened.

For the first time, he was curious to know what lay outside. He looked at a wall to look through it, but he couldn't. Either they were too thick or made of a material impenetrable to his eyes.

Voices from outside drifted in, followed by the sound of footsteps. Soon after, a huge figure appeared in the doorway, human in appearance, almost as tall as Wren but twice as wide. At first, Max thought he must be looking at a Hunter but quickly decided that this person, like Tarin, had too much kindness in his face. Jenta, and to a lesser degree

Bayen, had a cold look. This person, scanning the room with joy, was very different.

"Nabiim," he rejoiced in a deep but tuneful voice, bowing before the Maker. "We have waited for so long," he said, in a language Max mostly understood. "You bring hope to us, a hope we thought was lost a long time ago." He caught himself. "I'm sorry. You have no idea who I am. I am Ramat." He bowed once more. "I was leading the search for you on Earth. Not Giadeen's search, I should add, but Lami-ir's search. She is eager to see you again."

Foss smiled graciously, but again, Max sensed his unease.

Next, Ramat turned to Greta, a look of awe on his face. He didn't bow, but looked at her as one would examine a piece of exquisite art or intricate piece of machinery. He was taken aback when she bowed, and he nodded in return. "And you are our new saviour."

"Greta."

He laughed and circled her, looking her up and down. She didn't seem bothered, but watched him keenly.

Ramat then turned to Wren. "And Rahiir." He bowed once again, this time lower than he had for Foss. It was a bow that seemed more formal than his others. "We are indeed honoured to have a Watcher of the High Nim among our number."

Max noticed a startled look from Foss at Ramat's words and was surprised when Foss bowed in Wren's direction, mimicking Ramat, bowing with reverence.

"And this must be Max Cannon," he said, now in perfect English. "The one I have heard much about." He bowed again. "First, I must apologise for *how* we got you here; Bayen can be impulsive. But I am glad he did what he did." A grave look fell on him. "For we are in a desperate race, Max. And from what little I understand, you give us a great advantage." Max was about to ask after his friends, but the man turned quickly to Kira. He didn't seem to be expecting her and looked to Foss for the introduction.

"Oh, yes: this is Kira," said Foss. "Like Max, she is of Nim descent."

Ramat bowed his head subtly in Kira's direction.

"She is here to aid us in looking after young Max." Foss looked uncomfortable, as if seeking Ramat's blessing for her presence. When Ramat continued to look confused, Foss added, "and she is a promising Maker in the... well...making."

Ramat's face lit up in sudden appreciation. "Wonderful," he said, bowing low. Kira smiled and dipped her head self-consciously.

Ramat backed out of the dim space and into the corridor, one side of him lit by the light from the world outside. He admired the group assembled and then addressed Kira and Max. "Are you ready to look upon the home of your ancestors?"

Max followed Ramat down a corridor filled with a light unmistakably that of early evening.

He stopped as he got his first look at another planet. The small slice of world that he could see through the doorway filled him with confusion. Not because it was unusual or alien, but because it was normal — familiar. Suddenly, he felt like he'd been tricked. Because what Max saw, framed in that tall doorway, was clearly Earth; there was no doubt about it. Long grass was swaying in a soft breeze, and there was a tree trunk, dark and thick, like any he had seen before. Beyond that was a grey boulder covered in what looked like ivy.

He turned and looked at Kira behind him. Keen to see this new world for herself, she ducked down and moved her head from side to side to see more of it. Not wanting to hold her back, Max walked towards the exit and stepped outside.

It was not Earth.

The tree trunk he'd seen from the corridor rose high above him. It was the shape of a large pine tree, but instead of needles, long wisps of white grass hung from its branches and hissed in the wind. It was the largest tree he had ever seen, and there were thousands more of them dotted sporadically throughout what Max could only describe as a vast savanna. The horizon ran uninterrupted, and to Max seemed to go on forever, giving him the feeling he was somehow at sea.

Behind him, Kira emerged from the black rectangle of the ship's doorway, which appeared to be set within the semi-circle of a giant red sun peeking over that endless horizon, painting the distant saucer-like clouds in a thousand shades of red and orange.

As they made space for the others to exit, he noticed more black rectangles appearing in the grassland around him, people emerging from their hidden ships, three or four at a time. All of them were in human form and had presumably just made the journey from Earth. They stood in the tall grass at a respectful distance, not approaching, just watching, as Max and the others stepped out onto Nimar.

Just then, a murmur of excitement arose from the onlookers. There were smiles and celebratory pats on backs. Foss had emerged and was standing in the red-orange glow of the sun.

These people had been looking for the Maker for almost two hundred years, he thought. Now the Maker was here; he was going to save them. But he was here because Max was here. And if he couldn't do what he was supposed to do, the Maker had wasted a trip.

Max tried to push that thought away and began to look for his friends. He looked to all the faces still clustered around the doorways of the other ships, but his friends were not among them. He was about to call out when a huge hand settled on his shoulder. It was Ramat.

"Welcome to Nimar," he said. "To be more specific, welcome to Palian. Even in a world as sparsely populated as Nimar, Palian is considered remote. You are as far from Giadeen's Great Tower as it is possible to be. And the closest settlement is a thousand miles east, where they are loyal to our cause. You're safe here. Relax for a while and be reunited with your friends." He gestured towards the horizon, away from the sun where the sky was indigo. Max could see nothing there but more grass. "Walk that way, and you'll quickly find them. I'll prepare my craft for their return."

Ramat walked back to his ship, where Wren had now emerged from the doorway. He was scanning the horizon, a look on his face that Max couldn't quite read. Max turned away, and desperate to see his friends, he walked in the direction Ramat had suggested.

As he went, he allowed the tips of the alien grass to brush the palms of his open hands. Each blade was soft like velvet, and he wondered how something so delicate could withstand a world that could flatten Kira's hair. On one of the blades of grass he spotted an insect. He pulled his hand away. It was like a ladybird, only flatter and longer. Although ladybirds were one of the few bugs he'd happily handle, he thought it safer to avoid this one. He had no idea what was deadly on this world, possibly everything.

He looked behind to see how far he was from the ship and saw Kira doing the same as him, walking slowly, hands brushing the grass. She smiled at Max, then shook her head in disbelief.

He looked forward again, wondering where his friends were and in what direction he was heading. Did the Nimarian sun set in the west or the east? What he'd assumed to be sunset might be sunrise. Maybe the sun never set here. Perhaps something about the planet's spin and orbit meant it just constantly skimmed the horizon.

The clouds on the horizon could have been Earth clouds; they were a familiar sight. But the stars were different; where the sky was darkening, they seemed brighter and more vivid, closer perhaps. As he looked for a moon, his attention was drawn to a faint wave of green light cascading across the sky towards the sun, where it was lost in its glare. He'd only seen the Northern Lights on TV, but this, too, looked remarkably familiar.

With his focus back on the ground, he soon came to a section of grass pressed utterly flat into a long rectangle, as if something had recently been sitting there. It took him only a second to figure out that it must have been another ship, and then one more second to realise it was probably still there. He reached out a hand and felt a rough, warm surface under his fingertips. For a moment, he forgot his worries and smiled.

"Wondered when you were gonna show up," said Issac, stepping out from nowhere a few metres to Max's left.

A second later, Ellie appeared from the opening now visible, stark against the landscape. She ran to Max and hugged him. "I'm so sorry," she said. "I should've seen it coming. Of course, he'd try *anything* to get you here. I should've seen it—"

"The super-intelligent robot woman didn't see it coming," said Isaac, giving Max a welcoming slap on the shoulder. "So, don't beat yourself up."

"Didn't she, though?" Ellie said with a sideways glance as she continued to squeeze Max.

"It's not your fault," said Max.

"No," said Isaac as Bayen emerged from the doorway, his brow furrowed. "It's *his* fault."

Bayen passed them with barely a glance and hurried towards Wren and company.

"Wonder what got to him," Ellie said, letting go of Max and composing herself. "He was in a good mood a second ago."

"I *really* don't care," said Isaac, giving Bayen a vicious look as he left. He turned back to Max, his expression softening. "Can you believe where we are?"

Max laughed. "No," he said. And he still couldn't.

"It *is* amazing here," Ellie admitted. She took a deep breath. "I can't get over the air. It's so..." She took another breath. "I don't know...." She trailed off and picked a blade of grass.

"Take that grass back to Earth," said Isaac. "And you'd be a millionaire."

Ellie flicked her eyebrows, picked some more, stuffed her pockets full, and then patted them flat. "So, what now?" She looked at Max.

"You two are going straight back."

"And you?" she asked. "How long will you be here?" She reached out and held Max's hand as the three began to walk.

Max shrugged. "They want me to do the vision thing: see if I can see inside this tower of theirs. I have no idea how long that'll take, but once it's done, I'll be home."

"You got into GiaTek, "said Isaac. "This is the same. Just bigger with higher stakes, but you can do it. All of that was practice for this. You'll be back in no time."

"Will Wren be coming back with you?" Ellie asked.

Max shrugged again. "Just me, I think."

"He's going to look for your dad?" said Isaac.

"I can't see him leaving without at least trying. He's his grandson, after all."

"You know what sucks?" said Isaac

"Go on," said Ellie.

"I'm now the most famous human in Earth's history—"

"What?" Ellie started laughing.

"No, seriously, listen.... I'm now the most famous human in Earth's history, and no one will ever know."

"What are you talking about?" said Ellie.

"I'm the first human to set foot on another planet."

"Hah! So that's why you shoved me out the way earlier." She turned to Max. "When we first got here, this guy pushes past, saying he's going to vomit..."

"Damn straight, girl. I'm no Buzz Aldrin."

"Buzz who?"

"Exactly," said Isaac, trying to keep a straight face.

"People might find out when you get back," Max said.

"Why?" Isaac stopped and looked at him.

"Our departure wasn't very subtle. We had a lot of attention: helicopters, SWAT teams, TV news crews...you get the idea. Things'll be different when you get back."

Isaac breathed out, and his shoulders dropped. "Suddenly, I don't want to be famous anymore."

Ellie put an arm around them both as they walked back to Wren and the others. "Anyway, you're forgetting Max's dad." She gave Max a sideways glance. "If he really *is* here, then he was the first."

"Not technically human," said Max. "Like it or not, Isaac's right. And he's never going to shut up about it."

Isaac and Ellie were telling Max more about their arrival when Kira came running to them through the long grass. She looked distraught.

"Kira's here?" said Ellie as she approached. "What the hell's up with her hair?"

Kira stopped before them, out of breath. "Something's wrong!"

"With your hair?" said Isaac.

"What? Oh. Yes, something is *very* wrong with my hair. But no, I don't know what they're saying, but it's not good."

They looked past her.

An angry Wren was holding Bayen against the ship while Ramat and Foss tried to calm him.

Max ran to them. "Wren?" he called as he neared, "What's happening?" He'd never seen him like this before.

Unquestionably stronger than Wren, Bayen was showing restraint and not fighting back, looking calm but avoiding eye contact with everyone present.

At the sound of Max's voice, Wren let go of Bayen. There was a silence.

"What's happening, Wren?" Max asked again.

Ramat looked at Max. It was a sorrowful look, underlined with a sense of urgency. He then rushed off towards one of the other groups.

Max stepped closer to Wren. "Talk to me."

Wren sighed, dismissing Bayen with a nod, who then followed Ramat. Foss and Greta also left, leaving Max and Wren alone.

"Walk with me," said Wren, placing a hand on his shoulder.

Isaac, Ellie, and Kira arrived and joined them, looking concerned. The five of them moved away from the gathering of hidden ships, the swaying motion of the long grass suddenly bringing calm to the situation. As they neared a large disc-like boulder, Max looked to the darkening expanse of sky around him, his mind returning to the wave of green light that had spread across it just moments ago.

"We're trapped here," He said, looking up at Wren, "aren't we?"

Wren sighed and nodded gravely. "We *are* trapped," he said. "Soon after we landed, Giadeen activated the Mesh. He knew we were coming. He has closed our only route of escape." He turned to face the group.

Isaac looked skywards with his hands on his head. "You're kidding me." His eyes went from Wren to Max. "He's not kidding me...."

Max shook his head. "I think I saw it close," he said.

Wren nodded.

"There must be a way through it," Kira said.

"Yeah," said Ellie, grasping at the slightest hope. "We smash through it."

"I'm afraid not," said Wren. "The Mesh is too strong. It has to be to protect us from our violent sun. Even if we could break through, doing so would do more harm than good. A broken Mesh this close to the Fire Skies will mean death for many."

Ellie let out a short laugh of disbelief and turned away from the group, shaking her head. She ambled over to the wide, flat boulder, stepped onto it, and walked up to its centre. She emptied her pockets of alien grass, then slumped down, hugging her knees, staring at the horizon and the setting sun that was not hers.

One by one, the others followed. First Isaac, then Max, then Kira. A breeze stirred the tall grass, bringing a sweet smell that was new to them all, save Wren.

"Do they know where we are?" asked Isaac as Wren finally joined them. "Should we be hiding or running?"

Wren didn't sit. He stood, looking out across the savanna. "We are safe here for now," he said.

"Are we ever going to see our families again?" Ellie asked.

Wren knelt behind the group, placing one hand on Ellie's shoulder, another on Isaac's. "I'll make sure of it."

Kira turned to him. "What happens now?"

There was a pause as they all waited for Wren to answer, but Wren was looking at Max.

"We hope I can do what I came here to do," said Max. He was looking out at the sun, now lower than before. So it was setting, he thought. And it would soon be night. His first night on Nimar.

To be continued...

ACKNOWLEDGEMENTS

A huge thank you to everyone who rated and reviewed my first book. Reading those reviews encouraged me to write this book. Please review this book too. It really helps other readers find my work. A thank you has to go to my wife for being the first reader and helping me get the book across the line. Also, thank you to all my beta readers, especially Julie Baugh and Jackie Rushton, both amazing (terrestrial) librarians. And finally, my editor, Nick Hodgson, for making this a better book than it would have been and spotting all the mistokes. (See what I did there)

Rob Winters, April 2022.

rawinters@me.com

Printed in Great Britain
by Amazon

12772864R10192